Up until that moment Cathy had been under the impression that athletes were to refrain from sex before an important game. But it seemed that no one had bothered to tell this to Marcus.

Pressed up as they were against the dishwasher, soft and sweet kisses started bursting into white-hot passion. Just as Cathy tried to get her bearings, Marcus kissed her neck while he skillfully unbuttoned her shirt with one hand. When her shirt lay on the floor, his eyes widened at the sight of her ample caramel breasts. They were so inviting in her sexy black lace bra.

"You're gorgeous." He panted.

Thank God I wore a pretty bra, she thought to herself. *Somehow I don't think an industrial bra would have elicited this reaction.*

Before she could say a word he kissed her neck and breasts. With sleight of hand, he undid her bra and caressed her breasts slowly and deliberately. *Whoever said all you needed was a handful obviously didn't know what he was thinking about,* Marcus thought. *I'll take two handfuls any day.*

Marcus pulled this shirt off and threw it to the floor. Cathy suddenly forgot how to breathe. He looked good in pinstripes but shirtless he was amazing. She ran her hands down his toned chest to his six pack abs; her hands were anxious to explore more of his tight, muscular body.

Marcus continued exploring the softness of all her curves. He ran his fingers through her hair, down her neck and then ever so slowly down her back. He paused to unbutton her pants and slowly pulled the zipper down. He felt her body tighten as he inched ever closer to the sweet spot just beyond.

NOT HIS TYPE

CHAMEIN CANTON

Chamein Canton

ISBN-13: 9781495238611
ISBN-10: 149523861X
Manufactured in the United States of America

First Edition

DEDICATION

This book is dedicated to all the women out there who are afraid of rejection, may you be emboldened to take a chance on love. Your heart will thank you for it.

ACKNOWLEDGEMENTS

Writers lead somewhat of a solitary existence. However, no writer is an island. We need the support, love and encouragement of our families and friends, to whom we owe so much. I send my love to:

My fantastic family, most particularly my dad, Leonard Canton, Jr., who never gave up on me even when I wanted to give up on myself; my mother, Mary Wallace, whose Southern ways gave me an odd sense of humor; my younger and only sister, Natalie Sherman, who has turned out to be my best friend; my brother-in-law, Donell Sherman, who has made my sister happy and is a wonderful uncle to Sean and Scott; my brother in spirit, Joel Woodard, the big brother I never had but love just the same; to my twin uncles, Calvin and Cecil Canton, teachers who spent many summers nurturing my love of reading; and to my twin sons, Sean and Scott, who are simply the most wonderful sons any mother could have, I love them more than anything. And to all my family too numerous to mention, but no less important in my eyes.

My wonderful boyfriend, Michael Bressler, who opened my eyes and my heart to what real love is.

My grandmothers, Grandma Salley and Grandma Canton; my great-grandmother, Dorothy Donadelle; my Auntie Ruth, Aunt Edna and Uncle Willis who, although they're gone, made an impression on my life and the woman I've become. To Mrs. Frances Watkins whose sage guidance gave me the courage to speak up for myself and my choices.

To my small circle of friends: Ed Kemnitzer, Sheri Collins, Pearl Alston and Eric Smith. Thanks for being there, guys!

For my favorite team, The New York Yankees, and to NYY #2 for being the epitome of style and grace under pressure both on and off the field! There will never be another man like you to grace Yankees Stadium with your presence.

CHAPTER 1

In the moments before Cathy Chambers stepped out of bed to get her day started she turned on the TV to see what The Weather Channel had in store for her. More red than yellow on the map meant the three Hs, hot, haze and humidity, would stick around, at least for the foreseeable future. *Another hot day courtesy of the greenhouse effect.* She sighed. Then a light smile washed over her face as she remembered the days when she could count on a fall cool down in September. Cathy had been one of the nerdy kids who actually looked forward to going back to school. Growing up, her summers were filled with religious meetings five times a week and a daily door-to-door ministry during the dog days of summer. Back to school meant a reprieve from her summer grind. The only downside was the end of summer meant the end of the regular baseball season. It wasn't all bad, though. Her favorite men in pinstripes always made it to the post season.

Thinking about the Yankees, Cathy changed the channel to see the baseball results from the night before, but the ESPN scroll was showing results from the National League. *I missed it,* she sighed. Since it was already four twenty-five, Cathy knew she didn't have time to waste waiting for it to loop around to the American League again.

She had a business lunch and staff meeting in Manhattan.

Slowly but surely Cathy's morning routine unfurled: She washed her face, put her shower cap on and hopped into the shower. She preferred baths but the time manager in her opted for showers as a time saver. After a quick ten minutes, she hopped out, then dabbed a little Oil of Olay on her face, a tip courtesy of her mother. Although she tended to balk at some of her mother's other suggestions, this one she followed. Despite being over sixty, Elizabeth, Cathy's mother, had very few lines on her face.

Covered by a towel, Cathy stood in front of her closet and searched for just the right outfit. A full-figured woman for most of her life, she had a keen eye for what worked with or against her curves. After studying the closet's contents for a moment, she held a Yankee blue V-neck shirt dress up against her and examined herself in the full length mirror. The blue complemented her caramel complexion and the V-neck would enhance her biggest assets, her boobs.

Good choice, she mumbled aloud. *It's authoritative yet feminine, and a little sexy.* Cathy laid the dress on her bed and continued getting ready.

Makeup flawless and dressed to the nines, Cathy went outside to get the newspapers on her way to the kitchen. She glanced at the headlines, then flipped over to the sports page before she tossed the paper on the dining room table. A long time magazine junkie, Cathy's business was such that she rarely got the chance to catch up. But this morning was different; she put the latest *Glamour* on the hutch so she wouldn't forget to read it. *One out of eight, I guess that's not too bad,* she thought as she glanced at the pile of magazines she had yet to read.

However, there was one important piece of business to take care of first: her morning coffee, which she fixed in a flash. With *Glamour* in one hand and her coffee mug in the other, she sat at the kitchen table. The morning silence was broken by the sound of her sister rummaging through her closet. *Ten to one she's looking for shoes*, Cathy thought, snickering softly, knowing her sister to be quite the shoe horse.

The aroma of baked muffins from the night before was still in the air when Anna entered the kitchen. Four years younger than Cathy, Anna put the idea of the mousy accountant in the dust. At 6'1 she made a traditional skirt suit or pant suit look as if it belonged on the runways of Milan. Her shoulder length brown hair framed her high cheekbones and perfect oval-shaped face to give her a soft look that belied her frank and precise nature. Anna was definitely not the stereotypical accountant and it had taken a secure brother to win her heart. Her fiancé was Roger Beckett, an electrical engineer, who at 6'3 loved being seen with his tall mocha latte, as he called her, a reference to her glowing, even complexion. "Another morning filled with fresh baked goods. You know I'm going to gain at least ten pounds this summer." Anna patted her thighs.

"You can blame it on me," Catherine laughed.

"It should be so easy." She checked out Cathy's outfit. "You look nice this morning. "

"Thanks, Anna. I'm heading into Manhattan later on."

Anna nodded her head before turning her attention to the muffins. "How many carbs are in the muffins?"

Cathy thought for a moment. "Twelve. I used Splenda to lower the sugar."

Anna, an insulin dependent diabetic, programmed the number into her pump.

"Are the papers here yet?" Anna asked.

"They're on the dining room table." Cathy pointed to the table.

Anna retrieved the papers from the dining room table. She stopped to giggle.

Cathy looked up. "What's so funny?"

"You didn't see this?"

Cathy raised her eyebrows. "You know I'm only interested in the sports page in the morning."

Anna chuckled. "I'll never understand why. You watched the game last night. You know your Yankees won."

"True, but you know how I am during the season."

"How could I forget?" Anna paused to read the back page. "I see your man was on point last night."

Cathy let out a dreamy sigh. "I'll say. He was three for four last night."

Smiling, Anna shook her head. "Why can't you be into basketball like the rest of the sistahs?"

Cathy looked up with a wry smile. "Because basketball wasn't our summer reprieve, baseball was."

Reminded, Anna backed down. "You're right about that. I don't know what came over me."

"So what's happening in the gossip columns?" Cathy said as she turned her attention back to the magazine.

"It seems the gossip columns can't decide whether the it girl of the moment has lost or gained weight after having a baby. Then there's another blurb here about a model who had a month to get the baby weight off for a fashion show."

Cathy hung her head, disgusted. "Nine months to put it on and thirty days to take it off. You see why I stick to the sports page. That's ridiculous."

"Tell me about it." Anna tossed the newspapers on the table while she made her tea. "If you're not reading the paper, what's so interesting?"

"An article in this month's *Glamour* I've been meaning to read."

Anna sat down with her muffin and tea. "What's it about?"

"Sex, of course," Cathy chirped.

"Figures."

"The article is fascinating. Women are revealing their true number of sexual partners."

"Must be anonymous."

"Of course, women never reveal such things unless it's to complete strangers."

"So how do we stack up?"

Cathy laughed. "We're in the embryonic league."

"Speak for yourself. I'm no heavy hitter, but I can't be that bad."

"You're also engaged."

Anna beamed at her princess cut diamond engagement ring. "True. When's the last time you had sex?"

"It's been so long I think I might be a reconstituted virgin. Mother will be so proud."

"I wouldn't go around telling anyone that," Anna cautioned.

"Career wise, I'm a 21st century woman."

"With a sex life from the 1800s. We're not living our lives to please Mom anymore. We can't."

"We couldn't please her if we wanted to. As far as she's concerned we might as well install a revolving door and put golden arches over our bedrooms." Cathy leaned back in the chair.

"You're right about that," Anna said sipping her tea.

Ten years ago Cathy and Anna had been members of a religion that didn't celebrate holidays or birthdays. Dating was permitted with a chaperone or in a group as long as the couple intended to get married. This rule applied to twenty-somethings to forty-somethings and beyond.

Needless to say, premarital sex was definitely way off limits. After years of feeling confined, Cathy and Anna left the fold to pursue a more normal adult life without restrictions. Although they didn't go buck wild, Elizabeth, their mother, was concerned that was exactly what they did, and there was no talking her out of that belief.

"My lack of a sex life has nothing to do with Mom. I just decided to take some time off from relationships and dating. I'm concentrating on my health and my business," Cathy said.

"You're hopeless. Ivy League education and this is what you do with it. You know there is only so much cooking, cleaning, walking and working you can do to work off your sexual tension."

Cathy was floored. "What sexual tension?"

"Listen, sister, I've caught you detailing the kitchen floor grout with a toothbrush at two o'clock in the morning."

"So you caught me once or twice, that's not a big deal."

"You also bake like a fiend in the early hours too."

"So? I like to bake."

"So you had a little after hours energy and you really wanted to do someone, not something." She sipped her tea. "On the other hand, you could be Madison and lose count of who's warming the sheets every other night."

"He's a legend in his own mind. A divorce attorney with a capital D. I think he leaves his cell phone on vibrate to save time on his off nights."

There was a knock on the door.

Cathy looked at her watch. "It's about that time. It's Madison."

"What's up with him?"

"His car is in the shop."

"That figures. The door's open!" Anna yelled.

Doing what could only be termed as his George Jefferson strut, Cathy and Anna's first cousin Madison walked in. Madison had been one of the few African Americans to make *Law Review*. He had since taken his degree and translated it into a thriving matrimonial law practice. His reputation as a hard line negotiator and prenuptial agreement buster kept his appointment calendar full. Always concerned with his appearance, Madison put the metro in metrosexual long before *Queer Eye for the Straight Guy*. At 5'6 he was one of the shorter people in the family. However, what he lacked in height he made up for in attitude and style, winning over clients and judges alike. His motto was, 'Barrister defend thy clients as thy would defend thyself.' It was a lesson he learned early after getting burned by his own divorce. Now Madison lived his love life à la carte, sampling as many women as humanly possible. This was a habit which got him in more trouble with women than it was worth.

Head held high, Madison strutted in. "I could have melted waiting for you two to open the door."

"This isn't the courtroom. You don't have make such a dramatic entrance. You surely do not impress us." Anna crossed her legs.

"Not to mention you're wearing your custom suit from Brooks Brothers."

Cathy sipped her coffee. "Your car's in the shop. How did you get over here?"

"Rena gave me a ride in her shiny new Jaguar." "Rena.

The one woman you can't have," Cathy said.

He grabbed a muffin. "She is a lesbian, you know. While the thought appeals to me, she's not having it."

"Rena has a new Jag?" Anna asked.

"Yeah, even lesbians drive chick magnets."

"Except they call it a clit magnet and they know where to find it, which is more than I can say for some men, my fiancé excluded."

"You are most certainly not talking about me; I'm familiar with the terrain."

Cathy covered her mouth. "God, you know how to ruin someone's appetite in the morning."

"He said terrain. Talk about a misnomer," Anna quipped.

"Ha, ha, very funny." Madison barked.

"I still don't know why you bought that linen suit; your pants will look like an elephant's butt at the end of the day," Cathy teased Madison.

Anna burst out laughing.

"I look damn fine. Would it kill you two to agree with me once in a while?"

"You already have a harem for that," Anna joked.

He turned to Cathy. "So what are you wearing, Ms. Chambers?"

She put her magazine down. "Cotton. I don't want people to feel compelled to throw peanuts at my butt every time I get up."

Anna snickered but again Madison wasn't amused.

"You're heading into the city, right?" Anna asked. Cathy nodded. "We have a staff meeting."

Madison looked surprised. "You're not doing the home office thing today?"

"No." Cathy sighed at the thought of a long day. "It's a mandatory meeting, but I won't be in Manhattan for too long."

Anna stood up. "I'll call the president on my way to work and remind her that you're not going to be home today."

Cathy cracked a smile. "That's right, she wanted to go shopping. I have to neglect my duties of state." She tapped her hands on the table to the beat of 'Hail to the Chief.'

The president thing was a running joke with Cathy and Anna. Somehow their mother hadn't gotten the message they're adults.

"Don't worry, she'll probably go with Ingrid," Anna shrugged it off.

"Imagine that, and I wore the right bra and everything," Cathy joked.

Anna laughed while Madison looked confused.

"You broke out the industrial brassiere?"

"Definitely. If there is anything I don't want to hear anymore, it's a state of the union address on tits, gravity and the woman."

Anna nodded in agreement "Oh yes. The pencil analogy. If you place a pencil underneath one and it falls, you're firm. If it doesn't fall, you're drooping."

"Which in essence means you can double as a bat rack for the Yankees," Cathy added.

Madison feigned being uncomfortable. "I don't want to hear any more of this talk; it might damage my gentlemanly sensibilities." He pretended to cover his ears.

"Mr. Vibrating Cell Phone in My Front Pants Pocket has gentlemanly sensibilities," Cathy quipped.

Anna laughed. "So you'll be heading home after the meeting."

"Yes, but I'm meeting Jim for lunch before the meeting."

Anna raised an eyebrow. "Are you sure it's lunch and not therapy?"

Cathy laughed. Anna thought she was more of a therapist than agent sometimes. "Yes, I'm sure it's lunch. There's always something going on his life."

Anna picked up her briefcase. "I guess that's why I'm an accountant. I know you get a percentage of his royalties, but it seems to me that you're more than earning it."

"Hey, it took two years and God knows how many rejections before we found a publisher for him and now he's writing bestsellers. If he wants to vent and moan that's fine with me. Anyway, I don't consider him just a client, he's also a friend."

"Better you than me." Anna turned to Madison. "Don't you need a ride to the train station?"

"As a matter of fact I do, since you're offering," he answered.

"I know that's the only reason you came over," Anna said.

"Certainly not for my ego."

"If you want your ego massaged, call one of your little harem girls."

He winced. "I wish you wouldn't call them that."

"Would you rather we call them your stable of hoochie coochie mammas?"

"I like the sound of harem better."

"I thought so." Anna put her sunglasses on. "See you later, Cathy."

"Have a good one, Cathy," Madison smiled. "I'll see you two later."

Cathy hadn't started her career as a literary agent. Armed with a B.S. and a B.A. in business management from Yale, Cathy entered the work force as a paralegal. She was ten times smarter than the lawyers she worked for and they knew it. It was Cathy who researched the case law, wrote briefs and did everything short of appearing in court. It was an uptight existence. She gave becoming a lawyer serious consideration but she was a divorced mother of twins with mounting bills and major headaches.

To relieve stress Cathy would bake all kinds of goodies, using her great grandmother's recipes from the Caribbean and her grandmother's Southern recipes. On a lark, Anna told her to write a cookbook and the thought appealed to her. She gathered all the recipes, put together a book proposal and marketing plan. Then she pitched to every agent she could, including E.D. Smith. He decided to take a chance on her and together they got her book published successfully. In fact, they worked so well together E.D. suggested they become partners. Cathy had leaped at the chance to leave law behind. That was ten years earlier. Today the Chambers-Smith Agency represented 30 authors with a staff of two junior associates, two assistants and one office manager. E.D was the senior partner and Cathy the managing partner. Although sounding glamorous, the life of a literary agent took a lot of work and flexibility. Sometimes it called for Cathy to be a referee, a therapist or a hard line negotiator. Other days she was a sweet talking dealmaker, a challenging editor or a cheerleader. Nevertheless, it was a job she relished doing, most of the time.

The house quiet, Cathy took her briefcase downstairs. As she placed her briefcase on the table she checked the time. It was still early so she had a little time to watch *Good Morning America* in peace and get her thoughts together before heading into the city. Just as she got comfortable her cell phone rang.

“Wishful thinking,” she muttered, then took a deep breath before she hit the talk button.

“Hello?”

“Cathy.” It was the unmistakable voice of Jan Peters, Steven Anderson’s editor.

“Good morning, Jan. How’s it going?” She braced for the answer.

“Not bad but it could be better. Have you heard from Steven?”

“I spoke to him last week. Is there a problem?”

“I’m still waiting for him to complete the revisions on his current project.”

Cathy rubbed her forehead. “When I talked to him last week he said he was working on the final touches.”

“Really? I haven’t been able to reach him at all.”

“I’ll find out what’s happening and have him get in touch with you.”

“Thanks, Cathy. I’ve been trying to get in touch with him for the past week. I finally figured that I was better off calling you.”

“I understand. I’ll take care of it.”

“Thanks a million, Cathy.” “Not a problem,” she lied.

Cathy groaned as she searched through the programmed numbers on her phone. Steven Anderson was of her prima donna authors. He hated to be edited in any way. Cathy knew she had a fight ahead of her.

She got his machine. “This is Steven. I’m not available. Leave a message.”

"This is your agent, Steven. I just spoke to your editor. Please get your manuscript to Jan as soon as possible and that includes the third chapter as you agreed to do it. I'll be in the city office this morning if you need to get in touch with me."

She closed the phone.

Each of his three books had been with a different editor. He had already gone through two deadline extensions to finish this manuscript. *If Steven gives me one more ounce of trouble I will kick his uppity butt 'til hell wouldn't have it again,* she resolved. *One day I'm going to get a life. At least I'd be worked up about a man I'm actually sleeping with*, she thought as she unmuted the television.

Cathy watched the metropolitan news scroll on the bottom of the screen for the sports results. *Yankees 3 Oakland 2. Yes!* Anna had it right: She had watched the game and knew the final score but seeing it again just reinforced her Yankee smugness.

Being a Yankee fan had been a tradition in the Chambers family since the days of Babe Ruth. Cathy's paternal great grandfather used to take her grandmother to see Ruth and Gehrig play back in the days when you could bring your wife and daughter for a quarter. The tickets had been a bit more expensive for Cathy's dad but Yankee

Stadium was the only place she could be a normal teenager. No one knew she didn't celebrate birthdays, Christmas or holidays. At the stadium Cathy blended in with the crowd. In every other area of her life religious dictates made her stand out like a sore thumb.

Secretly she had wished her father would stand up to her mother so she and Anna could have a normal life, but as long as her mother could point to him as an adulterer, he was hard pressed to do anything but make sure he paid child support and alimony on time if he wanted to keep the peace.

Eventually Cathy and Anna rebelled in the only way they knew how: They got married young. Cathy thought it would deliver her from her mother and her religion's controlling ways. As it turned out, her deliverance was scored by dueling banjos. Her husband cheated and left her to care for her twin babies, Alexander and Andrew, alone. She got divorced but stayed amongst the faithful for a while before disassociating herself in favor of giving her sons a chance at a normal life with all those things that had been taken away from her life, including real dating.

By the time Cathy got around to her love life after the divorce, she was 29 years old going on 16. With no dating experience she thought she'd hit the jackpot when she met Paul at one of her first real social functions as a single woman. They dated for seven years before she caught him in the act with one of his students. It had broken her heart.

As the sports report wrapped up, Cathy rummaged through her bag for her train ticket. Her cell rang.

"Hello?"

"Mom?" the voice screeched.

"Alex? Is that you?"

"Yeah, Mom."

"You have a cold or just a sore throat?"

"My throat is sore, Mom."

"I can hear that. What have you done for it?"

"Nothing yet. That's why I called."

Cathy stopped herself from laughing. At 6'3 and 6'2, respectively, her baby boys were quite grown. "You called me because you have a sore throat?"

He cleared his throat. "Yes."

"You realize I am over 400 miles away on Long Island, right?"

"I know, Mom. What can I take?"

"I told you to pack the sore throat medicine."

"What sore throat medicine?"

"The one I've been giving you for the past four years every time you got a sore throat."

"Oh right. I forgot."

"Don't they have a place where you can buy something on campus?"

"Yeah."

"Ask your brother to get it for you before he goes to his next class. Okay?" "Yeah, Mom."

"In the meantime, have some tea with lemon and honey. Don't forget to gargle."

"Okay. Did you see the game last night, Mom?"

"Of course I did."

"Marcus Fox is the man," he boasted.

"You'd better believe it."

"You know, Mom, I didn't think I'd find you at home."

She looked at the clock. "I am going to the city a little later today. I have a business lunch and a staff meeting."

"Sounds like a busy day, Mom."

"It looks that way."

"All right, Mom. I'll let you go. I have to see if Andrew can pick up the medicine."

"Okay."

"I'll talk to you later, Mom."

"Okay, but don't forget to take something for your throat so you don't miss too many classes."

"I won't. Talk to you later, Mom."

"Okay."

She un-muted the television again.

At the end of her relationship with Paul nearly three years earlier, Cathy had decided she didn't have the time or energy to devote to dating. The only man in her life now usually took her on a rollercoaster ride of highs and lows for six months before leaving her to pine away until it was spring again. That man was shortstop extraordinaire, Marcus Fox.

Marcus, the go to guy for the Yankees, was a convenient crush for Cathy. He personified all she could want in a man: He was good looking, smart, a gifted athlete and best of all, unattainable. After all, she'd been up to the plate once with her husband and once with Paul. Win or lose, it was the perfect relationship.

***

Marcus' stomach made it hard to concentrate during the business meeting. It had taken his agent several weeks and God knows how many phone calls, emails and faxes to set up this endorsement deal for the car dealership. Marcus certainly didn't want to blow it but he hadn't eaten since seven that morning. He glanced at the highlighted numbers on the proposal. *Who would have guessed that a kid from the suburbs of Michigan would have a payday like this?* He thought. He was also fully aware that with the addition of more zeroes, he'd come under greater scrutiny. While Marcus welcomed the money, he wasn't crazy about the surcharge, the loss of his privacy. He started to fidget at the thought.

Ben Bradford knew that look all too well. His favorite and his only client was restless, so he made a move to wrap up the meeting. A spectacled, tall, distinguished looking, athletic WASP with salt and pepper hair, Ben was more like a favorite uncle than sports agent.

Ben stood up with his hand out. "All right, gentlemen. I think we've covered everything."

Abe Bryant shook Ben's hand. "I'm glad we got this worked out. I'll have my attorney's office fax over the final papers to your guy and if everything checks out we'll messenger the contracts over."

"Sounds good to me." Ben smiled and turned to Marcus. "What do you think, Marcus?"

Marcus, who was staring blankly out the living room window, snapped into action. "I think it's good." He shook Abe's hand and escorted him to the door.

Both Ben and Abe looked a bit discombobulated at how quickly Abe was being ushered out. Ben recovered the moment. "I know you have another meeting so we appreciate your taking the time to see us personally."

"Not a problem. I was happy to do it." He turned to Marcus. "Good luck at the game."

"Thanks."

Once Abe was out of the door Ben turned to Marcus. "My God, Marcus, you practically gave the man the bum's rush." He smiled. "He did just offer you a pretty big payday."

Marcus slipped into his sports jacket. "I'm sorry, but man, I'm starving." He patted his stomach as if to quell the beast.

"You want to order something in?"

"No. I'm in the mood for a nice steak." Looking in the mirror, Marcus straightened his jacket. It fitted him as if someone had poured fabric over his broad shoulders and down to his trim waist. He looked razor sharp and he knew it.

"How about Keen's?" Ben asked.

Marcus grinned. "Now you're talking. You're also buying, right?" he teased Ben.

"I'm not the one with all the zeroes in my paycheck," Ben joked.

Marcus put his arm around Ben. "I guess I could spot you this one time."

The two men laughed as they left the apartment to wait for the elevator.

After stepping on, Ben pressed the button for the main floor. The elevator stopped two floors down and a lovely, lanky brunette got on. She batted her eyes at Marcus.

"Good afternoon, Mr. Fox," she practically purred.

Marcus smiled. "Good afternoon."

"Looks like things are heating up today. Wouldn't you say, Mr. Fox?" she asked.

"It certainly does," Marcus answered, ready to play her game.

"It will cool down soon enough, though," Ben said, injecting himself into the conversation. Marcus got the hint.

For all his triumphs on the field, Marcus Fox hadn't had much success with relationships. Some people thought it was due to all his high profile choices, while others said it was the race factor.

Marcus's mother was Irish and his father African American. Naturally Marcus had his father's skin tone. Most people, especially African Americans, identified him as black. Therefore, he'd taken a lot of heat for not dating black women exclusively. Occasionally he got some hate mail chastising him about it.

When they arrived on the main floor, Ben pulled Marcus back to let the brunette get a head start.

"What did you do that for?" Marcus complained.

Ben looked at him knowingly. "You know why I did it."

Marcus dismissed the thought. "It was just a couple of letters, Ben. No big deal."

"Well, you'll have to excuse me if I take it more seriously than you do. I don't take threatening letters lightly and you shouldn't either. There are some crazy folks out there."

"I know. Still, I don't want to live in fear about my choices. If I date a woman it's not because she's white or black, it's because there is something about her that attracts me. "

"I know the heart wants what it wants. You should still be careful."

Marcus patted Ben on the back. "I'll take it under advisement. Right now I have to call for the car."

"The car's here." Ben pointed to the front entrance.

"Cool. When did you do that?"

"That's my little secret." Ben laughed.

CHAPTER 2

There was something about being in New York that despite the heat put a little pep in Cathy's step. She had a rhythm as she walked through Penn Station. A person seeing her might think she was walking the fashion runways to the beat of the Bee Gees' "Staying Alive" or the intro to Beyonce's "Crazy in Love". Cathy was as confident as she'd ever been in her life with her size 16/18 body.

Cathy stepped off the escalator near Herald Square and continued her strut before she stopped to look at her reflection in the window of Macy's. Turning her body slightly, she made sure the V-neck shirt dress revealed a hint of her size 40 DD cleavage in just the right way. With her breasts she made quite an impression when she entered a room. She gave herself one last check. Everything as it should be, she continued her booty-licious assault on 34th street.

A welcome rush of cool air greeted Cathy as she arrived at Keen's around twelve forty-five. Though she'd enjoyed her walk, she didn't feel much like waiting around to get a table and Keen's was crowded. Lucky for her she didn't have a long wait.

"Cathy!" Dahlia, Keens' exuberant and beautiful hostess, came over with arms outstretched for a hug. "How are you, darling? You look wonderful." Dahlia had a way of making everything she said sound like a song. "I'm good, Dahlia. How are you?"

She shrugged her shoulders. "I can't complain." Dahlia's warm smile brightened once again. "How about we get you a table?"

"That would be lovely," Cathy sighed.

"Follow me." She grabbed a couple of menus.

Cathy followed Dahlia through the dining room to a place near some gorgeous young women, all of whom looked like models; the table was a virtual kaleidoscope of beautiful women of all colors. Cathy felt a sense of dread. *Oh God, it figures I'm actually hungry this afternoon. Should I wait and let Dahlia find another table further away?* No sooner did the thought enter her mind, than she dismissed it. Keen's was rather crowded and she was hungry; that was the bottom line. Besides, her client, Jim Weil, would surely appreciate the view more than she.

"Here you go, darling." Dahlia placed the menus on the table.

Cathy sat down. "Thanks, Dahlia."

"Anything for my favorite literary agent."

Cathy grinned. "I told you, when you're ready to do your book let me know. I know you have stories to tell."

Dahlia leaned closer to the table. "You don't know the half of it." She winked.

"Well, I can't wait to find out."

"I'll send the waiter over to take your drink order. *Bon appétit.*" "Thanks again."

***

NOT HIS TYPE

Across the room Ben and Marcus were discussing a little business with a good steak lunch. While Ben had a cold beer, it was game night for Marcus and he nursed a Pellegrino with a twist.

"So are you excited about this deal?" Ben asked as he sipped his beer.

"Sure."

"You don't sound excited."

"Of course I'm excited. I think signing with Abe's dealership was a good idea."

"I'm glad you think so. I wasn't sure you were paying attention."

He chortled. "I was paying attention. Just because…" Marcus stopped mid-sentence when he saw Cathy. Hair bouncing, she smiled at her waiter, obviously engaged in a minor flirtation. A born breast man, his eyes immediately zeroed in on her cleavage. Driven to distraction, he kept missing as he tried blindly to slice a non-existent slice of steak on his plate.

Ben chuckled as he wiped his mouth. He'd seen this look before. "Marcus?"

He snapped out of his trance. "You were saying, Ben?"

Ben put his napkin down. "You haven't heard a word I said." He looked around. "So where are they?"

"Where are who?"

"The breasts that have you mesmerized. I know they have to be around here somewhere." His eyes searched the room.

Marcus knew he was caught. He laughed. "The hostess just seated a woman in a blue dress."

Ben tried not to be too obvious. "Yeah, I see the hostess."

"I'm not talking about the hostess. I'm talking about the woman in the blue dress." He looked closer. "She's almost directly across from us. I think it's a Yankee blue dress."

Ben scanned the room, then spotted Cathy. "Oh, I see her." He shook his head. "Do you have sonar or something? You always manage to scope out the biggest breasts in the room."

Marcus shrugged. "What can I say? It's a gift."

Ben pushed his glasses off the tip of his nose. "Okay, breast man, we'd better eat and get out of here soon. You have a game tonight."

"I know. But there's no law that says I can't look." "Not yet." Ben mused.

"Well, if they passed one, I would happily go to jail."

Ben conceded. "You and me both."

Marcus went back to his porterhouse but not before smiling in Cathy's direction.

***

Completely unaware of Marcus' presence, or interest in her, Cathy ordered lunch. Jim always ran late. She actually enjoyed the quiet, reader friendly buzz of the restaurant. However, today the quiet buzz didn't last for long as the table of supermodels suddenly came alive with girlish giggles and chatter. Cathy knew there was only one thing that could elicit such a reaction: a man. And not just any man, a famous one.

Cathy mustered up her cool and as nonchalantly as possible she scanned the restaurant to see who the supermodels were so worked up about. When she saw Marcus Fox she nearly broke into a giggle herself but thought better of it. After all, she was a dignified 40-year-old literary agent and mother. She'd giggle when she got home, like any other star-struck fan over 35. *Gorgeous.* She felt a chill down her spine but she reminded herself she wasn't there to ogle, but to discuss business with a client. She checked her cell phone again. No message from Jim.

Food in front of her, Cathy amused herself with a little lunch theater as the scene at Keen's became part circus, part drama and part fashion show. Each of the supermodels sashayed in front of Marcus's table but he ignored them all.

"Can you believe this?" he muttered.

"Believe what? The way those girls are walking around to get your attention? Of course I believe it." Ben sipped his water.

"Well, I wish they would sit down already. I've been trying to make eye contact with the woman in the blue dress and they keep getting in my way." He scowled.

"You're smiling in their direction. What else are they going to think?" Ben reasoned. "They don't know about your obsession with breasts. If they did, they would sit down. From the looks of things I don't think there's a B cup in the bunch. Hell, I'm not sure if you added them all together there would be a B cup."

Marcus laughed in spite of himself. "I think you're right about that."

"I know I'm right. Just relax. I'm sure they'll get the hint."

Marcus glanced at his watch. "I hope they get the hint soon."

For her part Cathy was surprised the supermodels didn't get any play from him. Every entertainment reporter in New York deemed Marcus Fox the stud of studs and a real player. Every other day one of the gossip columns reported on some aspect of his social life and the women (specifically singers, actresses and models) he dated. Yet with a virtual smorgasbord of models to choose from, he passed. The bewildered girls looked as if they'd been voted off *Survivor* by a tribal council of one, and they were none too happy about it.

Fascinated, Cathy watched the latest castoff go back to the table.

"Are you sure he's not a down low brother?" one of the models asked.

Cathy covered her mouth as she nearly choked on her steak.

"He doesn't look like a down low guy," another answered.

"Isn't that the point? They never look like down low brothers. Otherwise they'd be out."

"I don't think he's interested."

"Isn't he seeing that girl from that entertainment news show?"

"I read the gossip column and it said they're just friends."

"Well he's smiling at someone over this way. If it's not one of us, who is it?"

"Forget about it. Let's just pay the check and get out of here. It's his loss."

As the dejected supermodels made their way out, Cathy realized she wasn't the only one watching. *If I didn't know better I would say Marcus Fox looks relieved*, she mused.

Marcus did in fact breathe a sigh of relief.

"Marcus, are you ready to bounce?" Ben was a little anxious about the time.

"Not quite. I need to get the waiter."

Ben looked incredulous. "Are you telling me that you want something else after that porterhouse?"

Marcus wasn't fazed. "Yeah. Signal the waiter for me."

In the meantime Cathy answered her cell phone.

"Cathy? It's Jim. I'm so sorry about lunch."

She pretended to be annoyed. "You could have called me earlier, you know."

"I know, I just got caught up in things."

"By things you mean either cigars with your crew or some new young thing."

"I'm through chasing after young things."

"Spoken like a man who is nowhere near ready to give up chasing younger women no matter how much trouble they get him into," Cathy quipped. "Can I get a rain check on lunch?" "Eventually," she teased.

"You know you're the best."

Cathy smiled but she didn't let on. "Yeah, sure. Yada, yada, yada. I'll talk to you later."

"Okay."

Just as Catherine put her cell phone away the waiter came over.

"Something for dessert?"

Dessert. What could be better? She thought as she eyed the menu.

Her eyes widened at the very words, *chocolate mousse*. "I'd love the chocolate mousse."

"Certainly."

Wait a minute, Marcus Fox is still here. I can't let him see me make a pig of myself. A little wave of guilt glided over her. "No, I changed my mind. I'll just have a cup of coffee."

"Sure."

In an instant Cathy silently chastised herself for changing her mind about dessert. *With all my talk about feeling sexy in my own skin I still didn't want Marcus Fox to see me eat dessert. Never mind that I powered down a New York strip, baked potato, salad and steamed vegetables. I might not have pranced in front of him but I was as bad as the supermodels,* she sighed. Every day was a battle in the crusade for real self-acceptance of her body.

***

Ben signaled for Cathy's waiter to come over.

"Yes, sir?"

"Did the lady in the blue dress order dessert?" Marcus asked

"No, sir. She ordered coffee."

"What was she going to order?"

"The chocolate mousse."

"Okay. Get it for her and put her lunch and dessert on my tab." He gave the waiter a $100.00 tip.

His eyes lit up. "Thank you, sir. I'll take care of it." The waiter went into the kitchen.

Arms folded, Ben asked a silly question. "We're not leaving yet, are we?"

Marcus smiled. "Nope."

A few minutes later the waiter placed the chocolate mousse and coffee in front of a very puzzled Cathy.

She took a whiff of her coffee for hallucinogens or liquor. Then she pinched her arm to make sure this wasn't some post lunch traumatic stress thing.

Satisfied that she wasn't nuts, she looked up at the waiter. "I'm sorry. I changed my mind about the mousse."

"Yes ma'am. However, this is compliments of the gentleman."

He motioned towards Marcus's table but only Ben was there.

Cathy was confused. "I don't think I know him."

The waiter glanced over and saw Ben. "That's not him; it was the other gentleman."

"What other gentleman?"

The waiter seemed genuinely surprised. "He was there a few minutes ago." He paused to scan the room. "He wanted you to enjoy dessert and lunch is on him."

She was floored. "Well, tell him thank you if you see him." She went for her bag. "At least I can get your tip."

"No need, he took care of that too."

She was dumbfounded. *Who in the world would send me dessert and then pay for my lunch right down to the tip?* Catherine stared at the mousse as if it were a magic eight ball but staring wasn't going to answer her question; she decided she might as well enjoy.

Like a little girl, Cathy slowly put a spoonful in her mouth. She closed her eyes and let the delightful whipped texture melt on her tongue.

As Marcus approached he watched her full lips glide over the spoon and felt a sudden rush of heat under his collar.

Unaware of her audience, Cathy leaned forward to read her magazine, which pushed her breasts further into view.

Marcus hung back for a moment and stared at Cathy's assets. His eyes traced her body along the V-neck opening of her dress. The little freckle on her left breast was like a cherry on the top of Marcus's version of a sundae, perfection. He was more than hot under the collar. Another moment and the whole restaurant would know just how hot he was.

He cleared his throat. "Now that's what I like to see. A woman enjoying dessert."

The minute Cathy heard the voice she felt hot and cold at the same time. She struggled to put her thoughts together before she looked up but it was too late, she was helpless and breathless. It was as if her eyes had reached the summit of the Mount Everest of men. At 6'4 Marcus, with his light cappuccino complexion, tight body and hazel eyes was the epitome of gorgeous. Taking him in almost completely overwhelmed her senses. Cathy, usually never at a loss for words, searched for something smart to say. *What the hell is wrong with me? Why am I drawing a blank?*

He grinned. "Do you mind if I join you?"

"Sure. Be my guest," she finally managed to respond.

As he sat down and checked out the object of his distraction, his warm smile reflected his approval. "I'm glad I finally have your attention."

She was at a loss. "Finally have my attention? I didn't know you were trying to get my attention," she stuttered. Marcus struggled to keep his eyes on her face.

"The women at the table behind you noticed."

Cathy was surprised. "I saw you looking in this direction but I assumed you were interested in the supermodels." *I can't believe I said that out loud*, she thought to herself.

"I guess you read the gossip columns." He titled his head back and laughed.

Cathy's face felt flushed. *Look at those sexy lips. I wonder if they taste as good as they look.* Cathy was grateful he couldn't read her X-rated mind but she blushed just the same. "Sometimes."

He enjoyed making her blush. "You're blushing. That's so cute."

"I don't feel cute. I feel silly. I'm too old to blush like this."

"Says who?"

Her heart raced. "No one important."

"You know why I noticed you instead of them?"

Cathy leaned forward, which made her cleavage more noticeable. Again her breasts put Marcus in a trance. He just stared.

"Let me know if they answer you," she said softly.

He snapped out of it. "I'm sorry. What did you say?"

"I said let me know if they answer you."

Marcus was a little confused. "Who?"

She batted her eyes. *Now who's blushing?* "My boobs. You are apparently talking to them. I just want you to let me know if they answer because that would be one hell of a party trick."

He laughed. "I apologize."

Cathy smiled warmly. "Apology accepted." She leaned back. "So was I the only woman in the restaurant actually eating and not just pushing my food around the plate?"

He enjoyed her playful yet sardonic sense of humor. "I wasn't going to say that, but that's a good one." She shrugged.

"I noticed you because you were so busy working in the midst of all this noise. Nothing fazed you."

And here I thought it was boobs. She chuckled. "Funny, that's the same thought I have when I see you step onto the field. How in the world do you manage to perform under such a noisy microscope?"

"I love what I do and I owe it to our fans to do the best I can."

"It's kind of the same for me except I don't work in front of 50,000 plus fans at Yankee stadium. Not to mention God knows how many watching on television. I just do my best for my clients."

"What line of work are you in?" Marcus asked.

"I'm a literary agent."

"Really?" He leaned in to listen more closely to this beautiful and smart woman. It was a nice change. She was an even better balance: brains and breasts. She could be a challenge. He decided to play devil's advocate. "A literary agent. In your opinion what's the difference between sports agents, talent agents and literary agents? Don't all three basically serve the same essential purpose?"

"Yes. We represent artists in different mediums. I'm sure I'd get an argument from sports and talent agents, but I think literary agents have the toughest job."

He was intrigued. "Why's that?"

"For one thing, with the exception of nonfiction, which we can sell based on marketing research and hard facts, it's harder to get fiction published these days than ever before." She paused for a moment. "Come to think of it, nonfiction's not a picnic either."

"So why do you do it?"

"Because a yes washes away hundreds of rejections and makes it all worthwhile."

He was impressed with her sincerity. "You really have to love what you do."

"Absolutely, otherwise you wouldn't last one day. Frankly, you're just as vested in their project as they are."
"You said vested in their project and not their success. Doesn't their success mean money?"

"Oh, don't get me wrong, the money part is a good thing. It's just not the only thing. I don't know how to explain it." Catherine reflected a moment to make sure she didn't sound like an idiot. "Writing a book is like being pregnant, only gestation goes way beyond nine months. Fiction or nonfiction, the ideas are nurtured, fed and protected by the author. Then they turn the baby over to me, the agent, and it's my job to find the best home for it so it can be shared with the world."

Cathy wasn't sure if the look on his face meant he thought she was the craziest broad he'd ever met or not. She held her breath.

"That's an interesting way to describe it."

It was getting late so Marcus risked one more glance at her bodacious breasts. He liked that she hadn't let him get away with it before, but he was a breast man and couldn't keep from looking again.

Cathy was hip to even the slickest dip of the eye but this time she decided to let it slide. After all, he was *the* Marcus Fox. She figured she'd enjoy the attention while it lasted.

Marcus looked disappointed as he glanced at his watch. "I would love to talk more but I have to head over to the stadium."

"Of course, there's a game tonight at seven."

"Do you have tickets?"

"No. I'll have to settle for watching it on television."

"At least this time. But before I leave, can I ask you something?"

"Sure."

Cathy's heart fluttered as he pulled his chair closer to her. "Can I at least get your name?"

"How embarrassing. I'm Catherine Chambers."

They shook hands. "Pleasure meeting you, Catherine. By the way I'm Marcus Fox."

"As if I didn't know."

He chuckled. "Do you have a business card, Catherine?"

She reached into her bag and pulled out a couple of cards. "Here you go."

"Thank you." He studied the card. "The Chambers Stevens Literary Agency. Catherine Chambers, Managing Partner. Wow, managing partner. That's impressive."

"Thanks." *It should also say head bottle washer*, she thought.

He took a pen out. "This card lists your business numbers. Would it be possible for me to get your home number?"

She was taken aback. "My home number?"

"Yes, if you don't mind. I promise I won't write it on the wall of the clubhouse."

She laughed, then realized he was serious. *Oh my God. He really wants my home number. What's the harm in giving it to him? He's not going to use it.* She figured it couldn't get any more surreal than it already was. "It's 631-555-9864."

He jotted the number down. "I'll be giving you a call sooner rather than later." He winked.

The butterflies in her stomach moved. "Okay. By the way, thanks for lunch and dessert."

"My pleasure." His eyes were so intense Cathy was a little unsettled.

They shook hands. Cathy watched him as he walked over to Ben.

From his position Ben had watched Marcus interact with the lovely lady in the blue dress. He'd been around the block a few times with Marcus's dating/love life and knew the type of women he usually went for. And a full-figured woman was definitely outside his zone. *What do you know, Marcus might actually be growing up,* he thought.

Marcus walked up to Ben. "Are you ready to bounce?" Marcus said as he slipped her business card in his wallet.

"Sure. Are you ready? I thought you might want to spend a little more time with…"

"Catherine Chambers," Marcus filled in. "Catherine Chambers, literary agent."

"Impressive."

"I thought so too."

A young boy walked over and interrupted the conversation.

"Excuse me?" The little voice asked.

Marcus looked down. "Hi there. What's your name?"

The little boy tried to quell his excitement. "Kevin."

Marcus stooped down and shook his hand. "Nice to meet you, Kevin. I'm Marcus Fox."

The little boy giggled with delight. A breathless woman appeared. "There you are, Kevin." She let out a sigh of relief. "I've been looking all over for you."

"Sorry, Mom. I wanted to get Mr. Fox's autograph."

"I'm sure Mr. Fox doesn't have time for that."

"No, ma'am, that's quite all right. Where's your camera?"

His mother produced her cell phone.

"Terrific." He handed the camera phone to Ben. "Take a picture of the three of us, Ben."

"Sure."

"Do you know how to use the cell phone camera?" Marcus asked jokingly.

Ben ignored him and took a couple of pictures. He handed the phone back to Kevin.

"Thanks, Mr. Fox."

"Not a problem."

"Have a good game."

"Thanks, Kevin."

As Marcus and Ben walked out, Marcus turned to Ben. "Why don't the photographers ever print those pictures?"

"Pictures like that don't pay the bills, my friend."

From her table Cathy admired how graciously Marcus treated his fans. She was tickled that he'd asked her for her number, despite having had to call him on the boob stare. Deep down she thought, *There's no way he's going to call, but it sure felt good to give him my digits.* She could hear her sons moaning now. 'MOM! Digits is so lame.'

Suddenly she was hit with a thought. *I didn't think I had a snowball's chance in hell of actually meeting Marcus Fox, yet I met him today. He asked for my phone number, and I gave it to him.* She rubbed her forehead. *What have I gotten myself into?*

Cathy checked her watch. It was time to bounce if she wanted to make it to the staff meeting on time. Even though the office was a relatively short walk from Keen's, she hailed a cab.

Cathy got in the cab and stared out the window. *Will he call? If he does, what will I say or do?* Every question begot another and soon she had her head spinning.

"Miss?" the cabbie said.

She came back to earth. "I'm sorry."

"You're here."

"Oh thank you." She jumped out and paid the cabbie. "Keep the change."

"Thanks, lady."

Cathy paused outside. *It's time to get serious. I have to leave all this Marcus stuff on the curb.* Entering, she passed the reception desk and pressed the button for the elevator. *It's all about work and nothing else. Besides, why should I worry? There's no way he'll call. I read the papers. He dates women with legs that start at their shoulder. I'm definitely not his type.*

CHAPTER 3

As the managing partner of the Chambers-Stevens Literary Agency, Cathy's name went first on the stationery. More importantly, she was more hands on with the clients and publishers.

When Cathy arrived, the office had been in full swing since eight thirty. The office manager, Sylvia, opened around eight every day to enjoy the calm before the neuroticism level rose significantly. A tall, full-figured girl from the South, Sylvia made the office run like a well-oiled machine. Stationed near the entrance, she was the first one Cathy saw.

"Good afternoon, Sylvia."

She looked up from her computer. "Afternoon, Catherine. How are you?"

"I'm good. Do I have any messages?"

Sylvia handed her two message slips. "One is from Jennifer and the other is from Steven's editor. She called early this morning."

"I've already spoken with both of them today." "You can't resist dealing with the office stuff at home." "It's kind of hard to avoid when you have a home office. I used to have the kids' activities as a buffer, but now that they're in college it's full metal jacket."

"At least the Yankees make you happy, most of the time. Did you see Mr. Fox last night?"

Reggie, one of their interns, walked over to Sylvia's desk. "Talking about the Yankees' win, I bet." He grinned.

"Of course. My men in pinstripes pulled it out," Cathy chimed.

Reggie, a Mets fan, shook his head. "You Yankee fans with your roster of stars are something else."

"Don't talk to me about stars; you know my position on that." That was the one place she and the Yankees' boss differed: He was star struck and she believed in growing players.

Reggie conceded, "Well it was the farm system players who did their thing last night."

"That's right. Just look at the history. Mickey Mantle and Maris to name two. All the great players come from the farm system."

"Including Mr. Fox." Sylvia raised her eyebrow.

Cathy grinned like a Cheshire cat. Seeing him in person was her little secret for now. "He's the man."

Sylvia chuckled. "You are a do or die fan."

"Most definitely. I find that my dad, my boys and the men in pinstripes rarely disappoint me. I can't say that about most men."

"Ahem!" E.D cleared his throat as Reggie quickly scurried away.

"Check that, Sylvia. I'll add E.D to my short list."

"Thank you."

Cathy gave him a little peck on the cheek.

"Feel better, my poor under-loved and under-appreciated baby?"

Sylvia cracked up. "You two are too cute. Why don't you just get married already?"

"And ruin a perfectly good partnership? Nothing ruins a friendship quicker than sex."

"Amen to that, E.D."

"You two certainly seem married."

"We are married in a literary sense. What publishing has joined together let no man or woman pull apart," E.D. expounded.

Sylvia shook her head. "I don't think that's how the vows go."

"What do you expect, Sylvia? Neither E.D. or I have been married in eons and it shows."

Cathy settled into her little nook and booted up her computer. Sylvia poked her head in.

"Staff meeting at 2:15."

"Cool. Thanks."

"How was lunch with Jim?"

"He didn't show. I had lunch by myself."

Sylvia nodded her head. "You ate alone in the middle of a big restaurant? I don't know how you do it." Having been married for 20 years, dining alone was not a concept Sylvia got.

"It's no big deal. A girl's gotta eat."

"True." She paused. "You really don't mind eating alone?" she pressed.

Cathy shrugged it off. "I don't mind at all." *Besides, I wasn't alone for long.* Before she could stop herself, she grinned.

"What's that little grin about?" Sylvia asked.

Cathy played coy. "Nothing. I'm just in a good mood." She changed the subject. "Is Michelle in?"

Sylvia moved on. "Yes. I think she's coming down here to see you. Something about Beatrice Collins and Sandra McCoy."

"Oh good God! They're not at it again, are they?" Cathy cringed.

"As a matter of fact, they are," Michelle said as she leaned against the door.

Michelle Young, their 40-year-old junior associate, had been one of Cathy's closest friends since high school. An avid reader, she was just starting her second career after divorce. She was usually bright-eyed and bushy-tailed, but this afternoon she looked completely worn out.

"I'm almost afraid to ask."

"You have no idea." Michelle covered her eyes.

"Oh yes I do. I've been in the middle of this author/publisher tug of war for two years and four bestsellers."

Beatrice and Sandra represent one of the most contentious publisher/author relationships Cathy had ever dealt with. Separately both women were sweethearts, but for some unexplained reason they occasionally rubbed each other the wrong way. Normally Cathy handled them, but she'd put Michelle on the case to strengthen her diplomatic chops.

"Can you give me some tips on how to get oil and water to mix?"

"You use Good Seasons and shake things up. Let Beatrice know that we're prepared to go elsewhere. There are at least four other publishers of children's books who are just chomping at the bit to sign Sandra. We had to play it Beatrice's way in the beginning but now we have options *and* a contractual clause that allows us to shop." "Brilliant." Michelle beamed.

"Listen, whether I'm working here or at home, if she gives you any more grief pass her on to me. I'll handle it."

Michelle looked relieved. "Thank you. How in the world do you do this every day and still look unflappable?" "Just lucky I guess." Cathy shrugged.

Michelle stretched out on the sofa.

"You look tired, Michelle. Rough night?"

"Sort of." She sighed. "Not in a bad way though."

"I take it you had a date."

"Yeah. I met him at one of those Big Beautiful Women events. He's a real nice guy and a lot of fun."

Michelle usually kept Cathy in her dating loop; this time she'd played it close to the vest. "You stinker, you didn't say a word."

"I didn't want to jinx it. You know how I am."

"True. So how long have you been going out with him?"

"About two months."

"And you didn't think to tell one of your best friends?"

"Sorry, but I didn't want to hear any I told you so in case it didn't work out."

"And?"

"I think it's getting serious."

"I'm so happy for you, that's great." Cathy smiled.

"You should go to a BBW event; it's great and really empowering."

Catherine had been around the block on this subject more than a couple of times. She could almost set the questions and comments to music.

"I know. I've been to a few events. I met some great people and had a good time."

"There's a *but* coming."

"There's no *but*. I'm just not ready to date again."

Michelle sat up. "Come on, Cathy, it's been at least a year since you broke up with Paul."

"Two years. Almost three, really."

"All the more reason to get back out there. Your sons are in college and you're still young. Live a little."

Cathy was getting a little irritated. "I'll take it under advisement. Don't you have a staff meeting to get ready for?"

"Don't you ever get lonely?" Michelle insisted.

"That's why God made chocolate, sleeping pills and double A batteries, thank you very much."

"Maybe. But there's nothing like an energizer bunny of your very own."

Cathy laughed and tossed a paper clip at Michelle, which she quickly dodged.

"Hey, it's the truth," Michelle laughed.

"You should really get ready for the staff meeting. From the looks of E.D.'s memo this is going to be fun."

"I'm going. You're not the boss of me, you know," Michelle joked.

"As a matter of fact, I am your boss."

"That's right. Oops, my bad. Guess I'd better get ready for the staff meeting."

"Good idea."

***

Back in the Bronx Marcus was about ready to take batting practice. Ben kept his eye on his star player who looked a little distracted.

"Hey man, what's going on?" Marcus's teammate, Mark Vasquez, patted him on the back. Mark, a four time All Star, was a bit of a sex symbol. A mix of African American and Latino blood, he had a beautiful light bronze complexion and slim, strong build that attracted the ladies in droves. Nevertheless, he was somewhat of an anomaly in sports: He was happily married.

Marcus shook it off. "Nothing."

Mark knew better. He liked to subject Marcus to a little good-natured ribbing about his love life. "I've seen that look before. What's her name?"

Marcus tried to play it off. "What makes you think it's a woman?"

"Experience."

Marcus laughed. "It's that obvious?"

"To me it is. But then again, I've known you a long time now. So what gives?"

"Nothing. I met a nice woman this afternoon. Her name is Cathy."

"Is she a model, actress or singer?"

"None of the above. She's a literary agent."

Mark looked impressed. "A literary agent? That's interesting. But something tells me it wasn't her brains that caught your eye."

Marcus tried to sound offended. "Is that all you think I look at?"

Mark ignored his weak protest. "Yeah. I have to go by your track record. You're a breast man. A worshipper at the temple of the breasts."

Marcus got a little annoyed. "All right already. Enough with sayings." He paused. "There's more to her than breasts."

Mark was game. "Okay. Describe her to me."

"She's kind of tall, full-figured, with long red hair and sort of a caramel complexion. She's very attractive." Marcus paused to wait for a reaction.

Mark didn't give him the one he expected. "Smart and pretty, that's a good combination."

"That's all you have to say about it?"

"Why should I say more?"

"I thought you would trip over the full-figured part."

"Why should I trip over that? It's not something that makes a difference to you, so why should it bother me?"

Marcus felt a little ashamed of himself. "You're right. So she's full-figured. Big deal."

"It won't be a big deal unless you make it into one," Mark observed. "You approached her right?"

"Yeah."

"So there was something about her that drew you to her. Don't sweat it. Enjoy it."

Marcus tied his sneakers. "She does have a lot of cute freckles on her face and her…" He stopped before he went further.

Mark got the implication immediately. "She has freckles on her breasts, too, right?"

He smiled. "Just one on her left breast."

Mark playfully pulled Marcus's baseball cap down over his eyes. "You're hopeless," he joked as he walked away. "Call her. You know you want to."

Marcus thought about it and pulled his cell and her card from his jacket.

More than a little aware of how E.D. ran a staff meeting, Cathy kept meticulous notes on clients, publishing trends and publishers. While her printer shot out a few copies of the latest sales figures, she made some last minute additions.

Sylvia poked her head in. "I'm heading in. Are you coming?"

Cathy looked up. "Tell E.D. I'll be there in a minute. I'm just getting some of my projections and trends together."

"Okay."

Just as she pulled the last sheet off the printer the phone rang. With everyone in the conference room Cathy answered the call.

"Good afternoon, Chambers-Smith Agency."

"Hello, Cathy?"

Cathy's eyes got wide in a hurry. "Yes? Marcus?"

"Hi."

"Hi." Cathy was uncharacteristically speechless.

"I just thought I would give you a call. I really enjoyed meeting you this afternoon."

"The feeling is mutual. How's batting practice going?"

"I haven't actually taken it yet, but I'm sure it will be fine."

"Oh, I see."

Michelle knocked on her door.

"Are you coming, Cathy? You know how E.D. gets."

"Would you hold for just a minute?"

"Sure."

"Thanks." Cathy pressed the hold button and handed Michelle the reports. "Tell E.D. I will join you in progress."

"Okay." She turned and left.

Cathy took Marcus off hold. "Sorry about that. I have a staff meeting this afternoon."

"Oh, I'm sorry. Am I keeping you from it?"

"Yes, but I can afford to be a few minutes late. What's the point of being a managing partner if you can't arrive late to a meeting every now and again?"

He laughed. "It must be nice to be the boss. You get the cool office and the big money."

Cathy was amused. "I do have a cool office but the big money is debatable. Maybe your boss has the big money."

"That's the truth."

E.D. walked in. "Cathy, are you coming? You know I hate to begin the meetings without you."

She covered the receiver. “I’ll be there in a minute, E.D.” Her patience had worn a little thin.

“Okay.” He walked out.

She uncovered the receiver. “Sorry about that.”

“It sounds like they need you. I’ll let you go.”

“I’m sorry. The natives really are getting restless.”

“I’ll call you later, okay?”

“Sure. Good luck tonight.”

“Thanks. You’ll be watching?”

“I never miss a game.”

He smiled. “Have a good afternoon meeting.”

“Thanks.” She smiled. “Bye.”

“Bye.”

As soon as Marcus flipped his phone shut, Ben handed him a bat.

“You’re up.”

“Thanks, man.” He smiled and jogged to the batter’s cage.

Then Mark jogged back into the dugout and patted Ben on the back. “So Mr. Agent, in your opinion is this a twenty-four hour bug or what?”

“To tell you the truth, I think this one might be a keeper.”

The two men watched a smiling Marcus in the batter’s cage.

“I think you might be right, Ben. This one bears watching.”

***

Two hours after the staff meeting Cathy managed to take the last off peak train home. Staring out the window, her mind drifted to lunch and Marcus Fox. A part of her wanted to dwell on and enjoy the moment, but the other part was deathly afraid of getting her hopes up. She was afraid to get happy. It wasn't so much a case of Murphy's Law as it was about being punished by God for leaving the church.

According to her former church, anyone who left the fold was like a dog that returned to its vomit. Whether or not God intended the reference to be used in this manner, it was a graphic and effective guilt tactic pulled from the pages of the New Testament. She could expect no blessings to come her way due to her disobedience. As a result, Cathy always waited for the other shoe to drop. Today, however, Cathy made an exception. She was buzzed without one sip of alcohol. She'd had a shot of Marcus Fox straight with no chaser and she was unapologetically on cloud nine when the train stopped at her station. Dreamy-eyed, she walked through the parking lot to her car. Just as she turned the ignition she closed her eyes and recalled his gorgeous light eyes and slim muscular build. *I could just eat him up.* She sighed. *God, his butt was even cuter in person, if that's humanly possible.* The sound of a car horn blaring jolted her back into reality.

"God! Give someone a chance to pull out, why don't you?" she shouted. Car in gear, she nearly slammed into the car behind her, causing the other driver to recoil. "Serves you right, you donkey," she huffed.

Her cell phone rang. It was E.D. She composed herself. "Hey E.D., what's the word?"

"I talked to Patrick and he says we'll have an official offer later today."

Cathy was delighted "That's great news. Have you told Tim yet?"

"I just did and he's going to call the Jacksons himself."

"Good. He deserves to make this call. I'm just so glad it worked out."

"Makes two of us." He breathed a sigh of relief.

"Okay, we'll talk later."

"Okay, Cathy."

That was just the kind of news Cathy needed to hear. The Chambers-Smith Agency now had 25 writers with publishing contracts. Flying high, she caught her second wind in time for a quick trip to the supermarket.

A bit of a bon vivant, Cathy picked up a few things for the evening menu. She bought organic butter, shallots, jumbo shrimp, basil, fresh-made pasta, mixed salad greens, Pellegrino, light cream, prime aged parmesan cheese from Italy and a large bag of Kona coffee beans. It was just enough to fit in one bag. Now that her sons were away at college, she had to lug the grocery bags into the house. Just as Cathy was putting things away, the house phone rang.

"Hello?" Balancing a bag of shrimp, salad, basil and butter, Cathy struggled to keep the phone to her ear.

"Hey, Cathy," Madison said.

"Hi, Madison, hold on for a minute."

"Sure."

She set everything down on the counter. Cathy knew Madison never had much in the way of groceries in his house, unless she counted his *9 1/2 Weeks* stash. The call was about dinner so she put it out there first.

"So you want to come to dinner tonight?"

"Oh, you're inviting me over for dinner?" He tried to act surprised. "I accept. What are we having?"

"Whatever I make for dinner since you don't cook and your harem is kitchen impaired as well."

"That's not entirely true; some of them are quite good in the kitchen."

"Getting busy on the butcher- block table doesn't count as a culinary skill," she shot back.

"Maybe not but it sort of rhymes with culinary."

Image flashing in her mind, Catherine grabbed her stomach. "This is a first. A Maalox moment before dinner. You sure know how to ruin an appetite."

"Ha. Very funny."

"Listen I'm hot, tired and I just walked in from the store. I'll see you a little later. Bye."

"Bye."

Cathy glanced at the clock as she put the shopping bag in the recycle bin. *I guess Madison wrapped his pillaging up early.* She giggled to herself. When they were teenagers

Cathy always said Madison was going to be a lawyer or a gynecologist. For her part, she was glad he'd gone into law.

Cathy felt a twinge in her back when she reached down to get a saucepan and she gingerly straightened. The twinge served as a reminder of a car accident she'd had years ago. Hit by a drunk driver, she had been fortunate to walk away with minor cuts and bruises. The real damage to her back was invisible then, but as she'd gotten older she'd had to deal with more nagging aches and pains.

Erring on the side of caution, Cathy put cooking aside for the time being and headed to her room to take a couple of Advil. Back aching, she climbed the stairs as if she were scaling Mount Kilimanjaro. Finally reaching the second floor, Cathy smiled as she passed the autographed poster on Alex and Andrew's bedroom door. The cold air wafted over her as she opened her bedroom door. *Thank God for central air.* Advil popped, Cathy kicked off her shoes and shimmied out of her dress and into her favorite Thurman Munson shirt and lounge pants. She had a few hours before the game to get dinner ready.

CHAPTER 4

Game time was near. Players, sports reporters and commentators milled around the field and the clubhouse. The pre-game show was underway and with the pennant race around the corner, they were looking for stories. Although there wasn't much dirt to be had at home games, a few tabloid reporters hung around searching for back room scenes or liaisons.

It wasn't a total waste though, of tabloid reporters' time. Single players were often easy fodder. Tabloids paid good money to get the story of their latest paramour with pictures. Most people thought a high profile single baseball player shouldn't have any trouble meeting women. The truth was somewhat different. Baseball was their life for six to eight months of the year, counting spring training. So they had limited options and sometimes got involved with someone who was simply convenient. Such had been the case with Marcus's involvement with a local sports reporter.

Barbara Ann Jones, a sports reporter with the number one news program in New York stood near third base as she gave her report. A petite brown-eyed, brunette beauty, she and Marcus had dated for a few months before deciding they were just friends.

The 6'2 native Californian and second baseman, Tim Dugan, pointed to the television. "Hey look, Barbara's on." Everyone looked up but Marcus.

"Wait. Are my eyes deceiving me?" Tim was incredulous.

"I've seen her on television before." Marcus was dismissive.

"Didn't you guys date at one time?"

"That was a while ago. We're just friends now."

Tim looked again at the television. "She's something to look at. Not that I'm looking at her in that way. I'm married but I'm not blind," he joked.

"We know. Just don't say it too loud. Tabloid reporters and their sources are everywhere," Mark warned.

Tim turned to Marcus. "It's nice that you guys are still friends."

Marcus nodded. "I think so, too. She's a great person."

Catcher Juan Lopez walked over from his locker. "So which model is it?" Juan asked. He and Marcus had signed with the Yankees the same year.

Marcus played cool. "What do you mean, which model is it?"

"Come on, man, you must have traded up," Juan insisted.

"He just met someone," Mark interjected.

Marcus flashed Mark a dirty look.

"I knew it," Juan said excitedly.

Marcus was quickly surrounded by the infield players.

"She isn't a model, actress or singer," Marcus said.

"She isn't?" John Ames seemed quite shocked.

"You don't have to sound so surprised. I don't just date models, actresses and singers," Marcus insisted.

The clubhouse broke into a roar of laughter. John Ames, the good-natured first baseman, patted him on the back. Tall and plagued with injuries in the beginning of the season, John was back in the groove with a hitting streak.

"Thanks, man, I needed a good laugh," he grinned.

"Okay, guys, that's enough. We need to leave the captain alone," Mark piped up.

"Okay, we'll stop giving you a hard time," Juan said.

Marcus sat down in front his locker. "Thanks."

Tim waited a couple of minutes before approaching Marcus again. "So what does she do?" Tim asked.

"She's a managing partner of a literary agency," Marcus said.

"Oh, she's a smart girl." John stopped. "Not that the other girls weren't," he quickly added.

"I know what you mean, John." Marcus nodded his head.

"Is she here?" Mark asked.

"No. I'm thinking of asking her to our next afternoon game."

"You should go for it."

He thought about it for a second. "You know what, Mark, I think I will. I'll be right back." He left the clubhouse.

Marcus had a plan and he needed to talk to Ben, who was talking to someone outside the general manager's office. "Excuse me, Ben. Do you have a minute?" he asked.

Ben excused himself. "What's up?"

"You didn't have to end your conversation. I could have waited a few minutes."

"That's okay, we were just shooting the breeze. What's on your mind? Or should I say, who's on your mind?"

Marcus smiled. "It's a little of both actually. I'm going to invite Cathy to tomorrow's afternoon game and I'd like you to set her up in the Hall of Fame Suite for me."

"You don't want much, do you?" Ben said facetiously.

"Do you think you could arrange it for tomorrow afternoon?"

"Consider it done."

Marcus smiled and patted Ben on the back. "Thanks, man. I knew I could count on you."

Madison finished the last bit of wine. "Great dinner, Cathy."

"Thanks."

"Now I guess Madison can load the dishwasher," Anna suggested.

Madison looked dumbfounded. "I'm a guest."

"Guest my behind. Load the dishwasher." Anna laughed.

"I'll do it after I finish my wine."

"Fine." Anna turned to Cathy. "How was your day?"

"Interesting."

"What's going on in the world of publishing?" Madison asked.

"We got an offer for the auto book today."

"Good, I know you're relieved. Those folks left you messages practically every day," Anna said.

"Oh, that's the Jackson thing you were working on, right?" Madison asked.

"Right. I'm not sure about the details yet but at least we have something concrete on the table." Cathy swirled the wine in her glass. "How about you, Anna?"

"Now that we've been auditing school districts, things are really getting interesting. I didn't find anything monumental today, but it's still early." She smiled.

"How's life in the world of matrimonial law?" Cathy asked.

"Not bad. Today we did half a dozen depositions and filed court papers in a few different counties. Other than that, nothing out of the ordinary."

"Speaking of out of the ordinary, how was lunch with Jim?" Anna asked. "I'm sure he's as neurotic as ever."

"Jim is Jim. Anyway, I didn't have lunch with Jim. He couldn't make it."

"So I hope you went anyway," Madison added.

"Did I mention he called to cancel when I was at the restaurant?"

"That wasn't nice," Madison said.

"No, but that's Jim. He means well but sometimes he's easily distracted. I didn't sweat it."

"Still, it's not fair. Your time is valuable," Anna said like a true accountant.

Before she could stop it, Cathy had a Kool-Aid grin on her face.

Anna looked puzzled. "What are you smiling about?"

"Nothing. It's silly."

Madison looked serious. "Cathy, you don't do silly."

She hesitated for a minute. "Well, if you must know, I saw Marcus Fox at lunch."

Anna looked skeptical. "You just *saw* him at lunch? There is no way that grin has anything to do with just seeing Marcus Fox in a restaurant. There's got to be more to it."

"Okay, so I met him."

Madison's eyes widened. "You met him? I don't follow baseball but I know he's a legend when it comes to women." He was impressed

Anna scoffed. "Down, boy!"

"You know a guy mistook me for him in court once," he boasted.

"How many times have I told you the guy was trying to pick you up, Madison?"

"The guy really thought I was him, Anna," he said defiantly.

"Marcus Fox is about 6'4, tight and muscular. His complexion is like coffee with extra cream, extra heavy cream," Cathy observed.

"So? What's your point, Cathy?"

"I'm 5'8 and I'm a good six inches shorter than him, which makes you eight inches shorter than *the* Marcus Fox."

Anna laughed. "I rest my case, counselor." "You two are some mean heifers," he huffed.

"Hey, Cuz, if having a guy try to pick you up is one of your hall of fame moments, more power to you," Anna snapped and pointed to Madison.

"Oh, shut up. This isn't about me anyway. It's about her meeting Mr. Fox."

"That's right. We got off track. So how did you meet him?" Anna asked.

"He bought me lunch."

"He bought you lunch?" Madison echoed.

"Yes. Only I didn't know about it until the waiter told me."

Anna's mind was at work. "So he just bought you lunch out of the blue like that?"

"I know it sounds strange but it's true."

Madison thought for a minute, then tapped his temple. "Now I remember. You wore your Yankee blue dress today."

"So?"

"So, it's a V-neck dress that shows off your girls there." He pointed in her breasts' direction. "I'll be damned, Marcus Fox is a breast man."

"I think you're right for once, Madison," Anna added.

Cathy moved right along. "Be that as it may, he bought my lunch. We talked for a few minutes and he asked for my business card and home number. End of story."

She conveniently left out the part about Marcus's call to her at the office earlier. Cathy just sipped her wine as the two of them looked at her in silence.

"Are you two all right?"

"I can't believe how nonchalant you're acting. You met the Marcus Fox and he asked you for your number. This is huge," Anna said excitedly

"Why is it huge, Anna? He's not going to call. He was just being polite."

Anna looked disgusted with her. "Madison, since you're a player, I think you should school this one."

"Listen, Cathy. He asked you for your home number. When a guy is interested in a booty call thing, he just takes your cell number. If he wants to know something like your business number and home phone, then he's interested in you."

"Is that why you only get cell numbers now?" Cathy's inquiring mind wanted to know.

"Hey, I'm a divorce attorney. I learned my lesson after my own divorce. You remember what Theresa was like."

"That woman put the W in witch," Anna quipped.

"That woman totally singed my mind and soured me on relationships. Screwing without strings is much less complicated."

"Is that why you date in quantity as opposed to quality?" Anna asked.

"As long as you haven't plowed through the Eastern Seaboard." Cathy qualified his mission statement.

"I've had enough high maintenance relationships to last me two lifetimes. I have no intention of screwing and trying to please any more Martha Stewarts."

"Martha Stewarts?" they chorused, puzzled at the choice of words.

"You know, the type of woman who gives directions on the things you can and cannot do in bed. Screwing goes something like this: Would you prefer I call it a penis or use the 'd' word? I'm not using the 'c' word. You're an educated native Easterner so we'll use the correct terminology, which is penis. Let's begin. First you enter me. Good. Now move two centimeters to the left and you'll find my clitoris, but remember, only go two centimeters and not two and a half. Wonderful! Now with three successive circular motions followed quickly by three counter-clockwise circular motions, work your hips and this will coax a delighted moan from me. Feel free to make a similar, not loud, moan. Next, position your hips slightly parallel to mine and continue with thrusting while maintaining the clitoral angle we established when we commenced screwing. This will result in heightening my enjoyment while giving you the pleasure and privilege of pleasing me. It's a good thing."

Anna and Cathy had tears streaming down their faces they laughed so hard.

"You are no good." Cathy howled with laughter.

"It's the truth," he said.

"We can't handle the truth," Anna chuckled.

"Anyway, Cathy, my point is, Marcus Fox is interested. I wouldn't be the least bit surprised if he called you."

"Then you'd be by yourself because I would be floored."

"Did you get his number?" Anna asked.

"And why would I do that?"

"To call him, of course."

Cathy was exasperated at having to explain over and over. "Listen, Anna, I really enjoyed talking to him. He's charming, well-mannered and intelligent. He's even more of a treat to see in person but I'm a realist. Today was as close as I will ever get to him in life and that's okay with me."

"I will never understand why you always sell yourself short." Anna was dismayed.

"We have the same mother, you know why."

"You have to put that out of your head. You can't let your mother's obsession with religion, weight and size rule your whole life," Madison added.

"You're right. I shouldn't and most of the time I don't. But come now, you've read the tabloids and seen the entertainment reports, Marcus Fox dates models and actresses with legs that start at their shoulders. My legs start at my knees. I am *so not his type.*"

Anna was clearly aggravated with Cathy. "That is total bull. Then how do you explain his interest in you when he only dates supermodel types?"

"I have no idea. Maybe he needs new contact lenses."

"That man could be the one and you're too afraid to find out."

"You know for someone who takes risks on new writers, you sure play it safe when it comes to your own happiness," Madison added.

"I'd rather have no expectations this way I won't be disappointed." Cathy maintained her position. "It's the way I want to live for now, Madison. Maybe it will change down the road, but for now it's working for me. And speaking of the Yankees, it's almost game time."

"We'll leave you alone for now but you can bet we are going to revisit this topic," Anna said.

"I know you will. By the way, Madison, don't forget to load the dishwasher."

Cathy headed upstairs as quickly as her legs would take her. She rushed into her room and flipped YES on. It was 7:10 P.M. and she'd missed the top of the first. However, her immediate concern was the score. Thankfully, the top of the first was a one, two, three inning. It was time for her man of the hour to step up to bat. Catherine watched the count intently when Marcus hit a triple.

"All right man! That's how you do it!" She clapped.

Cathy knew her sister and cousin meant well but the way she figured it, speaking to Marcus bought a little more time for her self-imposed moratorium on dating. They just wanted her to be happy. She settled in to watch the rest of the game in peace. Today had been a fluke. As Chris Rock said, "Here today, gone today." For Cathy it was a matter of being realistic. Not everyone got their happy ending.

The YES post-game report ended and Cathy was ready to turn in for the night. It was a good night for her. The Yankees had beat the Oakland A's 11-4 to wrap up the series. Life was good.

***

Back in the Bronx, life was very good in the Yankee clubhouse. The team was on a winning streak and the press was happy. Marcus had given his obligatory interviews and now he wanted to find a quiet nook to make a call.

"Hey, guy." His agent patted him on the shoulder. You had a pretty good game tonight."

Marcus searched for Cathy's business card. He'd written her home number on the back. "Thanks."

"Is everything okay?"

"Yeah, man. I'm just looking for something." He finally found the card in his duffle bag. "Got it."

His agent raised an eyebrow. "Are you calling that cute little devil in the blue dress?"

Marcus smiled, but he was wary of his agent's opinion. "Yeah. You want to say something about it?"

"Not at all. I think she is a looker."

Marcus was surprised by his candor. "You do? I thought for sure you'd have something to say."

"Why? Because she's full-figured? I don't care about that stuff. Personally, I like a woman with meat on her bones."

"I never knew that, Ben."

"You never asked." He looked at his watch. "I'm going to head over to the GM's office. Make your call." "Okay, man. I'll see you later."

Whether in the city or at home. Cathy was a workaholic. When her kids were home she'd had their activities to keep work and home balanced. With them away at college, Cathy worked around the clock. In a last ditch effort to get more down time, she'd tried establishing clear boundaries between her rest area and office, but judging by the *Publisher's Weekly* on the night table, had failed miserably. Just as she leaned over to pick it up, she was startled by the phone. She looked at the caller ID but didn't recognize the number. *I better answer just in case. I don't want someone leaving a message on the wrong answering machine.*

She picked it up. "Hello?"

"Hello. Cathy?"

Who in the hell is this? She didn't immediately recognize the voice.

"I hope I didn't wake you. Did you catch the game?"

Catherine was stunned for a moment. Marcus Fox was actually calling her.

"I sure did. It was a good game and a win. You can't beat that."

"So you finally recognized my voice."

She felt flushed. "I was in shock. I didn't expect you to call."

"Why?"

"Well, I'm ashamed to say it, but I thought you were being polite when you asked for my home number."

Marcus leaned against the wall. "Let me assure you I didn't ask for your number to be polite. I meet a lot of women who give me their number whether I've asked for it or not." Marcus's tone was clear and definite.

Cathy's heart jumped into her throat. It took her a moment to gulp it back down. "If today's impromptu fashion show was any indication, I don't know how you do it."

"It comes with the territory." He laughed.

Cathy seized the opportunity to change the subject. "So you had a good night, 3 for 5 with three RBIs."

"Everyone on the team did their part." "Always the good leader," she said.

"So are you a night owl, Cathy?" He sounded playful.

"I have my moments, and most occur during baseball season."

He laughed. "I was calling about tomorrow afternoon's game."

"I'm sure you don't need any batting tips from me," she joked.

"I like a woman with a sense of humor." He paused. "I wondered if you would like to come to the game?"

She felt positively gleeful. "I'd love to."

"Great, then maybe we can go out for dinner afterwards."

Cathy tried to get her heart back into her chest again. "Sure." She tried to sound casual.

"Good. I'll send a car to pick you up."

"That won't be necessary. I can take the LIRR into the city and hit the subway from there. Do you know what hell it is to drive to Yankee Stadium from the boroughs, let alone Long Island?"

"I know it's hell, but I'm trying to impress you. So please let me send a car," he insisted.

She grinned. "Okay."

"Good. What's the address?"

"4312 Great Neck Road, Amityville."

"Amityville? As in the Amityville Horror?"

"The one and only. Except I live in North Amityville. The horror house is in South Amityville."

"So tell me, is the house really a horror?" he asked jokingly.

"The only real horror in Amityville is the property taxes and possibly the dating pool. Beyond that, it's a pretty cool place to live."

He let out a big laugh. "That's too funny." "I try." She smiled.

"So let's firm this up. I'll have the car get you tomorrow morning between ten thirty and eleven o'clock. Louis will probably be there sooner rather than later."

"Smart guy."

"He knows what hell it is to drive to the stadium. Even from Manhattan it's a real bitch."

"I bet." She yawned. "Oh, I'm sorry. Excuse me."

"Don't worry about it, you're entitled to be tired. I'll let you go."

"Thanks for calling."

"You're welcome. I'm looking forward to tomorrow."

"So am I. Have a good night."

"You do the same."

Cathy slipped under the covers, turned the light off and stared into the darkness. She simply couldn't believe it. A few days earlier she'd thought she was on the edge of growing into a single woman without cats. Cathy wondered what the fates and Marcus Fox had in store for her.

***

Just as Marcus closed his phone Ben walked over.

"Okay, you're all set for tomorrow."

"Great."

"I even got Melvin to be her attendant for the game."

"Fantastic." He patted him on the back. "No one can say you're not earning your money." Ben laughed.

CHAPTER 5

When Cathy's alarm clock went off at 4:15 A.M., she was already awake but dawdling in bed. She finally got up when her eyes focused on the time display. Fumbling around, she grabbed her workout clothes and headed into the bathroom where she washed her face, brushed her teeth, pinned her hair up and changed.

After stopping in the kitchen for a water bottle she was on her way. Contrary to the view most people have about full figured women, she made working out a part of her regimen four times a week. Even though the gym had every workout machine imaginable, Cathy walked the track. It helped to clear her head before the day began at the literary agency. However, today was different. She had to clear her head before her 'date' with Marcus Fox.

Leaving the house, Cathy walked into a wall of humidity.

"They'd better have on the air conditioning," she mumbled to herself. "God knows they collect enough dues to pay for it."

Five minutes later Cathy pulled into the parking lot. There was a line outside the door. *Honestly, you'd think they were giving good bodies away on a first come, first serve basis.* She laughed to herself.

Less than an hour but a world away from Cathy's life, Marcus was awakened by the sound of his trainer leaning on the doorbell of his posh Manhattan penthouse. Mornings like this Marcus wished he'd never given his trainer's name and photo to security. He dragged his body out of bed to answer the door.

"Hold your horses, George. I'm coming," he grumbled.

As he opened the door Marcus cringed at the sound of George clapping his hands. "Come on, Marcus. You have to get the lead out." Even after 10 years of working together his cheeriness still reminded Marcus of a demented elf, which wasn't too much of a stretch since George was about a minute tall. However, what he lacked in height he made up for in muscle and unbridled enthusiasm.

"We have to keep your win streak alive. Come on now."

Marcus grudgingly went into his bedroom to change while George waited in his circuit training room. He put a club music
CD on.

"Aww man." Marcus covered his ears. "Do you have to play that stuff?"

"It pumps you up!" George shouted.

Marcus threw on his sweats and a t-shirt.

"It gives me a headache. Put on something with a little beat, please. If I have to exercise this early in the morning I at least want some music I can dance to."

"As you wish." George changed the CD and put on some old school rap.

Marcus bopped his head to the beat. "Now that's more like it. I can exercise to this."

Cathy was into her third lap when Melody Dickson came in. Melody was one of those women who possessed star quality and an almost royal-like presence whenever she entered the gym, or a room for that matter. A former model, she stood 6'1 without shoes. Her well-toned cocoa brown body was enhanced by long shapely legs that seemed to start at her shoulders. As if she needed any more charm, her sparkling smile had the magical ability to turn grown men into deer in headlights. One of the subjects in her realm was Jason Martin, a personal trainer and musician. A racquetball enthusiast, he had a court every morning and every morning he was distracted by Melody. Cathy couldn't figure out how he avoided getting whiplash or hit by the ball.

Melody dashed upstairs to join Cathy on the track. For the most part Cathy didn't mind the company even though she knew the two of them looked like the female African American version of Laurel and Hardy. That didn't bother her one bit because she liked Laurel and Hardy.

"Hey girl. What's up?"

"Not much, Melody. How about you?"

"Same old thing, work stuff at the restaurant."

"What's going on there?"

"The usual nonsense since I'm the only female and I'm the line manager. Guys don't like women telling them what to do. It's just stupid."

Cathy nodded. "I don't know how you take it."

"It's all about the Benjamins."

"I hear that."

Melody looked around. "Speaking of Benjamin, have you seen him today?"

"I don't think he's come in yet."

A forensic accountant, Benjamin Green was a little bit older, in great shape, smart, married and had a harmless crush on Melody.

"I have to keep an eye out for him. I need to ask him a couple of questions."

"You're still having trouble with your father's estate? I thought that was resolved."

"Are you kidding? We're still fighting over money and real estate. It's a mess."

"It's amazing what money does to people."

"Tell me about it."

Cathy noticed Jason staring at them. "We have an audience this morning."

"I know." Melody had a sly grin on her face.

"What's going on? Or should I say what happened?" Cathy asked.

"Let's just say we got together for a little television." Cathy watched in disbelief as Jason bench-pressed over 200 pounds with a smile on his face.

"That must have been some program."

Melody flashed her million-dollar grin. "I'll say."

"If you're not going to give me details, at least tell me which show it was. If nothing else I can at least TIVO it for a rainy day."

"You are too funny. What are you up to today?"

"I'm heading into the city later this morning."

"Is it business or pleasure? That sounds good. At least you travel off peak."

"It's business," she lied. However, Melody seemed satisfied with the answer.

"Oh, before I forget, I wanted to ask you if you know of a good esthetician."

"I know several. What do you need done?" Cathy asked.

"A bikini wax. A Brazilian bikini wax."

"Oh that's easy. I go to Lana's Day Spa in the Village."

"Really? She's good?"

"Oh yeah. I was there about a week ago."

"A bikini wax? Are you planning on getting busy with someone you haven't told me about?" Melody asked suspiciously

"Just because tourism has fallen off down the Brazilian way doesn't mean I shouldn't keep the streets of Rio clean and presentable on a moment's notice. I do pride myself on being ready to entertain." Cathy grinned.

"Girl you know you are too funny."

"I try."

"You should get back in the game."

"I will."

Melody didn't look convinced. "You always say that. In fact, you've been saying that for the past two or three years."
"I know I'm all talk."

"Your boys are in college and you are all of 40 years old. Do you know how many people would kill to be in your position?"

"What? Overworked and overextended?"

"One day we're going to have a serious conversation about this."

"I know, but I just can't have that conversation today." Cathy looked at her watch. "It's time for me to bounce. I have to get my day started."

"Okay, girl. I'm going to the ab room." She patted her non-existent stomach. "My stomach is getting so big."

Cathy squinted to see what she was talking about. "Melody, you don't know what a real mid-section looks like." She patted her stomach. "Now here's a real tummy."

She looked. "You aren't all that big there."

"You know, I do love the smell of fiction in the morning. I'm not sure I even have stomach muscles anymore," she said jokingly.

"You had kids. Twins no less."

"Eighteen years ago. I think that excuse is way past its expiration date." She looked at her watch again. "I've really got to go. I'll see you tomorrow." Cathy walked over to the steps.

"See you later."

***

Finally it was the cool down portion of Marcus's workout. George handed him a towel.

"You worked hard today." George smiled

"Don't I work out hard every day?"

"Yes, you do."

"What was so different from any other day?"

"Nothing, I guess."

George tossed him a water bottle as he got off the treadmill.

"You want to stay for breakfast? Marta's bringing something in."

He looked at his watch. "I would love to but I have another appointment in about 45 minutes"

"Okay."

"See you next time, Marcus. Good work."

"Thanks."

Marcus stood in his big empty luxury apartment for a moment before he headed for the shower.

***

Cathy's post workout treat was an extra-large cup of coffee from Dunkin Donuts. She didn't go for the coffee, per se. It was more about the people who worked there and the service. Her coffee was served light, sweet and ready to go without her uttering a word. If only she could find a boyfriend with the same talent in other areas her life would be perfect.

When she got home, instead of making her usual pit stop in the kitchen, Cathy went straight upstairs to take a bath and figure out what to wear. Water running, she washed her face in the sink with her Olay facial cloths. Patting her face dry, she studied it up close for signs of a breaking out or errant facial hairs. *They tell you forty is the new 30, but no one said a thing about facial hair,* she thought. She zeroed in on two taunting hairs sticking out on her chin and plucked them. *And people wonder why I carry tweezers in my pocketbook.* "I have to see the dermatologist soon.

If I wait much longer I could wind up at the barber shop for a shave," she muttered aloud.

A little while later Cathy's mind was racing and her nerves were shot as she slipped into warm bath water. She hadn't been on a date in eons and frankly, she wasn't sure if she remembered what to do or how to act. Despite not admitting to it in public, she'd glanced at the tabloid headlines, even read a few articles about Marcus's love life. How could she help it? The man was a sex symbol and a baseball icon. Sure, Cathy sashayed with the best of them but she knew she wasn't the norm for him. Marcus dated a parade of rail-thin beauties whose pouts added three pounds to their frames. Cathy fidgeted as the floodgates of insecurities over her size rushed over her. Then she got pissed with herself. After all, she'd fought hard to gain self-esteem and to finally love herself, weight, warts and all. In the past she'd never gone on a date with any expectations, so she'd avoided disappointment. Yet this date was different; it actually mattered. When she stepped out of the tub she knew all her calculated plans of self-protection had gone down the drain with the bath water. Today she ran the risk of having her hopes dashed on the bleachers. Her heart betrayed her when it started to care about the outcome.

Cathy beat her insecurities back long enough to get ready. She slipped into a sexy lace black bra and panty set with her *Cat on a Hot Tin Roof* full black slip. She wouldn't go bare-legged; instead, she put on a pair of thigh highs and topped them off with a pair of strappy sandals. She held up two Marilyn Monroe type dresses against herself.

"I didn't know you were going back into the city today," Anna said from the doorway, startling her.

"I'm not."

"So why do you have those two dresses out if you're not going somewhere?"

"I didn't say I wasn't going out."

Anna stopped eating cereal out of the box. "You have a date?"

"I'm going to the Yankee game if you must know."

"When did you get tickets for the game?"

"I didn't get tickets. " She turned and held up both dresses. "Which one?"

"The blue one."

"I thought it was a good choice too. Thanks."

"You're not answering my question. How are you going to a game if you don't have tickets?"

"Anna, I don't have time to sweat the small stuff. I have to get cleaned up and ready by the time the car gets here."

"By the time the car gets here? What car?"

She tried to escape to her bathroom but Anna's long legs were no match for her.

"I said, what car?"

Cathy was a bit peeved to have to share. "The car Marcus is sending for me." Anna

let out a scream.

"Damn, girl! My ears!"

"I thought you said you wouldn't hear from him. When did he call?"

"Last night after the game."

"Will wonders never cease?" Anna said rhetorically. "So did you guys make small talk or did he get right to the point?"

"It was late but we talked for a little bit. Then he asked me about coming to the game."

Anna took a closer look at the blue dress Cathy planned to wear. "He must be taking you out afterwards; this isn't your usual Yankee game gear."

She had a point. Cathy's usual game gear consisted of a Yankee tee shirt, shorts or jeans and naturally a Yankee baseball cap.

Cathy let out a heavy sigh. "As a matter of fact he is. Now, Anna, if you really want to see what happens you're going to have to let me get the rest of my toiletries from the bathroom."

She stepped out of the way. "I wouldn't want you to miss this."

"Thanks."

Cathy debated over whether to wear perfume. She'd gotten a gift set of Dolce and Gabanna's Light Blue for her birthday in August. She'd joked it was the closest she'd ever get to Dolce and Gabanna anything, but the perfume was the perfect fit.

Soft and sweet, she stumbled into her dress. It was nine fifteen. She had to move on to makeup.

Anna opened the door. "Are you trying to kill yourself?"

She buttoned the front of the dress. "I'm just a little off my game."

"What time is the car coming?"

"Ten-thirty or possibly earlier."

"Then we have to get the lead out. Sit down. I'll put the rest of your makeup on."

Cathy breathed a sigh of relief. "Thanks. I already put my moisturizer on."

"How made up do you want to be?"

"Enough so I'll look good without too many reapplications."

"Can do."

Anna put a towel around her neck to protect the dress. Neither of them believed in a lot of makeup so it only took Anna 10 minutes and she was done.

"There you go." Anna stepped back to admire her work.

Cathy looked in the mirror. "Looks good. Thanks."

"You're welcome. What are you doing with your hair?"

"I think I'll wear it down. Or do you think up is better?"

"What I think is you're really nervous and you need to calm down."

"You're right. I just have to breathe."

Cathy didn't want it to seem that she was trying too hard, even if she was. She wore her hair down. It was the least fussy thing she could do. She looked at her reflection in the full length mirror. The dress accentuated her curves in all the right places. Even though Cathy called it her Marilyn Monroe dress, at 40DD she had the upper body of Jayne Mansfield.

Her stomach in knots, Cathy tried to eat at least a piece of toast. She decided to forgo her usual, a large mug of coffee

She didn't want to be running to the ladies room every five minutes.

Anna peered out of the living room window in between pacing the floor. Pacing was a Chambers family trait. Whether on the phone or waiting to go somewhere, they were pacers. Just as Anna peered out the window again, Cathy walked in.

"Don't you have an audit this morning?" Cathy was puzzled.

"Yes. It's local. I can be there in 10 minutes."

"Oh." Cathy paused to watch her go to the window again. "You know a watched pot never boils."

"Gee, thanks for telling me, Mom," she said sarcastically. "Wait. I think I see a limo."

"He's not sending a limo. It's probably just passing by."

Anna's eyes widened. "Ha! I told you! It's stopping right in front of the house."

He sent a limo, Cathy thought. "I need to make one last check of my bag." She quickly grabbed her pocketbook.

"Hurry up, the driver's getting out of the car."

She rummaged through her bag to make sure she had all the essentials: breath mints, spasm medication, Advil and her Blackberry.

Anna opened the door to a stately looking African American gentleman with silver hair. "Good morning. I'm here to pick up Ms. Chambers."

"She'll be right out."

"Thank you."

She checked herself again in the hall mirror. "So do I look all right?"

"You look great. Now go. Enjoy yourself," Anna said.

"Thanks." She took a deep breath. "I'm off."

Cathy walked out to the waiting car. The driver held the door open for her. "Good morning, Ms. Chambers. My name is Louis."

"Good morning Louis. It's a pleasure to meet you."

"Likewise."

"Do you need any help?"

"No, thank you." Cathy eased herself into the car. "See." Thankfully her dress was long enough for her to scoot into the seat without any 'I see England, I see France, I see Cathy's underpants.'

"Very good then. Just be comfortable we'll be in the Bronx in no time. I hope." He

closed the door.

CHAPTER 6

After breakfast Marcus got ready to head over to the stadium. It was an early afternoon game set to start at one. Knowing he wanted to take Cathy out after the game, he took his Jag.

Just as he neared the stadium his phone rang.

"Hello?"

"Mr. Fox? It's Louis. I just wanted you to know that I picked up Ms. Chambers and we're on our way in."

He smiled. "Good. How's the traffic?"

"We're on Northern State and so far, so good."

"I guess you have to wait until you get closer to the city to see what traffic is really like."

"It looks that way."

"Okay, Louis. Good job. Thanks."

"It's my pleasure, Mr. Fox."

Marcus pulled into the players' lot. He breathed a sigh of relief to see there weren't many tabloid reporters. Then out of the corner of his eye he spotted Lisa Spellman. *Does this woman ever get tired?* he thought to himself. Lisa, a freelance reporter, had been the bane of his love life's existence almost from the moment he signed with the Yankees. One of her biggest scoops had come at his expense when she witnessed the scene where he and a former girlfriend broke up. She hadn't been far away since. However, he'd learned to live with her presence. One could even say they were friendly.

Hoping Marcus wouldn't see her Lisa quickly ducked behind an SUV.

Marcus laughed softly. "Hello, Lisa. No use in hiding, I saw you."

She stepped out and tried to be nonchalant about it. "Hi, Marcus, how are you?"

"Fine, thank you. How are you?"

She kicked the ground playfully. "Not bad. Is there anything new happening?"

She walked with him to the door.

"No."

She smiled. "Not that you would tell me if there was."

"You're probably right about that," he said with a wry grin before he opened the entrance door. "How's Stanley?"

"He's good, thanks." She backed off as he was about to enter. "Have a good game."

"Thanks. Tell Stan I said hello."

She saluted him. "Will do."

Marcus always wondered why on earth such an attractive and intelligent woman worked for gossip rags. It just didn't make sense.

Cruising through the hallway, Marcus saw Mark leaned up against the wall talking on his cell.

Mark closed his phone. "How's it going, man?" They gave each other a pound. "You look like you've just seen a ghost or something."

"Lisa Spellman isn't a ghost, she's more of a shadow I can't get rid of."

Mark nodded his head. "I have to give it to her for persistence. She's like a pit bull with a bone."

"Don't I know it?"

"You're the reason she's got such a name in gossip."

Marcus looked agitated. "Listen, you don't have to remind me. I lived through it."

Mark backed off; he knew that look all too well.

Melvin Cain, one of the luxury suite attendants, approached them.

"Hey Melvin."

"Hi, Mr. Fox. How are you?"

"I'm not too bad. And you?"

"I can't complain." He stopped. "Mr. Bradford tells me you have a guest today for the Hall of Fame Suite."

"I certainly do."

"Well, don't worry about it. I'll take good care of her, I promise."

"I appreciate that."

"But I have a question for you."

"Shoot."

"Do you want me to bring her to the clubhouse to see you first and then take her up?" It was an honest question and one Mark was eager to hear the answer to. "No, that's okay. Just take her up to the suite." "Why?" Mark asked.

Marcus turned to Mark. "Don't you think that's a little much for a first date?"

Mark scoffed. "Well, let's see. You had a car pick her up, you set her up in the Hall of Fame Suite and you have dinner reservations at Chanterelle. So you tell me, what's one more thing?"

Melvin had the good sense to retreat to a corner.

"So you think I should bring her to the clubhouse. It will probably scare her to death."

"Come now, Marcus, have faith. Besides, she's an agent. They don't scare easy."

Marcus turned to Melvin. "Okay, Melvin, bring her to clubhouse first."

"Sure." Melvin had the good sense to make a quick exit.

Mark patted Marcus on the back. "Now that wasn't so hard, was it?"

"No. Ask me again tomorrow."

***

The celebrity treatment had its good and bad points. While she loved being chauffeured, it gave Cathy too much time to think. At least if she were driving she'd be distracted by construction delays and idiot drivers. Now she was stuck in the backseat with her own thoughts and expectations. It would be so easy for her to build up this afternoon into more than it was and for Cathy that spelled trouble. *An ounce of prevention is worth a pound of cure,* she told herself as she administered the ultimate antidote, work. She dialed the office.

"Good morning, the Chambers-Stevens Agency."

"Hey, Sylvia."

"Hi, Cathy." She heard another line ring. "Could you hold on for just a second?"

"Sure."

"Sorry about that. The phones are going crazy here this morning."

"That's okay. Is E.D. available?"

"Sure. I'll put you right through."

"Thanks."

She was on hold for a minute. "Hey, Cathy," E.D. said cheerfully.

"What's going on, E.D.?"

"Not much at the moment. The phones are busy with status calls."

"It's September. Every client comes out of the woodwork now."

"Tell me about it."

"In the meantime you have to check on Laurel Matthews, Janet Roberts and Lisa Todd. All three of them have projects in final editorial review."

"That's right. I'll have Sylvia pull their files to get the editors' names."

"Do you have a pen, E.D.?"

"Yes."

"Write this down. Laurel's gift book proposal is with Wendy Miller. Her number is 212-555-8742. Janet's business proposal is with Drew Elmore. His number is 212555-9632. And finally Lisa's cookbook is with Barry Stein. His number is 516-555-7855." She rattled off. "Do you need me to repeat any of that?"

"No, I've got it."

"Are there any fires to put out today?"

"Not yet, but it's early. That might change."

Just then the limo was cut off and the car stopped short. She dropped her cell. Louis leaned on the horn.

"Are you all right, Miss Chambers?"

"I'm fine, Louis."

"Damn idiots on the road," he grumbled.

"Tell me about it." She picked the phone up off the floor.

"You still there, E.D.?"

"Yes. Where are you?"

"I'm on my way to the Bronx."

"The Bronx? You mean Yankee Stadium, right?"

"Yes, it's in the Bronx."

"You are obviously not driving yourself, because if you were…"

She cut him off. She knew where he was going. "I'd be cursing like a sailor."

"Right. What gives?"

"I got a special invitation from Marcus Fox to come to this afternoon's game." Cathy attempted to sound nonchalant.

Silence.

"Are you still there, E.D.?"

"When did you start dating Marcus Fox? Hell, when did you meet him? Scratch that. When did you start dating again?"

"I *met* him yesterday at Keen's. We are not dating."

"What happened to lunch with Jim?"

Cathy rolled her eyes. "You're not serious, are you? Answer that for yourself."

"He met a new woman."

"Right. I had lunch by myself."

"Don't try to duck the subject. How did you meet Marcus?"

"He bought me lunch. Only I didn't know he had until he came over to my table."

"And then?"

"We talked for a little while, he asked for a business card and my home number. End of story."

"There's no way that's the end of the story. Did he invite you to the game at lunch?"

She looked out the window. It figured they'd be stuck in traffic so she had no way to avoid answering such pointed questions.

"No. He called me after yesterday's game."

"That game didn't end until after ten."

Cathy was shocked. E.D. didn't follow baseball. "How did you know the game ran over?"

"I was channel surfing. Now don't change the subject. He called you after the game, right?"

"Yes."

She knew the wheels were turning in E.D.'s head "It's not a big deal and it's not a date. Maybe he wants to write a book or something. I am a literary agent."

"Now who's kidding who? If he wanted to write a book he would have his sports agent get the ball rolling. He certainly wouldn't call directly and he definitely wouldn't call after hours. The man likes you."

"Why are you trying to drive me crazy? I can't let myself go there."

"Why not? Is it so hard for you to believe he could be interested in you?"

She glanced at Louis and lowered her voice. "I'm going to say to you what I said to Anna: I'm not his type."

"You're a woman, right?"

"Yeah."

"Then you're his type. You need to feel as confident as you look, Cathy."

She looked up and saw there was a dead zone ahead. "Listen, I'm probably going to lose you in a minute. Just remember to check with those editors."

"I will. But you…"

The phone cut off. She turned off the ringer.

While Cathy was busy checking her makeup in her compact mirror, she realized they hadn't stopped at any of the entrance gates. Confused, she looked at Louis.

"Louis?"

"Yes, Ms. Chambers?"

"I don't mean to sound silly, but I've been to Yankee Stadium countless times over the years and I have no idea where we're going."

She saw Louis grin in the rearview mirror. "We're going to the players' parking area."

"Oh. Okay." Like a child on a school bus, Cathy's face was practically pressed up against the car window. *God, it's practically a luxury car lot*, she thought. When the limo came to a stop, Cathy reached for the door handle but an eager young man beat her to the punch and helped her from the car.

"Thank you very much."

"You're quite welcome."

Louis handed her a pass for a luxury suite. "Here you go. Enjoy the game."

"You're not coming with me?" Catherine looked like a little girl on the first day of school.

He was amused. "No, Ms. Chambers. This nice young man here will assist you."

"Oh. Well, thank you for the nice ride in."

"You're quite welcome."

She turned to the attendant. "I guess I'm putting myself in your capable hands."

"I'll take good care of you. By the way, my name is Melvin."

She shook his hand. "Nice to meet you, Melvin. I'm Cathy Chambers."

"Well, Ms. Chambers, if you would, please follow me."

"Sure."

He opened the door. "After you." "Thanks."

She walked in.

A strange sense of déjà vu came over Cathy as she followed Melvin down the hall. *Now I remember, I came this way for a stadium tour with Alex and Andrew a couple of years back.* She breathed a sigh of relief. At least she wasn't losing it totally. Suddenly a chill went up her spine when the realization hit that they were headed for the Yankee clubhouse. *Please God, don't let me make a fool of myself in front of all the Yankees*, Cathy prayed, her heart pounding.

"Would you excuse me a moment, Ms. Chambers? I'll let Mr. Fox know you're here."

"Okay. Thanks." Cathy waited nervously. She might have geared up for the game and dinner, which was a big deal, but she wasn't prepared for a detour to the clubhouse.

Still nervously awaiting Marcus, Cathy wanted to pace but she figured that would make her look nuts. She turned and faced the wall to get her composure back.

With her back turned Marcus got a good look at her rear end and beautiful hourglass shape. *She looks good coming and going.* He smiled. "Hey there, Cathy." "Hi." She turned around.

Marcus closed his eyes and breathed in her sweet perfume as he hugged her. Her sweet smell and soft curves hit just the right note, almost overwhelming his senses. He pulled away from her gently. "Don't you look pretty today? Is this for me?" He pointed to the dress.

"I wanted to look good today." She grinned.

"Well, you've succeeded."

"Do I get to meet this young lady, too?" Mark asked as he walked over.

Marcus was a little startled. "Oh, I didn't hear you walk out."

"That's because you were hugging this lovely woman." He turned to Cathy with his hand extended.

"Hi. I'm Mark Vasquez." 'Mark, this is Catherine Chambers," Marcus said.

I would have to live under a rock not to know him. My sons would die if they knew I met the MVP of the league, she thought as she shook his hand. "Sure. It's a pleasure to meet you, Mr. Vasquez," Cathy said shyly.

He feigned being shot in the heart. "Please, call me Mark. Mr. Vasquez is my grandfather."

"Okay. You can call me Cathy."

"It's a pleasure to meet you, Cathy."

"I hate to break this up but we're nearing the pre-game show," Marcus said.

"Oh, I guess that's my cue to leave, huh buddy?" Mark joked. "Next time we'll have to talk more, Cathy." She smiled. "I'd like that." He went back into the clubhouse.

Marcus turned to Cathy. "I'll see you after the game."

"Okay. Good luck. Let's keep the streak going." He smiled with that gleaming white grin.

Cathy waved. "All right, Melvin. I guess I have a date with a luxury suite."

"You sure do. Follow me."

Cathy felt a warm sensation run down her neck and along her back. Marcus was watching her walk away; she didn't need to turn around to be sure. She didn't want to disappoint so she added a little extra swing to her walk. *Just giving the audience what they want.* She smiled coyly.

Marcus raised his brow. *Sorry, Jay-Z, but Beyonce's got nothing on Cathy.*

Back in the clubhouse Mark softened his glove with the ball. Marcus sat next to him.

"I told you she'd be cool. Agents are like that," Mark said.

"I was afraid she would be like a deer in headlights."

"Far from it. Not to sound crude but speaking of headlights, she's built."

Marcus remembered how her curves felt in his arms. "I know." He smiled.

"The woman is a brick house. That's some nice figure she has."

"You think so?" Marcus asked.

"Don't you?"

"I'm just surprised to hear you say that."

"Why?"

"Your wife looks like a model."

"Cathy looks like a model, too, you know." Mark studied his friend's face. "They do have full figured models you know."

"I know."

"So what's the look on your face for?" He paused. "You're not worried about what any of these guys would have to say, are you?"

Marcus looked uncomfortable. "No. I'm prepared for the comments."

"Guys will be guys. You know that, but as for your friends, they'll be cool with her."

"I know."

Mark sat down. "I'm not going to say you won't get some negative comments. Some people are shallow and that's just the way it is. You can't let them bother you. Cathy seems like a lovely woman and she's a nice change for you."

"I know you're right about that."

"So have a good time and see where it goes."

"I'm looking forward to getting to know her better. So far what I already know is great; she's smart, funny and easy on the eyes. It can only get better from there."

Mark patted him on the back as he stood up. "It sounds like you have a game plan. Now speaking of game plans, we should head to the dugout."

"I'll be there in a minute."

While he worked on his glove, Marcus reflected on what Mark had said. His family, agent and teammates had weathered the many storms of his love life, the last one being Hurricane Cybil. Out of all his girlfriends she was a category five storm and their breakup had played out in public.

Cathy was a nice change from the melodramatic attention seekers he usually dated. He thought about her long red hair and the way her eyes smiled at him. *It's going to be a great day and night.*

***

The luxury suites were something of an urban legend to Cathy. Her family usually camped out in the Loge section, which was a major step up from the bleachers where her grandparents had watched Gehrig, Ruth, Mantle, Guidry, Munson and DiMaggio play. So to say she wasn't prepared for the air conditioned room, cushioned seats, three monitors, bar and private restroom was an understatement

Cathy listened with wide-eyed eagerness as Melvin described the suite's amenities.

"Impressive, aren't they?" He smiled.

"Oh my God, I can't believe this." She was awestruck.

Melvin thought it was too cute. *Luxury suite virgins are the best,* he thought. *They really appreciate the experience.*

"Well, Mr. Fox wanted you to be comfortable."

"I don't think my house is this comfortable."

"Do you have any questions?"

She was still awestruck. "No, I'm just tickled that it's air-conditioned. For once my behind won't be stuck to the seat." Cathy quickly covered her mouth when she'd realized what she'd let slip out. She was completely embarrassed. "Sorry, you can't take me anywhere."

"No need to be sorry. We've heard much worse even here in the luxury suites." He showed her to a seat. "Thank you."

"If you need anything someone will be glad to help you."

"Thank you."

"Enjoy the game."

"Thanks."

As Cathy looked around she couldn't help thinking about her family's earlier days at Yankee Stadium. "Talk about coming a long way, baby, this is unreal," she mumbled to herself. Generations of her family had occupied seats in Yankee Stadium since the 1920's as the original bleacher bums. Today she was in the luxury suites. *Too bad Grandma isn't here*, she sighed. Her thought was interrupted by her vibrating handbag. She quickly grabbed the phone.

Although it was a big no-no, Marcus had found a quiet spot to call Cathy before the Yankees took the field. "Hello?"

"Hey. I know we just saw each other but I wanted to give you a quick call to say hello again before the game."

She was tickled. "I'm glad you did. I want to thank you for the lovely accommodations."

"My pleasure. I'm going to meet you there in the suite after the game. The clubhouse is too crazy with reporters and cameras for you to come here."

"You don't have to tell me, I watch the post-game report."

"Okay. Then I'll see you later."

"Okay. Good luck."

"Thanks."

As Cathy disconnected the phone, her stomach fluttered, a sure sign Marcus was doing and saying all the right things. *I can't fall for this guy, even if he's my dream guy. I'm done with love and my track record proves it. There's no way this is going to work out*, she told herself. Needing to get her mind off a romance with Marcus, she decided to call the other big Yankee fan, her son Andrew. He would help her stay grounded.

"Hey Andrew. It's Mom."

"Hey Mom."

"How's school going?"

"Good. I like my classes."

"Great. What about work-study? Do you have your assignment yet?"

"Yeah. I'm working in the game room. Alex is too."

"That's interesting. You're working different shifts then."

"Oh yeah."

"Good. Guess where I am this afternoon?"

"Where?"

"I'm in the Hall of Fame Suite at Yankee Stadium."

"Get out of here, Mom! How did you get in? Don't you need special tickets?"

"Actually, you do."

"Wow, someone gave you a pass?"

"In a manner of speaking. You know I love to catch a live game."

"Wow, Mom, I'm jealous."

"Maybe one day your old mom will be able to afford it and bring you guys."

"That would be sweet."

"Anyway, I was going to call your brother. Does he have a class now?"

"He's with a study group. Want me to tell him to call?"

"I can't have my cell on during the game."

"Okay, Mom. Listen, I gotta go, Mom. I have to meet with my advisor."

"I'll talk to you later. Love you!"

"Love you too, Mom."

Cathy's cell rang before she could turn it off.

"Damn!" She nearly bobbled her phone in her hands before she caught it. "Hello?"

"Thank God I got you."

"Hi, Fran. What's going on?" Cathy waited for the other shoe to drop.

"Nothing really. I just wanted to let you know I sent the manuscript to my editor today. I'm going away for a couple of days so I needed to give you a heads up."

"Thank you, Fran. I appreciate that. Could you do me a favor and email E.D. and cc Sylvia and Michelle.

"Not a problem."

"Thanks. You enjoy your vacation."

"I will. Thank you. Talk to you soon."

Cathy turned her ringer off as quickly as possible. She didn't want to risk getting another phone call.

For the next few hours, Cathy enjoyed a real nail biter of a game in air-conditioned luxury. She wanted to get up and scream as she did at home, but the dignified surroundings made her feel self-conscious about it. It was funny since the people seated next to her were cursing up a blue streak with more yelling than she'd ever heard in the bleachers. By the seventh inning the Yankees had tied the game 5-5. The eighth and top of the ninth was a real pitcher's duel. Then came the bottom of the ninth and it looked as if the game was heading into extra innings. There were two outs, one man on and her guy Marcus was up. Talk about pressure. The count was 2-2. He swung and Cathy heard that distinctive crack of the bat. The fans rose. It was going, going…gone! Marcus had hit the game winning homerun. The stadium erupted as if were a World Series game. Catherine jumped up and down.

What a ballgame! What a man! *What am I getting into?* She thought to herself. Something told her she was definitely in over her head.

CHAPTER 7

Flashbulbs popping, Marcus stood in a sea of microphones, cameras and reporters. It was September and as captain he was used to addressing questions about the game and the state of the team especially as the race for the pennant now began in earnest. However, today was different; homerun or not, he was distracted and anxious to get to Cathy.

"So Marcus, this was a real nail biter this afternoon. What do you think the team did differently in the sixth inning?" Bill Martin of *The Chronicle* asked.

"Well, Bill, we started getting some timely hits to build towards a rally."

"You really crushed Juan's slider, which is a pitch that hasn't been kind to you in the past. What was the difference today?" Gina Allen of *The Post* asked.

Marcus took a breath. "Juan usually has good location on his pitches but he left it a little high and I was able to make contact." Marcus motioned to Ben, who instinctively knew what he wanted.

Ben walked to the fore of the group. "Okay, guys, he's answered your questions. How about we let today's hero get some food in his stomach?"

"What about our deadlines?" Jack Ford asked.

"He's given you plenty to write about with photos. We'll make it up to you on the way to the Series."

"You think the Yankees are going to make it this year, Marcus?" Bill asked.

"I'm sure the best teams will. Okay, fellas, I've got to go." His answer was the right blend of confidence and political correctness. Marcus politely excused himself. Once he was in the hall he ran straight into Barbara Ann Jones, who had a sly grin on her face.

Marcus was startled. "Hi, Barbara, how are you?" He kissed her cheek lightly.

"I'm good, Marcus, although I'm not as good as you are today. That was some homerun blast."

"Thanks." He kept looking at his watch.

Barbara was intrigued. "You're in a hurry. Do you have a date with a dinner plate, a woman or both?"

Friends or not friends, Marcus and Barbara had dated and he thought it would be unkind to talk about someone new he was dating. "I'm hungry."

She didn't believe him. "I see. What's her name?"

He tried to play it off. "What are you talking about?"

"Come on, Marcus, we used to date. I know that look. What is her name?"

He knew the jig was up. "You don't know her."

Barbara was flabbergasted. "Oh my God, you really like her. If you didn't, you'd give me her name without a second thought. You want to keep her to yourself for a while." She nudged him. "I can respect that."

"Thanks." He looked at his watch again. "I really have to go. Maybe we'll get together for a drink or coffee."

"That sounds good to me."

He began walking away. "I'll call you."

She waved him on. "Okay." Barbara watched as he went down the hall. "I never thought I would see the day when the Marcus Fox would look nervous going on a date." She shook her head. "Will wonders never cease?"

Shades on, Marcus looked like his calm, cool and collected self on the outside; inside it was another story. He was actually a little nervous and jumpy. *What the hell is wrong with me*? He thought. After all, he'd only met Cathy the day before and outside of the phone conversation he'd only spent maybe a little over a half hour with her in person. On paper it didn't make sense to be nervous.

Yet Barbara Ann had called it accurately. He'd never had a problem sharing the name of his latest flame and neither did the woman. Most women loved to see their names paired with his and went so far as to make sure the papers correctly spelled their name. Marcus knew there was something different about Cathy and it had nothing to do with her size. True, she was the first full-figured woman he'd ever dated but there was something else he just couldn't put his finger on until he entered the luxury suite.

There she was, back straight, legs crossed and leaning forward just enough to enhance her cleavage. Busy on her Blackberry, Cathy had a laid back, easy going sex appeal. Marcus unconsciously took a page from LL Cool J's playbook and licked his lips. He'd seen many women contort their bodies to appear sexy but Cathy's sexiness was as natural as breathing in and out.

He cleared his throat. "I haven't kept you waiting that long, have I?"

Cathy was a little startled and quickly put the Blackberry away. "No, you haven't kept me waiting long."

"At the risk of repeating myself, I have to say you look gorgeous."

Even with the air conditioning her face grew hot. "Thank you. So do you, Mr. Homerun." Marcus

felt a little bashful in front of her.

"Thanks. How did you like your accommodations?"

"I could get used to this. I can't afford to, but I could get used to it."

"I'm glad you enjoyed yourself. Are you ready to go?"

"Absolutely."

"Cool. Let's go."

When Marcus took Cathy's hand, she smiled like a teenager. She'd halfway expected his hands to be rough and was pleasantly surprised at how soft his hands were.

Marcus took a lot of teasing for using a special hand cream, but as a ladies man he knew full well that while most women appreciated the feel of an alligator bag or shoes, alligator-like hands didn't cut it. Marcus didn't want to let go of her soft hands but he knew he had to prepare Cathy for what awaited them on the other side of the door. He stopped suddenly, throwing Cathy off balance.

He caught her before she could fall. "I'm sorry. Are you okay?"

Cathy regrouped. "I'm fine. What's wrong?"

"You might want to put your sunglasses on."

She complied. "The photographers are that bad?"

"Worse. Just hold my hand and we'll get through the obstacle course together in no time."

She took a deep breath. "Okay."

The minute he opened the door the flashbulbs were in rapid fire mode as were the questions being hurled their way. Cathy and Marcus ignored them and kept smiling.

"Are you the new woman in Marcus's life?" a female voice shouted.

"Marcus is she your new lady?" a male voice shouted.

Cathy found the pace of the questions dizzying. She'd never heard so many ways to ask the same incessant question. Was she the new woman replacing Cybil, his supermodel ex? Inquiring minds apparently wanted to know. In truth, Cathy wanted to know, too, but she was afraid to entertain the idea of being Marcus's girlfriend even for a minute.

Cathy kept her focus until they finally got to his Jaguar. Marcus helped her in, threw his bag into the backseat and dashed over to the driver's side.

"Are you okay?" he asked as he climbed in.

"I'm fine."

He slammed the door. "That was fun, wasn't it?" he said with a little mischievous smile.

"Oh yeah, that was a blast," Cathy said with her tongue planted firmly in her cheek.

"So now that we're alone we can talk for a little while without photographers or reporters." He started the engine.

In the side mirror Cathy saw another Yankee star emerge. The reporters were on him as quickly as they surrounded Marcus and Cathy. "I would guess the only time you can have a little peace is when you're in the car."

Marcus shook his head. "It certainly seems that way." He drove out of the lot.

Cathy nodded. "I give you credit. Between the press watching and judging your performance and the tabloids obsessing over your personal life, I don't know how you take it."

"I guess I'm used to it."

"Which is easier to handle, the sports press or the tabloids?"

He didn't miss a beat. "The sports press is easier. At least with them we're talking about concrete statistics or technicalities of baseball. With the tabloids anything goes."

"How do you deal with stress? You're always so calm and collected."

"I go to the batting cage or the driving range. That helps. What about you?"

Cathy was surprised by his interest. "I walk for six miles or so in the mornings before my day gets going."

"You walk six miles or so?"

"Between my client roster and my children I *need* to walk; now that my sons are in college I mostly walk because of clients."

"You have sons in college?" He was incredulous.

"Yes."

"You don't look old enough to have children in college."

Her dewy caramel complexion boasted a few freckles but there wasn't a line on her face. Her smile was bright and her dark brown eyes had a youthful glimmer.

Cathy bashfully looked down at her legs. "Thanks for the compliment, but I do."

He still couldn't believe it. "You're pulling my leg."

Cathy chuckled at the idea of debating her age with a younger man. "Okay then, how old do you think I am?"

He looked at her. "Maybe thirty-three."

Cathy was floored and confused. Was this simple flattery or was he sincere? "I was a young parent but I would have had to get pregnant at fifteen using your math. I didn't have my sons until I was twenty-two."

Marcus did the math in his head. "You're forty?" he asked, shocked at the number.

Cathy smiled warmly. "I would show you my driver's license but it looks like a mug shot."

"Okay, then I have to take your word for it." He took another long look at her. "You look great."

"I look great for my age, right?" she teased.

Marcus's expression was serious. "I'm giving you an honest compliment. I think you look wonderful, period."

She could see from the look on his face that he was serious. "I was just teasing. Thanks for the compliment."

His warm smiled returned. "You're welcome." He paused. "You said sons plural."

"I have twins."

"You have twin sons. Are they identical or fraternal?"

Cathy looked to the sky. "Fraternal, thank God. Half the time I can't call them by the right name. If they looked alike I'd be in real trouble." She opened her bag to take out Alexander and Andrew's latest pictures.

"This is Andrew and this is Alexander."

Sitting at a light he glanced quickly at the pictures. "Fraternal? I bet people still can't tell them apart."

"You'd be surprised just how many can't."

"I bet you can tell them apart."

"Some days that's debatable. Catch me when I'm yelling at them. I'm lucky I remember one name." He laughed. "They're good looking young men." "Thanks." Cathy smiled as she put her wallet back.

"Who's older?"

"Andrew is by two minutes. I can't tell you how funny it is when Andrew holds it over Alex's head."

"If there's a first place, then there has to be a second place."

"True. Still, the two minutes made the biggest difference to me. After all, I was the one in the delivery room."

He laughed. "So they go to the same school?"

"Yes. There was talk about going to different schools but we went where the money was."

"Are they rooming together?"

"No."

Cathy answered so quickly Marcus had to laugh. "I guess that answers my question. You didn't waste any time thinking about that answer."

Cathy laughed. "Listen, they've been sharing space since the womb. It's one thing to break up any arguments at home; it's another thing when they're over 400 miles away. Besides, any more togetherness and they'd kill each other for sure."

He chuckled. "Just the two kids and no more after that?"

"Jackpot! I figured I would retire with a high batting average."

"You did bat a thousand."

"Exactly. How about you? Do you have any children?" As soon as the words left her lips she realized what a silly question she'd asked.

Marcus chalked the question up to nervousness, then answered without missing a beat. "Wouldn't that be something else?"

"Oh yeah. There's no way you could have a love child and not have the press dig it up."

"Exactly."

"Do you want kids?"

"Eventually, with the right woman."

"I hear that. You have to make sure you've got the right person who's in it for the long haul."

"That sounds oddly like the voice of experience."

"It is."

"How long have you been divorced?"

"Hmm. Lets see." She counted in her head. "Almost seventeen years."

He was taken aback. "Wow. You never wanted to get married again?"

"I thought about it, but a divorced mother with two kids didn't rate high on the date-ability meter, especially back then. I focused my energy on my children."

"Which you obviously did well since they're in college."

"Thanks. Knock on wood." She knocked on the dashboard. "What about you? Have you ever been engaged?"

"No. I came close a couple of times, but it didn't work out."

"I'm sorry to hear that. I hope it didn't end badly."

"It kind of did."

"Oh, I see. Enough said." She paused. "Well, on the bright side you are still one of the most eligible bachelors in the world. Women break their necks to get close enough to get your attention."

"You think so?"

"I know so."

"What about you?"

"What about me?" she asked.

"You didn't break your neck to get my attention. In fact you barely even noticed me."

Cathy cracked up. "I barely noticed you? I noticed you."

"Really? I kept looking over at you, trying to see if you'd look up even for a second. You were so sure I was looking at the women behind you."

"I'm sorry. I was going with the odds. I figured I was a long shot."

With the car stopped at a light Marcus turned toward Cathy and looked at her in all seriousness. "You are definitely not a long shot." His eyes were so intense she was unsettled.

He dialed it down a notch. "What's the matter? Hasn't anyone ever said you're beautiful?"

"I wouldn't say that. I have turned a head or two, only they're not usually on such handsome shoulders."

Marcus liked what he heard. "Ah, so you're a woman who knows a little something about the art of flirting. I'm impressed." He grinned.

"Thanks." Although she was apprehensive Cathy decided it was as good a time as any to ask him the $64,000 question. "So Marcus, I'd like to ask you something."

"Sure."

"I don't want you to take this the wrong way but I am a big, no pun intended, change from the usual women you go out with, so I guess I'm a little curious as to why you asked me out."

"That's a fair question." He paused for a moment. "I liked the confident way you just strolled into the restaurant. Your date didn't show and you ordered lunch without skipping a beat."

"Why should I starve because my client didn't show?"

"Exactly. Do you know how many times I've taken a woman to dinner only to have her not eat or just push her food around the plate? Even innocent gestures of affection are taken as code for you're getting fat."

"Oh so since I'm full-figured I couldn't possibly be as neurotic." Catherine's tone was playful and a little serious.

"No, I'm not saying that."

"Good. Because you'd be wrong. All women are neurotic on some level regardless of size. Some of us handle it better than others."

"True. You got me there."

She laughed so she wouldn't seem like a stick in the mud or some kind of full-figured militant. "I'd better stop giving you a hard time before you never ask me out again."

"I don't think you have to worry about that. I definitely plan to ask you out again." Cathy smiled.

They were at another light. Once it changed Marcus slowed down so Cathy assumed they were close to their destination.

"How do you feel about dinner at Chanterelle?"

She was pleasantly surprised. "I love the idea. Am I dressed for Chanterelle?"

"You look perfect to me."

Cathy was embarrassed when she turned red for the umpteenth time. "I don't think I've blushed this much in my entire life."

Marcus thought it was sweet. "Really? I'm surprised. You're such a pretty woman I would think you'd be used to receiving compliments."

"Now who's the old-fashioned flirt?" She winked

"Hungry?"

"Starving."

"You didn't eat at the stadium?"

"No, I didn't want to spoil my dinner."

"Spoken like a mom."

By the time they pulled into a parking garage on Leonard Street something had changed. Both Marcus and Cathy began to feel that they were on a normal, real first date like anyone else. However, that quickly changed when the attendant greeted them.

"Oh my God!" he said excitedly. Cathy turned and smiled at Marcus, who was a little embarrassed to have a grown man fawn all over him in front of his date. The attendant, whose name was George, opened the door.

"That was a beauty of a pitch you hit today. Man, I loved the look on Juan's face, he knew you would crush that pitch the minute he released it."

Marcus stepped out of the car. "Thanks, man." He shook George's hand and gave him the keys before walking around to open Cathy's door.

George smiling ear to ear, said, "Don't worry. We'll take care of your car, Mr. Fox."

Marcus was gracious as always. "Thanks, dude."

Marcus put his arm out for Catherine to hold on to, which she did. "I'm not cutting off the blood supply to your arm, am I?" he laughed.

"Not at all." She patted his arm. "This is the same arm pitchers seem to be gunning for."

"It does seem like that sometimes, doesn't it?"

"I get so mad when they try to hit you."

Marcus could see she was sincere. "That's sweet but baseball is a contact sport. It's a risk."

"I guess that's why they pay you the big bucks. I've seen the speed of those pitches. It's got to be painful."

"It doesn't tickle but you learn to shake it off."

Marcus looked at Cathy as they walked down the street. She had the face of an angel when she smiled. He stopped walking abruptly.

"Did you forget something?" Cathy asked.

"Yes."

"You want to go back to the car to get it?"

"That's not necessary. It's right here."

Before Cathy could say a word he pulled her to him. Cathy melted the moment his lips touched hers. Marcus was excited at the tentative way she parted her lips; it made them all the sweeter. He wanted to pull her in closer but he knew if he held her just a moment longer she would know how much he wanted her. Breathless and a little surprised by the passion, they came back to earth.

"I've wanted to do that all afternoon. I was going to wait until I took you home, but I couldn't wait."

"I'm glad you didn't."

"So am I."

CHAPTER 8

The moment Marcus and Cathy walked into Chanterelle, the place nearly went silent. Cathy could feel her level of insecurity rise with each passing glance as the maître d' showed them to their table. She wondered if they were thinking the one thing she'd been trying not to: why her? Then Marcus turned and smiled at her and she felt silly for letting negative thoughts get the best of her.

Marcus was a near perfect gentleman as he held Cathy's chair for her, but he couldn't help being drawn to her cleavage yet again as she sat down in her Marilyn Monroe *Seven Year Itch* dress. He was dying to scratch and when he finally looked up and met Cathy's gaze, he knew he was caught, again.

I'm busted again, Marcus thought. He was embarrassed. "I'm sorry. You must think I'm a pig."

Cathy was amused. "Not at all. Believe me, you're not the first."

"You're awfully magnanimous. Doesn't it piss you off?"

"Let's put it this way: I haven't had a spill in my lap since I was ten. So I'm used to the attention."

His eyes widened. "Did you say ten?"

"You heard correctly." She nodded. "So you can imagine how much I hated recess." Cathy sighed. "They snapped my bra straps every chance they got."

He raised his brow. "You know boys will be boys. Besides at that age they only bother the girls they like."

"True." She paused. "But once I slapped one of the leading offenders they stopped."

Marcus pretended to be worried. "Oh, I guess I'd better watch where my eyes wander."

Cathy was a little embarrassed; she'd made herself sound like a real tough cookie. "I'm not that bad anymore. I only get pissed when it's done in a business setting. On a date it's not so bad as long as you remember that a person comes with the breasts. We're a package deal."

Marcus wanted to howl with laughter but he remembered where they were. "I like your sense of humor." He chuckled.

Cathy was still giggling when the waiter took their drink orders. As she glanced around the restaurant, it honestly looked as if everyone had forgotten they'd come there to eat.

Marcus glanced around. "Welcome to the fish bowl," he said, seeing all the attention register with her.

Cathy laughed as she looked around the room again. "How strange is this?"

"You know how I said earlier that you get used to it?"

"Yeah?"

"Truth is, you never get used to it, you just learn to adapt. It's not easy." "I can see that."

Cathy perused the menu. "My goodness, everything looks so good."

The waiter brought their drinks.

"Would you like to start with an appetizer?" he asked.

Cathy faced a moment of truth. Would she show restraint and graze on a salad? Or give in to her growling stomach? She hadn't eaten anything that day other than a couple of bites of toast without coffee. A little uncomfortable, she continued to scan the menu. *I might as well swing for the fences and see what happens,* she thought.

She stepped up to the plate. "I think I'll have the butternut squash ravioli with oxtail ragout and bay leaf cream." Cathy was afraid of Marcus's reaction but when she looked up he was smiling.

"Good choice." The waiter turned to Marcus. "And you, sir?"

"I'll have the tasting of fresh wild mushrooms." "Very good, sir. Do you want to order your entrée now? Or do you need more time?"

Marcus looked at her. "Are you ready to order?"

Feeling a little emboldened she spoke up. "As a matter of fact I am. I'll have the sea scallops sauté with caramelized endive."

"And I'll have the breast of free range chicken with preserved lemon and Greek olives."

"Thank you. I will be back with your appetizers shortly."

The vibe between them was relaxed and easy, just like that of two old friends. Marcus studied her soft, cherry colored lips as she sipped water. Friends didn't watch friends like that and he knew it. His mind raced at a hundred miles a minute and he needed to rein himself in. *Slow down, get to know her first,* he told himself. *Talk about her kids*. He piped up, "You know, I'd love to hear a little more about your sons, Cathy."

At first, Cathy looked at Marcus as if he'd grown another head. She rarely met men who wanted to talk about her kids. Whether he knew it or not, he'd just scored big time. Alex and Andrew were the only subjects she liked talking about more than the Yankees. And this night she had the best of both worlds.

"Oh, haven't I bored you enough with that already? You know how we parents are. Once you get us started you're hard pressed to get us to shut up," she said playfully.

"I'll take my chances." He took a sip of water. "Do they have middle names?"

"Yes, and they're going to sound truly pretentious."

"How pretentious can it be?"

"Andrew Michael Chambers Carlyle and Alexander Matthew Chambers Carlyle."

"I think they sound great. They will be quite a mouthful for a bride to remember, however."

Cathy winced at the thought of her babies getting married. "Oh, bite your tongue. I'm still trying to get used to the dating stuff."

He laughed. "I guess it's the same for all moms everywhere."

"It's not like I've stopped them from dating. I've lived through a couple of teen romances."

Marcus made a face. "Teen angst combined with teen romance? That couldn't have been easy."

"You have no idea."

"Kind of makes you wonder how our parents did it." He laughed

Cathy chuckled softly; she obviously knew something he didn't.

"Girls today are really different. They are much more assertive," Cathy said.

"I know what you mean."

"It used to be that guys would ask you for your phone number. I don't think my sons have ever had to. Girls give them their home and cell phone numbers, along with their email address and instant messenger IDs."

Marcus laughed. "It sounds like they cover all their bases."

"Cover their bases? Hell, they blanket them." A

passing thought made Marcus laugh.

Cathy was intrigued. "What's so funny?"

"I was just thinking about today's more aggressive young women and their contact information."

She was still a little puzzled. "What about it?"

"I guess I went old school when I asked you for your number."

"I guess you did."

The two laughed together.

"It's not easy watching your boys grow up, is it?"

"Yes and no. They are still my babies even though Andrew is 6'2 and Alexander is 6'3. Somehow they never stop being those little bundles I brought home from the hospital."

"Those are some pretty big babies."

"I know."

The waiter returned with their appetizers.

"That ravioli looks good. Mind if I have a bite?" Marcus smiled.

"Be my guest," she said.

Marcus liked that she was so willing to share. Cathy wondered if she'd passed some kind of test.

He took a bite. "This is good. Would you like to try my appetizer? Do you even like mushrooms?"

"I love mushrooms." Before she could put her fork up to get a mushroom he fed one to her.

A little taken aback, Cathy didn't know whether it was Chanterelle or Marcus's feeding her the mushroom that made it taste especially good. Chances were it was the latter that had amped up her taste buds. "That's terrific." She dabbed her mouth with a napkin.

"I know." He paused to enjoy a few mushrooms. "So what are your sons' majors?"

"Andrew is a business finance and economics major and Alexander is an adolescent education major with a concentration in African American and American history."

He was impressed. "Wow, their majors are totally different. They obviously have distinct personalities."

"It's been that way since birth. When they were babies I got tired of looking like Rocky Raccoon breast feeding for three months."

Marcus was surprised. "You breast fed twins for three months?"

She nodded. "I was a regular 7-11. That's why I switched to formula to make life easier. At least that was the idea."

"I guess they had other ideas."

"Oh boy, did they ever. They didn't even take the same kind of bottles. Andrew went on Enfamil, Alexander went on Isomil. I knew right then and there it was going to be interesting."

"So after all the late nights, bottles, formula, cuts and bruises, would you say it was worth it?"

She answered without hesitation. "I couldn't have better sons if I'd mail ordered them." She leaned in a little closer. "Now what about you? What were you like growing up?"

Marcus settled into his seat. "I think I was a pretty well-adjusted kid. My parents were really involved in the school so my sisters and I always had them in our corner."

"Interracial couples are a little more accepted now, but back then it wasn't easy." She'd read about his mother and father.

"That's the truth. Even though we lived in a Northeastern state we were still close enough to farm country to have a problem every now and then."

"I give your parents a lot of credit. They managed to give you and your sisters a good sense of yourself and your heritage on both sides."

Cathy was horrified by the strange look that came over Marcus's face. She thought she must have put her foot in her mouth up to her knees. When the busboy came over to clear away the appetizer plates, she said, "Listen, I apologize if I said something out of line. It just came out." She apologized as fast as she could.

"You don't have to apologize. I'm not mad. It just sounds like you have a better idea than most of what it's like to be bi-racial."

Cathy tried to brush it off. "Didn't you go out with…" she blurted out. Horrified, she realized she'd inserted her foot back into her mouth, only this time it was thigh high. "I'm so sorry. I usually engage my brain before my mouth gets in gear."

"Don't be sorry. You're right, I have dated a few women who are bi-racial like me. But it seems like you get it."

"My maternal grandmother who was born in South

Carolina in 1904 had a white mother and a black father."

"That couldn't have been easy."

"It wasn't, especially after her father died and her mother went back to her family. Grandma Salley was raised by her father's family."

"Her mother never came back for her?"

"No. It was probably just as well. Her family wouldn't have accepted her and only God knows what would have happened."

"It's a shame but that's probably true," he conceded. "Is your mother an only child?"

"No. She has an older sister, Aunt Peg."

"Your grandmother had only two kids?"

"Yes, but she helped to raise five, including three grandchildren. When my cousin Madison was born my grandmother lived with Aunt Peg until he went to pre-school. Once my mother got pregnant with me, she came to live with us and she took care of my sister and me." Cathy rubbed her eyes to hold back the tears. She had been close to Grandma Salley and many of her happiest memories were of times with her grandmother in the kitchen. Her feelings stirred, Cathy exhaled to regain her composure.

"Are you all right?"

Cathy smiled warmly. "I'm fine. I just find myself missing her at the oddest times." She paused. "Anyway, I remember how much I hated it when my friends would ask us who that white lady at my house was."

He made a face. "I know how that feels."

"I guess that's why I have such empathy for what you and your family must have faced from people wanting to draw color lines."

"That's a powerful observation."

She nodded in agreement. *This is getting a little heavy for dinner conversation.* "So how about we change the subject just a little. I read somewhere that you were in the National Honor Society."

"I held my own."

"Held your own? You were class valedictorian."

He seemed bashful. "I did okay."

"Am I making you uncomfortable?"

"No. This is just really different for me."

"Different? How's that?"

"Most women talk about the accoutrements of sports and celebrity but not you."

"I sound like a college interviewer, right?" Cathy's self-effacing humor made a brief appearance.

He laughed. "Not at all."

"Well, to be honest, I find intelligence to be very attractive. In fact, that's why you're my favorite player."

"Really?" He seemed pleased.

"Yes. You're a great object lesson for teenage boys."

"Oh, so this is a parental thing," he joked.

She laughed. "Yes and no. Yes, because I could always point to you as an athlete and a scholar who was voted most likely to succeed."

He sipped his water. "And no because?"

"Well, you were very cute in high school," she said coyly.

"I certainly hope you think I've improved with age. High school was such a long time ago."

"I do think you've improved with age."

He smiled. "After all, I graduated almost 16 years ago."

"If you think that's a long time ago, I better not tell you how long it's been since I graduated." She winked and he flashed her that megawatt smile of his.

The waiter brought the entrees to the table. They continued to chitchat about different things from politics to movies. Cathy found his easy going manner disarming, while he took note of her distinctive North meets South blend of cosmopolitan sophistication and Old South gentility.

"So you grew up watching the Yankees, too," Cathy noted.

He smiled. "Yeah, I just knew I wanted to wear pinstripes and be just like those guys."

Cathy put her fork down. "Things are a lot different these days. Years ago you only saw athletes during their regular season. Now with all these endorsement deals athletes are in the spotlight 365 days a year."

Marcus's mind went back to the deal he'd signed the day before. "You're right." He tried not to grimace.

Suddenly Cathy remembered Marcus had several endorsements and quickly used a Seinfeld catch phrase. "Not that there is anything wrong with that."

He laughed. "No offense taken. You're right, it is a different business. We're offered hefty endorsement deals and most athletes, including me, take them." "I'm not passing judgment," she insisted.

"I didn't think you were. It is what it is and most of the time it's a mixed blessing," he reassured her. "Nowadays there is a lot more money and a whole lot more exposure and responsibility."

"Do you ever think about that kid who might have your poster on his bedroom door?" Cathy was thinking about her own sons.

He got serious. "I think about that kid all the time. That's why I do my best to set a good example and keep my nose clean. It doesn't make for good copy, but it keeps me out of trouble."

Marcus wished just keeping his nose clean was enough. The media focused a lot of attention on his love life so a night without the paparazzi or Lisa Spellman was a rare treat. If only for one evening Marcus was like any other guy trying to make a good impression on Cathy.

"You're a very wise man, Marcus."

"Thank you." He found it easy to talk to Cathy.

Cathy felt the same way, so much so that it threw her for a loop. *Okay, calm down, Cathy,* she admonished herself.

Keep it together before you fall for him right here and now.

"Would you excuse me for a moment?"

"Sure." He stood up to get her chair.

"Thanks. I'll only be a minute."

"Take your time." He smiled at her.

Cathy rushed to the ladies' room, went straight into a stall, sat down and buried her face in her hands, all her insecurities suddenly surfacing. *He seems sincere but he is a playboy and everyone knows it.* She rubbed her forehead. *I need to chill out.* Cathy's rational side slowly emptied into her consciousness. She was having a good time, so why not leave it at that? She'd smiled more in this one evening than she had all year. It was time to stop playing dime store psychologist, overanalyzing every word and motion. Not only was it a waste of time, it never helped.

After five minutes, she flushed the toilet and emerged from the stall. Cathy gave the two women at the sink a fake little grin. Once they left, she checked her makeup and then inspected her teeth for endive. *All clear,* she thought. Just as she was about to leave, her cell phone rang. Cathy quickly picked up.

"Hello?" Cathy spoke softly.

"Cathy?"

It was her moody client Steven. "Steven? What's going on? Are you sick?" She tried not to seem annoyed.

"Kind of." He was melodramatic.

"What do you mean, kind of?" Now she was perturbed.

"I sent off the manuscript but I'm not sure how I feel about it."

"It's writer's remorse. All of us get it. Just put it out of your mind." She spoke quickly.

"I know you're right. I just needed to hear you say it."

"Good. I'm glad you feel better." She looked at her watch. She didn't want Marcus to think she'd fallen in. "I really have to go."

"It doesn't sound like you're at home." He seemed perplexed since usually Cathy indulged his neurotic spurts. "I'm not, Steven. I'm on a date." "You're on a date?" He was shocked.

She grew more annoyed. "I know it's shocking but you didn't have to make it sound so incomprehensible."

"You should have hung up on me. I'm just being nuts."

"I pick up the phone out of habit. But I can assure you I am going back to my date."

"Have a good time."

He hung up. Cathy regrouped and returned to the table. Marcus got up and held her chair again. "Are you all right?" He was concerned.

"I'm fine. Sorry it took me so long."

"That's okay. I think there's another world in the ladies' room."

"You have no idea how right you are."

With a gleam in his eye Marcus said, "So do you feel like dessert?"

Catherine leaned in to give it right back to him. "Sure. What did you have in mind?"

"You mean to eat?"

"Of course."

"How about bittersweet Napoleons with five spice chocolate ice cream and star anise anglaise?"

"Ooh, sounds good and rich. Can we share?"

"That's cool with me."

Marcus ordered dessert.

"It's not chocolate mousse, but it's good. I think you'll like it."

"I'm sure I will. Everything has been good tonight. The food was good, the service was great and I haven't had such a good time conversing in a while."

"I take that to be high praise coming from a literary agent. Don't you converse for a living?"

"Oh yes. I spend my days talking about book projects, editors, book tours, publicity and publishers. And that's when I'm not soothing my authors' feathers."

"How many clients do you have again?"

"Thirty total. More than half of our clients have signed publishing deals and the rest we're working hard to find deals for."

"So you and your partner split the responsibilities?"

"I'm a little more hands on." *Since I don't have a life*, she scoffed to herself. "E.D. handles the submissions, along with the junior associates. If they find something interesting, it gets reviewed and we see what happens next."

"Sounds like a good system. What kind of projects do you represent?"

Cathy did a quick mental inventory. "I could go on all night with the cross-section of fiction and non-fiction, but I'm sure it would bore you to tears."

"I don't think you could ever bore me."

"You're sure about that? You just met me." She was skeptical.

"It's just a feeling I have." "I

see." Cathy was flustered.

Marcus put the conversation back on track. "Do you have any books I might recognize?"

"Have you heard of *Swiss Journey*?"

"The wife of one of my friends read it and thought it was great. Is the author a client of yours?"

"Yes. James Weil. In fact, he's the one I was supposed to meet yesterday for lunch."

"You know what? I think I'm going to get a few copies of the book and maybe I'll send him some cigars too. It's the least I can do since he's the reason we met."

She grinned. "He loves his cigars. You will have made a friend for life."

Just then the waiter brought dessert over, along with two spoons.

"Ladies first."

Cathy swirled her spoon over the ice cream like a little girl. "I think I'll try this first."

"Be my guest." Marcus laughed quietly.

She took a spoonful of the ice cream and let it melt on her tongue.

The expression on her face said it all.

"What do you think?"

"Mmm. I wouldn't have thought to combine spices with chocolate. Sweet but with a little bite. Have you had this before?"

He dove into the ice cream. "Yeah. It's sweet and spicy. Like you."

She raised her eyebrow. "You must have a graduate degree in flirting. You don't miss a beat." "I do my best." He winked.

Without so much as another kiss Cathy's stomach filled with butterflies, a sure sign she could fall head over heels for him. She had been so careful with her heart for so long she knew she had to derail the conversation before it went to her head or worse, her heart.

"I'm going to take a little bite of this Napoleon. Join me?"

"I thought you'd never ask." He smiled like a naughty little boy.

Cathy knew any more conversation might de-construct her resolve so she was quiet through dessert. She even let Marcus get the last bite. He paid the check.

"I hope you enjoyed dinner as much as I did."

Marcus got up and held her chair, only this time he managed not to stare at her cleavage. It wasn't easy but he'd learned his lesson, for the time being.

"I really did. It's been a long time since I've been out to dinner for something other than business."

They left the restaurant and slowly strolled down the street. "You know, I'm really interested in what you said before," he said.

"What would that be?"

"You only go out to dinner for business?"

"And lunch. We can't forget lunch," she joked.

"Why is that?"

"It's been a while since my last relationship. I wasn't really interested in hopping back on the dating treadmill right away so I focused my energy on my sons and building the agency."

"At what price though?" he asked.

"True." But haven't you ever reached a point where you were just tired of doing the whole dating ritual?"

"Oh yeah."

"I guess that's hard for someone in your position."

"I'm damned if I do and damned if I don't. If I'm keeping my options open and seeing different women, then I'm a player. On the other hand, if I decide to take a break and just hang out, then it's like I must be gay."

"Pardon my French, but that sounds like a royal pain in the butt."

He laughed. "It is." He got quiet for a minute. "Still, when you meet someone you click with, it's worth it." He looked directly in her eyes. "So Cathy, what about you. Do you think it's worth it?"

Cathy was almost in a complete trance. "Definitely." She sighed.

She'd been living vicariously for so long that she'd nearly forgotten how nice it was to go on a date.

"I hope you enjoyed yourself as much as I have," he said.

"It's been a wonderful evening. Thank you."

"No. Thank you. I haven't had an evening this pleasant in a very long time."

She smiled, glad that her red face wasn't visible in the streetlights.

Arm in arm they strolled down the street to one very happy parking attendant.

CHAPTER 9

Smiling like two cats that had feasted on a couple of canaries, Marcus and Cathy on the way home quietly reveled in the excitement of a good first date.

Cathy broke the silence first. "You have a game tomorrow night. I could just as easily hop the train and get home. You don't have to drive all the way out to Amityville." He was very quiet.

"Marcus?"

"Oh, I'm sorry. I was ignoring your suggestion. There is no way in the world I would let you take the train home."

"I appreciate that but I think you should be fresh and rested for tomorrow's game. It's September and you guys are making your push for the playoffs."

"The game is in the evening. Don't worry about me, I'll be fine."

"If you say so. Don't say I didn't offer."

"You're sweet to worry about me, Cathy, but there's no need to."

When he kissed her hand she got goose bumps. "Okay, you win."

"Good. So what are we doing tomorrow?"

She was surprised. "I'm sorry. What?"

"For our second date."

"Our second date?" She tried not to seem too anxious.

"I can have Louis pick you up and bring you to my place. I'll give you the grand tour, then maybe we can have lunch or an early supper before we leave for the game."

"Sounds good to me."

"Great. Since it's a night game I'd like for you to sit where I can see you. Is that okay with you? Or should I get you a seat in the luxury suite again?"

"The luxury suite is nice but not necessary."

He kissed her hand again. *He's definitely a charmer*, she thought.

"You know, I haven't seen much of Long Island."

"I would be happy to be your tour guide."

"I'd like to take you up on that."

"Please do. It would be my pleasure."

Between holding hands and flirtatious glances, time passed quickly. After what felt like the shortest drive ever they approached Cathy's exit on the parkway.

"We're here already. That wasn't too bad of a drive at all."

"Wait a minute. How did you know how to get here?" She was puzzled.

"You didn't see the navigation system?"

"No. I can't say I was paying attention."

"All you have to tell me is when we reach your house."

"It's just before the third intersection."

"I really hate for this night to end, but I will see you tomorrow, right?"

"Definitely." She paused. "My house is just after the green one on the right side."

"That's good to know." Cathy was confounded when he drove past her house. "You know that was my house."

"I know. I thought that maybe you could take me on a little tour of Amityville."

Cathy looked at him as if he were crazy. "You're kidding me, right?"

"You did say you would love to be my tour guide, didn't you?"

"Yes, but I didn't expect to be called to duty tonight."

He pulled over to the side of the road. "I'm having a lot of fun with you and I thought we could just extend it a little while. I promise I will get you home." She

waited for the punch line.

"If you'd rather I could just turn around."

"No. You don't have to do that. What would you like to see?"

"Well, the Amityville Horror house comes to mind."

She smiled. "That's South Amityville."

"So are we headed in the right direction?"

"Yes. I'll tell you where you're going."

He smiled. "Cool."

It only took a few minutes to go from North to South Amityville by the water. "Okay. Make a left here. This is the infamous Ocean Avenue."

She smiled as she watched Marcus study the neighborhood. "It's really nice here."

She nodded her head. "I told you it was. They actually don't take too kindly to tourists, especially when it comes to this block."

"I bet they don't. How many Amityville Horror movies have they made?"

"At least three I can think of off the top of my head."

"And that's not including the sensation the book caused."

"I know." As they approached the house she pointed it out. "Slow down you're looking right at it."

He stopped the car. "Wow, all that hoopla about this house? It's a nice house."

"I know."

"It is infamous, though."

"True, but for all the wrong reasons; an entire family was killed back in '73 or '74, yet somehow all the focus is on flies in winter and pig's blood."

Marcus had to crack up at the absurdity of it all. "That is pretty bad, isn't it? I guess that's why they don't take too kindly to tourists or movie companies."

She looked over her shoulder. "We have company."

"We have company?"

"Yes." Cathy watched as one of Amityville's finest approached the car.

The officer tapped on the window. Marcus rolled the window down. "Yes, officer?"

The officer bent down. "I was just wondering what's going on with you folks."

"My friend here was just showing me the neighborhood."

She watched as the officer's eyes went from normal to at least three times their normal size. "Aren't you Marcus Fox?"

"Yes."

"Oh my God. I can't believe it."

She spent the next ten minutes watching a man re-visit his inner child. Marcus gave him an autograph and she got into the act, taking their picture with the officer's camera phone. All in all, it was an eventful trip down Ocean Avenue.

"I'm sorry if that bored you," Marcus said.

"No, not at all. To tell you the truth I think that's why I love baseball so much."

"Why?"

"It's silly. Forget I said anything."

"No. I really want to know."

"Why? It's silly."

"Well, you're kind of an unusual fan."

"I'm an unusual fan? What makes me unusual?"

"Well, you're an African American female baseball fan."

"So?"

"There aren't many black women who go nuts over baseball."

Cathy's mind wandered back to the days when she was growing up. "I've always been different."

"Everyone thinks that when they're growing up. I'm sure you weren't an outsider or anything."

Cathy stared out the window. "You might be surprised."

"Oh really? So tell me about it."

Cathy wondered for a minute. *Do I tell him about the religion thing?*

"I'm waiting," he joked.

"Well, my favorite group was the Beatles and I had all their albums."

Marcus snickered. "You've got to be kidding, that's nothing."

"Maybe to you, but my parents were so worried that they bought an Isley Brothers album, along with the 'Yellow Submarine' my grandmother gave me for my ninth birthday."

He chuckled. "That's not so bad. So how did you come upon your love of baseball?"

"It came from my grandmother."

He looked genuinely taken aback. "Your grandmother loved the Yankees?"

A warm smile lit up her face. "Oh yeah. Her father used to take her to games when Babe Ruth and Lou Gehrig played. Then after her dad died in 1934, she used to go to games with my great uncles."

"That's amazing. So baseball is a matter of family tradition."

Cathy liked the way the statement rolled off his tongue. Baseball as a matter of tradition in her family. Deep down she knew she'd handed him a carefully spun

PR story. Baseball was a tradition in her family, but she couldn't exactly tell him that Yankee Stadium was her haven from a religious life of quiet desperation and a refuge from weekend door to door field service.

She nodded her head. "It is a tradition on my father's side. My mother's family wasn't into baseball. My grandmother continued the tradition with us when she came over to watch games on a Sunday afternoon. She died when I was ten so those memories are precious to me as well. Sue me. I'm a sap. "

He smiled. "I don't think you're a sap. There's something special about you, Cathy."

She was touched. "You think so?"

"Definitely."

Out of the corner of his eye Marcus noticed Cathy staring up at the stars. It was a clear fall night and the dark sky seemed to go on forever. She looked lost in thought as she closed her eyes.

" 'Star light, star bright, first star I see tonight. I wish I may, I wish I might have the wish I wished tonight.' "

Cathy was surprised. "What made you say that?"

"I saw you looking up at the stars and figured you were making a wish."

Cathy glanced up at the sky again. "I was just admiring the stars. Besides, what I really wish can't happen."

"You mean you would wish for your grandmothers to be here."

Cathy quickly wiped a tear away. She'd always thought that if her grandmothers were around her parents would not have broken up or at least her life after the divorce would have been more bearable. "Yes. I'd give anything to have them back."

Marcus reached out and touched Cathy's shoulder. He knew it wasn't the time for words and she appreciated not being pushed into talking about it. When they pulled into Cathy's driveway she could see the curtains moving upstairs. She knew they had an audience.

"I see you remembered how to get here with no problem."

"Told you I'd get you back in one piece."

Cathy's heart raced as Marcus came around the car. Even though he had already asked about a second date, she knew good chemistry, an amazing kiss, would seal the deal for sure. He helped her out and they held hands like teenagers as they walked to the front door.

He looked around. "It's a nice house. Maybe one day soon you'll invite me over for dinner."

"That can be arranged."

"What time should I send Louis to pick you up?"

"Same time as today is fine with me."

"Good. So we're just saying good night for now." He rubbed her hand.

"Not goodbye, just good night."

Marcus leaned in for a good night kiss. He wanted to give her a gentle kiss but the moment their lips touched a spark ignited. Cathy's whole body tingled as things quickly escalated into a deep, passionate kiss, the kind she hadn't had in a while, and after tonight she wasn't sure if she'd ever had one in the first place.

They were both breathless when Cathy reluctantly pulled away. "If you're going to get back home in good time we have to stop."

"I know you're right. We'll see each other again tomorrow."

"Right. Can you do me a favor?"

"Sure."

"I know this is going to sound stupid but could you call me to let me know you got back okay?

Marcus thought that was such a cute thing to say he kissed her again and both their knees almost buckled.

"I knew you were special. I'll call you when I get home."

"Thanks."

"Good night."

Cathy put her key in the lock. "Good night."

Her heart still pounding in her ears, she watched him for a couple of minutes until he was out of sight. She sighed and started to turn the knob. Her sister Anna pulled the door open so fast Cathy nearly fell on her face.

"Hey!" She barely caught herself.

She walked into an inquisition of two, with Michelle, arms folded, sitting on the sofa. "What's going on? Did I miss something or is this the Inquisition?"

Michelle sat up straighter. "Now who's the one keeping secrets?"

"Oh no, you don't. I'm not the one who's been dating someone for two whole months without saying a word."

Anna looked surprised. "You've been seeing someone for two months?"

Michelle was a little defensive. "Wait a second. This is not about me. It's about her." She pointed to Cathy.

"That's right, you're the one who's dating Marcus Fox."

Cathy walked to the hall closet to kick off her shoes. "Is it a crime to date him?"

"Ah ha! So you are dating him!" Anna exclaimed. "When are you going on the second date?"

"If you must know, tomorrow. He's sending a car for me."

A chorus of oohs and ahs came from Michelle and Anna.

Anna shook her head. "I can't believe this all happened because Jim didn't show up for lunch. You know, Cathy, I think you owe Jim a big bottle of champagne or something. Standing you up for lunch was the best thing he's ever done for you."

"Aside from the royalty checks, right?"

Michelle was coy. "Oh, honey, you earned those checks."

They laughed. Cathy flopped between them on the sofa. She hadn't felt like a girl in a long time. It was as if she were sixteen only this time she was allowed to date.

"So give us the details." Michelle was practically salivating.

Cathy felt pleased with life. "It was a great day. He set me up in the Hall of Fame Suite. You know, I've been to Yankee Stadium a bunch of times since we were kids, but today I saw a part of the stadium I'd never seen." She paused. "I knew about the suites but I sure as hell didn't expect to ever get *near* one, let alone be a guest."

"I heard they're really nice." Michelle was envious in a nice way.

"Michelle, really nice doesn't begin to cover it."

"That's all fine and well, Sister, but let's get to the good part. Where did you go for dinner?" Anna had never been one to mince her words. She wanted the real skinny.

"Chanterelle."

"Woo hoo," Michelle shouted.

"Sounds like you had a good time."

"Dinner was fantastic. The food was unbelievable and the conversation was great." She paused. "He wasn't at all what I thought he'd be like. He's a great ball player, has a foundation to help kids, five World Series rings and the man's name is synonymous with a cottage industry. He's got the goods and he's totally relatable." She shook her head. "You know, I've been on dates with guys with executive titles who can't get out of their own way they're such jerks."

"Wow," Michelle sighed.

"So? Did you kiss him?"

She shook her head. "It's too funny. All these years have gone by and you still manage to ask the little sister questions. To answer you, yes, we kissed and it was great."

"We know that much. We saw you."

Cathy swatted Anna. She laughed as she ran away. "You did say I am still the quintessential younger sister."

"Quintessentially the younger sister."

"You know, your sons called for you."

"Oh God. I was supposed to call Alex back. I totally forgot."

"Are you going to tell them about Marcus?"

"I don't know, Michelle. I really would rather wait and not get their hopes up."

"You mean your hopes up. You really like him."

Cathy sighed. "What's not to like? I haven't felt like this in eons."

"Well, it's getting late and from the look of things we'll be handling a bit more at the agency tomorrow." Michelle smiled.

"Oh God! That's right. I forgot to check with E.D. about Laurel, Janet and Lisa." She had a twinge of guilt.

"Don't sweat it, Cathy, all three received good offers today."

She was so tickled she clapped. "Fantastic. We've gone from 25 signed authors to 28 in one fell swoop."

"You should be proud of yourself, Cathy. You were the one who worked extra hard to make it happen and now here it is. You're the one who takes the after-hours calls, the panic attacks, the negotiations and the author/publisher skirmishes. You deserve some time to yourself, if for no other reason than to make sure you don't go postal," Michelle said as she put on her jacket.

"I second that. It sounds to me like you deserve to have some fun without guilt. Besides, when was the last time you took a vacation?"

"Does taking time off to drive Andrew and Alex to school count?" Catherine asked timidly.

"No!" Michelle and Anna spoke at the same time.

"Well, I guess that answers my question."

All joking aside, Anna got serious. "And you know E.D. is the last one to begrudge you any time off. He's been trying to get you to take it easy for years now."

"You need a time out." Michelle paused. "Now that we have 28 signed clients there are only two without publishing deals and we can handle that."

"Now that we're not taking on any new clients, it should be okay."

"And even if we were, that's what you have yours truly for, to go through the representation queries."

"Okay, ladies, you've convinced me. I'm going to head upstairs, take a shower and get some rest."

Cathy kissed Michelle on the cheek. "Talk to you tomorrow."

"Okay."

"Good night all."

"Good night."

Although she'd had an exciting and physical day, Cathy didn't have any problems with her back going upstairs. When she passed by her sons' room she couldn't help smiling at Marcus's poster.

***

Marcus walked back into his apartment, using his remote to turn all the lights on. He walked over to his picture window and looked at all the red and white lights of traffic below.

The phone rang.

"Hello?"

"So I take it you had a good night?" Ben asked.

"I did. One of the best nights I've had in a long time."

"Good. So you really like this girl?"

"I do. She's sweet, smart and very sexy in a way I never thought about before."

"What do you mean?"

"I've never been out with a full-figured woman before and now I'm wondering why. She's just as sexy as any woman on the runway."

"Beauty is beauty no matter what package it comes in. What you really have to look for is what's inside the package."

"You're right about that. Anyway, Ben, thanks for calling."

"Anytime. See you

tomorrow." "Good night."

Marcus dialed Cathy.

Cathy was still floating when she got into bed.. When the phone rang, she glanced at the clock.

"Hello?'

"Hey there. I'm back home in one piece."

"Good. Now I can go to sleep."

Hearing his sexy voice, she closed her eyes and thought back to their good night kiss.

"Sweet dreams,

Cathy." "You too,

Marcus." She hung up.

"It'll take a crowbar to get this grin off my face," she mumbled out loud.

***

Marcus looked at his watch. "They're an hour behind us so they should still be up," he said out loud before he dialed the phone.

"Hello?"

"Dad."

"Marcus. How are you, Son?"

"I'm good, Dad. I didn't wake you, did I?"

"No, I was up going over some case files. What's up?"

"Is Mom up?"

"No, she went to bed early. They've been doing inventory for a day or so and she's really worn out."

"Oh. Give her a kiss for me in the morning."

"I will. So what's on your mind, Son?"

Marcus knew better than to dodge a direct question from his dad. "Remember what you told me about meeting Mom?"

"Sure."

"You said that you knew she was the one for you by the end of your first date."

"I did know. Not that you ever believed that could happen."

"Well, it seems that I might be a convert to that way of thinking."

"I see. So you've met someone."

"I have. Her name is Catherine Chambers."

"How did you meet her?"

"I know this is going to sound like a cliché but I saw her across a crowded restaurant."

His father laughed. "So your old dad isn't such a sap anymore, huh?"

Marcus chuckled. "They say the apple doesn't fall far from the tree."

"So what is it about this Catherine that's made you a convert?"

Marcus paced in front of the window. "It's not just any one thing, it's a combination of things. She's smart, pretty, open and down to earth. When she smiles her eyes have a little sparkle in them. Most of all, she was herself and I felt comfortable enough to be myself."

"That's great, Son. I'm happy for you. I take it then she's not in the entertainment industry."

"She's a literary agent."

"Nice."

"She's divorced and she has twin 18-year-old sons in college upstate."

"She has eighteen year olds? She got married young. How old is she? If you don't mind me asking."

"She's forty."

"So she's only six years older than you. That's not bad. At this stage in the game age is relative."

"She's a full-figured woman, too."

"Great. Your mom wasn't a Skinny Minnie when I met her. I like women to have some meat on their bones."

Marcus smiled. "She does have curves in all the right places."

His father laughed again. "There's nothing wrong with that, just in case you needed to hear someone say that out loud."

"Dad, I can see the gossip captions already. They're going to zoom in on her body."

"Listen, Son, she may not be part of the entertainment industry but I'm sure she knows and she said yes to a date anyway."

"She's coming to the game tomorrow night."

"Oh yeah? Maybe your mom and I can fly down for the game."

"I would love for you to meet her."

"Tell you what. I'll think on it and give either you or Ben a buzz."

"Okay, Dad."

"Now I really have to get these files done. I'll talk to you sometime tomorrow, Son."

"Okay, Dad. Good night."

"Good night, Son."

Marcus stared out at the city again. Cathy was on his mind and under his skin already. He could smell her perfume on his shirt. He took a deep breath as if he were drinking her in again and headed to his bedroom to call it a night.

***

Just as Cathy was about ready to call it a night she heard banging on the door downstairs. She got up and fumbled around to get her robe. When she stepped into the hall she heard her sister cursing up a storm. Then she heard a man's voice. It was Madison.

As she walked downstairs, Cathy rubbed her eyes. Madison looked as if he'd been thrown down a flight of stairs. She rubbed her eyes again because there was no way he would allow himself to looked ragged. As she got further down the stairs she realized his clothes were damn near shredded.

She turned to Anna. "What the hell happened to him?"

"I can't seem to get the story."

"He looks like he was rode hard and put away wet." "Ahem. I am standing right here." "So speak already!" Anna was annoyed.

"He's a real son of a gun! That's all I can say."

"Who's a son of a gun?" Cathy was too tired to play guessing games. "Did you get into a fight with one of your girlfriend's ex-boyfriends or something?"

"No. This was courtesy of a client's now ex-husband."

"*Your client's ex-husband did this to you*? You're not sleeping with a client, are you?" Anna was flabbergasted.

"No, Anna. He knows better than that. Don't you?"

"Yes, of course I know better. That's not why this happened."

"Then what got him fired up enough to go after you?" Anna asked.

"We'd been tracking this guy's finances for more than a year. In fact, I had you look over some papers and you recommended a forensic accountant. Remember, Anna?"

"Oh yeah, I remember that. I gave you the number of a professor I had in grad school."

"Well, he was worth the money because he hit pay dirt. We found accounts in the Cayman Islands, buildings being managed by a dummy corporation and several properties in California's wine country." "Oh my

God." Cathy was shocked.

"You hit the mother lode."

"Naturally we reported it to the judge to have the matter of property division, child support and alimony revisited in light of this new information."

"So this guy's major pissed with you."

"Tell me about it. Today the judge handed down his decision and he really cleaned this guy out. It's not that he has nothing left, but he has to pay."

"Judges don't take kindly to hiding assets," Cathy said.

Anna was doing the calculations in her head. "You're talking millions here."

"He probably ordered him to pay the attorneys' fees too."

"He did."

"So what happened exactly?"

"I was walking outside my office and I see a man coming down the block towards me. I couldn't make out who it was at first and then I realized it was this guy." "What did you do?" Cathy's eyes widened.

"I put my briefcase in the car and I waited for him to reach me. He was screaming at me about his money and how I helped that money grubbing misspelled witch get his money. I'm a divorce attorney; it wasn't anything I haven't heard before."

"Right," Anna interjected.

"I figured I'd just let him vent and get it out of his system. Next thing I know, it gets physical. He's throwing punches at me. There was no talking to this guy. I knew

I had to get back to my office or the building lobby to call security or this guy was going to kill me."

Anna looked at his ripped clothes. "It looks like he made a good start."

"He did. I was almost home free when he picked me up and threw me down the steps in front on the building. He was going to finish me off but the police came and grabbed him before he could do anything else."

"Who called the police?" Cathy breathed a sigh of relief.

"My secretary Nancy called. He'd been to the office ranting and raving. She called the police right away." "Good thing she did. It's a wonder he didn't kill you." "Don't I know it, Cathy? I had him arrested for assault. I'm just coming back from making my statement."

"Did you go to the hospital and get checked out?" Anna asked.

"No. I just wanted to get out of there." He looked in the mirror over the mantle. "I'm a little the worse for wear, but I'll be okay."

Cathy got up and poured him a glass of wine. "You might make a lot of money as a divorce lawyer, but no one can say you don't earn it." She handed him the glass and watched as he drank it all in two gulps.

"I hate to say this, but do you have anything stronger? I need a stiff drink."

Anna went to the bar and took out the Johnny Walker Blue, a gift from a client. She poured him a double. "You want ice?"

"I'll take it straight." He was shaken.

He downed it. "Hit me again."

Anna poured him another double. For the most part they were a family of teetotalers, but if anyone needed a few tonight, it was Mad.

"You're staying here tonight. You can sleep in the boys' room."

Usually Anna and Cathy liked to kid around with Madison, but tonight wasn't the night for jokes.

"This was one of my favorite suits. He ruined my vintage Armani suit."

"You can buy another suit, Madison. It's your life we can't replace." Anna spoke calmly.

"Yeah. You know, this is the first time anything like this has ever happened to me. I know threats come with the territory, from both men and women, but this the first time I've ever felt so helpless." His voice cracked

"You fought back, right?" Cathy asked

"I got a few swings in, but this guy was like a bull. He was snorting and cursing and behaving like an animal." Madison was more shaken than he wanted to let on.

"The guy was trying to hide money so he didn't have to pay his wife anything and he was ducking out on child support. He got what he deserved. You did the right thing," Anna reassured him.

"I know. I'll feel better in the morning. Sorry I woke you two up."

"Don't sweat it, Mad, that's what family is for. "There's clean linen on the bed and fresh towels in the linen closet," Cathy said as she stood up.

"Thanks."

"I was going to go to bed unless you still want to talk," she said.

"No, that's okay."

"I'll stay up with you, Mad." Anna sat down next to him. "Besides I can give you the 411 on your other cousin there who went out with star baseball player Marcus Fox."

"See, I told you he was interested, Cathy."

She kissed him on the forehead. "Yes, you did, and you were right. Get some rest after the story hour. Good night."

"Good night," Madison said quietly.

She went upstairs to the linen closet, took out some clean towels and placed them on one of the beds in Alex and Andrew's room. Even though she was very concerned about Madison, there was still lightheartedness in her spirit tonight. She had a date Friday night and it was the first time she'd looked forward to Friday in a long time.

CHAPTER 10

Marcus got up early the next morning and showered. He was looking forward to a day with Cathy. Still clad in a towel, he made a phone call.

"Hello?"

"Hi, Louis."

"Mr. Fox. What can I do for you?"

"Nothing really. I just called to tell you that I think I'll pick Ms. Chambers up myself."

"Are you sure?" He sounded puzzled.

"Oh, yeah. I'll still need you for the game tonight."

"Okay."

"See you later, Louis. I've got to run."

"All right."

Marcus knew he had to get a move on if he wanted to get Cathy in good time. He looked forward to the chance to get to know her better on the drive in.

***

Cathy woke up and wondered for a moment if she had dreamt the whole date thing with Marcus Fox. She pinched herself. *Ouch!* So the answer was a resounding yes! Cathy felt so good she even read her horoscope, something she never did. According to the stars, there were good vibrations in her future and for once Cathy believed it.

She took a warm bath and got dressed. Although her mother ran a strict religious household, she was big on the idea of taking good care of yourself whether you were single or married. Cathy got regular weekly manicures and pedicures in addition to Brazilian bikini waxes. The Boy Scouts weren't the only ones who believe in preparedness. As usual she had The Weather Channel on while she got dressed. It looked as if the day was going to be another warm one but she decided to wear jeans anyway. Thankfully Cathy didn't have a pair of "mom" jeans in her closet. She was an all skirts girl before Anna took her out and made her buy jeans in every cut and style available. Anna didn't know that Beyonce had been a key in Cathy's conversion. Before Beyonce, Cathy was so used to seeing celebrities with field goal thighs wearing jeans that she didn't think she looked good in jeans. She smiled, remembering the first time she'd heard thighs that don't rub together described as field goal thighs. Beyonce wore jeans and she had real thighs and a motor in the back of her Honda. Jennifer Lopez had a booty but Beyonce had BOOTY. Cathy decided she could work a pair of jeans, too. Cathy turned around in the mirror to check out the rear view and gave a little shake, humming the "Milk Shake."

She was saved from embarrassment by the sound of a lawnmower. Mr. Little, their gardener, had obviously decided to beat the heat. Any other day the noise would have driven her crazy but today he saved her from singing out loud and letting others find out that she knew the words to a Kelis song. After all, she was a 40-year-old mother of two. What did *she* know about milk shakes?

Once she had the last bobby pin in place for her cool updo, she turned her attention to her makeup. Unlike yesterday, today she could manage to apply her mascara without putting an eye out with the mascara wand. The only thing she didn't apply was lipstick. The last thing Cathy wanted to worry about was lipstick on her teeth. She was good to go except for one thing. She absolutely had to straighten up her room.

As she made her bed with perfect hospital corners, Cathy suddenly realized how alone she'd been for the past two years. She'd been sleeping alone in a king size bed for so long that its size was lost on her. She wasn't exactly sure what was going to happen between her and Marcus, but she hoped she remembered how to share, if the situation arose. She caught herself smiling. "Cut that out, Catherine!" she scolded herself.

***

Marcus was on his way to Amityville when his cell rang.

"Hello?"

"Hey, Marcus."

"Hey, Ben. How are you?" He felt good.

"Good. But the question should be, how are you?"

He smiled. "I'm fine."

Ben groaned. "I take it you haven't seen the paper today."

"I grabbed it on the way to my car but I haven't looked at it yet. Why?"

"There's an item on the gossip page about you and Cathy."

Marcus smacked the dashboard. "You've got to be kidding me. What does it say?"

"It's just a photo with the caption 'Is Marcus Fox Living Large with New Larger Lady Love?' They can't just leave well enough alone."

"Like it or not, it's a part of their job."

"I wonder if Cathy's seen it."

"I think it's a safe bet to assume she has seen it. If she didn't see it herself someone else has told her about it by now."

"You know, I was hoping that we wouldn't have to deal with this stuff so soon."

"I'm sorry buddy, the honeymoon with the press is over.
Don't worry, I'm sure she understands."

"How do you know that?"

"Well, she's Jim Weil's agent and they've had some real fun with him over the years."

"How do you know he's one of her clients?"

"I did my homework."

"I guess she and I are going to have to talk about it."

"Good. It's one thing to have your client get a lot of publicity; it's another thing entirely when you're the subject."

Marcus let out a loud sigh. "Okay, man. I'll see you later."

"Okay. I'm sure everything will be fine."

"I hope so."

Marcus looked up for a moment. He'd so wanted to make sure he had time to talk to Cathy about the gossip circus that surrounded his life, but the press had beat him to it. He hoped her agent's skin extended to her own life.

***

Just as Cathy finished fluffing the pillows she heard her sister yelling. She rushed out to the hall where she heard her cousin and sister talking excitedly.

She went down the stairs as quickly as she could. When she walked in the kitchen she saw that Madison had borrowed one of the boys' sweat suits, which was about six inches too long. Nevertheless, she was a good cousin and didn't point it out.

"What's all the noise for?" she asked.

Madison smiled. "You made the papers."

"Glad to see you're feeling better, Madison," Cathy said.

"Thanks."

"Now what's all this noise about me making the papers?" she asked.

Anna handed her the paper. "It's right here." She pointed to an item in the paper.

Cathy couldn't believe her eyes. There was a picture of Marcus and her walking to his car with the caption, 'Is Marcus Fox Living Large with New Larger Lady Love?'

She put the paper down. All that energy and confidence she'd had earlier suddenly fell down around her ankles. Her countenance changed in slow motion as she read the words 'larger lady love.'

"They're not used to seeing him with anyone with a little meat on her bones. It's nothing to fret about. Marcus decided he wants some meat with his gravy," Madison offered.

In spite of herself, Cathy laughed.

"I couldn't have said it better, Madison. Every now and again you say something smart," Anna teased. She couldn't resist getting one crack in; she'd cut back. Cold turkey would have been too much to ask.

"Thanks a lot."

"He is a famous ball player and bachelor who usually dates actresses, models and singers. Though seeing me with him was way out of left field, it still doesn't make it any easier to see it in print."

"Don't let it bring you down." Anna rubbed her back.

"Shake it off, honey," Madison chimed in.

Cathy picked the paper up again and studied it for a moment. "It's not a bad picture of me, though." "I would call that the money shot," Madison agreed.

"The money shot?" Anna asked.

"Yeah, didn't you see the close-up of the cleavage?" Madison asked, surprised his cousins hadn't noticed. Both Anna and Cathy took a closer look. "Oh my God, they did zoom in on it!" "Don't you mean on them?" Anna kidded.

They broke up with laughter again.

"I guess I should have something to eat or at least some juice this morning."

Cathy went over to the refrigerator.

"You're not having any coffee?" Madison asked.

"Maybe later. I don't want two cups of coffee working on my bladder on the way into the city."

"Enough said. I get where you're coming from." The doorbell rang. It was only a little after nine o'clock.

"Who in the world could it be? I'll get it." Anna went to answer the door.

"It's probably a Jehovah's Witness." Madison shrugged.

"Not at this house. We're practically considered the anti-Christ." Cathy snickered as she poured a small glass of orange juice. "So you're sure you feel better, Mad?"

"So far, so good."

"Let's hope it stays that way." Mad and Cathy raised the juice glasses for a morning toast of solidarity.

Anna slowly walked into the kitchen.

"Was it the *Watchtower* people?" Cathy asked.

Before she could get a word out Marcus appeared.

"I don't know anything about the *Watchtower,* but I hope I bring good news," he said.

Cathy was completely taken by surprise. "I thought you were sending Louis."

He walked over and planted a kiss on her. "Good morning Cathy." He planted another kiss on her. "I decided to pick you up myself." "Good morning to you," she returned.

Madison cleared his throat.

Marcus turned around with his hand out. "Hi. I'm Marcus Fox."

Madison shook his hand. "I'm Madison Parker. I'm Cathy and Anna's first cousin." "Nice to meet you," Marcus said.

She stood up. "Marcus, this is my sister, Anna Chambers."

They shook hands.

"I guess we sort of met at the door."

"It's nice to officially meet you, Anna." He looked at her and Cathy. "You two really have some resemblance." "We hear that a lot." Anna grinned.

Cathy's eyes widened when she spotted the paper on the counter just behind Marcus. Guessing what was in her thoughts, Madison engaged Marcus in conversation. "I see the Yankees are doing pretty well. You're on a winning streak, right?"

"Yeah. We've won the last four games."

Madison's sports interruption allowed Anna to get the paper closed and out of the way. Cathy told herself she had to remember to give Madison his props for thinking on his feet. Especially since the only sports he watched were tennis and women's mud wrestling.

"It's been a tough season," Anna interjected.

"But I think we've seen the worst of it," Cathy said.

"I'm sure you know my sister and nephews are big time Yankee fans. In the summer we get a play by play every morning," Anna said.

Marcus laughed. "Works for me." He kissed Cathy's hand and the butterflies in her stomach went to work.

The television was tuned into the traffic report. Anna was a traffic report person. Cathy thought if she hadn't become an accountant she would be up in a helicopter reporting on traffic patterns.

"The traffic to the city should be lighter now since it's technically after rush hour," Anna reported.

"Are you ready to go?" Marcus asked.

"Sure."

"Do you have an overnight bag?"

If this were a sitcom the sound effect would have been that of a car screeching to a halt.

"An overnight bag? I didn't realize I would need one." Cathy felt panicked.

A light slowly dawned on Marcus. "Oh, I'm sorry. I just realized how you must have heard that. What I was saying is it gets a little chilly at night this time of year and since you're going to be in the stands, I thought you might bring something a little warmer for the game."

A feeling of relief came over the room and over Cathy in particular.

"I'll throw a few things in a bag for you. It will only take me a few minutes," Anna said before vanishing upstairs.

"I've got to take a deposition on the north shore," Madison announced. He picked up his briefcase. I also need to get home and change."

"It was a pleasure to meet you, Marcus." Madison and Marcus shook hands.

"Same here."

"I'll check you later, Cousin."

"Okay. See ya later."

Madison tried to make a smooth exit but he apparently forgot the pants were extra-long and he nearly fell on his face. Cathy quickly bit her bottom lip to keep from laughing.

"Are you all right, man?" Marcus asked.

Madison recovered quickly. "Yeah, I'm fine. Thanks. I'll see you later."

He rolled up the pants and made a quick exit.

"I'm not going to ask about the pants." "Good.

You don't want to know," Cathy said.

"Enough said."

Anna returned carrying an extra-large duffle bag. It looked as if she'd packed Cathy for a week.

"Here you go." She placed the bag near the door.

"Thanks." Judging from the look on her face there were likely a few surprise choices in the bag.

Marcus hoisted the bag onto his shoulder and kissed Anna on the cheek.

"It was a pleasure to meet you. I'm sure we'll be seeing more of each other in the future."

Anna grinned. "Sounds good to me."

Cathy grabbed her large Coach bag. "I'll call you." "Okay." She paused until Marcus was out of earshot. "Don't do anything I wouldn't do." She smiled mischievously as she closed the door behind Cathy.

Like a real gentleman, Marcus held the car door open for her and put her things in the backseat. A second later they were off.

CHAPTER 11

Both Cathy and Marcus knew about the newspaper item. No matter how you sliced it, the car wasn't the place to have the conversation, so the elephant stayed between them. Marcus didn't want anything to spoil the good feelings the two of them had shared the night before so he kept the conversation light and breezy.

"By the way, if I didn't say it last night, thanks for the late night tour of Amityville."

"It was my pleasure. Not only did you get to see the infamous house it, came complete with a fawning fan."

He laughed. "He was nice."

"It never gets tiresome does it?" Cathy asked.

"Not really." He turned the radio down. "So is your whole family from Long Island?"

"No. My dad lived in Harlem before the family moved to Amityville in the late forties. My mom is from South Carolina. Where are your parents from?"

"My dad was raised in Chicago and my mother grew up in Cleveland."

"How did they meet?"

"They met at Michigan State and became college sweethearts. Did your parents meet in college?"

"They met when my father was at Morgan State in Baltimore. My mother was living with some cousins and they met at a party. How long have your parents been married?"

"It will be 36 years in November."

"That's great. It must be nice to have parents who still like each other."

"Still like each other?"

"Mm hmm, as far as I can tell, love is the easy part. You can love someone deeply but if you don't like them it's hard to stay together."

"I never thought about it that way."

"Liking someone is a big thing in a relationship. Trust me, I know."

Marcus chuckled softly. "My parents still kid around and play with each other. My mom is ticklish and my father still loves to take advantage of it."

"Oh, that's so cute." Cathy giggled at the thought.

"My sisters and I never thought so; he always did it whenever our friends were over. It was so embarrassing."

"Embarrassing your kids is one of the little benefits of parenthood. What's worse is there's no age limit."

"So what do I have to look forward to?"

"Embarrassing your own kids, of course."

"I'm sure you don't do that to your kids."

"If I do it's purely unintentional, which probably makes it ten times worse. I'm the single parent of boys, excuse me, young men, so there are areas I plain don't understand."

"So it's just you and your sister? No brothers?"

"It was just Anna and me. The closest thing we have to a brother is Madison. Other than him, all the guys in my neighborhood were a lot older."

"Your ex didn't help out?"

"My ex fell off the face of the planet just a few months before they turned two."

He grimaced. "Oh, that's not right."

"He only followed what he knew. His father was a rolling stone and his mother allowed it. He blew in and out of my ex's life. I wouldn't have it for my boys."

"I don't blame you."

"I gave him a choice. I told him he could be in or he could be out, it was one or the other. If he decided to be in, he had to be all the way in, which meant being an involved parent. If he decided to be out, he had to go all the way out. There was no way in the world I would have subjected my children to all the instability of a revolving door father."

"You were right."

"Don't nominate me for sainthood yet," Cathy cautioned him. "I also told him that if he showed up for high school graduation to make sure he wore track shoes. Not only did I know how to use a machete, I knew where to find one. I gave him fair warning."

"Did he show up?"

Cathy snickered quietly. "No. He knew better. What's funny is that it wasn't so much about the divorce; we have divorced people in our family who managed to raise their kids without killing each other. He just didn't grasp the concept."

"How long have your parents been divorced?"

"Twenty-four years."

"That's a long time."

"I know. Now that I'm older I wonder if it's long enough."

"They say divorce is harder for adult children."

Cathy nodded her head. "I'd agree with that. When you're younger parents are very careful to make sure you don't take any of the blame; they want to protect your feelings. Then when you're older, they want you to be on their side."

"Sounds sticky."

"It is. Sometimes they talk to you like you're a friend of theirs or something. Like there was this one time my mother made a comment about her sex life with my father and before she could expound, I had to get all Regis Philbin with her."

"Get Regis Philbin?"

"I told her she could poll the audience or phone a friend but I didn't want to hear it and that was my final answer." They cracked up.

"You have some sense of humor."

"Hey, the way I figure it, you can laugh or you can cry; laughing is much easier." Cathy looked out the window. "I don't think I've ever driven into Manhattan this way before."

"I'm taking the scenic route."

"Oh, I'm not boring you to death? I don't live the glamorous life of a singer, actress or model."

"Don't be so quick to think they live such a great life. I enjoy talking to you. You keep it real. I like that."

"I like talking with you, too." She felt a little bashful but kept the conversation moving. Marcus noticed she had a sexy way of making her hair bounce when she turned her head. She did it so naturally Marcus knew it wasn't a put on.

"Now let's talk about your family. I know you're the oldest and you have two sisters. Tell me about them. Are they married?"

"My sister Lisa is a psychologist. She's 32. She just got engaged a few months ago."

"Do you like the guy?"

"Yeah. He's pretty cool. He's in law enforcement. My youngest sister Cecily, is a record company executive. She travels a lot and is in no hurry to settle down."

Cathy nodded. "She just turned thirty last month. You had a party for her at the Four Seasons."

"How did you know that?" He was a little shocked.

"My father, Anna, Madison and my sons took me there for my 40th birthday. The lobby restaurant was all abuzz about you being there. I think you were in the Fifty Seven, Fifty Seven restaurant."

Marcus couldn't believe that it was a small world after all. "That's right. When was your birthday?"

"August sixteenth."

"Her birthday is the sixteenth."

"How wild is that? We have the same birthday and I'm just a couple of years older." She winked.

He laughed. "You said your family took you there. Didn't your mother go?"

"My mother doesn't celebrate birthdays." *Here comes the million dollar question,* Cathy thought.

Marcus looked totally confused. "She doesn't celebrate birthdays? Is it against her religion?" he joked.

"As a matter of fact, it is."

Marcus was clearly baffled. "It is?"

"Believe me you don't want to get into it. We'd have to drive all over Manhattan for me to explain and you have a game tonight."

"Must be some story."

"Oh believe me, it is."

"I'll leave it alone then."

"Thanks. I promise I will tell you about it one day." She was grateful for the temporary reprieve.

"Okay." He seemed pensive for a moment. "I have to ask, she does celebrate for the grandchildren, right?"

"Nope."

Marcus's mouth seemed to hit the floor. "My parents are itching to become grandparents; they would love to go nuts for a grandchild's birthday."

"Most grandparents would but my mother isn't most grandparents. She didn't celebrate for my kids and once my sister has children, she won't celebrate for them either."

"That blows my mind."

"Imagine how we feel." She looked out the window again. "We're in Manhattan. Are we far from your place?"

"No. We'll be there in just a bit."

"Cool."

Marcus was quiet for a few minutes. Cathy wondered if she'd shared too much too soon. How was she going to tell him that up until ten years ago she hadn't celebrated either? She still kicked herself every day about it.

"Here we are."

"Oh, terrific."

Cathy got chills just looking at the Tower. She'd heard that it was a mix of celebrity tenants and entrepreneurial wealth, a place where a neighbor might have an Oscar or two on their mantle, or perhaps own prime real estate in Manhattan. As they pulled up to the front of the building, two doormen rushed out to attend to them. One opened Cathy's door.

"Good morning, miss." Although she was a bit of a feminist, at 40, *miss* felt like less of a demotion to Cathy. In fact, she actually appreciated being called miss.

"My name is Daniel." He helped her out of the car.

"Thank you, Daniel."

The other doorman took the bag out while Marcus grabbed Cathy's handbag.

"That's okay, Bill. I have it."

"Very good, Mr. Fox."

"Bill, if you could park the car and bring the bag up, that would be great."

"Not a problem."

Marcus held her hand as they entered the building.

Cathy's eyes lit up. Everything she'd read about the Tower was true. The lobby was simple yet elegant. Even the elevators had style. When Marcus pressed the button for the penthouse, her heart raced so she unconsciously squeezed his arm. Her wide-eyed expression made him smile.

"Here we are." He opened the door. "After you."

Cathy stepped into a place she'd seen only in *Architectural Digest* or in *In Style* magazine. Marcus's apartment was very modern, but the walnut colored walls balanced the room's nearly sterile aesthetic. As the sun shone, it bathed the room in warm light, giving it personality while it highlighted the Monet and Picasso prints that lined the walls.

"So what do you think?"

"It's amazing." She smiled. "It's very yin/yang. That's not easy to do."

"I had a great interior designer."

She nodded as she looked around. "You certainly did."

Cathy walked over to the window to a magnificent view of the city.

Marcus put his hands on her shoulders. "Would you like the grand tour?"

"Absolutely."

Marcus was tickled to take someone who appreciated architecture and interior design on a grand tour of his place. In the past Marcus had brought women to his place but he'd always felt that they had a mental calculator going. Cathy seemed genuinely impressed with the design aspect.

"Here we are. I just want to say this is only the tour stuff." He opened the door to his bedroom.

She walked in. "Oh, wow. This is gorgeous. I see you chose to continue the color from the living room in here. It's very soothing."

"You think so?"

"Absolutely." Her eyes lit up when she saw the bed. "I love sleigh beds."

"So do I. My decorator didn't put a lot of pieces in the bedroom. Something about creating a restful space."

"I think it's Feng Shui. I did the same thing with my room. You're supposed to leave work at the door to create a space for rest."

"Does it work?" he asked.

"Did it work for you? I see you have a plasma TV."

"Snuck it in afterwards. You won't rat me out, will you?"

"It will be our little secret. I have a TV in my room so I can watch and scream at baseball games."

"You scream?"

Cathy smirked. "You have no idea."

Marcus was skeptical. "You don't look like the type."

"We never do, but trust me, I sound like a longshoreman."

"I can't believe that."

"Trust me."

He smiled again. "I'll take your word for it."

"Please do."

He showed Cathy the master spa bathroom with a whirlpool tub and a separate enclosed shower.

Her mouth dropped open. "This is heavenly. It's definitely a place to tune out the world."

"That's true. Oh, let me show you one thing." He showed her the walk-in closet.

"My sister would kill for this kind of closet space."

"Is she a shoe or clotheshorse?"

"Both."

He laughed. "What about you?"

"I'd like to have a closet like this." She wasn't nearly as enthused.

"You don't sound convincing."

"I'm more of a kitchen girl." Cathy resisted the urge to say, *Can't you tell from my butt I'm a kitchen girl?*

"Then I've saved the best for last. Come with me." She followed him down the hall. He opened the door. "Voila."

Cathy stepped into a gourmet cook's wet dream: sleek floors, gorgeous cabinets, marble countertops and stainless steel appliances. There was an island, plus hanging copper pots, a Viking range, Sub-Zero refrigerator and every top rate small appliance she could imagine.

Marcus grinned. She looked like a child on Christmas morning.

She went over to the Viking range. "I love this. It's a range I could drive." She ran her fingers over the range and opened the double ovens. "It has a double oven and a warming drawer?" She placed her hands on the range. "This is my version of the Holy Grail."

He burst out laughing. "I never heard that before."

She started to ask Marcus about the staples, but it didn't look as if he spent much, if any, time in the kitchen. The place was pristine.

"Are you hungry?" he asked.

"I could eat."

"It's still early. How about we go out for a late breakfast?"

"What do you have in your kitchen? I could make something if you'd like."

Marcus looked at her in disbelief; most women jumped at the chance to eat out. "You're willing to cook?"

"Yes. Why wouldn't anyone want to cook here?"

"I hate to tell you but I haven't met many women who want to cook."

"I'm not most women and I'm the mother of teenage boys. I had to cook."

"Teenage boys are like having human garbage disposals."

"Tell me about it. You should have seen my grocery bill before they went to college. My purse screamed for mercy in two places. One was the grocery store."

"What was the other place?"

"The shoe store. Andrew and Alex wear a size 14 and 14 1/2 respectively."

"Wow."

"Whenever the shoe guy would bring boxes out I'd ask him if he was sure there were sneakers in the box. It always looked like he was bringing me logs."

He cracked up. "I bet they're skinny to boot."

"Skinny hardly begins to cover it. I love them to death but they're shaped like the capital letter L, straight lines and all feet."

He cracked up again. Her sense of humor made her all the more attractive to Marcus.

"So would you like me to make breakfast?" she asked sweetly.

"That would be a real nice change of pace. I usually eat out a lot."

"Do you like pancakes or waffles?"

"Yes."

She chuckled. "Okay, how about Belgium waffles?"

"Cool. I can send someone out to get the mix."

"Mix? I don't need no stinking mixes," she joked using a voice from an old movie she couldn't remember the name of.

"You make them from scratch?" He seemed suspicious.

"Sure. Tell you what, boot up your computer, log onto Amazon or Barnes and Noble and then type in my name."

"Okay. But maybe I should tell you where everything is."

Cathy knew Marcus didn't have a clue but she asked anyway. "Do you know where everything is?" "No," he said sheepishly.

"Don't sweat it. I'll figure it out."

Cathy assumed he had a cleaning and maid staff. All she had to do was think logically to find everything she needed, including the waffle maker.

As she was sifting the dry ingredients, Marcus swatted her on the butt.

She jumped "Hey!"

"You little sneak. You're not just some mild-mannered literary agent, you're a cookbook author with two books no less."

Cathy smiled. "That's how E.D. and I met. He was my agent before I partnered with him in the agency."

"Do you have any other little secrets you want to tell me about?"

"I'm not that interesting. That's about the extent of my secrets. Do you forgive me for not telling you earlier?"

"Of course. Who wouldn't forgive someone who can make Belgian waffles from scratch?"

"Plug in the waffle maker for me, please."

Within about 20 minutes Cathy made a full breakfast, including coffee. Marcus was quite impressed. Cathy ate a couple of waffles and left the rest for him.

Out of habit she cleared the table and loaded the dishwasher. As she finished loading, Marcus came up behind her and wrapped his arms around her waist. Cathy felt those butterflies again and this time some of them were heading due south.

"Are you just happy to see me or is your cell phone vibrating?"

Cathy had completely forgotten her cell was in her back pocket.

She checked the caller ID. It was E.D.

"Speak of the devil, it's my partner, E.D."

"Don't mind me."

She smiled as she picked up. "Hello, E.D. What's up?"

"Hey, Cathy. I just called to tell you we got the paperwork on the offers from the other day. Since they were your babies I thought I should let you know."

She knew better than that. He had something else on his mind. "Good. Now tell me what's happening?"

He paused. "I saw the paper this morning and I wanted to make sure you're all right."

"Thank you. I'm fine."

"What did Marcus say about it?"

"Haven't talked about it yet."

He finally caught on. "He's still in the room."

"Right."

"We'll talk later."

"Okay. Bye." She closed her phone.

Marcus was still behind her. "Everything cool at the office?"

"Oh, yeah, everything's fine." She slipped the phone back into her pocket.

"You know you can leave the dishes. I do have someone who takes care of that."

A little embarrassed, she put the dishes down. "Sorry. It's a habit."

Marcus turned her around to face him. "That's all right."

As he looked into her deep brown eyes, he softly outlined her face and lips with his finger, then kissed her sweetly. "I think we have to talk about something. I know you must have seen the paper." "First thing this morning."

Marcus tensed up a bit. "You know, I thought I would have more time to prepare you for this fishbowl known as the reality of dating me."

"The media microscope."

"I hope the caption didn't bother you."

"Listen, Marcus, I've been a big girl all of my life. I used to spend all kinds of time obsessing over my weight and size until one day I decided I had better things to do."

"I think that's terrific. Still, it's one thing to deal with it in private and quite another to deal in public."

"I won't lie. I had a moment this moment this morning when I let it bother me, but I let it pass. If I'm going to be around you I have to take the good with the bad. I'm not made of glass."

He pulled her closer to him. "I just want you to know that I think you're great the way you are."

Up until that moment, Cathy was under the impression that athletes refrained from sex before an important match and/or game. No one had bothered to remind Marcus.

Pressed up as they were against the dishwasher, soft and sweet kisses burst into white-hot passion. Just as Cathy tried to get her bearings, Marcus kissed her neck while he skillfully unbuttoned her shirt with one hand. When her shirt lay on the floor, his eyes widened at the sight of her ample caramel breasts. They were so inviting in her sexy black lace bra. "You're gorgeous," he panted.

Thank God I wore a pretty bra, Cathy thought to herself. *Somehow I don't think an industrial bra would have elicited this reaction.*

Before she responded, he kissed her neck and breasts. With slight of hand he undid her bra and caressed her breasts. *Who ever said all you needed was a handful obviously didn't know what he was talking about,* he thought. *I'll take two and half handfuls any day*. Marcus pulled his shirt off and threw it onto the floor.

Cathy forgot how to breathe. He looked good in pinstripes but shirtless he was amazing. She ran her hands down his toned chest to his six pack abs; her hands were anxious to explore more of his tight, muscular body.

Marcus explored the softness of all her curves. He ran his fingers through her hair, down her neck and then ever so slowly down her back. He paused to unbutton her pants and slowly pulled the zipper down. He felt her body tighten as he inched ever closer to the sweet spot just beyond.

She pulled away suddenly. "Wait a second." She could barely catch her breath.

"Is something wrong?" Marcus worried.

"No. I just want to be sure this won't affect you later."

"Affect me later?"

"I'm afraid this will affect your performance."

She looked at his expression. *He thinks I mean need a little blue pill performance.* "Affect your performance for the game," she clarified.

He let out a relieved laugh. "I thought you meant…" He shook his head. "Never mind what I thought. I can assure you making love to you before the game isn't going to affect my performance on the field."

She was still tentative. "Are you sure? I don't want to be the Yoko Ono of baseball, especially here in New York. The fans would never forgive me."

"You won't drain my mojo. I will be just as ready for this game as I am for any other."

"So it's just a myth?" She still wasn't quite convinced.

He leaned in to kiss her again. "I'll prove it."

Cathy's heart raced as he took her hand in his and led her back to the bedroom. She worried about how her body looked. Even though she'd given birth nearly twenty years earlier, no amount of cocoa butter had rid her of all the telltale stretch marks. Within a moment her jeans and lacy panties were off. She closed her eyes and braced herself as Marcus looked at her.

He was puzzled. "Why did you close your eyes?"

She felt bashful. "It's been a little while since I've been with someone and I am not exactly the model type."

"You don't have a thing to be bashful for, you're beautiful."

He laid her across the bed. "Keep your eyes open. I don't want you to miss one second."

His lips caressed the back of her neck and spine to the very small of her back. Cathy's passion ignited; she didn't know whether he kissed her one hundred or a thousand times and she didn't care. Her senses were awakened from their long exile. She wanted him then and there but he held back, touching her softly and deliberately. Cathy felt fluid and as light as silk.

Completely excited, she quickly turned the tables. "Now it's your turn," she whispered.

Never much of the aggressor in the bedroom before this, Cathy took command of Marcus's body, tantalizing and titillating him with her lips. She hovered over his chest to let her tongue slightly tease him. She softly kissed him every other moment or so to keep him guessing. His breathing grew more intense. Nearly crawling out of his own skin, he lifted her chin. "I have to have you now."

He reached over into his nightstand to get a condom and a minute later they were two bodies intertwined making love in the afternoon…twice.

Marcus showered and dressed while Cathy dozed. She looked like such an angel, he thought better of waking her up and decided to make alternate arrangements. He called Louis.

"Hello?"

"Hi, Louis."

"Mr. Fox. Do you want me to come for you now?"

"No. I'm going to take another car over. I need you to come and pick Ms. Chambers up between five and five thirty."

"Not a problem. I'll be there."

"Thanks."

Just as he hung up the phone rang again.

"Hello?"

"Marcus?"

"Dad?"

"Yeah. I just wanted to let you know that we decided to fly down for the game. We should be at the stadium in plenty of time."

"Terrific."

"Is Cathy going to be there?" he asked.

"Yes."

"Good. We're looking forward to meeting her."

"Okay, Dad, I'll see you after the game."

"See you then."

Marcus looked at his watch. He had time for one more phone call.

"Hello?"

"Ben?"

"What can I do for you, Marcus?"

"My parents are coming tonight so I need to make sure they can sit in their usual spot, plus one."

"You're seating Cathy next to them? Does she know about this?" he asked, knowing it was a big deal for one of Marcus's girlfriends to sit with his parents at a game.

"Not yet."

"Don't you think she should? If you seat her next to your parents, you're telling the world that she's the one."

Marcus thought for a minute. "That is exactly right."

Ben was floored. "So you think you've found the one?"

"I know it sounds strange, especially for me, but yes, I can see a future with her in it."

Ben smiled. "Okay then, I'll make a phone call and get it all straight."

"Thanks." He looked at his watch. "I hate to run, but I have to finish getting ready."

"See you tonight."

Marcus made a quick call for another car and went back into the bedroom where Cathy was just beginning to wake up.

Cathy opened her eyes and there was Marcus, dressed in khaki pants and a pin-striped shirt.

He smiled at her. "Hey there, sleepy."

She pulled the covers up before she sat up. It took a minute for her to get her bearings.

"How long was I asleep?"

"Not long. It was more of a cat nap."

She looked at the clock. "It's time for you to head to the stadium."

"I know. But I ordered a couple of sandwiches for us. I wasn't sure what kind to get you, so I ordered roast beef. We didn't exactly make food a priority. It's on the counter in the kitchen."

"Thanks. I love roast beef."

"Good." He looked at his watch. "I don't have much more time to get to the stadium."

She took in a whiff of his cologne. He smelled fantastic. "You look like you just stepped off the cover of *GQ*." He smiled. "You think so?"

"Definitely. You look and smell good enough to eat."

"Promise?"

"You are so bad," she chuckled.

Marcus was so hungry for her soft lips. He leaned over to kiss her.

"You were amazing this afternoon." He was an inch from her face.

"You weren't half bad yourself."

They kissed again.

"Think we can pick up where we left off a little later?"

"I'm game if you are."

He winked. "Good."

"I have to get going, but Louis will be here to pick you up for the game later. He's going to drop you off in the players' lot, and just like before, Melvin will meet you there to take you to your seat."

"Great. Melvin's a nice young man."

"Should I be jealous?"

"You're such a joker." She playfully hit him. "He's not much older than my sons."

"Well, you are a beautiful woman. I wouldn't blame him if he tried."

She blushed again. "I can't believe I'm still turning red. You've seen me naked and still I blush like a teenager."

He kissed her. "I think it's cute."

She patted his butt. "Now get a move on. We need a five game winning streak."

"Yes, ma'am, I aim to please." He joked. He picked up his bag. "Louis will be here between five and five-thirty."

"I'll be ready. See you later."

Once Marcus left, she stretched out to enjoy the butter soft sheets. Although she missed Marcus, she was glad no one was there to see the goofy grin on her face.

At forty years of age she had just had the best sex of her rather sheltered life. She had only been with three men: her ex-husband, her ex-boyfriend Paul and now Marcus made number three. Today she felt as if she had traded way up.

Even though she didn't want to leave the comfort of the bed, her stomach had different ideas. She was ravenous. Standing up in the kitchen, she finished her sandwich in record time. Satisfied on two levels, she took a bath in Marcus's spa-like tub. Wrapped in a towel twenty minutes later, she opened her bag and saw that her sister had packed several of her sexiest bra and panty sets, along with four changes of outfits, a couple of sweaters, her makeup bag and toiletries, enough stuff for Cathy to stay at least a week. "Maybe she knew something I didn't know," she said out loud.

Cathy began to get herself ready for the game. She wanted to make sure her hair, makeup and clothes were on point. Cathy knew being with Marcus Fox meant time in the spotlight, whether she liked it or not. Over the years, every hot spot in the city had had a picture of Marcus stepping out with the latest 'it girl'. But Cathy was the first full-figured woman he'd ever dated and in a strange way there was a lot more riding on this than her heart.

She went into the bathroom to quickly finish her makeup. The phone rang a few times before the machine picked it up.

"Hi, this is Marcus. I'm not available at the moment. So please leave a brief message and I will call you back."

"Hey, baby," a voice purred. Cathy quickly became interested in this phone call.

"It's Sarah. I'm in town and I wanted to see if we could get together. Give me a buzz. You know the number."

All of a sudden Cathy's confidence vanished. Every insecurity she'd ever had flooded back in an instant. "I'll bet he does know the number," she growled. *Damn it, Cathy! Stop the madness before it starts,* she scolded herself. *The fact is that though I feel like I've always known him, it's only been three days. I don't have the right to get mad. Marcus didn't live in a monastery. He had a social life, a very active social life before me.*

Cathy nearly jumped out of her skin when the intercom buzzed.

"Yes?"

"Miss Chambers, Louis is here. Do you want us to send him up?"

"No. I'll be down in a minute. Thank you." Cathy grabbed her bag and headed out the door.

***

There was a lot of activity in the clubhouse. The players were in the zone and getting ready to take the field. Game face on and all suited up, Marcus worked on his glove. Tim Dugan joined him.

"How's it going, Marcus?"

"Not bad, Tim. How about you?"

"I'm good." He hemmed and hawed a bit. "Are you sure everything's okay?"

"You saw the paper this morning, right?"

"Yeah. I think we all saw it."

"I'm not worried about it. As long as she didn't get upset, that's all I need to know," Marcus said calmly.

"Good. She's pretty, Marcus."

"Thanks. I think so, too."

Just then, rookie Miguel Torres entered the clubhouse. He seemed excited to see Marcus.

"Hey, Marcus!" he shouted.

"Hey, Miguel." Marcus smiled at his enthusiasm.

They shook hands.

"You know, Marcus, I met some old friends of yours last weekend."

Marcus moved on to cleaning his cleats. "You did?"

"Do the names Melinda and Zoe ring a bell?"

The names rang a bell, but not in a good way. Melinda and Zoe were baseball groupies.

"I know them." He was very matter of fact.

"They're outside and they want to say hello."

Marcus realized Miguel didn't know any better. They were good time girls and that was it.

"That's all right. Just tell them hello for me."

"Are you sure?"

Marcus got up. "Absolutely. If you'd excuse me…"

He walked away.

Tim looked up. "Man, don't you read the papers?"

"Yes. I mean, sometimes," Miguel answered.

"Did you see today's paper?"

"No."

"Marcus has a new girlfriend."

"Oh."

"So he doesn't want to get caught up with a couple of baseball groupies with new boob jobs."

"How did you know about that?"

Tim grinned at his teammate's greenness. "Everybody knows about it." He patted his back as he got up.

Juan jumped into the conversation. "I think Marcus is serious about his new girl. He walked away without so much as a second thought."

"I never thought I'd see the day when Marcus Fox settled down and forgot about all these crazy chicks." Tim shook his head.

"I don't think Marcus did either but it had to happen eventually," Juan added.

CHAPTER 12

Cathy had plenty of time to think about things on the ride to the stadium. Memory of how Sarah's voice had practically purred into the machine annoyed the hell out of her. *Am I destined to be another Sarah purring into the machine like some cat in heat? Am I just a booty call? Could I live with that? Obviously Sarah is fine with it.*

Cathy fidgeted in the car, then sighed out loud. *I broke my own cardinal rule and slept with Marcus after one date. Breakfast doesn't count as a second date. Oh my God! Am I a ho?* She worried. *After all, what man takes a woman seriously who slept with him after one date? God, I can hear my mother now. 'You were out there being one of those slutty gals.'* She stared out of the window as they neared the stadium. *I guess I'd better enjoy the evening; it just might be my last.*

Melvin stood at the curb waiting for her.

"Thanks for getting me here safely, Louis. I got to enjoy being a passenger for today anyway."

He looked confused. "You're welcome, Ms. Chambers, but I will see you after the game."

I hope so. She smiled as Melvin opened the door.

"Hello, Ms. Chambers. Good to see you again."

"Hi, Melvin."

"If you will please follow me. We are going to take a slightly different route today."

"Lead the way."

Melvin led her past all the different seating levels.

"Have you ever been field level before, Ms. Chambers?"

"No. I usually come for day games and I can't be in the sun."

"Oh. You won't have that problem tonight."

As they walked down a bit more, Cathy glanced ahead and came to a dead stop.

"Ms. Chambers, are you okay?"

"Are you sure I'm supposed to be over here?"

"Yes. Mr. Fox specifically requested that you be seated behind the Yankee dugout."

"Yes, but his parents are there. Am I sitting nearby?"

"You're seated next to them."

"Oh, okay." Her voice squeaked. She sounded like Alvin the chipmunk.

There they were, Evelyn and Joseph Fox. Everyone in New York knew Mr. and Mrs. Fox. "Here you go Ms. Chambers," Melvin said.

"Thanks."

Mr. Fox stood up to let her in the row. "Joseph Fox." He shook her hand.

"Pleasure to meet you, Mr. Fox. I'm Catherine Chambers. Please call me Cathy."

"Nice meeting you. This is my wife, Evelyn."

They shook hands. "Pleasure to meet you, Mrs. Fox." She sat down.

"Marcus told us we were going to have company."

Cathy did not want to look like a deer in headlights so she smiled. Marcus surely hadn't told her.

"He did, did he?"

"He says your family has a tradition of being Yankee fans."

"That's very true. My great grandfather would take my grandmother to games when Babe Ruth and Lou Gehrig played. So naturally the tradition has continued through the years."

"Wow, isn't that something?" Mrs. Fox smiled.

"So I will be on my best behavior. The only time I ever yell and scream is at home." They laughed.

"Marcus tells us you have two young men in college. You must be so proud."

"I can't even begin to explain how proud I am, Mr. Fox, but I think you and Mrs. Fox know a thing or two about being proud parents."

Before they could say any more the Yankees took the field. Cathy reached into her bag to put her cell on vibrate just in case. The game was underway.

The top of the first was a one, two, three inning and then the Yankees came up to bat. Marcus was on deck. He looked around at the stands and spotted his parents. Cathy wasn't in sight because her watch had slid off and she had bent down to get it. Mrs. Fox tapped on her shoulder. "Cathy, I think Marcus is looking for you dear." She quickly sat up.

Marcus smiled and mouthed, 'Hey Cathy,' and winked before he stepped up to the plate.

Cathy felt her face break out in that goofy grin. She silently prayed to God, 'Please don't let me be on camera. I have a dumb grin on my face.'

The count was 0-1. Cathy was so tense about his first at bat she thought she would wring her hands off. Another pitch, a curve ball that went a little too inside, the count was 1-1. She clapped her hands together. "Come on, baby," she whispered.

Cathy needed to see a base hit to prove she hadn't played Delilah to his Samson. Then the bat made contact, and she watched as Marcus drove the ball into the gap for a single.

"All right!" She clapped and smiled at his parents. It was the beginning of a good night.

By the third inning the Yankees were up 4-2 over the Blue Jays. Marcus's second hit of the game was a double that drove in two runs. Cathy was so caught up in the game she didn't realize her cell phone was vibrating in her bag.

Mr. Fox woke her from her trance. "I think your cell phone's vibrating in your purse."

"Oh, I'm sorry. Thanks for telling me."

She quickly got it out. The text message read, 'Mom call us as soon as possible.' Cathy got onto her feet quickly and turned to Mrs. Fox.

"I'm sorry to put you to the trouble of getting up, but I have to call my kids. They sent me an emergency message and I don't want to disturb anyone."

"That's quite all right, dear. I hope everything is okay."

"Thank you, Mrs. Fox. So do I."

Mr. Fox got up to let her out of the row. Cathy dialed Alexander as she walked the steps to the corridor. She silently prayed again, only for a different reason. 'Please

let them be okay, please don't let it be an accident. Please God.'

"Hello?"

"Alexander, it's Mom. What's the matter?" Cathy was freaked.

"Hi, Mom." He seemed relaxed.

"Alex, you just text messaged me about an emergency. Are you and your brother all right?"

"We're fine, Mom. We were calling about you."

"About me? Why?"

"We were watching the game and then the cameras panned over to Marcus Fox's parents and you're sitting next to them."

"Yes, I'm sitting next to them and that was enough to make you call me like it was an emergency?"

"Sorry, Mom, we were just excited. How did you get that seat?"

Cathy was relieved and pissed at the same time. *Dear God, these kids are going to wind up paying for my next visit with Miss Clairol.* "The game is still in progress. I'll give you a call later on and I'll fill the both of you in. Okay?" "Okay, Mom." He seemed suspicious.

"I promise. I'll talk to you afterwards."

"Okay, Mom. We'll talk to you later then."

Cathy took a deep breath to see if she could somehow get back the ten years he'd just taken off her life. She returned to her seat.

"Is everything all right, Cathy?" Mr. Fox asked as she scooted past him.

"Thankfully yes. They called me because they saw me sitting next to you on camera."

Both Mr. and Mrs. Fox chuckled.

"I told them I would talk to them later." She laughed. "What did I miss?"

"It's the top of the fourth and it's still 4-2."

"Thanks, Mr. Fox."

Cathy went back to concentrating on the game for the rest of the evening. The Yankees won by a final score of 7-3. Marcus had a good night; he was 3 for 4. She sighed, knowing she hadn't derailed him.

After the game she waited with Marcus' parents outside the clubhouse while the reporters and photographers jockeyed for post-game positions. Ben Bradford walked out to greet them.

"Ben."

"Joe." The two men hugged.

"Evelyn. You're just as lovely as ever."

Mrs. Fox smiled. "Good to see you, Ben." They hugged.

Ben turned to Cathy. "Hi, Cathy. I'm Ben Bradford, Marcus's agent."

"It's a pleasure to meet you." She smiled and shook his hand.

He looked at her. "I can see why Marcus is so taken with you."

Cathy turned red as a beet. "I've blushed so much this week I think I have a condition." They laughed.

"It was a good game, Joe. Your boy is doing his thing."

"I see that. He knows what he has to do and he does it." A few more reporters and cameras joined the melee.

"Amazing, isn't it?" Mr. Fox asked

"It's fascinating to see the attention up close."

Mr. Fox leaned against the wall. "New Yorkers take their sports seriously."

"Truer words have never been spoken," Cathy said.

"If you will excuse me for a little bit, I think I just might have to rescue your son," Ben said.

***

Ben braved the crowd to get through. Seeing that Marcus was being interviewed by two local metro channels, Ben hung back and waited until it looked like a wrap. He waved to get Marcus's attention.

"Hey, man. Are my parents out there with Cathy?"

"Yes."

"How's it going?"

"They seem to be enjoying their conversation. I didn't have a chance to poll them or anything." Ben's sarcastic wit surfaced.

"Very funny. I guess I'd better get out there."

Ben held his shoulder. "You might want to wait. I have something to tell you

Marcus felt dread. "Now what?"

"I just got a heads up from one of my buddies at the paper. They're running an item and photo in tomorrow's paper about you and Cathy."

Marcus looked disgusted. "When did they get another picture of the two of us? It's not like we've been all over town together."

"They took a picture of you kissing and one of you and her entering your building."

"Maybe it won't be too bad. She's still a mystery woman," Marcus rationalized.

Ben looked away.

"Don't tell me they have her name."

"Her name and what she does." Ben took his glasses off.

Marcus tried to downplay it. "I'll tell her about it myself."

"I could talk to her if you'd like."

"No. It's better if she hears it from me."

Ben patted his back. "I know you can handle it."

"I just hope she can."

***

Cathy and the Foxes were still chatting away.

"So how are your kids doing in school?" Mrs. Fox asked.

"Not bad. They've adjusted to college life, which was my biggest worry."

"Marcus says you raised your boys as a single parent."

"I did. But I had a lot of help from my parents and my younger sister."

"Are they your parents' only grandchildren?" Mrs. Fox asked.

"As a matter of fact they are. My sister's engaged but she doesn't have children yet."

"So your family focused on your sons."

"They say it takes a village to raise a child."

"I can tell you this, Mr. Fox. If it takes a village to raise one child, it's takes a county to raise twins."

Marcus watched his parents and Cathy for a few moments before joining them. He could see her bubbly personality charmed them as it did him.

They were laughing when he joined them.

"So what did I miss?" Marcus asked as he hugged his mother.

"We were just talking about kids." Marcus and his father hugged.

Cathy enjoyed seeing Marcus's bond with his parents. She was a little taken aback when he kissed her in front of them.

"So you've met the parents." He put his arm around her.

"Yes, and they are wonderful."

"Good game, Son."

"Thanks, Dad."

His mom walked over and brushed her hands through his hair. "You look well. Have you finally been getting enough sleep?"

"Yes, Mom. I'm getting my rest."

"Good." She kissed his cheek.

"Well, Son, your mom and I have to get back to the hotel. It's back to the grind for us."

"Okay, Dad. I'll give you a call later."

Cathy was surprised. "You're not staying for the series?"

"As much as we'd love to, I have to get back to my practice and Evelyn has inventory at her store."

"Oh."

"Don't worry, they'll be back." Marcus rubbed her shoulder.

"It was a pleasure meeting you, Mr. Fox." She went to shake his hand and he hugged her instead.

"You take care, dear, and hopefully we'll see you again soon," Mrs. Fox said as she hugged her, too.

"I will."

As Mr. and Mrs. Fox walked toward the exit, Cathy turned to Marcus.

"By the way, if I didn't tell you before, great game."

He put his arm around her waist. "Thanks, sweetie."

"Your parents are terrific."

"Thanks. I think the feeling is mutual."

"They just met me…Hell, you just met me."

"You know, it doesn't always take an eternity to figure out how you feel about someone."

Cathy didn't know how to respond to that statement so she just smiled as they walked to the players' lot and she changed the subject. "Did you drive your car here?"

"No. I came by car earlier. Louis should be outside waiting for us."

As soon as the door opened Cathy was nearly blinded by flashbulbs. Questions were hurled at them from every direction. She tried to see where Louis was parked. Marcus took her hand. "The car is over here."

The flashbulbs popped so rapidly Cathy could barely see where she was going for the spots in her eyes, but finally she could see the outline of Louis holding the car door open. Marcus quickly helped her into the car. Louis closed the door and both men entered on the driver's side.

"Are you okay?" Marcus rubbed her hand.

"I'm fine." She kept her eyes closed until the spots disappeared.

"Are you sure?" Marcus was concerned.

"I don't need a doctor, Marcus. I promise I'm fine." She opened her eyes.

"As long as you're sure."

"I am." She rubbed her eyes one last time. "Now I have a question."

"Shoot."

"Why didn't you tell me your parents were going to be at tonight's game?"

"I thought I would surprise you.

"You succeeded. I was surprised, all right. It scared me to death."

"You were scared? Why?"

"I wasn't expecting to meet them. I like a little notice. I almost passed out when I saw them."

"I'm sorry. You recovered nicely."

"That's not the point." She shook her head. "Next time I'll be sure to let you know ahead of time." *Next time?* Cathy thought to herself.

"Thank you. That's all I ask."

"Done."

"Now I have another question."

"Go ahead."

"What was all of that with the photographers about? This didn't happen yesterday. I mean, they've taken pictures and we made the paper but tonight they're frenzied. What's got them worked up?"

"You were sitting with my parents in the stands."

"I'm sure other people have sat next to your parents during games. What's the big deal?"

Cathy caught Louis's glance in the rearview mirror. He was pretending not to know anything.

"Wait a minute. I have the distinct feeling there's a 'but' coming down the pike."

"No, there's no but. I do have to tell you something."

"Should I brace myself?"

"No. It's not that kind of thing."

"Just spit it out. The suspense is making me nervous." Cathy's heart was in her throat.

"My agent gave me a heads up on a news item a couple of papers are running tomorrow."

Her heart was in the pit of her stomach. "A news item? What's being reported in this news item?"

"It's just a little blurb with a couple of pictures." "A blurb with a couple of pictures," Cathy repeated. "Pictures of what?"

"Pictures of us kissing the other night and a photo of us going into my apartment building."

Cathy almost stopped breathing. "Good Lord, I don't remember seeing any photographers."

"Some of these guys missed their calling. They should have joined the CIA."

Suddenly a lightning bolt hit Cathy. "Is it in the gossip section of *The Journal*?"

"Yes."

Of all the papers, *The Journal* ranked as the premiere source for learning who was doing what with whom.

"I definitely have to call my sons before they read about it. Does it mention me by name? Or am I still the mystery woman?"

"They mention you by name."

"Great. Just great." She took a deep breath "You know, so what? All that really matters to me is that my sons not find out about us in the paper. Even way up there at Geneseo they get all the papers."

"You don't think they saw the item in today's paper?"

"No. If they had they would have called me right away, like they did tonight."

"They called you tonight?" he asked.

"Yes." She laughed. "They saw me sitting next to your parents on television."

"What did you tell them?"

"I told them I would fill them in later."

"You can give them a call from the apartment."

She looked at her watch "It's a little late, but they're college students, and college students are always up late."

"Are you upset with me for causing all this upheaval in your life?"

"Why would I get upset with you? It's not as if I didn't know you live your life in the spotlight."

He came closer to her. "I'm so happy you're not freaked out."

"I am a little freaked out, but as long as you're around it's okay with me."

He kissed her forehead. "You are something special."

Cathy truly hoped he meant that. She knew small town gossip was just that, small. This stuff was the big time, not the kind of thing she wanted her sons to read about in *People* magazine

Once they were back at Marcus's place she didn't waste time. She made the call.

"Hello?" Andrew sounded groggy.

Cathy could not believe her ears. As the technical oldest by two minutes, Alexander had always been her night owl since he was in utero, a fact Cathy determined after many late nights on the floor with him as a baby.

"Andrew?"

"Yeah, Mom."

"Wonder of wonders. Were you actually sleeping?"

"Yeah, Mom. I fell asleep after the game."

"Oh. Sorry, but I need you to wake up for a few minutes. First, I'm going to patch your brother in." "Okay."

She flashed over to the other line and dialed Alex.

"Hello." Alex sounded sleepy too.

"Alex, it's Mom. You were sleeping, too?

"Yeah, Mom."

"Why couldn't you have done this when you were babies?"

"I know."

"Hold on a second. I have to patch your brother back in."

She pressed the flash button.

"Alex? Andrew?" "Yes, Mom," they chorused.

"Good. Now that I have both of you on the line I have to tell you something important before you see it in the paper."

"What's the matter, Mom?" Andrew asked.

"Nothing, nothing bad." She took a deep breath. "You know how you saw me sitting with Marcus Fox's parents tonight and I told you I would fill you in later?" "Right," Alex said.

"There is a little more to it."

"A little more to it?' Andrew asked.

Cathy decided there was no beating around the bush. She had to come right out and say it. "I just started seeing Marcus Fox, as in dating him." She blurted it out so she wouldn't lose her nerve.

There was dead silence.

"Are you two still there?"

"You're seeing Marcus Fox?" Andrew was stunned.

"Yes. I have to give you a heads up about tomorrow's paper. There's going to be a picture of the two of us out on a date in a few of the gossip columns. I just didn't want the two of you to find out that way."

"So it wasn't a coincidence that you were sitting next to Mr. and Mrs. Fox tonight?" Alex surmised.

"So Marcus Fox got you into the Hall of Fame Suite at Yankee Stadium," Andrew added.

"Right."

"This is mad hot!" Alex was excited.

Cathy wasn't up to date on the latest sayings. "Is mad hot a good thing?"

"Yeah." Andrew, Alex and Marcus chorused.

Cathy flashed a look at Marcus, who covered his mouth after the fact.

"Sorry," he mouthed.

"Too late," she mouthed.

"Mom? Is someone there with you?"

"Yes, Marcus is here." "Oh

my God!" Alex yelled.

"Alex! Stop yelling. You are going to wake up your entire dorm."

"Wow, Mom!" Andrew was low key with his excitement.

She abhorred lying so she crossed her fingers. "We're on our way back to the island."

"How did you meet him, Mom?" Alex asked.

"It's kind of a long story. Suffice it to say we met and we liked each other."

"This is something else." Alex was still in shock.

"Are you sure you two are okay with this?"

Marcus's interest picked up on Cathy's end of the conversation.

"Whatever makes you happy, Mom," Andrew said.

"You're both sure?"

"Yes," they chorused.

"Besides, Mom, it's not like you've dated much in the last two years. So it's time for you to meet a nice guy and Marcus Fox seems like a nice guy."

"You're right, Alex. He is a nice guy."

Marcus smiled.

"So we're cool," Andrew added.

"That's a load off my mind." She yawned. "Now that I've talked to you two, you should get some rest."

"How can anybody sleep after this kind of news, Mom?"

"You just go back to bed, Alex. You have classes."

"Tomorrow's Saturday, Mom."

"Go to bed anyway."

"Okay, Mom." Another tandem answer.

"I'll talk to you two later. Love you."

"Love you too, Mom."

She turned her cell phone off. Marcus cuddled up to her on the sofa.

"Sorry about before. It just slipped out," he said.

"That's okay, it happens."

"It's cute the way you are with your sons." Cathy laughed, knowing they must sound strange.

"Were they okay with you dating me?" Marcus asked.

"What do you think? You're only their favorite player. Alex got excited and nearly woke up the dorm, while Andrew was also excited but quiet." She chuckled. "If I hadn't been the one on the delivery table I would never guess they were twins."

Marcus smiled. "I can't wait to meet them." The words nearly bowled her over.

"Why the look?"

"No reason. I'm just surprised."

"You're surprised I would want to meet your children?"

"Some men aren't crazy about meeting your kids, regardless of their age. I know for a fact my sons would love to meet you."

"I'm not most men."

"Isn't that the truth?"

They kissed.

He looked at her strangely.

"What?"

"Is there anything else you want to talk about?"

"No. Why do you ask?"

"I heard the message from Sarah and judging from the time stamp, I think you did too. Is there anything you want to ask me about that?"

"So I heard the message. It's not a big deal." Cathy tried to sound real casual about it.

"Don't you *want* to ask me about it?" he pressed.

"Marcus, we met a couple of days ago. I know you had a life before. I do not expect it to disappear."

"Are you saying you don't care?"

"No, it's not that I don't care. I don't have the right to get upset or ask for any explanations from you."

"You don't think you have a right?"

"Marcus, I've made the mistake of going into new relationships with expectations and I got burned. I refuse to do it anymore."

"So you learned to accept less."

"I guess that's exactly what I did," she conceded.

"You don't have to do that anymore."

"I don't?

"You know, the reporters aren't that far off the mark."

"What do you mean?"

"Yes, people have sat next to my parents at the stadium before, but I've never had a girlfriend sit next to them until tonight."

Cathy was speechless.

"All I'm saying is, give us a chance. My father always said when you meet the right person, you'll just know it. I think we're on that track."

"You do?"

"Yes, I do. The moment you walked into the restaurant I saw this confident and beautiful woman sit down at a table in the middle of the place by herself. Then I saw you smile at the waiter. I thought to myself, I'd love to have her smile at me the same way. That's why I had to meet you."

"You *had* to meet me."

"Yes, I did. Sarah and I weren't an item. We had fun together and that was about it. I'm not a saint. I've dated a lot of women but now I'm ready to give a real relationship a try. All I want to know is if you're willing to do the same."

"I would like that." Cathy was lot more emotional than she'd been in a long time.

"Good."

Tears streamed down her face. "Damn. Now my face is leaking." She wiped her eyes. They looked at each other and howled with laughter. Marcus handed her some tissues. "Your face is leaking. That's a new one."

"It's an expression Alex used to use when he was little. Whenever I peeled onions he'd say, 'Mommy's face is leaking.' It was so cute I haven't stopped using the saying; it reminds me of when they were babies." She looked down at the floor. "I know, I'm a cornball."

"You know what? I like corn."

"You do?"

"Oh, definitely."

They kissed each other tenderly, letting the passion build with each moment that passed. Once again Marcus took her by the hand to the bedroom.

Face to face in the bedroom, Marcus took Cathy's sweater off and he stopped her before she could undress herself. "I want to do it."

She let him. After years of submitting to religious doctrine, Cathy had a need to maintain control so it was a big deal to let him undress her a second time.

Things were different for Marcus too. In the past he'd watched a woman get undressed just to get to the ultimate finish. Now he wanted the pleasure of taking his time. Piece by piece he gently removed her clothes.

Having been a big girl all her life, Cathy felt he treated her as a treasured porcelain doll he was afraid to break. He made her feel delicate, even fragile.

Marcus turned the lights down low, but not off. He stopped for a moment. "I love looking at you."

Cathy's stomach fluttered. Marcus teased her with stop and go kisses down her neck and shoulders. It tickled but she didn't laugh. She stood behind him and took his shirt off. She rubbed his sculpted back. *Michelangelo's* David *has nothing on him*, she thought.

The hairs on the back of Marcus's neck stood straight up from the warmth of her breath. *If she kisses the nape of my neck, she's going to have to peel me off her.* Just then she lightly kissed the nape of his neck. *It's on.* He quickly turned around and kissed her; within minutes their bodies were so entangled it was impossible to tell where he ended and she began

Cathy's hands grabbed the covers to anchor her body to the bed as Marcus took her higher and deeper to a place where she didn't know her own name, but knew his. "Oh God, Marcus," she moaned. *Oh my God! Did I just moan his name?* She asked herself for just a moment and then quickly forgot her own question as making love turned into a religious experience like none other.

Nestled in each other's arms they drifted off to sleep.

During her limited sex life, Cathy had never been comfortable sleeping with someone else after they'd made love. However there was safely in "his nook," which she thought was strictly a *Sex and the City* concoction since she didn't think her body was made to fit with that of anyone else. Something was different this time; she could sleep with Marcus near her. It felt as if he and she fit together so well that she could rest her body, mind and maybe even soul without reservation.

CHAPTER 13

Saturday morning meant an afternoon game. Cathy left Marcus sleeping soundly in bed. They'd had quite a night and he needed to get some rest. She quietly slid out of bed and grabbed his robe before going to the kitchen.

Once she opened the bedroom door she could see the sun was shining brightly on New York City. She stopped to enjoy the breathtaking view from Marcus's living room.

Feeling more like the happy homemaker than the happy hooker, Cathy went to the kitchen to make breakfast.

She wasn't quite sure whether it was elves or a secret team of maids that came in and re-stocked Marcus's refrigerator. Whoever did it didn't matter. She was happy to see the ingredients she needed to make blueberry pancakes. While she made up the batter for pancakes, she turned the griddle on and placed a couple of plates in the warming drawer before making blueberry compote, scrambled eggs and sausage to go with the pancakes. Orange juice and coffee rounded out the breakfast tray.

Bringing the tray out of the kitchen, Cathy set it on the dining room table for a moment. The only thing that was missing to complete her breakfast in bed service was a newspaper. In a fancy building like this, she figured all the newspapers would be right outside the door. So she poked her head out the door and hit pay dirt. All the papers were there.

As she started to put the newspapers on the tray she remembered what they'd talked about last night. She hurriedly opened *The Journal* and scanned the celebrity section for her name. She didn't have to look too hard; there were two photos of her and Marcus just as he'd said.

New York Yankee Marcus Fox was seen canoodling with Catherine Chambers, literary agent and managing partner of the Chambers-Stevens Literary Agency in New York. Onlookers said the two were quite chummy over dinner. Fox, whose last main squeeze was supermodel Cybil George, seems to be quite taken with the voluptuous

Chambers. Sources close to Fox say Chambers has even met his parents. Could this be the real thing? Stay tuned.

Cathy breathed a sigh of relief. *At least they said voluptuous* rather than fat. She was sorely tempted to read the other papers but decided to quit while she was ahead. She refolded *The Journal* and put it on the tray with the other papers.

Marcus was still asleep when she brought the tray in.

"Hey, sleepy head."

He turned over and slowly opened his eyes.

"Hey."

"Good morning. Are you ready for a little breakfast in bed?"

It looked as if his eyes were slowly getting focused.

"Would you look at that? You made me breakfast?"

"Yes, I did. Now sit up so I can put this tray down. It's kind of heavy."

He quickly sat up. "Okay, babe. Is that better?"

"Much." She gave him the tray. "Now you are almost all set. I just have to get the half and half for your coffee. Or do you use milk?"

"Half and half is fine."

"Okay. I'll get it and the sugar."

Just as she was about to leave he grabbed her hand. "Can't a guy get a morning kiss?"

She smiled and gave him a kiss. "Now let me get the cream and sugar. I'll only be a minute or two."

"Hurry back."

She went to the kitchen and returned with the cream and sugar in hand.

"See. I told you it wouldn't take me long."

Marcus was a little too busy chewing. "Thanks. This is fantastic. Don't tell me you made the compote, too."

"If you don't want me to tell you I made it, then I won't."

"You are a little character."

"Thanks. Is everything okay?"

"It's great. I can't tell you how long it's been since I've had a breakfast like this at home. Not including yesterday's breakfast."

She climbed back into bed. "You mean your other girlfriends never made breakfast for you?" Cathy couldn't believe she'd said 'girlfriends,' as if she were sure she ranked right in there.

"No. I never had a girlfriend like you before."

She was secretly tickled to have him refer to her as his girlfriend.

"Cooking was not their strong suit." He stopped to eat.

"Aren't you having breakfast?"

"I already ate."

"You didn't want to have breakfast with me?"

"It's not that. I'm just not much of a breakfast person this early. Toast and coffee this time of day is more than enough for me."

"If you say so." He opened up the paper. She'd put *The Journal* on top.

"Did you read the paper?" he asked.

"I glanced at *The Journal*, but that's the only one. The rest I don't know about." As he opened up to the gossip pages she watched for his expression.

"They crack me up with this stuff."

"They do have a flair for words. But you did date for a while."

"We dated for three years."

"That's practically a lifetime in fashion and Hollywood."

"I can tell you it wasn't all glitz, glamour, high profile outings, fashion shows and premieres. There were some not so pretty times with the beautiful people."

"Be that as it may, this is the kind of stuff that sells papers and gossip magazines. You were dating the ideal woman, a sex symbol and top model. Now you're dating a woman six years your senior, divorced with two kids and to top it off she's full-figured. I can see why they're baiting her."

Marcus dismissed the idea. "Cybil can't be bothered enough to read in the first place. She used to leaf through the fashion magazines for the photos. The only time she read was if some outfit or bag caught her eye."

"Marcus, you may have dated her for three years, but I know women and regardless of whether she sees this or not, someone is going to tell her and then it's just a matter of time before there's another little item in the paper or on *E Hollywood News*."

"That relationship is in the past for the both of us."

"I'm sure it is, but right, wrong or indifferent, the press is seeking to stir things up."

"Maybe. They did get a few things right." He put the tray on the night table and came towards her. She pretended to try to get away.

"Really? What part did they get right?"

"The part about me being taken with you. Come here, my voluptuous woman."

He kept kissing her neck.

"Wait a minute, Marcus. Are you trying to give me a hickey?"

"Mmm? Me? Would I do that to you?" he asked coyly.

It tickled her. "Stop, Marcus. Not only am I too old to have a hickey, it's still a little bit warm. I can't cover up with a turtleneck."

He ignored her. After another couple of minutes of her protesting, he stopped.

He looked at his handiwork. "There it is."

Cathy put her hand on her neck then dashed to the mirror. "Oh, Marcus. What am I supposed to do?"

"If anyone asks, tell them I did it."

"You know how long it takes to get rid of the mark?"

"No. How long?"

"I don't know. I was asking you. I haven't had a hickey since I was…" Cathy stopped to think. "When was the last time I had a hickey? I think I was 29."

"Twenty-nine? You never got a little love bite as a teenager?"

"No. Together my parents were strict but once they split up my mother tightened the religious reins.

"Your dad didn't have a say in it?" He was incredulous.

"Not really."

"So you weren't allowed to date?"

"No. According to the rules of this religion you couldn't date until you were ready to get married."

Marcus was floored. "What?"

"You heard right. We didn't date, period. We didn't get to go to the junior or senior prom either."

"What was wrong with going to the prom? It's just a rite of passage."

"A night of degradation."

"So you never really dated until you got married."

"Right."

"Is this the same religion that doesn't celebrate birthdays?"

"Yes."

"So you couldn't celebrate birthdays and you had to be ready to get married in order to date."

"There was a high rate of young people getting married in this religion."

"With rules like that, I bet there was."

"It's still like that. I was an oddball because I stayed in college after I got married. It was the one thing my father really put his foot down about."

"I think that's great. Where did you go to college?"

"Haven't I told you before?"

"No."

"Oh. I went to Yale," Cathy said nonchalantly. "All three of us did. Madison is a graduate of Yale Law School and Anna has her master's in finance and accounting from Yale. I have degrees in political science and business management."

"That's some accomplishment for all of you. How in the world did you combine being married, having twins and college?" He was impressed

"I didn't have the twins until I was 22. By then I was a senior. I graduated and gave birth in the same month. I got divorced when I was 23."

"Was your ex-husband part of this religion thing too?"

"Yes, he was. He still turned out to be lousy." Cathy was surprised at how matter of fact she was with Marcus. "Still, I had to prove I was one of the faithful and I stayed the religious course until I was twenty-eight. By then I was done living like a nun without the habit. So I didn't get my first hickey until I was 29." It happened so long ago it was as if she was talking about another person in another lifetime.

"So you really didn't start dating until you were almost 30."

"Pathetic, isn't it?" Cathy said.

"No, not at all." He looked thoughtful. "You said your last relationship was about two years ago, right?"

"Almost three years ago."

"So you dated him for a while."

"Eight years."

Marcus looked as if he was finally doing the math. "So I'm only the…" The light bulb flashed over his head. "Oh my God."

"That's right, and I'm forty years old." Cathy looked in the mirror again. "This thing is getting more black and blue by the minute."

He playfully threw his pillow at her. "Wait a second. Is that my robe you have on?"

"Yes."

"You didn't bring a robe?"

"No."

"In that case I want my robe back."

"You can't have it back, otherwise I won't have anything to wear."

"That will teach you to come prepared."

"Oh, so it's like that now?"

"Uh huh."

Cathy dropped the robe to her ankles. "Satisfied?"

"Very." He got out of bed, came to her, put his hands around her waist and kissed her.

They didn't make it back to the bed in time.

After stealing the robe back while Marcus was sound asleep, Cathy quietly got lost in the majesty of New York City spread out in front of her.

"Gorgeous. Simply gorgeous." Marcus slipped his arms around her waist.

"I didn't know you were awake." She was a little startled.

"I was just dozing. The view was too enticing to miss."

"It is. The city looks so beautiful from here."

"I wasn't talking about the city." He kissed her neck. "You're gorgeous."

"You better watch out, you're spoiling me," she said bashfully.

"I think you deserve to be spoiled."

She closed her eyes. "I could get used to this."

"I hope you do."

She turned around and kissed him. "You are so sweet." She caressed his face.

He looked into her eyes. "I know you're happy but there is a little something in your eyes."

She walked away from the window and sat on the bed. "It's probably guilt."

"Guilt? What do you have to feel guilty about?"

"Everything and nothing at all."

He sat down next to her. "You can talk to me. I'll listen. I won't judge you."

"Nobody could be a harder judge than I am."

"Why are you judging yourself?"

"It's so hard to explain, Marcus." She sighed. "Even though I haven't lived that religious life for more than a decade, still there are remnants."

"Like what?""

Remember we talked about celebrating birthdays?"

"Yes."

Cathy was ashamed to say it out loud. "I didn't celebrate my sons' birthdays until they were about eight years old. They had no parties or anything for eight years and I feel like I let them miss out."

"But they've had parties for the last ten years, right?"

"Oh yeah. I've been crazy about giving them the biggest parties ever since."

"So you're a good mom. I'm sure they don't hold it against you."

"But I hold it against me."

He hugged her. "Well, you should stop."

"I know."

"But this guilt isn't just about birthday parties, is it?"

"No."

"This is about dating and sex."

"Those are two areas I still feel guilty about." "Cathy, it's obvious to me that you are a moral person. I know you aren't the kind of woman who sleeps around."

"I know, but that doesn't stop me from feeling guilty."

"It should."

"You're right. It should. I used to feel guilty about my last relationship too. So when he cheated on me it felt like God was punishing me for not doing the right thing in the first place."

"If the guy was stupid enough to cheat, that was on him, not you. It certainly wasn't God punishing you."

"Intellectually I know it, but I was in a religion that teaches if you leave it, God won't bless you, and you're on the same level as a dog returning to its vomit."

Marcus cringed. "They teach you that about God? I'm not terribly religious but I don't think God goes around handing out punishments. People reap what they sow."

Cathy nodded her head. "You're lucky you don't have my mother's voice in your head."

Marcus thought about his mother's relationship with his sisters. "It's real easy for me to tell you not to think about it, but she is your mother so I get why you're so bothered."

"It would be nice if she'd be more of a mother and less of a religious zealot." She sighed. "I guess I have to get over it."

"I do have a solution to take your mind off it for tonight," Marcus said sweetly.

"You do?"

"Yes. How about we go out to dinner and then maybe a little dancing tonight?"

Cathy was thrilled. "I'd like that."

"Good. I'll make all the arrangements. All you have to do is look pretty."

"Oh no. I can't go anywhere. I don't have anything to wear out tonight."

"Don't be silly. You can go shopping before the game."

"I did see a dress I liked about a week ago. I bet they still have it."

"Good." He looked at the clock. "It's still early enough for me to leave in time for practice. I'll take my car. This way

Louis can take you shopping, then drive you over to the stadium."

"A night on the town sounds wonderful. I'm really looking forward to it."

"Me too." He stood up and took her by the hand. "Now let's say we do our part for water conservation."

"Do our part for water conservation?" Cathy was puzzled. "I didn't know there was a water alert in the city."

"There isn't. But who says we can't be environmentally conscious anyway?" He had a naughty look in his eyes.

He untied the robe and slowly led Cathy into the bathroom.

"Are you sure you want to be in the cold spot?"

"What cold spot? There are shower heads on both sides."

"I see."

He turned on the water.

"What if you don't use the same shower gel as me?"

"We'll use yours. I don't care if I smell like a flower." The robe fell to the floor.

"A raspberry, you'll smell like a raspberry. Or we can use the vanilla if you like."

They stepped into the warm shower

"Vanilla and chocolate. Sounds good to

me." He closed the shower door.

After Marcus went to the stadium, Louis took Cathy shopping for a robe and a dress to wear for an evening of dining and dancing. He dropped her off in front of Lane Bryant. She went straight to the lingerie section. Even though Cathy had been bold enough to drop her robe and be completely naked in the daytime with Marcus, she wasn't sure if she'd have the nerve again. So she picked up two robes, one sexy silk and the other functional terrycloth. As Cathy was locating her size, she noticed a couple of salespeople looking at her. She couldn't understand the fascination and didn't have time to figure it out. Robes in hand, she went to the sales counter

A very pretty young woman was at the cash register. "Good morning." She smiled.

"Good morning."

"Will you be using your Lane Bryant card?"

"No. I don't have one."

"If you open one you can get 10% off your purchase."

"Thanks, maybe next time."

"No problem."

One of the two sales girls tapped her on the shoulder.

"Yes?"

"I'm sorry. I don't mean to bother you, but aren't you Catherine Chambers?"

Cathy was surprised she knew her name. "Yes, I am."

One girl turned to the other. "See, I told you it was her."

Cathy was flabbergasted. "Have I met you before?"

The salesgirl smiled. "No, I saw your picture in the paper today. You're the big girl dating Marcus Fox."

The girl at the cash register dropped the hanger. "Get outta here." She had a strong Brooklyn accent. "You're dating *the* Marcus Fox?"

The other salesgirl came over. "We were just talking about it this morning. I think it's great."

Cathy was overwhelmed. "Thanks."

"No, really thank you. It's nice to see a big girl get the dream guy."

Cathy smiled. "I think so, too." "He is fine," the cashier cooed.

"You won't get any argument from me." Cathy grinned.

The clerk rang up her purchases and bagged them. "Thanks for shopping at Lane Bryant. I hope the black one is for Mr. Fox," she whispered.

Taking the shopping bag, Cathy whispered back, "It is a good day ladies!"

They waved as she walked out. She couldn't believe how her dating Marcus was the plus-size community's cosmic version of "Run, Forest, run."

Cathy went from Lane Bryant to Ashley Stewart to pick up the halter dress she'd admired earlier last week. She'd tried the dress on before so she knew what size fit her.

Once in the store, Cathy went straight over to the rack, searched for her size in the black print and headed for the register. The saleswoman behind the register had the paper open on the counter.

"Good morning. Will this be all?"

"Yes."

"Is that cash or credit?"

"Cash."

As she pulled the security tags off she glanced at the paper and then looked at Cathy.

"What paper is it?" "*The Journal.*"

"Then it's me."

She dropped the dress on the counter. "Girl, you've got it going on."

She laughed. "Thanks."

"It's about time he stopped with those skinny witches."

Cathy laughed because the clerk had said what she couldn't say.

"And from the looks of things I'd say he's been hungry for someone to fill his arms."

Cathy was completely confused.

When she pointed to the hickey on Cathy's neck, she blushed. She was so embarrassed.

"You don't have to be embarrassed. Wear it like an accessory, because this dress is hot."

"I know. I saw it a few days back but I couldn't think of where I would wear it."

"And now you've got someplace to wear it. You go, girl!"

Cathy paid for the dress and the saleswoman put it on a hanger to bag it.

"Here you go." She handed the dress to Cathy.

"Thank you."

"Thank you for shopping at Ashley Stewart. Enjoy the dress and the man. Not necessarily in that order." "Bet on it." Cathy got a good laugh.

She called Louis on the cell phone and he brought the car around. He took her bags and put them in the trunk while she got in.

Louis looked in the rearview mirror. "Ms. Chambers?"

"Yes?"

"I like the way you shop."

Cathy chuckled. "Hey, I like a bargain as much as the next person. I just don't want to bring a shovel to dig through each and every layer. It drives me crazy." "You're a woman after my own heart," he said.

Cathy winked and sat back in the seat.

Her cell phone rang. It was E.D.

"What's shaking E.D.?"

"The question is, what's shaking with you? I see you made the papers again today."

"Isn't that wild?"

"It's certainly raised our profile. We've gotten so many calls we've run out of room on the machine and it's Saturday."

"Wow. That is something then."

"You do sound relaxed and happy. It's nice to call you and not have you fire off a list of clients, editors and publishers. It isn't all about work."

"You're right."

"Is this really Cathy?"

"Very funny."

"I'm just kidding. You deserve some happiness."

"I'd better go before the score from *Beaches* starts playing."

"Okay, I'll go. Have a good weekend."

"Thanks, I will. Marcus is taking me out for dinner and dancing tonight. It should be fun."

"Nice. Have a good time."

"Thanks. Later, E.D."

Up until a few days ago Cathy had no idea how to stop and smell the roses. E.D. always said she'd find the man who was truly right for her, and when she did she'd finally be able to exhale and enjoy life. He'd also told her she would not find that man in publishing. He was right.

Melvin was waiting to greet her for the afternoon game.

"Thanks for driving me, Louis." She started to get out of the car. "Oh, Louis, I have these bags. Should I take them with me?"

"I'll take them back to the apartment. I have a key and it will only take a minute."

"Thanks, Louis."

"You're welcome, Ms. Chambers. I hope you enjoy the game."

"I'm sure I will." She got out of the car and turned to Melvin. "Hello, Melvin. How are you?"

"I'm good, Ms. Chambers. How are you?"

"Good. So where are we headed today?"

"You're going back to the suite this afternoon so you don't have to worry about the sun."

"I have to tell Marcus I don't mind sitting in the Loge section. It's in the shade too."

Melvin smiled. He knew not to say too much. She followed him to the suites section again.

"Here you go."

"Thanks, Melvin. You're a doll."

"Don't forget that if you want or need anything, there is someone here to get it for you."

"I won't."

Although Cathy looked forward to an evening of dancing, she didn't want Marcus to be out too late. She'd never met his boss in person but she knew hanging out late dancing wouldn't sit too well with him. Her cell phone rang.

"Catherine Chambers."

"Hi, Mom."

"Hi, Andrew."

"Are you at the game?"

"As a matter of fact I am. I'm not in the stands. I'm back in the suite."

"Cool."

"So is anything going on? Did you see the paper?"

"Yeah, we saw it this morning. It wasn't bad like you said."

"I told you not to worry. So the pre-game is on now, right?"

"Yeah."

Cathy heard a little something in his voice. "Andrew, is something on your mind? Do you need to tell me something?"

He hesitated. "You know we listen to the radio station out of Buffalo or Rochester."

"Yes."

"Today they did a gossip report and it was about you, Mr. Fox and Cybil George."

"Really? What did they say that got you upset?"

"They said after Cybil read about you and Mr. Fox, she said she didn't know he was a…" He was reluctant.

"Go ahead, Andrew. You can say it."

"She said Marcus Fox was a chubby chaser."

The words pierced Cathy's skin but she didn't let on. "Well, you know, honey, she has to say something. They were probably pressing her about it."

"It doesn't bother you?" He was relieved.

"No, honey, it doesn't. Unfortunately, it's just the kind of thing that sells newspapers and feeds a gossip happy public."

"I'm glad you're okay with it, Mom."

"You feel better now?"

"Yeah. Thanks, Mom."

"Maybe I'll give you a call after the game. Okay?"

"Okay, Mom. Talk to you later."

"All right then."

Although it wasn't unexpected, it didn't make it any easier for Cathy to hear. She knew the press baited Cybil.

Still it didn't feel good to be right. Her remark had hit the target.

Tall, blond and willowy thin Cybil George was one of the most successful and in demand models in fashion.
She was high fashion, high priced and high strung. No shrinking violet, her tirades were legendary.

Then it hit her. If this sound bite was on the stations upstate, then it was downstate as well. She had to find someone who still listened to those stations.

With ten minutes to go before the game started, she dialed Michelle first, but got no answer. Then she took a chance that her sister might have her cell on.

"Hello?"

"Hey, Anna, it's me."

"It's about time you called. I read the papers this morning. You and Marcus are big news. So how's that going?"

"It's going pretty well. But listen, I need to ask you something."

"What?"

"Have you heard anything on the radio about Cybil George?"

"Cybil George? Marcus's ex-girlfriend? Other than what I read in the gossip section I haven't heard anything else about her."

"Andrew just called me to tell me about an entertainment report he heard on a station upstate. According to him, George was quoted as saying in response to the story that she didn't realize Marcus was a chubby chaser."

"Oh no. This was on the radio up there?"

"Yeah, and now I'm thinking if it was on the air way up there, it has to be down here."

"It's Saturday. Most of the stations play rebroadcasts of shows earlier in the week, but I'll keep my ears open. I'll check a couple of the radio stations' websites; they usually have links for entertainment and people in the news."

"Thanks. The game is about to start. Buzz me if you find anything out."

"Okay. Later."

Though the odds were not in her favor, Cathy hoped it was nothing. But something told her she'd be on the wrong side of a sucker bet.

CHAPTER 14

Cathy was grateful for the suspense of a close game. It kept her from wondering what was going on in the world outside Yankee Stadium. She was on the edge of her seat. It was the bottom of the seventh inning and the score was tied 2-2. There was one out and two men on base. In the distance she saw Marcus lean against the dugout as intense as ever. She wondered what was going through his mind. The count was 2-1 on Juan Lopez, who was having a roller coaster of a season. Yet somehow Juan usually came up with key hits or walks a younger catcher wouldn't have the experience to do. Finally there was a crack of the bat. She got to her feet. The ball was hit hard to left field for a base hit.

She screamed as the crowd broke into a roar. Marcus clapped his hands together and she saw his million dollar grin on the monitor.

A two-run double. Hallelujah!

Just as Cathy grabbed her water bottle her phone rang.

She picked it up quickly.

"Hey. You're still at the game?" Anna asked.

Cathy was concentrating on the field. "Yes. We just went ahead 4-2. So what's the word?"

"There have been a couple of reports on the radio."

Cathy felt the wind go out of her sails. "I had a feeling." "But what do you care? You're with Marcus and she's not. She had to say something when they printed her name in the blurb. That's all it was, Cathy, just a sound bite. Who gives a rat's behind?"

"I know."

"It doesn't make you feel better does it?"

"Not really. I mean, I'll keep my chin up but it hurts."

"Are you going to talk to Marcus about it?"

"It's not his fault. There's no reason for me to say anything. I'll get over it."

"Cathy, I know it's going to bother you. I think you should talk to Marcus. I'm sure he'd want to know how you feel."

"Hell, Anna, I don't want to know how I feel. But you may be right; I need to get this off my chest before we go out tonight. Maybe I'll talk to him before dinner."

"Good."

"Listen, I'd better go. We're still in the bottom of the seventh."

"Okay. Talk to you later."

She closed her phone.

Cathy didn't have a doubt that Cybil's dig was aimed at her, even though she'd said it about Marcus. She decided to put her feelings on the shelf and enjoy the rest of the game in relative peace.

The seventh inning proved to be the Yankees' rallying point and they went up 6-2. The bullpen came in and shut down Toronto's offense. The Yankees won and their winning streak was extended to five.

***

There was a sense of jubilation in the Yankee clubhouse.

The first part of the season had had even the faithful questioning their team's chances. Then the Yankees had started to pull out seemingly from nowhere. A crowd of reporters surrounded Juan Lopez as he was the man of the hour. Already changed, Marcus sat down to put his shoes on. Mark sat next to him.

"Good game," Mark said.

Marcus turned towards him. "You too. You're really pulling off some good defensive plays out there. Don't be surprised to see them replayed on ESPN's top ten."

Mark laughed. "If they choose it, cool. If they don't, I won't lose any sleep. We've got to make the drive for October." "I know. How are Pamela and Mark Jr.?"

"They're good. He keeps the both of us hopping at home."

Marcus laughed. "He's a little over two years old, right?"

"Yep. It's the terrible twos for sure."

Marcus nodded. "I can't believe that at one point Cathy had twin two-year-olds." He shook his head in awe.

"And she survived."

"Yes, she did."

"How's she making out with all this press stuff?"

"So far she's seems okay. I'm taking her out for dinner and just a little dancing tonight. You know, to take her mind off things."

"That's sounds like fun."

"I hope so." He stood up. "Listen, I'll see you tomorrow."

"Okay."

***

After the game Melvin brought Cathy to the clubhouse area where she waited for Marcus. It was busy enough to keep her distracted. She watched the usual suspects, the intrepid sports reporters and photographers. Marcus emerged from the clubhouse looking fresh-faced and happy. He kissed her.

"Great game, honey. You extended the win streak. I heard the reporters buzzing about it."

"It is a big change from how we started out at the beginning of the season."

"My dad always says that baseball has such a long season; it's the end of the season that matters, not the beginning."

"He's right about that." He put his arm around her waist. "Ready to go?"

She put her sunglasses on first. "Sure am."

With security in front, Marcus and Cathy stepped outside where they were nearly surrounded by an onslaught of reporters and photographers.

Security separated them from the newshounds.

"Marcus! Care to comment on Cybil's statement?" a female reporter asked while her photographer took pictures.

Marcus was annoyed. "What statement?"

"How do you feel being called a chubby chaser, Marcus?" a male reporter asked.

"What?" Marcus shouted.

They never stopped walking to the car. Marcus unlocked the doors by remote. The questions and camera flashes came at them so fast Cathy could barely distinguish a woman's voice from a man's; to her, they were all sharks.

"What about you Ms. Chambers? How do you feel about it?" another voice shouted.

Cathy ignored the question and Marcus helped her into the car. Security covered him long enough for him to get in the car and pull away from the melee.

Cathy and Marcus were quiet for a moment. Marcus silently fumed over the comment and subsequent press feeding frenzy. Things with him and Cybil had not been civil after the breakup but in the last few months it had seemed that she finally let go.

"I'm sorry about all of this."

"It's not your fault, Marcus. You didn't have any control over this."

"I had no idea Cybil talked to the press."

"Honey, it was just a matter of time. She couldn't let it go."

"You're not bothered by this?

"It's par for the course. The media has focused on our obvious differences, which is size, and our commonality, which is you. I can't be bothered about it. Otherwise I wouldn't be able to listen to the radio again."

"This was on the radio?" He was alarmed.

"Yes. My son Andrew called me about it during the game. He heard an entertainment/gossip report on one of the stations he listens to upstate."

"What did you say to Andrew?"

"I let him know I wasn't bothered." "Are you sure?" He didn't quite believe her.

"Listen, Marcus, I promise you I've heard worse."

He didn't look completely convinced. "Are you sure?"

She put on her happiest face. "Trust me. I don't think I'm being punished by God. Somehow I don't think he'd use Cybil as a tool to do that. This is a pure media thing, not divine retribution."

"You're telling me the truth?"

"Of course. I have too much to look forward to tonight to let Cybil George bring me down."

"You know, we don't have to go out. We could just make a night of it at home."

"No. Why should we change our plans over something so ridiculous?"

"Good. I can't wait to take you out and show you off."

She smiled. Of course it bothered her. It had taken Cathy years to make peace with her body issues, to find a way to incorporate self-esteem into her life. Now one of the most beautiful women in the world was raising the issue again.

Cathy thought about Madison's philosophy to stop feeling sorry for herself and shake things off. Cybil George had called her chubby, but in the end all that mattered was that Marcus was with her, not Cybil. Even if the world thought she was not Marcus's type, as long as she didn't buy into it, too, they had a shot at being happy together.

***

As promised, Louis had left Cathy's purchases in the apartment, in fact on the bed. Marcus picked up the bag. "Ooh, what's this?"

She played coy. "Just a little something I picked up before the game."

"Can I take a peek?" Marcus said playfully.

She grabbed the bag from him. "You just have to wait. It's a surprise."

He looked like a little boy. "Come on. Can't I have one tiny peek?"

"Sorry, you just have to wait." She hung the dress up. "Now do you want to get cleaned up first?"

"We don't have to call dibs on the bathroom. I'll use the guest bathroom. This way you can build up to your revelation." He kissed her.

"I think you've seen too many makeover shows."

"You could be right. At any rate, my love, I will leave so you can get ready."

"Thanks, sweetie. I won't be long."

"Take your time. You're worth the wait."

Cathy had everything she needed to give herself a real attitude adjustment from frumpy to sexy. There was sexy lingerie, sexy strappy shoes, a sexy dress and the perfect accessory, a very sexy man to go with it all.

After a quick shower she got dressed and walked out into the bedroom to check her reflection in the full-length mirror. "Not bad," she said out loud. All that was left for her to do was her makeup.

Just as she sat down her phone rang.

"Hello?"

"Cathy?"

It was Cathy's mother. At sixty-three, Elizabeth Anderson outwardly appeared to be a docile woman but Cathy and Anna knew better. She walked softly and was licensed to carry a concealed weapon, her tongue. She didn't curse a person out, however. It was all in the delivery.

Elizabeth could pump Cathy full of holes in no time flat.

"Mom?" Cathy was now filled with dread.

"I haven't heard from you in a while."

"It's been less than a week, Mom."

"Even so, you could have called."

"I left you a message, Mom."

"I know. You just don't want to hear my mouth."

"You aren't exactly supportive about things, Mom."

"You know why. You and Anna know what's right."

"We know what's right for us, Mom, which happens to be the opposite of what you think."

"Imagine how I felt when Ingrid told me all about what's been happening in the news with you."

"Mom, I'm dating Marcus Fox."

"Well, he's new."

"God, Mom, you say that like I change men like I do underwear."

"You were just going out with that Paul guy."

"Mom, we broke up nearly three years ago. I haven't been out with anyone else until now."

"So you are going out with this Marcus Fox?"

"Yes, Mom. In fact, we're going out for dinner and dancing tonight."

"I hope you have something appropriate to wear."

"I'm wearing a nice dress."

"You don't have too much cleavage showing or anything? You have to be careful when you're…" She didn't finish the sentence.

Cathy finished it for her. "Plus-sized. You know, Mom, I don't dress like nun nor do I dress like a hooker. I'm right in the middle."

"I'm just saying this man is a baseball player so people are going to watch you like a hawk."

"People always have something to say. It's just human nature."

"You don't have to get snippy with me. I am still your mother."

"I'm not getting snippy. I'm just stating a fact, that's all." She got defensive.

"Where are you going?"

"I'm not sure. Marcus made the reservations." She looked at her watch. "In fact, I'd better get going so we're not late."

"All right. We'll talk early next week."

"Okay, Mom."

Cathy hung up, took a deep breath and put her lipstick on.

"Cathy?" Marcus called.

"Yes?"

"Are you ready?"

"Yes. I'll be right out."

She checked herself one more time in the mirror, grabbed her wrap and purse. "Here I come."

Marcus was waiting in the living room. His eyes widened.

"What do you think?" she said as she twirled around to give him the 360-degree view.

He stood up. "You look beautiful." He smiled.

"Thank you very much, kind sir. You look pretty fantastic yourself."

"Thanks." He put his arm out. "Your chariot awaits."

***

Cathy barely caught the name of the restaurant as they entered, but the décor and atmosphere were elegant and intimate. The maître d' showed them to a beautifully set table where a bottle of chilled champagne awaited them.

Marcus held her seat.

"Thank you."

He sat down. "So what do you think?"

"This is very nice."

The waiter came over. "Would you like me to open the champagne now, sir?"

"Absolutely."

The waiter opened the bottle and poured two glasses.

"Thank you." Marcus lifted his glass. "I'd like to make a toast."

Cathy raised her glass.

"To us."

"To us," she said as they clinked glasses together. "This is lovely, Marcus, thank you."

"Don't thank me yet. I took the liberty of picking tonight's menu. I hope you approve."

"How in the world did you find the time to set this up?"

"That's my little secret." He winked. "Besides, one good meal deserves another."

Cathy took another sip. "This champagne is fantastic. Now what's on the menu?"

"If you look on your plate there's a card with all of tonight's delicacies." It read:

Supper for Two:

Appetizer: Blini with Smoked Salmon

Soup Course: Zucchini Vichyssoise

Main entrée: Chicken with Morels and Haricots Verts

Dessert: Crème Brulee

"This sounds wonderful."

"I bet you've made a few things on this menu yourself before."

"Once or twice."

"I knew it. You know, I haven't met many women who love to cook. Where did you get your love of cooking from?"

"With a maternal grandmother from South Carolina and a great grandmother from the Virgin Islands, the food was always good and I watched them in the kitchen when I was a little girl."

"You watched your grandmother *and* your great grandmother?" He was incredulous.

"Yes, I had the best of both worlds. I wouldn't dare say I'm in their league but I can hold my own in a kitchen. I'm an all out foodie."

"So you're really into the Food Network."

"Definitely. Before the Food Network I spent Sunday afternoons watching cooking programs on PBS, one after the other."

"But raising two kids as a single parent, how did you find the time to hone your skills?"

"Remember earlier today you were doing a little math problem that involved me?"

He thought for a moment. "Oh, that math problem."

"Let's just say celibacy had its rewards. I had to put the unspent energy to use somehow. I used mine in the kitchen. I finally realized I'd gone overboard when I made bagels at home. Bagels, of all things. This isn't Paducah, Kentucky. This is New York. You can get bagels anywhere. I decided then and there I probably needed a more appropriate outlet for my energy."

He laughed. "In other words, a sex life."

"Exactly."

"That is too funny."

"Now of course my sons are spoiled. In college they've had to resort to packaged cookies, muffins and the like. Everything was and still is made from scratch at home."

"With the exception of bagels."

She laughed. "Right."

"You realize you've *really* spoiled them."

"Absolutely. I know my future daughters-in-law are gonna hate me for it."

"Of course they will. They won't have the excuse of work or anything else since you managed to do all of it as a single parent."

"Oh well." She shrugged.

"Since you've done this menu before, maybe you can make it for me someday soon."

"That's cool with me."

Cathy and Marcus had a lovely dinner. Cathy silently grew more impressed with Marcus's choices for the menu. From the appetizer to the entrée, every part of the meal complemented the next. Then it was time for crème brulee, always one of her favorite desserts. Cathy's eyes lit up as the waiter placed the ramekin in front of her. She took a deep whiff of the caramel scent as it wafted in the air. The raspberry coulis further tempted her palate.

Marcus was pleased. "This looks so good." He dove in

"It really does look wonderful. I love the presentation." Suddenly she was too self-conscious to eat with her usual abandon.

Marcus looked up. "Dig in. You'll love it."

Cathy quietly took a deep breath. "I know." Not wanting to draw attention to herself, she took the smallest spoonful and ate it slowly. She tried to make it look as if she were savoring the taste but she didn't fool Marcus.

"What's the matter, Cathy?"

"Nothing. I'm just savoring the taste."

Marcus put his napkin down. "I'm sorry, Cathy, this just isn't you."

She tried to act innocent. "What do you mean?"

"I've seen you eat dessert and I loved seeing the pure pleasure on your face. Tonight you look as if someone has a gun pressed to your temple. What's going on here?" "I am enjoying this," she insisted. "No, you're not. You're being self-conscious." "Maybe I am." She put the spoon down.

"You are."

"You weren't the one they called chubby," she retorted.

Marcus leaned back in his chair. "So that's what this is about?" He shook his head. "You don't look like the type who would let something so ridiculous and untrue bother you."

Cathy knew he didn't have a clue. "I'm ashamed to admit it, but yes, I'm not perfect. There are days I struggle with self-esteem without the glare of the media. Now that

I'm in their crosshairs, it just feels like it's going to take on a life of its own."

"Sweetheart, one of the things that attracted me to you was your independent spirit. At Keen's you sat down and ate your lunch without apology. So you'd rather deny yourself something you obviously enjoy just because of what other people might think?"

The words hit her like a hammer. "When you put it that way, it sounds shallow. I'm not a shallow person."

"I don't think so either."

Cathy knew Marcus was right. "The hell with them. It would be an insult to you and the chef not to enjoy it." She dug right in. "Besides, we're going to burn off some calories dancing."

"Right." Marcus dipped his spoon into the coulis. "Do they have a special name for this raspberry sauce?"

"It's a raspberry coulis."

"It's good."

"I know."

Cathy was glad Marcus didn't let her off the hook. Why should she let a few words ruin their evening after he'd planned such a lovely dinner? They were going to burn up the dance floor later and get their hearts pumping. Dancing counted as an aerobic activity with Marcus, only this time Cathy would be on her feet.

A short time later Louis pulled up to the front of the dance club. A valet opened the door and there were delighted sounds from fans when Marcus stepped out with Cathy on his arm. While he stopped to sign a few autographs and posed for a few pictures for the paparazzi, Cathy hung back.

Marcus smiled for the cameras. "Just a minute, guys, I forgot someone." He walked over and led a surprised Cathy over to the cameras with him.

"What are you doing?" she spoke through her smile.

Marcus kept smiling. "What kind of a gentleman would I be if I didn't introduce my girlfriend?" Cathy's heart leapt. "Your what?" "Who is this, Marcus?" a voice shouted.

"This is my girlfriend Catherine." He smiled as he looked at her.

A flood of flashbulbs nearly blinded Cathy but she didn't care. He'd just told the world she was his girlfriend. She was happy to smile for the cameras.

"Okay, guys, you got some pictures. I promised to take her dancing, so if you will excuse us…"

"Thanks, Marcus!" another voice shouted.

The one and only time Cathy had been to a nightclub was when she was thirty-three. She and Marcus walked hand in hand through the club. The music was so loud she could barely hear herself think, which when she thought about it, was probably the point. As they made their way to a table, people approached Marcus just to be in his orbit. He managed to remain gracious and still make his way through the crowd. They found a table.

"What would you like to drink?" he shouted.

"It doesn't matter to me," she shouted back.

"Okay. I'll just pick something and hope I get it right."

Cathy covered her ears. "Whatever you get will be fine."

Marcus smiled when he glanced back from the bar and saw Cathy moving her shoulders to the music. He hoped this little outing would be just the ticket to get things off her mind.

Just then he felt someone rub his back. He turned around quickly. It was Sarah, the brunette he used to fool around with. Her timing couldn't have been worse.

"Hey there, stranger, long time no hear," she purred.

"Hi." He was subdued.

She was genuinely surprised by his reaction. "Is that all I get?" she asked.

"How are you, Sarah?"

"I'm good, but I would be even better if you called me back. What gives?" She put her hand on her hip.

Marcus looked directly in her eyes. "I have a girlfriend."

He looked over at the bartender mixing the drink he'd ordered for Cathy.

"That never stopped you before." As she went to rub his chest, he gently grabbed her hand. "What gives?" she growled.

"I said, I have a girlfriend."

The bartender walked over, drinks in hand. "Here you go, Mr. Fox."

"Thanks, man. Keep the change."

"Thank you."

"It was good seeing you, Sarah. Take care."

Marcus coolly walked away from a shell-shocked Sarah.

Cathy scanned the A-list crowd of twenty and thirty somethings on the dance floor. *Wow,* Cathy thought, *I'm only 40 but in here it might as well be in dog years.* Marcus returned.

"Here you go."

Cathy smiled. "How did you know this was one of my favorite drinks?"

He played coy. "I made an educated guess. I figured you'd like something a little sweet but not too sweet."

"Good guess." Not much of a drinker, she sipped it slowly.

"The music is pretty good tonight," Marcus said as he moved to the music.

"Yeah, it's pretty good."

"As long as it's not that techno stuff, I'm good."

"I know what you mean. They sometimes play it at my gym in the morning. It drives us crazy." "Are you feeling okay?" he asked.

"I'm fine."

"Would you like to dance?"

"Sure, just let me finish my drink and I'm good to go."

"Whenever you're ready."

Cathy took one last sip for courage before she hit the dance floor with all the Beyonce and Usher wannabees. She prayed she wouldn't make a complete fool of herself or slip a disk.

She got up. "Let's go."

Whether it was fate or the good Lord smiling down on a fool for love, the club played R&B music from the nineties that Cathy could actually shake her groove thing to.

Marcus was pleased to see Cathy have such a good time. While the other women were grinding and dropping their groove thing, Cathy's smooth, sexy dance moves left more to the imagination, much more. Cathy noticed a few fellow big girls on the dance floor. She almost chuckled out loud when she thought about something Chris Rock had said about big women in the clubs. She smiled instead.

"What are you smiling about?" Marcus shouted.

"Nothing. I'm just having a good time." She continued dancing.

Before they knew it, they'd worked up a sweat for over an hour on the dance floor. Although younger, Marcus threw in the towel first.

"You really did your thing out there." Marcus put his tie in his pocket as they headed back to their table.

"It's nice to know I still can." Cathy was pumped. *Cybil who?*

"Want something?"

"Oh, yes, I'll take anything as long as it's cold and nonalcoholic. I'm going to the ladies room."

"Okay. I'll be here when you get back."

Cathy made her way to the ladies room and splashed a little water on her face. She was relieved to see it wasn't crowded so she wouldn't look like some old chick trying to catch her breath. She knew her makeup was a lost cause after sweating it off on the dance floor, but since it was her first night on the town with Marcus, she needed a little color on her mouth and she put some lipstick on. Cathy reached for another towel to blot but she'd used the last one.

"Damn, I threw the towel away." She looked around. "Tissue will have to do." As she went into one of the stalls she heard two women enter the bathroom.

"You got the stuff?"

"Yeah."

Cathy heard what sounded like snorts. She took a peek and sure enough, there stood two women snorting coke. *When the hell did doing coke in the bathroom become fashionable again? It's not the eighties.* The women continued talking between snorts.

"Did you see her?"

"Who?"

"The woman with Marcus Fox."

The minute Cathy heard his name she froze.

"Is she the one he left Cybil George for?"

"Yeah. Cybil called him a chubby chaser."

"Did you see how big she is?"

"I would die if I gained that much weight."

"Me too. I wonder how he screws her through all that flesh."

"If cows can screw, there's a way."

Suddenly Cathy felt as if she'd been punched in the stomach. She was upset and mad at the same time.

"She looks like she wears a size 20 or something."

Cathy stepped out of the stall. "It's more like a size 16." She was pissed.

Caught, the two gossipers made a hasty exit.

"We have to do this again sometime, ladies. It's been real!" she shouted after them.

She looked at her reflection in the mirror. *What the hell am I doing here? What made me think I could do this?*

Cathy went back to the table. Marcus's face quickly went from a smile to concern. "Are you okay?"

She could barely look at him. "I have a wicked headache. Can we go?"

"Sure. I'll call Louis." He looked disappointed but he made the call.

She felt bad for cutting the evening short but there was no way she could stay there a minute longer.

It only took a few minutes for Louis to bring the car around. On the drive back to the apartment, Cathy took a couple of Advil for her non-existent headache that was sure to become a reality in the penthouse.

The minute they walked in, Cathy kicked off her shoes and flopped on the sofa. Marcus sat down next to her.

"Now are you going to tell me the real reason you wanted to leave?"

"I knew you didn't buy the headache excuse."

"Does it have anything to do with your mother?"

"My mother?" she asked.

"We talked about this kind of thing earlier. I thought maybe dancing was against the religion too.

"I did talk to my mother before we left, but for once she doesn't have anything to do with it. There's no doctrine against dancing. The prom had more to do with not dating, I guess."

"They didn't let you go to the prom but you could go to a nightclub?" He seemed puzzled.

"No, they don't approve of nightclubs, but dancing is okay. You could dance at weddings and some gatherings had music for dancing."

He laughed. "So you mean this very religious woman likes to shake what her momma gave her?"

"Yes, she does. It is kind of funny when you think about it. Whenever there's a wedding, all we have to do is look in the middle of the dance floor and there's Mom, shaking and moving. It cracks us up."

"Sounds wild."

"It is."

"Well, if it isn't about your mother, something else happened. It's written all over your face."

Cathy's smile ran away from her face. She sighed.

"Take your time, I am not going anywhere."

She could see he meant it. "I overheard two women talking about me in the bathroom." Marcus's stomach sank.

"I'm not thin-skinned but it was hard to hear people who don't know me from a hole in the wall talk about me."

"What did they say that got you so upset?"

She didn't want the words in the air again but Marcus wanted to know. She took a deep breath. "They couldn't figure out how you could have chosen me over Cybil. Of course, I'm paraphrasing."

There was something about the way Marcus took her hands that touched her emotions. She fought to keep the tears at bay and tried to pull her hands away but Marcus wouldn't let her.

"I want you to know you're safe. You can talk to me." Cathy looked away. The tears began to well in her eyes. "That's a tall order, captain. You want me to let my defenses down. Don't you know I need my quick wit and self-effacing humor to hide in plain sight? You can't just call me out on it. What will I have left?"

"The truth."

"The truth will set you free," she said half-heartedly. "What they don't tell you is self-truth is much harder to face." She bent down and wiped her eyes with her arm.

She had a far off look in her eyes. The memories played in her head like a movie reel. "I've always been the big girl growing up but it was harder for me because of religion."

"You felt like an outsider?"

She shook her head. "Yes. I couldn't participate in the very things that would have validated me. I didn't get to be pretty in pink for my prom. I didn't date. I spent my

Saturday nights studying or reading Jane Austen. It's not so much that I was the only big girl in my class, I wasn't. I was just the only one who never went out."

"God, those are all things most of us take for granted."

"It made it that much harder to learn how to be comfortable in my own skin. My mother always fought her weight but divorce took care of that for her once and for all.

She was definitely from the school of Ivana. She got everything and she looked good doing it."

"Oh, I see."

"She became one of those former fatties who suddenly got onto this soapbox about weight. She said it was about health, but that was a load."

"What about your dad? What did he have to say?"

"He never said anything about weight. He was more interested in school work. Grades, tests, things like that."

"He never said you were beautiful or pretty?"

"He did but I developed way ahead of other girls so he was more protective than anything else. I wore a B-cup in the fifth grade and by the time I graduated high school I was a DD-cup."

Marcus was impressed. "You were a DD-cup in high school. Wow."

"I know."

"So your parents' split was less than amicable."

"That's putting it mildly. My mother was awarded custody and froze my father out whenever she could just shy of violating the court's visitation order. Her nitpicking about my weight got worse and now 24 years later we're sitting here dealing with my hang-ups."

"Have you ever talked to your dad about it?"

"No. It's not exactly an easy subject to chat with your dad about." She paused. "I still don't have a clue how to even bring the topic of body image up."

"As a man he could have helped you deal with your insecurities by giving you a man's point of view."

Cathy wiped her eyes. "You may have a point there, but everything was so tense back then. He couldn't talk to my mother. He had an affair so he was the last person my mother would listen to."

"He was and still is your father. No matter what happened between them, he should have had a say."

"Not on Elizabeth's watch he didn't. She did back off a little when we got older but by that time, I had my issues under control, at least most of the time."

"You know, you don't seem like you have any issues with your body at all. I watched you dance tonight. You have some great moves."

Cathy couldn't help but laugh softly. "Thanks. You know, I thought I'd dealt with it, but the truth is these feelings die a thousand deaths only to be resurrected over and over. It's an emotional cha-cha dance." Unable to hold them back any longer, Cathy felt tears stream down her face.

"I can't say I understand it completely, but I want to."

"I'm grateful that you want to understand but it's just not the same for men."

"Why don't you think it's the same for men?"

"Because when my cousin Madison gained weight from medication and went from a 34 to a 42 a few years ago, it didn't put a crimp in his social life. He still went out with gorgeous women; he had no qualms about his size. When it happened to me after my car accident, I wanted to crawl under a rock."

"You were in a car accident? When?"

"A long time ago I sustained a back injury after being hit at a light. I put on weight due to the medication my doctor prescribed. I knew it was a side effect that would go away once I stopped taking the pills but it didn't make me feel better. I went from a size 16 to a 22. It took me a year to get back down to a 16. That's why I started dating at 29 instead of 28."

He shook his head. "I knew there was pressure on women to be thin but I never realized how much pressure."

"Pressure?" she repeated. "Do you know most big girls would never even think of approaching a hot guy? Not to say there aren't some that would. But if you hadn't come over to my table at Keen's, I would have been satisfied telling people I saw you in person."

He was taken aback. "Satisfied with never taking a chance to get to know me?"

"As bad as it sounds, yes. I would never have dreamed in a million years that *you* would find *me* attractive."

"Why?"

"For one thing, I've never seen you with anyone who remotely looked like me size wise. Whenever I opened the paper, there you'd be with some long, lithe, leggy creature. That's why I thought you were interested in the women at the table behind me at Keen's."

"I notice beautiful women, period. You are a beautiful woman, Cathy."

She felt flushed. "Thank you Marcus but right now it's a little difficult to feel beautiful with all the attention my size is getting."

"I know and I'm sorry."

She caressed his cheek. "It's not your fault."

"I wish there was something I could do."

"You're doing something right now. You're listening to me vent." Her eyes started to tear up again.

"It's still very fresh for you, isn't it?"

She wiped her face. "It's a shame but all I had to hear was chubby, fat and cow and my hard won self-esteem was totally obliterated."

"Why didn't you just tell me how you really felt? You didn't have to tell me what you thought I wanted to hear. I wanted the real story."

"I'm used to putting on a happy face for everyone. Then I deal with it later by myself. It's the way it's always been."

"You don't have to do that anymore. I want to be there for you." His sincerity was touching but Cathy had to ask the question.

"Tell me the truth, Marcus. Did you like being called a chubby chaser? And what about your teammates and fellow baseball players? Are you saying they're not giving you grief? Mind you, I've seen their wives and girlfriends."

Marcus was ticked. "I don't give a rat's behind about what other people have to say. If being a chubby chaser means I've finally found a wonderful woman to be with, then Cybil and anyone else can call me a chubby chaser every day and twice on Sunday. Now as far as my teammates are concerned, as long as I'm happy, they wish me all the best. After that, who cares about anyone else? All that matters is you and me."

Cathy started to crack a smile. "I don't know what I did to get so lucky."

He was relieved to see her smile again. "I feel the same way."

"So are you ready to deal with all of my insecurities when they raise their ugly heads?"

"Yes. Believe it or not, I know a thing or two about being insecure. Can you handle that?" he asked.

"You have insecurities?" she asked in disbelief.

"Of course I do. Every time I step onto the baseball diamond I worry I'm not good enough to be there."

"That's crazy. You're a fantastic athlete." Cathy shooed his doubts away.

"Thank you." He moved closer. "And you're a beautiful woman inside and out. I know I've dated what some people call 'perfect women' but I've never felt so close to someone so quickly." He caressed her face. "I say all the right things in front of the cameras but I don't let anyone in easily. There's just something about you that just feels right to me. It feels like home."

"I'm a bit guarded too. I've never trusted anyone enough to really let my guard down."

He looked deep in her eyes. "I know we haven't known each other long but I think I'm falling in love with you."

Just as Cathy started to speak, he kissed her. His lips were filled with an urgent hunger he needed to satisfy.

"You're so sexy and so very sweet," he whispered in her ear.

The warmth from his lips against her neck made Cathy tingle. Together they pulled his shirt over his head and let it fall to the floor. Marcus held her face as they kissed. Her breathing intensified as she tried to unbutton her dress.

"No I want to undress you, again."

Marcus led her into the bedroom. He sat down on the edge of the bed as Cathy stood in front of him. Slowly he pushed her dress up her thighs to reveal the top of her stockings. He lifted her leg so that her foot was on his thigh. Cathy held on to his shoulder so she wouldn't topple over. He rolled her stockings down each leg, kissing her thighs, knees, calves, ankles and toes with every roll. Marcus turned her around slowly and unzipped her dress, then slowly untied her halter. Just as the straps fell around her shoulders he stopped the dress from falling to the floor. He whispered into her ear, "I love to reveal you slowly."

He unhooked her bra so her bra and dress fell to the floor simultaneously. Starting from the nape of her neck, he planted soft kisses to her shoulders. Her knees weak, she could barely stand up. Marcus kneeled in front of her to kiss her stomach and hips. When his lips got closer to her inner thighs, she tensed up.

"What's wrong, honey?"

Cathy was embarrassed to say anything. "Nothing, it's just that I've never…" She shook her head. "Never mind."

"You've never let a man please you there?"

She felt like a total neophyte. "No. I was taught it was wrong."

"What could be wrong with loving and pleasing every inch of your lover's body?"

She knew she didn't have an answer.

"Relax, sweetie, and let me take care of you."

She lay down on the bed. He kissed her knees, calves and then her inner thighs. The sensations pulsating through her overwhelmed Cathy. Marcus's silky touch loved every inch of her curves, even the dangerous ones. With panther-like moves, he hovered above her, playfully teasing her lips with his. Cathy's skin crawled with desire as he lowered his body. She'd never craved a man's touch like this before. They seemed to read each other's mind and in the midst of such exquisite ecstasy, their eyes locked.

"Cathy," he whispered. "I love you."
"Oh God, Marcus, I love you."

CHAPTER 15

The elephant was in the room. In fact, it was in bed with them. Last night in the throes of passion they had been as close as two can get; they had even confessed their love. But neither had brought it up this morning. So far it looked as if the elephant would be staying for breakfast.

Marcus stroked Cathy's hair. "Last night and this morning were amazing. They really were. I can't believe last night was the last evening I get to spend with you before we go on the road."

She waited for the other shoe to drop. "I know. The time just flew by."

"I just thought of something." He stopped for a minute. "Maybe you can join me."

Cathy was a little taken aback. "You want me to come on the road with you?"

"It doesn't sound that crazy to you, does it?"

"No. I don't think it's crazy at all."

"Do you think you could rearrange your schedule?"

Cathy thought about it. She could really use a real vacation. "It would be hard for me to flip it during the week, but maybe I can come for the weekend series in Tampa."

"That sounds good to me."

"I'll book a flight leaving Friday and returning Sunday."

"You can stay at the Hilton. I'll take care of the reservation and I'll have the concierge handle getting you to the stadium."

"Great. It's been forever since I've been to Florida. Maybe I'll check with the concierge for shopping and sightseeing recommendations, so I can keep busy while you're at the stadium."

"That's a good idea but you won't be on your own all of the time. We'll be able to do some stuff together."

She smiled. "Now that would be really nice." She kissed him, then sat up to see what time it was. "God, I didn't realize the time. Since this is our last breakfast together do you have any requests?"

"No. Whatever you make is fine with me. I love…" He stopped in the midst of his sentence. "…your cooking," he finished.

Cathy put on a smile even though he didn't say what she wanted to hear. She slipped her black robe on and headed to the kitchen to get her mind off the subject of love and into making breakfast. Some women find comfort in eating, Cathy found comfort in cooking. It was a cheap but therapeutic way for her to concentrate on something else instead of whatever was worrying her.

For the first time, Cathy had opened up to a man. She'd told Marcus her deepest fears and the life that had shaped her, something she'd never done in the past. Then when she thought their lovemaking couldn't get any better, they'd taken it to another place so amazing they'd uttered those three little words, 'I love you.' They went from 'I *think* I love you' to 'I love you' in the course of an hour or so. Only now in the light of the sun they couldn't seem to find those same little words they'd said so easily in the dark.

An hour later Cathy had channeled her uneasiness into blueberry muffins, a salmon frittata, sausage and fresh squeezed orange juice and coffee.

Although the elephant was likely to join them for breakfast, she didn't add a third place setting. She grabbed the collection of morning papers stacked by the front door. By force of habit she opened up to the gossip section and there was a picture of Marcus and her with the caption *Marcus Fox's New Ladylove Throws Her Weight Around At Club Z.*

Cathy couldn't believe her eyes. She quickly flipped to the item.

According to two women, New York literary agent Catherine Chambers verbally accosted them in the ladies' room of Club Z and chased them out of the ladies' room. The two women said they had no idea what made her go after them.

Cathy saw red. *Those two coked-out witches from the bathroom insulted me and I'm the bad guy. All I did was educate them with my real dress size.* She sucked her teeth. *It figures that this would back up on me. I thought I could put it behind me but now the whole dang world knows.* Lost in thought, Cathy unconsciously crumpled the paper. Marcus walked into the dining room. "Oh, honey, this looks wonderful."

She was silent.

"Cathy? Is something wrong?"

She handed him the paper. "Read this."

Marcus looked at the crumpled paper. "This doesn't bode well." He smoothed the paper and scanned down. "What the hell is this about?"

"I'd like to know, too," Cathy huffed. "I told you what happened last night. Those same two women were talking about me in between snorts of coke."

"So we have the word of a couple of cokeheads trying to score some cash with a bogus story."

Cathy was panicked. "What am I going to do, Marcus? I have children. My children are going to see this crap! How do I explain this to them? To my family? This is a nightmare for me on so many levels." Cathy paced the floor. "Then there are the business ramifications. I'm a literary agent with clients and a good reputation in publishing. This will totally ruin my life." Cathy stopped herself. "I'm sorry. I'm just so upset."

"Don't worry about it. You have the right to be upset."

Cathy tried to take it down a notch. "I wanted this to be a nice breakfast and here I am ruining it."

"It is a nice breakfast and you haven't ruined anything. It's the jackass that published this crap that ruined breakfast." Marcus was angry.

She sat down at the table. "I know what I have to do but there are so many things running through my head right now, I scarcely know where to begin."

Marcus stood behind her and rubbed her neck. "I'm going to call my agent this morning and we'll get this straightened out."

"Oh, Marcus, that's really nice of you but this isn't your problem. I can call Jessica Jennings; she handles PR for a few of our clients. I'm sure she can help."

"Really, honey, let me do this. It's my fault anyway."

"How is it your fault?"

"It's because of me that they are focusing on you in the first place. I have to and will put an end to it."

Cathy felt a little like she had her own knight in shining armor. "Thanks, honey. I think I'll get in touch with my attorney, too."

"Good idea."

Cathy had a headache but she quickly covered it up. "Now let's enjoy this breakfast."

He looked over the spread. "Are you telling me you made all of this with the stuff that's in my kitchen?"

"That's what I'm saying."

"It all looks so good. Do you mind if I dive in?"

"Please eat and enjoy."

They made a cozy looking pair sitting at the breakfast table. Then Cathy's cell phone rang.

"Why don't you let it go to voice mail?"

"It could be important and with the gossip column in the paper today I'd better be prepared to face questions sooner or later. I prefer sooner." She got up. "Excuse me."

She looked at the caller ID. It was E.D. She knew he'd be the first call.

"Hello, E.D."

"Cathy, what the hell is going on? I got the morning paper and I couldn't believe what I read."

She walked into the bedroom. "That makes three of us." Balancing the phone on her shoulder she sat down on the bed. "You know, I was going to ask you to send out a memo to let our clients know I had a social life. I guess that ship has sailed." She clapped her hands together.

"I know that's your attempt to lighten the mood." "You mean it didn't work?" she joked.

"What do you think? So, my friend, how the hell did it get started?"

"It started the minute I walked into that club. Scratch that. I was actually having a good time until I went into the ladies room."

"Forget the paper. What really happened?"

"To make a short story short, I overheard them talking about me while I was in the bathroom."

"Did they talk about you right to your face?"

"No, that would have required guts, which those two cokeheads didn't have."

"Cokeheads?"

"Did I mention they were doing lines at the time?"

"So they didn't see you."

"They were too busy to notice anything but they did have time to wonder how Marcus could screw me through all my flesh. One said, 'If cows can screw, there's a way.' Then they made reference to my dress size."

E.D. was silent for a minute. "Oh my God, Cathy, I can't imagine what that must have been like for you."

"It was a nightmare but what could I do? Hide in the stall all night? So I stepped out of the stall and told them I wore a size 16."

"Good for you!"

"The little heifers ran out. It felt good for about a minute. Then the more I thought about it, the more uncomfortable I got. We left the club not too long after that."

"Whose idea was it to leave?"

"Mine. I know I should have stayed and danced the night away, but once those words were in the air, I couldn't stay."

"Oh, Cathy, I know you're really upset because of your boys."

"There's my picture, this totally awful caption and a blurb full of lies. Even if I get in touch with the powers that be and get a retraction, it's too late. The damage has been done."

"Don't worry about business, talk to your kids first."

Speaking of mothers, I almost forgot about Elizabeth. She winced. "Oh my God. My mother is going to have a field day with this."

"Cathy, you cannot turn this into a punishment from God for your sins. I don't care what your mother and 'the truth' say."

Cathy fidgeted on the bed. "Why does it feel like I'm being punished?"

"Come on, Cathy. You know better. What did Marcus say about it?"

"He's mad as hell and he's contacting his agent about it since he thinks the whole thing is his fault."

"He can't be at fault for other people's eagerness to get an exclusive at any cost. However, I'm sure he has the right connections to get this handled yesterday."

"I know, but there's the matter of our clients. What's going to happen when they read this?" she asked. "You know they are going to call me about it." "I'll handle them."

"Then there are my sons. What am I going to say? What must they be thinking?"

"You didn't do a damn thing, Cathy. Your sons know you and there is no way they would believe such trash." E. D. was in motivational speaker mode.

"From your lips to God's ears," Cathy sighed.

"Don't worry. Concentrate on your kids. I'll handle the client stuff."

"Thanks, E.D." She looked at the clock. "I'd better get back to the breakfast table with Marcus. We'll talk later. Keep me posted."

"Will do."

Before heading back in, Cathy took a couple of Advil for her headache.

Marcus looked up. "Everything okay?"

"Yeah. That was E.D. I had to give him the rundown."

"I'm sure he's none too pleased."

"That's an understatement." She sighed. "My dad has been in Virginia for the last couple of weeks, but he's due back this evening. He reads every newspaper."

Marcus felt responsible for the whole mess. He watched as Cathy tried to downplay the way she was feeling but he knew better. Whether she knew it or not, he'd made up his mind about her and he planned to keep her in his life. In order to do it he had to take care of this mess yesterday.

Marcus got up. "Listen, honey, I need to make that phone call now. I'll be back in a few minutes or so. Okay?"

"Okay."

He kissed her before he left the room.

Marcus picked up the phone from the night table. He paced for a few moments to try to calm down before making the call.

He dialed Ben.

"Hello?"

"Ben? It's Marcus."

Ben knew what he was calling about immediately. "I've seen the paper, too, Marcus."

"What the hell kind of crap is this?"

"The kind of crap that sells newspapers."

"Well, I'm not standing for it. There is no way Cathy did what they said."

"I know, Marcus."

"There has to be something we can do about it. Call Martin."

"I was going to suggest that we do just that. Martin's a big fan of yours. Maybe he can help get to the bottom of it."

"You know, those women were doing drugs in the ladies' room. Cathy heard them. Wait a minute. Martin beefed up security at the club and I seem to remember there was a security camera outside of the men's room."

"Yeah. So?"

"If there is a security camera outside the men's room…" Marcus began.

"There has to be one outside the ladies room."

"Right." He looked over at the clock. "It's still early. Give Martin a call and see if he can cue up the tapes from last night. I know it's Sunday morning but this is important. Tell him if he does this solid for me his nephews can come to the stadium for batting practice before a game."

"Good deal. I'll get on it right away. By the way, how is Cathy this morning?"

"Not good. She's mortified, embarrassed and worried about her children."

Ben shook his head. "Poor thing."

"I really want to make sure this is handled today. She's put up with so much in such a short period of time, I'm amazed she's still standing."

"She certainly is a strong woman."

"I know but even the strongest of women have a breaking point and I'm afraid she's nearing hers."

"Don't worry, Marcus. I'll give Martin a call and get the ball rolling."

"Thanks, Ben. Keep me posted."

He hung up the phone and walked back into the dining room.

Cathy had her cell phone in her hand. As she stared at the number pad she thought about all the big conversations she'd had with her sons over the years. She'd had big talks about school, language, choosing friends, drugs, lying and sex. During the Lewinsky scandal the news had had more sex than an R-rated film and Cathy had to explain what oral sex was about ten years too soon. Now she had to call them and somehow it seemed far worse than a few stains on a blue dress.

Marcus entered the room. "Sweetie, did you make your phone call yet?"

"Not yet. I will in a minute."

"Okay. You can call from the bedroom if you like."

"Thanks. I think I'll do that."

She went into the bedroom, bit the bullet and dialed. It rang four times.

With a frog still in his throat, Alexander answered the phone. "Hello?"

"Alex? It's Mom."

He was still groggy. "Mom, what time is it?"

"I know it's early."

He yawned. "What's going on, Mom? You never call this early on a Sunday morning."

"I have to talk to you and your brother. Speaking of Andrew, is he in his room?"

"I think so. What's wrong, Mom?"

"Let me get your brother on the line and then we'll talk."

"Okay."

She pressed flash to get another line and dialed Andrew.

"Hello?" He was just a hair more awake than Alex.

"Hi Andrew. It's Mom."

"Oh hey, Mom."

"Just hold for a second and I'll patch your brother through."

She hit the flash button, "Alex?"

"Yeah, Mom, I'm here."

"We're both here now, Mom," Andrew added.

"I know it's not like me to call you so early on a Sunday morning, but just so you know, there's another item in the gossip column today with my picture and a story about me verbally accosting two women in the bathroom at Club Z."

"What!" How could they print something like that?" Alex asked.

"Simple. They had a couple of women who were willing to tell a tall tale to sell papers."

"You went to Club Z with Marcus Fox, right, Mom?" Andrew asked.

"Yes. I did go to the bathroom and I saw the two women from this story. I didn't accost them verbally but I did scare them enough to run out the bathroom when they saw me."

"What did they say, Mom?" Andrew pressed her.

"It's not even worth mentioning."

"Mom, don't let it bother you. We know it's not true."

Cathy quietly took a deep breath. "I wouldn't do anything to embarrass you."

"You could never embarrass us in a million years, Mom." Andrew said.

"Let's see if you still feel that way when I break out the baby pictures," she joked.

They both groaned. "Not the baby pictures, Mom."

She laughed. "I promise, no more baby pictures unless of course you bring a girl home."

"Oh, please don't, Mom." Alex pleaded.

"I'll take it under advisement, okay?"

"Okay," Alex agreed.

"I guess you can go back to sleep if you want."

"French toast is on the breakfast menu once a week and it's today."

"In which hall?" "MJ,"

Andrew answered.

"You're going to walk all the way over there from your dorm? That must be some French toast." Cathy was shocked.

"It's not as good as yours but we have to settle for it until we're home for the holidays," Andrew said.

She smiled. "When you come home for the holiday in November I'll make it for you." "Are you

okay now, Mom?" Alex asked.

"I'm fine. Don't worry about me. Now go on and get dressed before you miss breakfast. I'll talk to you both later. Have a good one."

"All right, Mom."

Cathy wondered how she managed to have such great kids. She thanked God every day for them.

Marcus walked into the bedroom.

"Did you talk to your kids?"

"I did. Since I told them before they could read about it in the paper, everything will be fine."

"How did they take it?"

"Pretty well. They know that kind of behavior is not my style."

"I know that's a relief for you."

"It is." She sighed.

"I spoke with my agent and we got the ball rolling to get a retraction."

She gave him a weak smile.

"Honey, we're taking care of it, I promise."

"I know you are. I've just got a little headache, that's all."

"Do you need an Advil or something?"

"Not right now. I think it's more of a tension headache than anything else. Maybe a hot shower will help."

"That sounds like a good idea. Let me know if you need anything."

"I will."

Once in the bathroom Cathy was on autopilot. She turned on the water in the shower, adjusted the temperature and stepped into the shower. As soon as the water hit her she broke down crying. She'd put on a brave face for Marcus, E.D. and the kids; she didn't want them to see or hear her cry. A part of her wanted to go back home, crawl into bed, pull the covers up over her head and hide. The other part of her wanted to stay and face the music to prove she could rise above this mess. She closed her eyes and hoped the water would wash the tears down the drain.

Unbeknownst to Cathy, Marcus was standing in the bathroom doorway. He watched her shoulders cave in under the weight of all the week's events including that morning. His precious porcelain doll was about to break.

Suddenly Cathy felt a hand caress her neck and shoulders. She was so far in her head she hadn't heard Marcus come in. She half expected him to say something but he didn't. He just held her tight. There was no need for words, even those three little words she'd wanted to hear this morning. Somehow he knew Cathy just needed to be held. Marcus turned her around to face him, and he shut the water off. Cathy slowly opened her eyes as he wiped the water from her face. He kissed her tenderly and she felt safe for the first time that day.

***

With her bag already packed, Cathy watched Marcus pack. She was impressed with how brief his routine was.

"I just can't believe how quickly and neatly you pack your suitcase. It takes me a week just to figure out what I'm going to pack."

He chuckled. "It's taken years of practice."

"I bet."

"So have you heard from anyone else today?" he asked.

"I'm sure I have." She looked away.

He looked confused. "You don't know for sure?"

"I turned my phone off."

"I can understand why you turned it off, but what if your family was trying to reach you?"

"I can call them later."

"I know you spoke with your kids. Now do me a favor and call your sister." He handed her the phone. "All right, since you put it that way." She dialed her cell phone.

"Hello?"

"Hey, Anna, it's me."

"Cathy! I've been trying to reach you since early this morning."

"I had my phone off."

"That was a silly thing to do. You could have at least called this morning." Anna was perturbed.

"I assume you read the paper so you know why my phone was off. I called Andrew and Alex."

"So you headed the bull off at the pass."

"It's not like I had a choice in the matter. I didn't want them to hear about it from anyone else."

"I hear that."

"The boys were good about it. Still, I think I may take a trip up there before parents' day next month."

"Just to be sure, right?"

"It can't hurt."

"Are you coming back tonight?"

"Mm hmm. The Yankees are on the road this week."

"Oh yeah. That's right. Where are they going?"

"Baltimore and Tampa. They'll be back at the stadium next Monday."

"Oh, okay. Before you ask, I stocked up on yeast and flour."

"Good. That was my next question. You got more than five pounds of flour, right?"

"What do you think?"

Cathy shook her head. "Good, I need as much dough therapy as I can get."

"I'll be sure to stay out of your way."

"Good idea."

"I guess we'll talk in more detail when you're not in the same room with Marcus."

"That's the idea." She sighed. "I have to get going.

Louis will be here soon. I'll talk to you later."

"Later."

As soon as Cathy hung up, Marcus looked at her strangely. "Dough therapy? What's that?"

"You know how you use the batting cage and driving range to de-stress." "Yes."

"Bread dough lets me work out my frustrations. Hauling off and hitting the person that pissed me off in the first place is a felony. At least my method results in some of the best bread you've ever had."

He laughed. "Is that your sense of humor peeking through?"

"I guess it is." She shrugged her shoulders.

Marcus's cell phone rang. He checked the caller ID.

"Oh, honey, I have to take this call. Will you excuse me?"

"Sure." Cathy stretched out on the bed and savored her last few moments of luxury.

"What's the word, Ben?"

"I contacted Martin and met him over at the club's office to go over the videotapes. The tape showed one of the club's waitresses going into the bathroom before Cathy. Martin contacted her and it turns out that she heard everything. So we called the paper so she could give her statement."

A weight lifted off Marcus' chest. "That's fantastic, Ben."

"The paper is printing a large retraction in tomorrow's edition. You know you owe Martin big for this, right?"

Marcus was overjoyed. "Not a problem. Tell him when I get off the road just bring his nephews to the stadium. I'll hook them up."

"Done deal."

"Thanks again for doing this, Ben. It will be music to Cathy's ears."

"What are agents for?"

"Good. See you over at the stadium."

"Later, man."

Marcus couldn't wait to tell Cathy but just as he entered the room the intercom buzzed.

"Mr. Fox?"

"Yes?"

"Your car is here."

"Thank you. We'll be right down."

Cathy checked around the room to see if she'd forgotten anything.

"Okay, honey. Louis is downstairs. I'll take your bag."

"Thanks."

They left the apartment and got into the waiting car.

Louis closed the door.

"Honey, I have some good news for you."

"As long as it's not about car insurance, I'm all ears," she joked.

He laughed. "It's not about car insurance. That was a good one Cathy."

"Actually it was a little lame but I'm trying to keep my sense of humor."

"Try no more. The paper is going to print a retraction in tomorrow's edition and it's going to be a great big, obvious retraction."

Cathy was elated. "Thank you so much. How did you do it?" She hugged him.

"Ben got on it and we found out there was another woman in the bathroom who heard the whole thing. She gave her statement to the paper today."

Cathy was stunned. "How did they know there was another woman in the ladies' room?"

"From the security cameras near the ladies room. We just asked the owner of the club to review it and bingo, a waitress went in before you and came out after you."

"I had no idea."

"You can still sue. They shouldn't have printed it without confirmation." He brushed her hair out of her face. "It's nice to see that cloud lift."

"It's nice to have it lifted."

"Good." He leaned forward. "Louis, we have a little time. Can you take the scenic route?"

"Absolutely."

"Thanks." He rolled the glass between Louis and the backseat up.

"The scenic route?"

Marcus unbuttoned the top of his shirt. "Yes, the scenic route."

Cathy grew nervous. "Ah, Marcus, what are you doing?"

He kissed her. "What do you think I'm doing?"

"I don't know. I'm just a poor girl from Long Island."

He laughed. "You know that's what I love about you; you are refreshingly honest and virginal." "What you love about me?" she asked pointedly.

His mind was on one track and could not be derailed. He was kissing her neck.

"Virginal? I have two children."

"I know. But in a way your lack of…"

She interrupted him. "My lack of sexual experience or track record, for that matter, makes me like a virgin touched for the very first time."

"Yeah, sounds good to me." His neck kisses intensified.

"Stop, Marcus. That's my weak spot."

"I know."

She whispered, "Louis is in the front seat."

"He can't hear a thing once I roll the window up."

"Oh."

"You know, I am so very glad you wore a skirt." He had unbuttoned and unzipped her skirt without batting an eyelash.

"Marcus," she weakly protested.

"I'm not going to see you until Friday. I have to wait all the way to the end of the week. " He kissed her again. "I need something to tide me over."

"A steady handshake won't do?"

"Not at all."

Cathy slid down the seat. "Marcus, I've never done this before."

He hovered over her. "That's okay, baby. I promise I'll be gentle."

She didn't have a chance to say another word. Cathy finally found out what it was like to make love in the backseat of a car, an experience usually reserved for horny teenagers. She might not be a teenager, and it wasn't your average backseat, but it was worth the wait. By the time they got to the stadium, the only scenery Cathy had enjoyed was the limousine ceiling, but as far as she was concerned, it was a better view than the Grand Canyon.

Cathy pulled herself together as they got closer to the stadium.

Marcus kissed her neck again.

"You are amazing."

"So are you."

"You're very limber and flexible."

She raised her eyebrow. "You have yoga and Pilates to thank for that."

"Thank you."

She giggled and gave Marcus a squeeze. "I can't believe you're not going to be here."

"Neither can I."

"Do you feel like you're all set and tided over until Friday?"

"Yes and no."

"I beg your pardon?" she said.

"Yes, I have been tided over." He kissed her hand. "And no, I could never get enough of you."

"You scared me for a minute."

He laughed. "Don't worry, you know I'm going to call you."

"There's email and instant messaging, too."

"Hopefully next week will go by quickly, until you come to Tampa of course." He winked.

"I'm looking forward to it."

Marcus rolled the window back down. They kissed until it bordered on making out. Louis cleared his throat to get their attention.

"Excuse me, Mr. Fox, but we're here."

They quickly regained their composure. "Thanks, Louis." Marcus helped her out of the car.

He put his arms around her. "I don't want to go."

"That's sweet, honey, but this is what you love to do for a living. Have a good game."

"Thanks, sweetie."

They nearly made out again while Melvin patiently stood waiting. Cathy reluctantly pulled away.

"I don't want you to be late."

"Okay. I will definitely talk to you later."

Cathy watched him as he walked away. Then something told her to turn around. There were a couple of photographers just shooting away.

"Don't they ever get tired?"

Melvin laughed. "Never."

"I think you're right about that, Melvin." "He's definitely right about that," Ben added.

"Mr. Bradford. How are you?"

"I'm very good, thanks. And you?

"Much better and I hear that much of the credit belongs to you."

"I do what I can." He turned to Melvin. "I can take her from here, Melvin."

"All right then. Enjoy the game, Ms. Chambers."

"Thanks, Melvin."

"How about we walk and talk?" Ben asked.

"Sure."

"So how are you really, Cathy?"

"I'm good. None the worse for wear."

"That's good to hear. It's been rather eventful, to say the least."

"Eventful is the word I'd use too."

He chuckled. "You and Marcus have only been seeing each other for a short time but I can see how much he cares for you."

She smiled. "The feeling is mutual."

He looked at her. "You're different for him."

"I know. I'm not exactly a small woman."

"No, no, no. Your being different has nothing to do with your size at all."

"Oh."

"You're the first woman I've seen in a long time who is interested in Marcus the man and not Marcus the celebrity ball player."

"It's hard not to be interested in the man Marcus is. I think he's wonderful."

Ben smiled. "I can see that. By the way, in light of this morning's paper, security will escort you to the car after the game. Louis will be waiting for you."

"Terrific. Thank you."

"You're welcome."

They were at the suite.

"Well this is me. Would you like to join me?" Cathy asked.

"Thank you, but I can't. There's a seat for me down there."

"Okay. It was nice talking to you."

"Same here. I know we will see more of each other."

"From your mouth." She grinned as she entered the suite.

Just before she sat down she decided to take advantage of the suite's bar service.

"What can I get you, miss?"

"A club soda with a twist, please."

"That's not a drink," the woman behind her announced. "You don't want anything stronger, honey?" She had a heavy Southern accent.

Cathy took a closer look. She was a tall, blond, voluptuous woman. "No, I don't."

"Neither do I. I was just pulling your leg. Hey, Mr. Bartender, could you make that two club sodas?" she joked.

"Yes, ma'am."

"Lord, I hate it when they call me ma'am."

The bartender served two club sodas. He even put a little umbrella in them.

"Thank you."

"Thank you kindly, sir." She put her hand out. "I'm Phyllis La Fontaine. My friends call me Fil." She spelled it for Cathy.

Cathy shook her hand. "I'm Catherine Chambers. My friends call me Cathy."

"Nice to meet you, Cathy."

"Same here."

"Let's just you and me get to know each other before the game starts." "Sure." They sat down.

"You know, I don't know how religious you are, but I believe God sent me here today for a reason."

Cathy was immediately wary. She had no intention of indulging any more heebie jeebie people. She'd had enough of that.

"I can see you're skeptical. You see, my husband and I were supposed to go to yesterday's game but everything got fouled up. So we had to switch to today's game."

Cathy was still wary. "I see."

She smiled. "Then I read about you in today's gossip column and I thought to myself that you might be in need of someone to talk to. Now here I am in the same suite with you."

Cathy immediately got defensive. "If this is about trying to get a story or some kind of dirt on me, I'm not having it."

"No. Not at all. I guess I'm not saying this as plainly as I should. You see Cathy, twenty-three years ago I was you."

She was jolted. "I beg your pardon?"

"I'm married to Jerry La Fontaine."

"The Jerry La Fontaine who played for the Kansas City Royals?"

"The one and only. You really know your baseball, don't you?"

"For as long as I can remember."

"That's why I said I think God sent me here today so I could talk to you."

Cathy relaxed slightly. "Maybe He did."

"I wanted you to know you're not alone. As you can see, I'm a big girl and I've been one all my life. Back then they didn't have as many nice stores to buy jeans, tops and dresses for full-figured women. We had those blasted catalogs with designs so frumpy your grandmother wouldn't be caught dead in one at her own funeral."

Cathy laughed. She remembered the catalogs. "I know that's the truth."

She smiled. "Seeing as I was always a pretty good seamstress I made all my own clothes. I would look at a regular pattern, then I would cut it to fit me so I would be as fashionable as the next girl. Then one night I went out with a group of friends and lo and behold who walked in but Jerry La Fontaine. Well, I can tell you almost every woman in the place went crazy. They strutted and shook their moneymakers and put tissue in their bras. Hell, they did everything they could, short of getting buck naked in front of him."

Cathy laughed. "I bet they did. If memory serves me he was one hot ticket with the ladies."

"Oh yes, he was. Women were prepared to do anything to get his attention—every woman in the place but me. You see, I was always the fat friend who came along to hold their purses while they danced. I didn't think I could get his attention. So imagine my shock when he asked me to dance, but I got un-shocked quickly and got right on my feet. That dance led to us dating. It also led to a lot of ugliness."

"Really?"

"People would say, 'Jerry's dating that fat chick,' and he got razzed about it by some teammates and other ball players. It wasn't easy for either of us."

"I know how you feel."

"Other women were always sniping at me, too. A lot of them let me know in no uncertain terms that I wasn't good enough to be with such a dynamic and good looking man." "I know how that feels, too," Cathy sighed.

"Even some of my friends would encourage me to lose a few pounds. I knew they had good intentions, but you and I both know the road to hell is paved with good intentions."

Cathy nodded her head. "You've got that right."

"It was hard but I didn't let it change me. Jerry saw something in me he liked, regardless of my size. I had no reason to go messing with a good thing. Now we've been married for 23 years."

"Twenty-three years. That's really nice."

"What I'm trying to say to you is this: For a lot of people athletes are the closest thing to physical perfection we have here on earth. Naturally they expect the physical perfection to include their lives outside of sports. They're used to seeing professional athletes with their cookie cutter girlfriends and wives."

"You know, I never thought of it that way."

"That's why they give you such a hard time. You don't fit into the mold and they can't understand what Marcus sees in you. Just like they couldn't figure out what Jerry saw in fat old me."

"You didn't feel persecuted?"

"I know it feels like persecution but we're not witches to be burned at the stake honey, we're fat girls."

She winced. "Don't say that."

"Why not? When I say it I take hold of the power and they can't use it to hurt me."

"You have a point there."

"I know I do. I didn't go to college or take psychology but I believe in that whole self-fulfilling prophecy thing. To me, if you act like you're fat and don't deserve anything good to happen to you, then that is exactly what will happen. It has nothing to do with the fates, other people or even God. You will have shot your own self in the foot. Only one person is to blame for that."

"You know, Fil, I think you just might be the smartest person I've ever met. Whatever brought us together today, I'm glad it did."

"Aren't you sweet? It's so funny. When I saw that column this morning I said to Jerry, 'I wish I could talk to her. She must be feeling totally isolated.' "

"I was. Marcus is very supportive and understanding but I don't think he could ever really know."

"It is something that comes over time. Do yourself a favor and don't freeze him out. I think he's the kind that can handle it. Anyone who plays for the Yankees comes from good stock." She looked over her shoulder. "Shh. Don't tell Jerry I said that, he might take issue.

Cathy chuckled. "I won't."

"Good. Now I know this game is fixing to start, but I hope I've been able to help."

"More than you know, Fil. Thanks."

"You're welcome, sunshine. Anytime."

Cathy reached for her bag. "May I have your number? I'd like to call you from time to time if that's okay with you."

"Aren't you sweet? Of course you can."

They exchanged phone numbers just before the first pitch of the game.

Cathy had to admit she felt better after hearing about Fil's experience. She even thought that maybe God, the fates or both had maneuvered things to get them together. Fil had made some good points about things she'd never thought of before. Athletes were raised to the level of gods in this country. They represented the embodiment of hard work and exceptional physical prowess. For Marcus to go out with a woman who represented what was average about this country's women was sort of blasphemous. Cathy knew she had to make sure she could handle it. She wondered if maybe she could be another Fil and hang in there for the long run.

Cathy had the opportunity to meet Jerry just before the bottom of the first and he was as sweet as his Fil.
Watching them together, she wondered how anyone could have given such a cute couple a hard time.

The afternoon was a boon for both Marcus and Cathy. She made a new friend and Marcus had a stellar afternoon after hitting the cycle; a single, double, triple and a homerun. Cathy was so tickled for him. The Yankees were able to keep their winning streak alive, seven straight.

CHAPTER 16

After the game Cathy had to run the gauntlet. Two security guys flanked her to shelter her from the throng of press people who lay in wait. Security had come up with an alternate way for her to get out of the stadium but her back was acting up a bit and she wasn't physically up to the challenge. Actually she was feeling unsteady so she used the guys for a little support until she got to the car.

Louis helped her get situated in the seat, then hopped in the car and they were off. "Ms. Chambers are you all right?"

"I'm a little shaken up, but otherwise I'm fine. Thanks, Louis."

"If you start to feel worse, tell me and we'll go straight to the hospital or your doctor's office. Whatever you need."

"Thank you, Louis, I'll keep it in mind. I'm going to rest my eyes for a little while."

"I think that's a good idea."

Louis was perceptive. She wasn't doing well. Even though the whole gossip column thing was essentially over, she worried about the next headline or caption. What clever, witty little sound bites would they think of next? But for now she closed her eyes and enjoyed the quiet of the car ride. Deep down she knew something was brewing with her back. All the signs were there and if she didn't take care, she wouldn't be able to make it to Tampa with Marcus this coming weekend.

She opened her eyes to Louis gently nudging her.

"Ms. Chambers? We're home."

She yawned. "That went fast."

"It always does when you're sleeping," he joked.

She had to laugh.

He assisted her in getting out. "Are you okay to walk to the door?"

"I'm fine."

Cathy realized her back was a little worse than she'd originally thought. She had to move slowly to get to the front door.

"Let me help you inside, Ms. Chambers."

"Thanks. I'm so embarrassed. I promise I didn't have anything to drink. I'm not drunk."

"I know Ms. Chambers. Your back is acting up." He kept her upright. "Do you have your keys? It doesn't look like anyone's home."

She had the keys in her pocket. He opened the door and helped her get to the sofa in the living room.

"Louis, how did you know it was my back?"

"How does the saying go? Been there, done that. I have a bit of a back problem myself."

"Isn't that something? How did you hurt your back?"

"I was in a car accident."

"Me, too."

He laughed. "Our bad luck."

"Tell me about it." He turned around. "I'll be right back with your bag."

"Take your time," she called.

It only took a moment. "Here you go. Where should I put it down?"

"My bedroom is on the second floor so you can leave it by the stairs. I'll ask my sister or cousin to take it up for me." "Very good."

"So, Louis, how long since your accident? If you don't mind me asking."

"I don't mind at all. It's been about six years now."

"I'm double that number."

"You don't suppose we were hit by the same guy, do you?" he laughed.

"I wouldn't be surprised," she grinned.

"You should take it easy and not let these crazy fools in the press bother you."

"That's easier said than done."

"The bottom line is you have to take care of yourself and let things roll off your back."

"That's a tall order but I'll try."

"I'm going to hold you to that." He looked at his watch. "Well, Ms. Chambers, I must be heading back. Are you sure you're all right?"

"I'm fine. Either my sister or my cousin will be along shortly."

"Very good then. Have a good evening."

"You, too."

***

Cathy was awakened by the rattle of keys at the door. "Hello? Is anybody home?" Madison called.

"I'm right here in the living room."

"Oh there you are. I didn't know you were back."

"I just got home a little while ago."

He sat down. "So it seems that I'm not the only one who had an interesting weekend."

Cathy's curiosity got the better of her. "What happened to you this weekend? Did you have another run in with that guy?"

"I took out a restraining order to cover all contact between him and me. Still, he's not listening. He's been sending me coded messages from someone else's computer," Madison said.

"But you're on to him. Have the police discovered where the messages are coming from?"

"Not yet. As far as the cops are concerned this is a low priority civil matter. Meaning, they will enforce the restraining order but they can't do much more than that. Unless he violates the order in a clear, definitive way, their hands are tied."

"But he's on record as assaulting you. Are you supposed to twiddle your thumbs?"

"That's what it seems like. I had to upgrade the security system at my apartment and I don't walk to my car alone now. The whole thing has me freaked."

"I know how you feel."

"Speaking of freaked out, I know you hit the roof when you saw that garbage in the paper."

"Freaked out hardly begins to cover it. I was really beside myself. Thank God Marcus had the kind of clout to handle it. There will be a retraction in tomorrow's paper.

"How did that happen? They usually hide behind the first amendment."

"There was a fourth woman in the bathroom. She heard the whole thing go down and will refute the story."

Anna casually walked in holding her briefcase. "Hey, you're back."

"I just got in a little while ago. Why the briefcase? It is Sunday right?"

"Yeah. I had to help someone with a tax question."

"Oh."

"It seems like I'm here in time to hear what really went down in the bathroom at that club."

"I'm actually getting sick of replaying this in my mind so I will only go through this once more. Okay? I don't mean to sound horrible but I'm tired." "Go ahead," Madison said.

Cathy recounted what happened in detail. The way she saw it, if she gave them the straight skinny they'd be able to tell everyone, including her mother and father, what went on.

Anna was pacing like a bull. "I can't believe you didn't jump out and beat their asses for that cow remark."

"Anna, I didn't do anything to them but say a few words and you see how much happened without me laying one hand on them."

"It's a good thing Marcus got a retraction, but you can still sue." Madison was emphatic.

"I plan to. I think E.D. is getting in touch with Frank tomorrow morning to set something up.

"Good. They should pay for this. That caption was God-awful. What would possess anyone to write something like that about another human being?"

"It's because being fat is the last form of acceptable discrimination in this country. Hell there's a whole multi billion dollar weight loss industry based on the fact that no one wants to be called fat. I never thought about it until Mrs. Phyllis La Fontaine brought a few things to my attention."

The name rang a bell for Anna. "That last name sounds really familiar. Is she related to Jerry La Fontaine from the Royals?"

"She's his wife *and* she went through the same thing when she and Jerry were dating. Her theory is athletes are perfect so there is a certain amount of perfection that's expected of people around them. So when a perfect man dates someone who is less than perfect, some people seem to go crazy."

"It's unfortunate that most of those people are in the media," Madison observed.

"Isn't that the truth?" Anna stopped to look at Cathy more closely; she could see something was wrong. "You don't look like yourself, Cathy. What's going on?"

"My back is acting up a bit."

Madison shook his head. "I think the stress is really setting it off."

Cathy shrugged. "It's because I haven't worked out in a couple of days. I have my meds. Things will be fine in the morning when I go back to the gym."

Anna raised her eyebrows. "I don't know if that's a good idea. I think you should make an appointment with Dr. Adams to be sure."

After the few days she'd had Cathy was defiant. "I'll make an appointment but I am heading to the gym in the A.M. as usual. I also plan to make it into the city office this week. Don't worry, I have to see Dr. Adams anyway to get checked out before I fly out on Friday."

Madison raised his glasses. "Fly where?"

"Tampa. The Yankees are playing the D-Rays at Tropicana Field and Marcus asked me if I would come down for the series."

"Sounds good to me. I think I'll come along. I have some vacation owed me from the state," Anna said. "I could use a break from my whole Cape Fear theme and going somewhere warm where the women are still showing some skin sounds like the right medicine to me."

"I don't need a couple of babysitters, you know," Cathy quipped.

"I'm not babysitting anybody. Roger might go so he can visit some friends who live in the area."

Cathy knew they wouldn't take no for an answer. It was nice to know she had family support. She was grateful but she didn't let on.

Just as Anna was about to leave, she noticed something a little different about Cathy again. "Are you using a different conditioner? Your hair looks really shiny and full."

Cathy automatically started fussing with her hair. "No, I haven't changed conditioners or anything."

"She has sex hair."

Cathy was taken aback. "What the hell are you talking about, Madison?"

"You've never heard of sex hair?" He seemed shocked. "It's basically the result of a lot of showers for two without wearing old lady shower caps and air drying your hair."

Cathy playfully threw a napkin at him. "Who asked you?"

"All of that gives you amazing looking hair?"

"Don't front, Anna. I've seen you with sex hair plenty of times."

"Cathy's right. Who the hell asked you?"

"I'm just calling it like I see it."

Anna put her hands on her hips. "Yeah. We'll just see how many ladies you meet wind up with sex hair this weekend."

Madison simply grinned.

***

Even though she was more active now than ever, Cathy still got up Monday morning at four for the gym. Besides, with Marcus in Baltimore her aerobic activities were now limited to power walking on the track.

As she walked out into the fall-like morning, Cathy took a deep breath. *Thank God, it feels like fall*, she thought. A few minutes later she pulled in the gym's parking lot. All the usual suspects were in their designated spots waiting for the doors to open.

Cathy turned the engine off when Melody tapped on the window. "Oh!" She rolled down the window.

"Melody, you nearly scared me to death."

"Sorry I scared you, girl."

"I didn't see you walk over."

"I figured I would come over to you before the rush."

"Before what rush? The rush to get in and get a good machine?"

She bent down. "I'll tell you in a minute."

In the rearview mirror Cathy could see the receptionist opening the doors.

"What's going on?"

"Come on and I'll tell you."

Grabbing her water bottle Cathy stepped out. They walked to the door.

"You're the talk of the gym."

Dread came over Cathy. "Oh God, the Sunday paper, right?"

"I'm afraid so. But I have to say that I didn't believe any of that crap anyway. However, I was a little insulted that you didn't tell me you're dating Marcus Fox."

"I'm sorry, Melody. I only started going out with him last week."

"Lord, you wouldn't know that from the way the papers print it."

Cathy stopped before they got any closer to the entrance.

"Do I want to go in there? The paper is printing a retraction today, but the damage is done, right?"

"As long as they spelled your name right, who gives a rat's tail about some sleazy old gossip column?"

"But these are the people I exercise with almost every single day."

"So? You have friends here and they support you. Not a one of them believed the newspaper."

Cathy took a deep breath and hoped she was right. "Let's go."

They swiped their cards and went upstairs to the track.

When Cathy and Melody began their six-and-a-half mile trek around the track, Cathy noticed they got a lot more attention than they had on other days. Some waved hello while others who only occasionally spoke broke their necks to look at her. *What on earth is everyone hoping to see?* Cathy wondered. *Marcus isn't in my back pocket.*

Melody took a cleansing breath. "Before we get going talking about anything else…how are you feeling?"

Cathy was relieved at the innocuous question. "I'm hanging in there. I came this morning in the hope of feeling better."

"Stress getting to you?"

"Yeah, just a bit."

Melody looked her over "You're glowing, but you do look a little uncomfortable. Are you sure working out is okay?"

"Sure. I've been working out five days a week for the last six or seven years and it's been good for me and my back."

Melody didn't look convinced. "Have you seen your doctor?"

"I have an appointment this week. Okay? Believe me, I have my hands full with my sister and cousin on my case. I promise I'm taking care of myself. Now can we just walk?"

"Okay. I was just checking. Now on to the news. Girl, people have been asking me about you nonstop since Saturday and Sunday."

"I'm sure they have."

"Of course they have. Marcus Fox isn't just any guy. He's a New York Yankee and that makes him damn near royalty in New York."

Cathy smirked. "You're right about that, too."

Melody pressed the point. "Don't hold out on me, give me the scoop."

"As soon as you tell me what happened with Jason."

"Touché! Well, if you're not going to give me details at least tell me something."

"As nice as he seems on television, Marcus is even nicer in person."

Melody looked disappointed. "That's sweet and all, but I wanted a juicy little tidbit."

"There's nothing little about him," Cathy said coyly.

Melody's mouth hung open. "Ooh, girl, you are bad."

They laughed.

"Seriously, Melody, it's been very nice with the exception of the press."

"I hear that."

"So how are things going with you know who?"

Melody's usually warm grim turned mischievous. "Not bad. He and I had dinner out the other night." Cathy was shocked. "Really?"

"He and Miss Thing broke up and now it's about him and me."

"Get out of here!" *Hallelujah! It's about time*, Cathy thought, though she knew better than to say it out loud. Besides, Melody was happy for the first time in a long time and so was she.

Before their high profile date in public Jason had treated Melody like his back door girl. It had come as a shock to Cathy that even Melody with her looks, charm and intelligence was insecure and would put up with someone like Jason. Cathy didn't think he was in Melody's league by a long shot.

While they chatted it up on their umpteenth lap, Cathy noticed a woman on the Nautilus equipment.

"Melody, the woman in the blue shorts and tank top keeps watching us."

"Where is she?"

"In the Nautilus room."

Melody slyly turned her head. "I've seen her before. She seems to keep to herself most of the time but I have seen her talking a blue streak a few times."

"Oh really?"

The five A.M. crowd was a lot like a family sitcom. There was a regular cast of players, and new people only guest starred until they met the required number of 10 straight early morning visits to the gym. In other words, when a new face showed up in the morning the regulars noticed.

Melody and Cathy continued their walk until six thirty when they completed their six and a half miles. That was Cathy's cue to leave. As she walked downstairs, she looked up to see the same woman from the Nautilus room on her cell phone, trying to act as if she weren't watching Cathy on her way out.

"Cathy!"

She looked over her shoulder to see Benjamin running to her.

"Hey, Ben. How are you?"

"Not too bad. I guess you're done for the day."

"Oh yes."

"Let me walk you to your car."

Cathy was a little taken aback but she went with it. Ben was an accountant like her sister and while he wasn't a stick in the mud, he didn't do anything just for the sake of doing it.

"So, Ben, we're outside. Anything wrong?"

"There's something I want to tell you about that new blond who's been working out here."

"Yeah."

"She's been asking a lot of questions about you. And if you press her she acts like she knows you."

Cathy was alarmed. "I've never seen her before in my life."

"I figured that. But there was all that stuff in the paper and you're going out with Marcus Fox, so I figured there was a connection."

"Thank you, Ben. You don't know how much I appreciate it."

"I have one more thing for you. Supposedly her name is Lisa Spellman. Maybe you can have somebody from Marcus' camp check her out."

"Thank you again, Ben."

"Anytime." He waved and went back inside.

Cathy hopped in the car to head to Dunkin Donuts to get her coffee and a paper. She filed away the name Lisa Spellman until she had a chance to ask Marcus about her.

The usual Dunkin Donuts crowd was lined up with Johnny, Itzhak and Avila running an assembly line of made to order coffee in various sizes.

"Haven't seen you in a long time," Johnny joked. "I've been out of town."

"Oh. Okay." He handed her an extra-large, extra light coffee with half and half and three sugars, along with a paper.

"Thanks. Have a good day all."

Coffee in hand, she opened the paper as soon as she got in the car. There was the retraction big and bold on the gossip page. She felt vindicated as she drove away.

Planning to work at home, Cathy took a quick shower as soon as she got home. Dressed in comfortable clothes, she went back to the kitchen to have coffee and read the paper. She heard her sister getting ready.

"Cathy!" she yelled.

"I'm right here in the kitchen!"

Anna walked into the kitchen. "Can I borrow your brown leather pumps? This black pair just isn't working with this outfit."

Cathy looked at Anna's feet, then at her chocolate brown suit. "I see what you mean. They're in my closet.

Want me to get them?"

"No you sit. I'll run up and get them." Cathy continued reading the paper.

Anna returned with the shoes on. "This looks much better. Don't you think?"

Cathy looked up. "Much better."

"Yeah. Wait a minute. You have the paper. Is the retraction in there?"

Cathy showed her the paper. "Big and bold."

"Good. So how were things at the gym today? Anybody ask questions or make you feel weird?" "Melody asked me directly for the straight skinny. Otherwise it was pretty routine except for this one blond woman. Ben told me she's been asking questions about me."

"Sounds like she's a reporter or something."

"Who the hell wants to know about me? By myself I am not that interesting. Anyway, I'm going to ask Marcus if her name sounds familiar."

"Good idea." Anna looked in the refrigerator. "What do you want to do for dinner tonight?"

"I haven't really thought about it."

"I'll pick up a rotisserie chicken at the supermarket. Keep things simple."

"Sounds like a plan to me," Cathy agreed.

Anna looked at the clock. "I have to get a move on. It's time to put fear in the hearts of school boards everywhere."

Cathy snickered. "You go get 'em, killer." "See ya later."

CHAPTER 17

The Yankees were in their designated exercise room for the morning. Some of the players weight trained with free weights while others used the Nautilus equipment or got their cardio in on the treadmills. Marcus spotted Mark while he did some old-fashioned crunches on the floor.

"Come on, man. You're almost there, just two more." Marcus sounded more like a drill sergeant than a teammate.

Mark groaned but managed to crank out the remaining two sit-ups.

Marcus clapped. "That's the way you do it!"

Arm over his face Mark lay on the floor. "Easy for you to say, you're not chasing a two-year-old all over the house."

Marcus helped him to his feet. "I guess energy is boundless at his age."

Mark wiped his face. "Are you kidding? When he goes to sleep Pam and I look for the energy outlet he's plugged into. The way we see it, we can either disconnect it or see if we can plug in, too."

Marcus laughed. "Let's get some water."

They grabbed a couple of bottles from the cooler and sat down.

Mark guzzled half the bottle. "That hit the spot."

Marcus looked up at the television. "Good, it's supposed to cool down here tonight."

Mark wiped his brow. "That's good. Baltimore isn't any fun in the heat. Camden Yards is a nice ballpark, but you would think someone would have suggested a dome."

"Somebody probably did but got shot down."

Mark nodded his head and changed the subject. "So. I didn't have a chance to ask you how Cathy is doing?"

"She's good now. She wasn't yesterday."

"I can imagine. I saw the paper."

"Can you believe what they print?"

"Actually I do. Nothing surprises me anymore."

"The woman is amazing; she raised her sons as a single parent and helped build a successful literary agency."

"True, but she's not made of steel."

"Sometimes you can forget that." Marcus sighed. "But when I saw how upset she was I really thought she was going to collapse."

"You handled it, right?"

"Got it straightened out before we got to the game."

"I was going to ask you how but I know the answer, Ben."

Ben had just entered the exercise room.

"Somebody say my name?" he smiled.

"Your ears must be burning. We were just talking about you," Mark said.

"Well, I just came by to deliver the New York and local papers personally."

He gave them to Marcus, who immediately opened to the gossip column.

Club Goers Fabricated Story About Marcus's Girl

The two women who reported they were verbally accosted by Marcus Fox's ladylove Catherine Chambers fabricated the story, according to a witness who overheard what actually transpired in the ladies room. The two club goers were arrested on drug possession charges Sunday evening and are awaiting arraignment. We at The Journal *wish to apologize for any grief the erroneous story caused Ms. Chambers, Mr. Fox and their respective families.*

"It's a retraction kicked up a notch. Bam!" Ben joked.

"Thanks again, Ben."

"I bet Cathy's happy about it," Mark said.

"Yeah." Marcus reached into his pocket. "I think I'll give her a call. Excuse me."

"Don't mind us," Mark joked.

He went into the hallway and dialed Cathy.

***

For Cathy there was no such thing as a light day. She delayed booting her computer up to see how many new emails she had. Normally Cathy got ninety emails or more a day but since she hadn't been online in a few days she knew there would be an electronic avalanche. Just as she was about to assess the damage, the phone rang.

"Hello?"

"Hey, baby." Marcus's tone was so low and sexy Cathy felt a chill run down her spine.

"Hi. I was just thinking about you." "You were? Did you see the paper?" he asked.

"Yes, and thank you again. I can't tell you how relieved I am."

"I know, honey." He paused and absorbed the sound of her voice. "I miss you, honey. I wish you could come down now."

Cathy smiled from ear to ear. "Me, too, sweetie but I have a lot of things to wrap up here. I'll be in Tampa on Friday."

"I can't wait."

"Neither can I." She paused. "I don't want to change the subject, Marcus, but does the name Lisa Spellman sound familiar to you?"

He groaned. "She's a freelance supermarket tabloid writer. Why? Wait a minute, is she snooping around you?"

"Apparently so. She's been coming to my gym for the past few mornings asking a lot of questions about me. Should I confront her?"

"Don't get in her face. You won't come off well when she writes about it."

"I don't want to have to worry about this kind of thing at the gym. I go there so I can work out and decompress before my day gets going."

"Ignore her. She will eventually go away when she figures out there is no story."

"If you say so, honey." Another thought came to her. "Oh, before I forget, I have to tell you my sister and cousin have decided to come with me. Is that a problem?"

"No, of course not."

"I'm glad. They won't cramp our style. Anna's bringing her fiancé and Madison is on the hunt for women."

"It's all good, baby."

"It really is."

"Well, sweetie, I'd better get back to the exercise room. I'll talk to you later."

"Okay, honey. Later."

Marcus was about to go back in when he stopped mid step.

He dialed his cell phone.

"Information."

"Yes. Can you give me a listing for a florist in Amityville, New York?"

"Sure. I show three listings for Amityville. Country Petals, Johnson's Florist and Wee Bee Country Florists."

"Can you connect me with Wee Bee?"

"Sure."

***

Even though her accident had happened nearly 12 years earlier, Cathy's back acted up every now and then. She even referred to herself as a barometer with legs since she seemed to be able to predict changes in the weather. However, today was a perfectly sunny and cloudless day and her back hurt anyway. She waited a few minutes and tried to get up again with the same result. *This isn't good. I can't have my back acting up this weekend,* she thought. She picked up the phone to see if Dr. Adams could see her sooner; thankfully he could. *My back hurts too much to drive. I'll call Dad.*

"Hello?"

"Hi Dad. How was your trip?"

"Not bad. I had a good time." He sounded chipper.

"Good. Are you doing anything special this morning dad?"

"No. Just leafing through all the newspapers and mail. Why? What's wrong?"

"I need to get to Dr. Adams and I can't drive."

"Your back again, huh? I'll be right over."

"Thanks, Dad."

Despite being in the path of Elizabeth's wrath, Cathy and Anna's dad, Ted Chambers, didn't live too far from them. Always an active man, he'd played a major role in raising his grandsons and with the boys in school, at 64 he was making up for lost time traveling. He still maintained a CPA office and a roster of clients but he made time for charity events, political fundraisers and appropriately-aged ladies. Anna and Cathy had friends whose fathers and mothers pranced around with younger men and women. They were really pleased that their Dad stuck to appropriately-aged ladies.

Cathy's dad made it to Dr. Adams's office in 20 minutes. It was a light late morning so they took her into the examining room immediately. The nurse took her blood pressure and temperature before Dr. Adams came in and did a full examination. Still not crazy about being naked in front of anyone, Cathy was happy to get dressed again.

"Knock, knock?" Dr. Adams was his jovial self as always.

"Hey, Dr. Adams."

He sat down on the stool." I'm only going to confirm what you already know. You're having intermittent back trouble." He put on his serious doctor face. "I read the paper and I know you've been under a lot of stress recently."

God, even my doctor reads the gossip page. Cathy groaned. "Basically I'm falling apart and I need to get back on track."

"So all of the symptoms seem to correspond to the upheaval in your life."

"Yes."

"The back problem might seem sudden but your back has probably bothered you for a while."

She thought for a moment. "I think you might be right about that. So what can I do? I'm planning to go away this coming weekend and I need this to go away."

"I know you are not one for the steroid course, so that will always be a last resort."

"Good."

"You're going to take pills. I think the medications combined with a lighter schedule this week might do the trick. I'll write the prescriptions but I want to see you back here on Thursday before you go away. Is that clear, young lady?"

"Crystal clear. I promise I'll follow doctor's orders."

"That's my girl."

He wrote three prescriptions and sent her home. Cathy had been with Dr. Adams since her accident and felt confidence in him. After leaving the office, they filled the prescriptions and went straight home.

While Cathy settled herself on the downstairs living room sofa for a while, her dad started pacing.

Cathy watched. She knew he was leading up to something.

"So what's going on, Cathy?"

"A whole lot, Dad. What do you want to hear about first?"

"You can start with what led to this emergency doctor's visit."

Her dad was a firm believer in the connection between the body and mind. Cathy decided it would be way too much information to talk about sleeping with Marcus. She simply answered, "Basically, Dad, I'm dating Marcus Fox."

"When did this happen?" He was taken aback. When he left for Virginia Cathy had been dating her computer.

"A couple of weeks ago."

"So far that doesn't sound all that bad to me." "Not until the gossip columnists entered the picture. They got a quote from his ex who called him a chubby chaser. I'm not exactly the type of woman Marcus Fox usually dates."

"He can't date who he wants? He has to please the public?"

"I know, Dad, but that wasn't the worst of it." She took a deep breath. "The gossip column reported an incident that supposedly took place in the ladies' room of Club Z between two women and me. They accused me of verbally accosting them and chasing them from the bathroom."

He looked completely baffled. "Wait a minute. They accused you of what?"

"You heard it right, Dad. My name was dragged through the mud Sunday morning."

He was alarmed. "Did you get it straightened out?"

"Actually Marcus did. There's a retraction in today's paper."

"Good. And that's what got you all stressed out?"

"That and a lot of other things."

"Like what?"

"It brought back a lot of stuff about growing up in Mom's religion and how I feel about myself in general."

"What does that mean?" He was perplexed.

Cathy's experience with the paper emboldened her to say what was on her mind. "Listen, Dad, I know you didn't want to have anything to do with her church so you got out. Anna and I didn't, we couldn't."

Her father's countenance changed. "I told your mother she was raising you two to live in a box."

"The box might as well have been a coffin. Any chance for a real life went out the window. We didn't have a choice. We had to conform or face the fallout."

"I've always said I take 99.9% of the blame for what happened between your mother and me. I shouldn't have done what I did."

"Once you left, Mom needed to be right more than ever."

"I never knew any of this before. Why didn't you tell me how you felt?" Her father looked confused.

"I wanted to be a good daughter to both parents. I put on a happy face and got on with it until I couldn't take it anymore. Once I was an adult the decision was mine but by then I was afraid to leave. Alex and Andrew are the reasons I broke out of the box; I never wanted them to feel out of place like I do." Tears poured down her face. "God, I don't think I've cried this much in my life."

Her father hugged her even though they'd never been a touchy feely family.

"I'm sorry. This dating stuff must be bringing the past to the surface." She wiped her eyes. "Suddenly I have to confront things I've kept bottled up."

"I see what you mean. You have to come to terms with yourself. Dating these high profile types you can't afford to wear your heart or your insecurities on your sleeve."

"I have to be a Teflon bombshell." She laughed a little.

Her father laughed. "That's true." He paused. "I don't know Marcus apart from his baseball stats. Is he a stand-up guy?"

Cathy smiled. "He is, Dad. He's really good to me."

"Good enough to seat you in a luxury suite?"

"Twice."

Her father laughed. "Now you know how the other half lives. All the big muckity mucks sit there."

"You know who I met there, Dad? Jerry La Fontaine and his wife Phyllis."

He was impressed. "Third baseman for the Kansas City Royals."

"They were really nice. I exchanged numbers with Fil. She's a Southern pistol."

"That's great." He nodded. "So you're really dating again."

"Yes, I am actually dating again after a two-year hiatus."

"I'm glad to hear it."

"I'm also going to Tampa for the series at Tropicana Field."

"Good. You know, Cathy, you kicked the walls of the box down a long time ago. Now all you have to do is let go of the guilt trip you feel for actually living your own life."

"I know, Dad."

"Maybe this weekend getaway is just what you need."

"I can't wait. Anna, Roger and Madison are coming too."

He stood up. "You'll have a good time."

"I think so too. It's the main reason I asked you to take me to Dr. Adams. I wanted to get checked out before the trip."

"You have to follow the doctor's orders."

"I will, Dad."

"Good. Oh, I almost forgot. I might need you to book a flight online for me."

"All right, Dad, whenever you're ready."

"Thanks. I'll give you the details either before the weekend or early next week."

He kissed her forehead. "Feel better. Love you."

"Love you, too."

Unlike Marcus, Cathy had never expected to live life in the spotlight. As his talent for baseball grew, the talent scouts began showing up in junior high and with them came the media. He went into the Yankee farm system with a star's aura everyone could see.

Things had been quite different for Cathy. She'd had a few friends in high school but was more focused on school work; it was a convenient cover for her lack of social life. Once she became a parent she hid behind Alex and Andrew, staying as involved in their activities as much and as often as possible. As a writer she hid behind her words. E.D. had practically had to force her to take a head shot for the book. Then she'd become an agent.

Being a parent and agent had given her an invisible cloak of sorts.

Now her sons had gone off to college and out of nowhere she'd fallen in love with a superstar. She was no longer invisible. She had to learn to deal with it.

***

A short time later Cathy awoke to the sounds of someone calling her name and banging on the front door. The banging got louder. She got up slowly. "Wait a minute! I'll be right there!" she shouted. "Who is it?"

"It's me Cathy, E.D."

She opened the door. "E.D., what are you doing here?"

He walked in. "Sorry for the banging but when I couldn't get you on the phone I decided to come out here and see how you were doing for myself."

"Thanks, hon, I appreciate your concern but I'm doing fine. Come on in. Have a seat."

She went back to the living room sofa.

He took his jacket off. "So what's shaking?"

"I went to the doctor this morning for a check-up." He sat down. "So what's the verdict?"

"He gave me medication to deal with my back flare up and told me to take it easy for a few days."

"But you're okay, right?"

"Yeah. I'm fine. I'm used to it. Now what's going on that you left the office to come out here?" He looked uncomfortable.

She had a lump in her throat. "Just spit it out, E.D. What is it? Are the authors upset with the publicity stuff?"

"Oh no. Nothing like that. If anything they were pissed about how the press treated you."

"Then what has you so tense?"

"We have a situation with the celebrity cookbook project."

Cathy was alarmed. "I thought that was under control. I just spoke to Jennifer a few days ago."

"She's having a little trouble getting some of the releases and the deadline is fast approaching."

"The releases or the recipes? She should have the photo and recipe releases along with the permission forms."

"Are you sure she has them?"

"Do me a favor. Go upstairs into my office and get her files out. I have copies of everything she's received so far. Thanks."

Within a couple of minutes E.D. was back downstairs with three thick files.

E.D. leafed through two of the files. "Cathy, it looks like we have everything we need as far as the releases and permission forms go."

"So we're covered. Check the recipe file. I have a list of every contributor and their representative. Whoever isn't checked off needs another friendly but firm call."

"Are you sure you're up to tackling this?"

"As long as we tackle it together it isn't a problem." She pointed towards the kitchen. "By the way there's a thermal carafe with fresh coffee in the kitchen if you want."

"Coffee always sounds good to me."

"Knock yourself out."

E.D. and Cathy spent the next couple of hours gently twisting arms. Normally these were the kinds of details they left to the author, but they made an exception for Jennifer since her project was much more complicated. Jennifer had to coordinate all the legal documentation and she had the added task of testing the recipes. E.D. and Cathy set about doing what they could to help make things easier as the deadline approached.

Cathy and E.D. were really in the groove when the doorbell rang.

"Are you expecting anyone?"

"No. But it could be a medical supply delivery for my sister."

"I'll get it." He got up.

The doorbell rang again. "Just a minute!" she shouted.

E.D. answered the door. Two minutes later he came in with a beautiful floral arrangement.

"This is all yours, Ms. Chambers."

She was tickled pink. "For me? Oh, how lovely." E.D. handed the flowers to her.

"Don't forget to read the card."

card read: *"Just wanted to you to know I'm thinking about you. I hope you enjoy the flowers. The flowers represent every day since I met you and every day to come until we're together again. Love, Marcus.*"

"It was so sweet of him to send me flowers." "Ahem! The florist isn't finished," E.D. said.

"What?"

Bouquet upon bouquet filed through the front door. An astonished Cathy had to get up to direct the floral flow of traffic. By the time they were finished she had a total of 10 very large floral arrangements.

E.D. looked around. "It looks like a floral shop in here."

"I just can't believe it. I don't think I've ever gotten as many flowers in my whole life." She beamed. E.D. smiled. "Then it's about time."

"Oh E.D., I think I left my bag in the kitchen. Could you please get it for me so I can give our delivery guy here a tip?"

"Sure."

"I appreciate that, miss, but it's been covered. Have a great day."

E.D. turned around. "And the man covers tipping the driver too. I'd better not let my girlfriend hear about this."

She laughed. "How much is it worth to you?"

"Oh now you're going to blackmail me, huh?"

"I said how much is it worth to you? Maybe a three day weekend pass from the office?"

"Hallelujah! It's about time you started to enjoy the weekends like the rest of us working people."

She threw a pillow at him. "I enjoy weekends."

"No, you don't. You hate weekends. You're a workaholic."

Cathy knew it was the truth and backed down. "Maybe there's a little truth to that statement. This weekend is different. This weekend I want to go on a little trip to Tampa."

"The Yankees are in Tampa this weekend."

"How did you know?"

"I saw it marked on your Yankee calendar. You have every game marked down."

"Oh. Anyway, do we have a deal?"

"Done."

"That also means no phone calls, emails or anything office related for three whole days."

"Fine with me. Are you sure you won't be tempted?"

"I'm sure I can find something to distract me."

"More like someone."

Cathy took in a big whiff of the flowers. "It smells so nice in here. How many more calls do we need to make?"

"Four. Tell you what, I'll get to them while you call and thank your guy."

"Thank you."

She dialed Marcus and got his voice mail.

"Hey, Marcus. It's Cathy. I just wanted to thank you for all the flowers. They are just beautiful. It really made my day, week, month and maybe even year. You're a sweetheart. Hopefully we'll have the chance to talk later but if we don't, good luck tonight. I'll be watching."

"It's so nice to see you happy," E.D. said when she disconnected.

"I like it too. Still, I'll be happier once we get this stuff out of the way."

"You're a real slave driver," E.D. joked.

"Hey, if it gets our clients where they need to be…"

***

Whether it was the coffee or the intoxicating smell of the flowers, by mid-afternoon E.D. and Cathy had secured all the missing recipes for Jennifer. Mission accomplished. E.D. put his coat on. "Well, that was productive."

"Good thing. Now Jennifer can concentrate on testing the recipes and has enough time to address any changes the recipes might need."

"I had them fax copies to this office as well as

Manhattan."

"With the hard copies going to Jennifer, right?"

"Right. I'll have one of the assistants fax over the information to Jennifer."

"Good. She'll be so relieved."

"Anyway, partner, we got the job done and I still have time to catch the off-peak ticket into the city."

"Okay. Thanks for helping me with my flowers."

"Enjoy them. I'll talk to you later."

"Cool. See ya."

***

With some time to spare before heading over to Camden Yards, Marcus, John, Mark, Juan and Tim decided to have an early dinner at Bo Brooks's Crab House. The men weren't shy; they enjoyed all the seafood delights Maryland is known for, along with light liquid refreshment.

Although they were in enemy territory, people were excited to see the Yankee players in person. After signing a few autographs they decided to head back to the hotel. As Marcus and the gang walked out, there was another bit of celebrity commotion outside.

"What do you suppose that's all about?" John asked.

Juan tried to get a look. "I can't see anything."

As they continued to walk, people parted like the Red Sea and there stood Cybil George, Marcus' ex-girlfriend.

"This can't be good," Tim mumbled.

Marcus was shocked. "What is she doing here?"

"I don't know but I think we're about to find out. She's headed this way," Mark said.

Blond hair bouncing, Cybil George practically glided over to Marcus.

"Hi, Marcus."

"Hi, Cybil."

"Fancy seeing you here." She tried to be light and breezy.

"We're playing the Orioles tonight. We just came out to get something to eat."

"Oh. Hi guys." She waved.

They waved back but no one said anything.

"Do you have a photo shoot or fashion show here?"

"No. You know how I always wanted to get into the movie business?"

"Yeah."

"I'm shooting a movie in the area."

"You're shooting around Camden Yards?"

"As a matter of fact I am." "Where's the crew?" Mark asked.

Cybil sighed. "We wrapped up shooting for the day. I was going to get something to eat with a couple of friends."

"I didn't know she ate," Juan whispered.

"So do you recommend this place?"

"It's good." He looked at his watch. "Listen, Cybil, it was nice to see you but we've really got to bounce."

"Okay. I understand."

"Thanks. Good seeing you. Take care." "Is that all I get?" she asked.

"I'm sorry?"

She smiled. "How about a little kiss for old time's sakes?"

Marcus was taken off guard when she suddenly kissed him dead center on his mouth.

"See? That didn't hurt, did it?" She grinned.

Cybil didn't get the rise she wanted. "Okay, Cybil. Take care." Marcus walked away as if nothing had happened. As soon as they were out of sight range Marcus wiped the lipstick off and got in the car.

"What was that all about?" Tim asked.

"I have no idea. She said she's shooting a movie nearby," Marcus answered.

"That's some coincidence," Mark said. "It

does seem suspicious," Juan added.

"You know what? I think so, too. But I really don't want to devote any more energy to Cybil's motives and machinations. I did my time, three years hard labor. I am not going back."

Another word didn't have to be said. The guys knew Marcus meant business. He was through with Cybil. But they weren't sure if she was through with him.

CHAPTER 18

Cathy took one arrangement upstairs with her and looked around her room to find the perfect place for it. She wanted to make sure the flowers were the first thing she saw when she got up in the morning and the last thing at night.

"Good God! Where did all these flowers come from?" Anna shouted from downstairs.

"Did somebody die? Or did somebody get married?" Madison echoed.

They came upstairs.

"Cathy! It looks like the florist set up shop in the living room."

"I know. Isn't it great?" She beamed.

"Marcus didn't just send you flowers; he sent you the whole damn shop," Madison said.

"That's fine with me."

"I guess we'd better get smoking on those plane reservations." Anna laughed.

"I'm doing just that." She tapped away on the laptop.

"Jet Blue goes to Tampa, right?" Madison asked.

"Yeah. I'm checking the schedule now. This is for Friday so we need to book it now."

"We're kind of last minute but it's nearly fall so the fares shouldn't be too jacked up."

"Okay, we can get a morning flight at 8:15 or 10:15 out of JFK."

"10:15 sounds good. It's a little after rush hour."

"What are you talking about, Madison? We have to get there before 10:15 so we'll be in the thick of rush hour."

"It's okay, Anna. We'll use my agency's car service," Cathy said.

"Good. I hate traffic and I really hate long term parking."

"You don't have to worry about either. A 10:15 flight will get us in just before two. And for our return trip we can leave at 5:45 P.M. and be back in New York a little after seven."

"Sounds perfect, Cathy. Book it."

Within a few minutes they were confirmed with tickets printing out on Cathy's office printer across the hall.

"So, Cathy, have you called to thank Mr. Fox? Or are you waiting to make it up close and personal?" Madison teased.

"As a matter of fact I called to thank him earlier. And you need not concern yourself as to how I might thank him in person."

He feigned illness. "Too much information."

"Okay, cut it out you two. I can't believe I'm the youngest and I always have to break you two up," Anna said.

"Give me a break," Madison groaned.

Anna rolled her eyes. "Anyway, moving right along, did you see the doctor today?"

"Dad took me this morning. I had a check-up and Dr. Adams put me on medication to help with my back."

"So no steroids?"

A chill went down Cathy's back. "Definitely not. I refuse to live through that again."

Madison nodded his head in agreement. "I hear that."

She closed her laptop. "I'm getting a little hungry. Did you stop by the store?"

"I did but all they had was honey mustard. I figured we could order in."

"Cool. I could go for a chicken gyro."

"Works for me. Greek food it is." Anna turned to Madison "You'd better write this down before you call to order."

"Since when am I the waiter?"

"Since I decided I might not be able to take you to work again this week."

"You are some controlling witches in here."

"Takes one to know one," Cathy quipped.

"Very funny."

"You don't need to write it down. We always get the same thing when we order from Athena's: three chicken gyros, hummus, a large Greek salad without anchovies."

Madison picked up the phone. Anna seemed a little distracted.

"What's the matter, Anna? Is your blood sugar dropping?" she asked.

"No. I'm fine."

Madison hung up. "It will be ready in 35 minutes."

"Good." Anna wrung her hands.

"Okay, Anna, what's going on? You're acting all nervous or something," Madison said.

She opened her briefcase and took out *The Tattler.*

Madison looked shocked. "Since when did you start reading that trash?"

"I don't read it." She sighed. "I didn't tell you the truth about the supermarket. I was standing in line all ready to pay for the rotisserie chicken when I saw this on the cover: *Cybil George Talks About the Heartache, Marcus and His New Lady Love.* I put the chicken back, bought this and headed home." She handed Cathy the paper. "Did you read it?" "I read some of it," Anna said.

"Any particular paragraph I should be interested in?" Cathy opened the paper.

"The third one." She scanned down to the third paragraph:

Breaking up with Marcus was one of the hardest decisions I ever had to make. He wanted more from me than I could give. I didn't mean anything bad by the chubby comment; she is just completely different than me, or any of his other girlfriends for that matter.

Cathy looked at the pictures. They had a photograph of Marcus and Cybil in happier times and one of Marcus and her kissing outside of the stadium. The caption read: *Tale of Two Women's Bodies.*

She closed the paper. She didn't want to read any more.

Madison picked up the paper.

"Are you okay Cathy?"

"I'm fine. It's almost to the point of being funny."

Madison threw the paper on the floor. "This is bull. I thought this girl had a modeling career. Where did she find the time to do this?"

"It's all about drama. Creating it and being the center of attention. What more could a girl want?"

"She certainly doesn't have a problem making that happen, does she?" Cathy crossed her legs and arms. She was tense.

"It's this whole generation. How old is she? Twenty-five?" Madison asked.

"She's twenty-eight."

"That's old enough to know better in my book," Anna said.

Madison stood up. "I'm going to pick the food up. I'll be right back."

"Okay."

When Madison left, Anna turned to Cathy. "Are you sure you're okay with this?"

"I just got twelve gorgeous flower arrangements and she got page 38 of *The Tattler*. Who do you think is doing better?"

Anna backed off and they went downstairs. When Madison got back they had dinner and watched television. Cathy checked on the baseball game but there was a rain delay. They settled for entertainment news.

Madison laughed. "Can you believe they actually cover this stuff? Who cares if Brad and Angelina shopped at the Piggly Wiggly? Why don't they just leave them in peace?"

"Then they wouldn't have anything to do," Anna said.

"It seems to me that the bigger stars get, the more people want to know every little detail about their lives. It's nuts." Cathy sat back in her chair.

The segment showed Marcus and Cybil talking outside a restaurant while the voice over reported: "Supermodel Cybil George who is in Baltimore shooting her first feature film was seen with her ex Marcus Fox. The two seemed to have a friendly meeting. Representatives from both camps have stated the two are just friends."

Anna quickly turned the television off. "Cathy, there is no reason to get upset."

Madison chimed in. "It's just a report. It doesn't mean anything. I mean, it must be a real slow news day." Cathy was still a little shocked.

"The man sent you ten floral arrangements because he misses you."

"I know, Anna. It just seems like every time I turn around here comes another report. First it was the papers, then the radio and now television. I've reached the media's holy trinity." Cathy threw her hands up in disgust.

"Don't get upset, Cathy, this is a part of what his life is about."

"Besides, this excess attention will be over after baseball season." Anna did her best to sound convincing.

"Anna's right. After the season is over there won't be so much coverage."

"So I just have to survive the next month and a half."

"Changing the subject, I have some news," Anna said.

"It's good news, right?" Madison asked.

"Naturally. Roger and I have set a date. November ninth of next year."

"That's terrific, Anna." Cathy was elated.

"Congratulations, Cousin."

"So of course, Cathy, you have to help me plan."

"I love the idea of weddings. There are so many fun things to do."

"I know." Anna nodded.

A thought hit Cathy. "You're not just telling me this to get my mind off the Cybil George thing, are you?"

"Of course not. Roger and I have been discussing dates back and forth for a while and we agreed on November nuptials."

"Good. I'm so happy for you, Anna. You're getting a great guy."

"I know." She smiled happily.

"Madison, do me a favor. Flip the television back on and turn to YES. I want to see if the rain has let up in Baltimore."

There was still a rain delay.

"So what are they going to do if they get rained out?" Madison asked.

"It's nearly the end of the regular season and they have to get the game in. If it gets called, they'll play a double header tomorrow."

The phone rang.

"I'll get it." Anna got up.

Cathy stared into space.

"Hey Cathy! Come back. Don't dwell."

She snapped out of it. "I hear you. I haven't lost touch with reality."

Anna walked back in with the phone and a mischievous grin. "Telephone, Cathy."

She took the phone. "Hello?"

"Hey, sweetie."

"Marcus?" She was relieved to hear his voice.

Anna and Madison watched her on the phone.

"I know it's weird to hear from me when there's supposed to be a game happening."

"It's raining. Does it look like it will let up so you can get the game in?"

"It might let up. But I didn't call you to talk about the game or the weather. I just didn't want you to hear about this from anyone else but me."

Her heart froze. "What is it?"

"I ran into Cybil today. She's filming some scenes for a movie around Camden Yards. We spoke for minute and she kissed me. I didn't know she was going to do it. If I had, I would have stopped her cold."

Cathy processed the information. "I see. She sandbagged you?"

"Exactly." He paused for a reaction. "Are you upset with me?"

"No. I'm just glad they didn't catch that on camera, too."

"On camera? What are you talking about?"

"I know you wanted to tell me first but the entertainment news programs beat you to it."

"What? Damn! Here I thought I was giving you a heads up." He was aggravated.

"As long as they missed her planting one on you, I'm okay with that. I'm not bothered by it or *The Tattler* story."

"What *Tattler* story?"

"It's nothing."

"Are you sure you're okay?"

"I'm fine, I promise," she reassured him.

"I got your message about the flowers and you are most welcome. Listen, if we do get the game in tonight, I'll call you tomorrow. If it's rained out I'll call tonight."

"Sounds good to me."

"I'm really not supposed to be on the cell, so we'll talk later babe. Miss you."

"Miss you too."

Both Anna and Madison had smug looks on their faces.

"Didn't we tell you not to worry?"

"Okay, so you were right. I'm happy to be wrong."

***

The rain did let up in time to get the game in. Cathy stayed up as long as she could before she dozed off. When she woke it was morning and her Yankees win streak had ended 5-4.

She followed doctor's orders and cut back her schedule. Instead of hopping right on the computer to see the day's business emails, she only checked her personal inbox. Alexander and Andrew had emailed her about the game but both were very sure the Yankees would get back on track that night. So was she.

A little later that morning Cathy put on a nice dress and headed to the supermarket to do some light grocery shopping. She even called her personal president, her mother, to see if she needed to go to the store. As far as Cathy could tell, Clint Eastwood didn't know a thing about being in the real line of fire.

Before she could stop herself, Cathy honked the horn when she went to pick up her mother. Her mother stood ready at the door.

"Hi, Mom."

Elizabeth got in. "Good morning."

Cathy's cell phone rang. She adjusted her hands free earpiece. "Hello?"

"Hey, baby. How are you doing?"

"I'm fine, thanks. You?"

"Not bad. I'm not happy we lost last night."

"I know, but Alex and Andrew have assured me that you guys will be back on track this evening."

"We're going to do our very best."

"Cathy? How can you drive and talk on the phone?"

"Marcus, excuse me a minute, please."

He chuckled. "Sure. Is that your mom?"

"Oh yes." She looked at her mother. "Mom, I'm using my ear piece so I won't take my hands off the wheel or my eyes off the road. I'm sorry Marcus. Go ahead."

"Your mother sounds like a pistol." He had to chuckle.

"A cannon is more like it."

He laughed. "That's a good one but I have an ulterior motive for calling."

"Ooh, sounds serious."

"Not that kind of serious. Did you book your flight for Tampa?"

"As a matter of fact I did that yesterday. We'll be in Tampa Friday afternoon."

"Fantastic. I reserved three rooms for you under your name."

"Thanks, honey."

"Who are you talking to?" Her mother's eyebrows rose.

"Mom, I'm on the phone." Cathy was growing more annoyed.

Marcus got a kick out of Cathy's mother. "Your mother sounds like fun."

"A regular laugh riot."

"I guess I'd better let you go before she starts interrogating you."

Cathy took one look at her mother's stern face. "That ship has sailed. It's more like the Spanish Inquisition coming up."

"Okay, babe. I'll talk to you a little later. If I can call you before and after the game I will."

"Okay. Is the weather better today?"

"Much better. We shouldn't have any trouble getting a game in tonight."

"Good. I'll be watching."

"Have a good one, baby. Don't let her put you on the rack."

"It's probably too late for that."

Cathy hung up, annoyed with her mother.

"Mom, why in the world do you talk to me when I'm on the phone?"

"You should be concentrating on your driving." She drove home the point with her finger.

"We're still in one piece, Mom. I didn't run a light or pop a stop sign."

"You have to be careful; so many people get into accidents talking on their phones."

"Okay, Mom. I'm being careful."

"Was that the baseball player?"

"Yes, Mom."

"What's the story with Sunday's gossip column?"

Cathy's heart sank. "Nothing, Mom. It was a lie and they printed a retraction on Monday."

"You're a 40-year-old woman and mother; you had no business being in some nightclub."

"Mom, I went there with Marcus. He wasn't worried about my age. We just went there to dance."

"Aren't you older than him?" "Yes,
Mom, I am. I'm six years older." "So
he's only 34?" her mother asked.

"What do you mean, only thirty four?" "He
isn't too old to be in a nightclub."

Cathy was stunned. *Oh no, she isn't going there*, she thought. Cathy used one of the few diffusers she had for her mother.

"Mom, may I remind you that you were 20 plus years younger than Mr. Anderson?"

"Are you buying a lot of groceries today?"

The diffuser worked. "No, I'm just picking up some groceries for the next couple of days. We're flying to Tampa Friday morning."

"What's in Tampa?"

"A Yankee game."

"I know you're not following this man everywhere. You have children."

Cathy rolled her eyes. "First, I'm not following him everywhere; otherwise, I'd be in Baltimore. Secondly, my children are in college. So I am not flaunting anything in front of them."

"Really? What do you call that article yesterday?"

"Fish paper."

"I just don't know. I raised the both of you to be better than that. I just don't approve of that kind of conduct." She shook her head.

"You did say I was 40 and Anna's 36, which means we are far beyond the age of needing your approval."

Although her mother didn't think Cathy was religious, Cathy thanked God when they pulled into the parking lot. Conversations with her mother tended to be interesting and eventful in a make-you-feel-guilty-about-the-choices you've-made kind of way. As they entered the store, Cathy and her mother grabbed a couple of shopping carts. While she might not follow all of her mother's beliefs, Cathy still stuck to the way her mother had taught her to shop. *Shop the outside, that's where all the good-for-you food is.* Naturally they were in the produce aisle.

"Ouch!" Elizabeth grabbed her arm.

"What's the matter, Mom?"

"The sprinkler came on."

Cathy took a closer look at her arm. "Mom, you have sunburn."

"I do not. I'm from the South. I used to work in the fields and I never got sunburned."

"That's because the hole in the ozone layer wasn't twice the size of Alaska back then. You know, Mom, sunblock isn't just for white people. Black folks get sunburned too."

Her mother scoffed. "It's just so ridiculous. As if I'm not paying enough for my medications, now I have to spend money on tanning cream? Summer is almost over."

"Not suntan lotion, Mom, sunblock. You can pick some up on the way out. The sun doesn't mix well with most medications, you know."

Cathy looked at her mother. After forty years she knew that expression on her mother's face. Her mother had just tuned her out and zeroed in on what she was wearing. "Before you say another word, Mom, I have on a good bra and a slip."

Her mother played innocent. "Why did you say that? I didn't say a word."

"Mom, I know you as well as you know me. And I recognize that look."

"I wasn't going to say anything about it. I was just going to say I'm going over to the organic section."

"Okay, Mom. I'm going to pick up some olives for my pasta salad later."

A few people watched Cathy as she filled a container at the olive bar. She was sure most of Amityville's 10,000+ population had either seen the paper or watched the entertainment news show. She filled the container with black olives.

"Cathy?"

She knew the voice immediately.

"Paul," she said in an even tone.

"It's good to see you."

"Thanks."

"How have you been? You look great."

"Fine, thank you," Cathy said.

She continued browsing the olive bar until he finally got the message. "It was good seeing you."

"Take care, Paul."

Cathy wasn't really mad at Paul anymore; she just couldn't seem to get the image of him in bed with his student out of her mind. It was hard for her to see him and not think of that night. Cathy found her mother and continued shopping. A few minutes later her mother slowed down to nearly a crawl.

"Okay, Mom. What is wrong with you?"

"There's some woman following us."

"What woman?"

"A blond."

"Where?" Cathy was furious.

"Over there. She's in frozen foods."

She looked over and it was the blond reporter from the gym, Lisa Spellman.

"Take my cart, Mom." She was hot.

"Cathy, don't do anything stupid."

"I'm not going do anything stupid, Mom. I just want to know why she's following me."

Spellman saw her coming and ran. The woman actually ran. But Cathy had a full head of steam.

"Don't you run! I want to speak to you." "I

have mace!" She fumbled through her bag.

"I'm not coming to eat you, little girl. I just want to know why you're following me!"

People stopped to watch the encounter.

"It's called freedom of the press."

"I know all about freedom of the press. But in the name of all things decent, stop following me for a story. I'm shopping with my mother. What the hell kind of story is that?" "It's my job," she insisted.

"I understand you're a working woman. So am I. All I am asking you to do is please back off. There is no story here. I may have squeezed a couple of melons but that's about the extent of my hijinks."

People started to laugh. Eventually Spellman laughed at the absurdity of the situation.

She stuck her hand out. "Lisa Spellman."

Cathy shook her hand. "Nice to meet you, Lisa. Even though you know my name, allow me to introduce myself anyway. I'm Catherine Chambers." "Nice to meet you, Catherine."

As the crowd dispersed her mother walked over. "Is everything all right, Cathy?"

"It's fine." She turned to Lisa. "Lisa, this is my mother, Elizabeth Anderson. Mom, this is Lisa Spellman."

She shook Lisa's hand. "So you're the stalker."

"Mom!"

Lisa took it in stride. "That's okay, I've been called worse. Nice to meet you, Mrs. Anderson."

"You certainly made grocery shopping interesting. By the way, Cathy, do you have everything?"

"Yes, I'm done."

"Good, I have to get back home. Ingrid wants me to go with her to her attorney's office."

"Okay. You go ahead, Mom. I'll be right there."

"So, Lisa, now that you're not my stalker, would you like to have lunch this afternoon, say around one P.M.?"

"Sure."

"Great. There's a place on Route 110 called Pete's Diner. The food is good and the patrons are colorful. I can meet you there."

"Cool. I'll see you then."

The customers were all abuzz in the checkout lines. They'd given them quite a floorshow for their shopping entertainment.

Cathy noticed *The Tattler* on the checkout stand. She wasn't worried about her mother seeing it. Her mother was more concerned with the amount of candy they had on display for children. Today her predictability worked in Cathy's favor.

***

Hobo came running out of his doghouse, at least as far as the chain would let him when Cathy pulled into the driveway. Cathy smiled when she saw him wagging his tail 90 mph. Cathy loved dogs but had decided against pets when her kids were growing up. Picking up after the kids was time consuming enough. Hobo sat and waited for Elizabeth to pet him, which she almost never did. Cathy gave him credit for persistence. She heard him whining when she turned off the ignition.

"Mom, did you feed the dog today?"

"No, I had to pick up some more dog food."

Cathy got out. "He tells on you every time."

Her mother dismissed it with a wave. "Old dog."

Cathy helped her mother get her grocery bags in the house.

"Which bag has the dog food, Mom?" Cathy asked as she put the bags on the table.

"I think I have it here." Elizabeth handed her a can of food.

Cathy got the can opener and went outside.

Hobo was actually older than her mother, in dog years, but Cathy loved to call him a puppy.

"Here you go, puppy." She patted him on the head and he immediately assumed the position for a tummy rub. "Aww. You are the sweet dog, aren't you? I know that Mom didn't feed you today, did she, big puppy?" She poured the food into his dish, changed his water and went back inside to wash her doggy hands.

"So, are you all set, Mom?" she asked.

Elizabeth put the milk in the fridge. "Yeah, I think so."

"I guess I better get back home and put my dairy away."

"Is Anna working out here today?"

"I think she's on the island this week."

"I have an appointment a week from this Saturday. I want her to take me."

"I think she and Roger have an appointment with a catering hall that day. I could be wrong but I think it's a week from this Saturday."

Elizabeth let out a heavy sigh. "A catering hall? Is she having a big wedding?"

"You could ask her yourself, Mom."

She shook her head. "I don't know why she's having some big wedding. It's not like she hasn't been married before.

Cathy turned to roll her eyes. "You know, Mom, Anna is very happy with Roger. He's a nice guy. Why can't you ever be happy for her?"

Elizabeth adjusted her glasses in that mother superior way of hers. "You know why."

"Right. Because he's not a part of the faith and we aren't either. So that means you can't be happy for your own daughter?"

"You know what the right standards are."

"Whose standards, Mom?"

"God's."

"Oh, give me a break!"

Elizabeth looked shocked. "What?"

Cathy was emboldened. "Give me a break. This isn't about God! It's about control."

"What control? Who's trying to control you?"

"You are. That's always been your M.O."

Her mother played the guilt card. "I struggled to bring you girls up the right way and then you just flush it down the toilet."

"We didn't flush you down the toilet, Mom. We just didn't want to be a part of that collective anymore."

"You know it means your life."

"It certainly does and that's exactly why I got out."

"It's like the two of you are dead."

"Guess what, Mom. Now you know how we feel about you. Do you know what it's like to watch your mother die and see this other person take her place?"

"What are you talking about? Another person?" Elizabeth was mystified.

"Yes, Mom. You are someone else and you don't even know it. How can you not be happy for your own children? We're not drug addicts or prostitutes. I wasn't an alcoholic child abuser!"

"I realize that."

"Do you? Anna is 36 years old, an accountant, and she has no children. Not one. Roger is a 40-year-old electrical engineer with no children and somehow they found each other. Any other mother would think this was the equivalent to finding the Holy Grail of love matches. Two people without children are getting married. You should be happy for her."

Her mother sat down. "You know what good principles are and neither of you is following them."

"According to you." Cathy went to the door. "There isn't any use in talking to you about this. We are just going to go in circles. I would like for you to show Anna at least a tenth of the joy you show those folks in the faith when they get hitched."

"I have to make some decisions."

"You go right ahead and make them, Mom. You've made decisions before and when something happens you come to us to for help. We may not always be your daughters, Mom, but you're still our mother because those are our standards."

She stepped out and then back in. "If you have a doctor's appointment that Saturday and one of your friends can't help you out I might be able to take you in the latter part of the afternoon."

"Fine."

This was the same dance Cathy had been doing with her mother for ten years. Most times it was Anna who took her on with Cathy just simmering in the background. Cathy suspected that some of Anna's power came from her relationship with Roger, that in Roger she'd found a true sense of happiness that protected her. Cathy was more vulnerable to her words and pronouncements from upon high. However, being with Marcus was making Cathy stronger. That was something no one, not even her mother, could take away from her.

CHAPTER 19

After an extra-long workout in the morning, Marcus had lunch in his room. Some of his teammates invited him to go out for lunch but he wasn't in the mood. He wasn't sulking about the loss the night before; he was anxious to see the article in *The Tattler* and didn't want an audience.

Ben slowly walked down the hall with a copy of *The Tattler* under his jacket. If it looked like a covert operation, it was. They couldn't afford to have anyone snap him with that rag in his hands. Ben knocked once and used the extra key card to let himself in.

"Did you get it?" Marcus was anxious.

"Simmer down. Here it is." Ben placed a copy of *The Tattler* on the table.

Marcus was appalled by the cover. "Good grief. Here's Cybil's tale of woe listed next to the latest sighting of Bigfoot."

Ben snickered. "No one takes this stuff seriously."

"Maybe not but there are other tabloid rags besides *The Tattler*."

"You should relax, Marcus. Cathy didn't take it seriously. It was just a passing raindrop. I wouldn't give it enough weight to call it a shower."

Marcus sighed. "I guess I forgot to mention that Lisa Spellman has been on the scene."

For the first time Ben looked alarmed. "She has? Since when?"

"Cathy's not sure how long but she did say Lisa was asking questions about her at her gym."

"What did you tell her?"

"I told her to stay away from Lisa, not to engage her."

"Good." He glanced at the television. "You can't help yourself, can you?"

Marcus looked up at the sports show. "I know it seems masochistic but sometimes these guys are on the money with their comments."

"And the rest of the time they're talking out their behinds," Ben retorted.

"It makes for good television, I guess."

"Did you talk to Cathy after the game?"

"No, I was going to call but it was kind of late. I talked to her this morning."

"That explains your chipper mood."

Marcus smiled. "I'm feeling pretty good."

"So she was really okay with that Cybil thing yesterday?"

"It didn't seem to faze her."

"I'm glad it didn't faze her but it sure fazed me." "I know, Ben. I think Cybil's up to something, too. What, I don't know."

"Keep a wide berth from her while she's here shooting her movie. The press would love to see any inkling of you two getting back together."

"You're preaching to the choir. I've been down this road before."

"You know where all the speed bumps and potholes are, just make sure you steer clear."

"I will. I promise."

"Let's get back to Cathy. When is she flying into Tampa?"

Marcus lit up. "Friday morning and I can't wait to see her."

Ben laughed. "You know, I wasn't sure about it until just now."

"Sure about what?"

"You're in love with her."

Marcus got flustered and bobbled his fork. Ben laughed and patted Marcus on the back. "Young man, if your nose was any more open, we'd be able to get two Mack trucks through it."

Marcus opened his mouth to protest then thought better of it. "I would prefer to say the words to her. If that's okay with you."

"Hey, that's all right with me."

Marcus wiped his mouth. "You like her, don't you?"

Ben smiled. "She's a keeper, Marcus. What's not to like?"

Marcus grinned. "Now who's preaching to the choir

***

Two most unusual lunch companions sat across from each other at Pete's Diner, a well-loved Amityville place to meet and eat.

"So how did you get into journalism? Was it your major?" Cathy asked.

"I majored in journalism and American literature," Lisa answered. She was relaxed.

"Sounds impressive. Where did you study?"

She hesitated for a minute. "You wouldn't believe it if I told you."

"Try me."

"Columbia University."

Cathy's interest was piqued. "My uncle got his doctorate in education from Columbia."

"Really? I bet he's doing something productive with his degree."

"He's the chairperson of the Criminal Justice Department at UC at Sacramento."

"Wow, that's something."

"What about you, though? I know freelancing for different tabloids probably pays the bills but just below the surface you seem to have a passion to do something else."

"Hi. Can I get you two ladies something to drink?" the waitress asked.

"Sure, I'll have a cup of coffee with half and half," Lisa said.

"I'll have the same."

"When I graduated I was filled with ambition. I was going to be an investigative reporter and write the great American novel."

"So you had a plan," Cathy said. The waitress brought the coffee.

"Are you ladies ready to order?"

Lisa looked at the menu. "What's good here?"

"Everything's good, but for lunch I like the turkey burger deluxe."

"Sounds good to me. I'll have that too."

"Very good."

"So what happened with your plan?"

"I got a job with *The Post* but instead of reporting I was a fact checker. It wasn't what I wanted but I toughed it out waiting for my big break." "And the break didn't come."

"Actually I got a break, just not the one I wanted."

"How's that?" Cathy asked.

"My boyfriend and I were total tourists on vacation in the Caribbean. One day I was on the beach to take some scenic shots when I realized a certain Republican senator was vacationing at the same resort. At first I brushed it off until I saw him making out with a woman who wasn't his wife."

"Not exactly the picture of family values."

"Tell me about it. I investigated the esteemed senator and sold the story with pictures for nearly 7K. It would have taken more than a couple of months of working crazy hours to make that kind of money at *The Post*."

"That was serious cash."

"And it led to more work, until eventually I stopped pursuing a traditional journalistic career, for a different one that paid very well."

"Sometimes it just comes down to economics."

"I have a nice house, my husband and I go on at least three vacations a year, and we're even talking about starting a family."

Cathy smiled. "That's terrific." She sipped her coffee to get her nerve up to ask the question she wanted answered. "Tell me, other than what was in the newspaper, why were you so interested in me?"

"I'm sure you're aware that I've been to your gym."

"There's not much you can hide from the five A.M. crowd."

"By the way, I just have to know. How in the world do you manage to get up at four every morning and go to the gym?"

"Is this on or off the record?"

She laughed. "Completely off the record."

"I hate to sound like a Nike commercial but I just do it."

"Good for you." She sipped her coffee. "Just so you know, I've been a member of the gym for five years."

"So you didn't just join to cover me? That's good to know."

"To be perfectly honest, you aren't the typical athlete's girlfriend. Especially for Marcus Fox." She qualified her comment. "No disrespect intended."

"None taken."

"He was just one of those players with innate star quality from the start. So naturally every singer, actress and model was all over him, which, let's face it, sells papers."

"I know it does." Cathy sipped her coffee. "What can you tell me about Cybil George?"

"Oh, I can tell you a lot about that one. She's a real piece of work.

The waitress brought their burgers to the table. "Thank you," they chorused.

Lisa took a bite. "This is good."

"I told you."

Lisa wiped her mouth. "Anyway, Cybil put Marcus through the mill. They were always on again, off again. She tried to do things to make him jealous and if she couldn't do that she would leak something to the press about him. It was a mess."

"Do you think they're really over? Or is this a break and not a breakup?"

"It's a breakup all right and it was Marcus who ended it."

"Really? She told *The Tattler* she broke up with him."

"*The Tattler?* Please. Just for the record, even I don't bother with that rag." She took another bite. "He definitely broke it off with her. He finally got sick and tired of the games."

"One of the entertainment news shows had a news link report about Cybil being seen with him in Baltimore. Marcus said she was filming an upcoming movie there."

Lisa sipped her water. "Cybil is filming a movie in Baltimore, but it's being shot in the same area they shoot *The Wire*, which is a long way from Camden Yards."

"So she was there just to see him." Cathy shook her head.

"I'd put money on it. At this point you're getting better coverage than she is. She had to take the bait and run with it.

"I told Marcus that."

"I think the final straw with her happened Friday night."

"What about Friday night?" Cathy was a little bewildered.

"In the three years they were together we'd see her at games every now and then, but never sitting with his parents. When you were seen sitting with Mr. and Mrs. Fox, I knew he was serious about you. I'd say it was the final insult to Cybil."

"I had no idea I was going to be seated next to them. I didn't even know they were going to be at the game."

Lisa had a strange look on her face. "I'm going to tell you something I haven't reported on."

Cathy was a bit cautious. "Okay. Are you planning to report it?"

"I gave it some thought and I decided against it."

"Now I have to know what it is."

"I heard his parents came in especially to meet you."

She was astonished. "They came all the way from Jamestown to meet me? I can't believe it."

"I heard it from a very good source. Apparently Marcus called them about you. They came down to check you out for themselves."

"In a way, then, I'm glad he didn't tell me. I would have freaked. Not that I didn't when I saw them." "Good thing." She went back to her fries.

"Wait. I've seen pictures of him with other girlfriends at events with his parents. What's so different about me?"

Lisa ate another fry. "God, you are going to make me tell you, aren't you?"

"Make you tell me what?"

"If you breathe a word of this I will go public with the supermarket thing."

She laughed. "I promise. I won't say a word."

"Not even to Marcus. Promise me. Swear on your Ivy League honor."

Cathy looked at her cross-eyed. "Do you know who else graduated from an Ivy League school?"

"I know. Politicians aside, swear on your honor."

Cathy held up her right hand. "I swear."

"His sister Cecily and I are friends."

"She works at a record company."

"Right. I've done some articles and puff pieces on several of her acts. She didn't want me to do a whack job on you. She said, 'Big brother really likes this one so back off.' "

"So I have her to thank for this kinder, gentler version of you?

"Sort of. Besides, you just seemed like a good person. I probably wouldn't have found a traffic ticket."

"You would have gotten a few late library fees."

She laughed. "Seriously, though, Cybil can't have it look like she was thrown over for a full-figured woman, no matter how beautiful she is. Make no mistake, Cathy, you are a beautiful woman."

Cathy got a little embarrassed. "Thanks."

"You're welcome but don't be so modest. Cybil is threatened by you. I'm surprised she wasn't at Club Z the night you were there."

"To be honest, so was I. I'm still trying to get over that nightmare."

"As soon as I read it, I knew Marcus would get a retraction. There was no way he'd let it go."

"That was such a relief." Cathy ate a couple of fries. "You know, if I didn't know any better I would say you and Marcus were friends, or at least friendly."

Lisa smiled. "I'm sure he had something to say about me but I am more of a pesky Chihuahua than pit bull as far as he's concerned. Cybil is another story."

"Doesn't sound like you like her much."

"I don't. Take my advice and watch your back with that one. She is some piece of work."

"I'll keep that in mind."

"Just don't let her get under your skin." She finished her burger. "Would you think I was a pig if I ordered another one? This was amazing."

"No, I wouldn't think you were a pig. FYI, it does come as a double deluxe entrée."

"Good to know."

Cathy enjoyed having lunch with her stalker, Lisa. She was glad to learn more about Marcus's relationships without having to pry it out of him. She realized she had to keep a watchful eye out for Cybil's shenanigans.

***

After lunch Cathy needed a little quiet time to think about what Lisa had told her and connect with her inner geek. For her money, there was no better place in the world to do it than the Barnes and Noble Café. Cathy had always loved going to the bookstore and as a literary agent, she had an excuse to hang out and check out the new releases, see if any of her writers were on the shelves and talk to the manager, Larry, to hear about things not reported on in *Publisher's Weekly*.

Larry walked over while she browsed the new cookbooks.

"Hey there, Cathy. How are you?"

"I'm good, Larry. How about you?"

"Can't complain. Checking out the competition, I see."

"You know me. I have to stay on top of these things."

"We sold out of your cookbooks this past weekend."

She was pleasantly surprised. "Really?"

"Oh yes. In fact I just ordered some."

"I assume this recent peak in interest coincides with my higher profile love life."

"You *are* dating baseball royalty."

"Don't I know it?"

"It sells books. Even a few of your clients' books have picked up."

"I guess I can't complain then, can I? It would be nice to say the work speaks for itself but this is a celebrity driven society. At least for now."

"I've even had a few orders for Cybil George's book and you know it's complete tripe."

She nodded her head. "It is amazing, isn't it?"

"Anyway, I have a few things to do in the back so I'll leave you to your research. Good to see you." "Same here, Larry. Thanks for the heads up." "Anytime." He went back towards his office.

You can't buy this kind of PR. My name hits the paper and now my sales have picked up. I suppose I shouldn't look this gift horse in the mouth.

Cathy treated herself to a decaf caramel latté at the café. *I know I had a burger and fries but I love to rationalize calories I don't chew*, she thought as she sipped.

"So this is what it takes for me to see one of my two favorite nieces."

Cathy looked up to see her Aunt Peg. At 65 she was as fashionable as ever. Cathy got up and hugged her.

"Hey, Aunt Peg. How are you? When did you get back?" They sat down. "I got back a couple of days ago. You know how it is. I had to sort through mail and try to get my house back in order."

"I know what you mean. You certainly look good, Aunt Peg."

"Thank you. So do you. I'd say this new man agrees with you."

Aunt Peg didn't miss a trick, never had. "He does."

"Imagine my surprise when I picked up a New York paper at Heathrow and saw a picture of my beautiful niece and this very handsome man hugging."

Cathy smiled. "It's been a bit of a shock to me too."

"I hope you're not still flipping out over the weight thing."

"I hate to say it, Aunt Peg, but you know my mother."

Peg rolled her eyes. "I don't know why she is so ridiculous with that. It's not as if we come from petite stock. Your uncle used to say when we got together with our cousins we looked like prison matrons."

Cathy laughed. "I remember hearing that."

"Remember, Anna's ex said he thought he'd wandered into a camp of female lumberjacks."

Cathy laughed even harder. "You know, I forgot about that."

"How is your sister doing? Has she set a date yet?"

"As a matter of fact they just set the date. November 9th of next year."

"That's wonderful. Does my sister know?" "She hasn't asked." Her Aunt Peg looked aggravated.

"Why is she still on this kick? I told her you were grown women and she had to accept your decisions, even if she doesn't like them."

"It doesn't stop her. I took her to the store this morning and she was talking about how she didn't approve of our conduct."

"Approve of your conduct? You're not seven years old," Aunt Peg said in disbelief.

"I know."

"Sometimes I think the worst thing that ever happened was that knock on the door more than thirty years ago. I don't have anything against religion but there has to be a balance."

"I think so, too."

"My God, they really did a number on you, and my sister only compounds it."

"It's all she knows now."

"No matter what your mother says, you and Anna are good girls."

"Thanks, Aunt Peg. It's a shame but even at 40 years old, I need to hear that."

"The two of you are always doing for your mom. You drive her places and take her to hair appointments. Hell, you even help dig her out when it snows."

"We have the aches and pains to prove it."

"I don't know why those folks don't come around to dig her out."

"They're busy doing God's work."

"Too busy for the widows in their midst?"

"Apparently. She says she has children so we can take care of it."

Aunt Peg shook her head. "Lord help us. We can talk a blue streak about this, but she's not going to change. So you have to move on and not let it get you down. You still deserve to be happy, Cathy."

"I know. I can't let anyone steal my sunshine."

"Right. So how are the boys doing?"

"They're good, Aunt Peg. I think they've adjusted to college life."

"You know, I was so glad when you told me you left that religion because you wanted your sons to have a normal life. I think it's been good for them."

"I do, too," Cathy agreed. "They haven't gotten into any trouble with drugs or drinking and they're good students. I couldn't ask for more."

"Especially these days. You have to count your blessings."

"You're right." Cathy paused. "By the way, Aunt Peg, does Madison know you're back?"

"I tried to call my son but I haven't been able to reach him. Have you seen him?"

"He stops by practically every single day. I'll tell him to call you."

"Thanks. Is he keeping out of trouble?"

"He's a good lawyer so trouble sometimes comes his way."

"Is there something going on?" She quickly became concerned.

"I don't want to alarm you, Aunt Peg. Everything is under control." Just then her cell phone rang. "Excuse me. Hello?"

"Hey, Cousin," Madison said.

"Well, speak of the devil. Your ears must be burning."

"Why?"

"I have someone here who wants to talk to you." She handed Aunt Peg the phone.

"Hello there, stranger, it's your mother."

Cathy stepped away to put some books up and give her aunt some privacy. With cameras in her own life,

Cathy had a new respect for privacy. Her aunt was still on the phone when she came back.

"I'm glad you're okay but you need to stay on top of this thing. People lose grip with reality when it comes to money. All right then, you give me a call at home later. I'll tell Cathy you'll talk to her later too. Okay, honey.
Love you. Bye."

She handed Cathy the phone. "Thanks, sweetie."

"Not a problem, Aunt Peg."

"Lord, I'm glad my son is a good attorney, but sometimes I think he is too good an attorney. You know what
I mean?"

"I certainly do."

Eager to hear more about her niece's new paramour, Peg leaned in. "So tell me about this Mr. Fox. I know he plays baseball. How did you two meet?"

Cathy liked the idea of being able to share her news about Marcus with her aunt; she knew she wouldn't judge her for the budding relationship with a younger man.

"We met at Keen's by chance. I was there to have lunch with a client who didn't show up and he happened to be there for lunch, too."

"I know you didn't go up to him. You have a bit of that wallflower thing when it comes to men. You don't have it in business, though."

Cathy was a little bashful. "You're right. He approached me." She smiled. "I really like him."

Her aunt gave her skeptical look. "You remember that old commercial that said it isn't nice to fool Mother

Nature? The same thing applies to me. Don't kid a kidder. You look like a woman in love. Are you?"

Cathy hesitated. She hadn't admitted it out loud to herself yet. "I am, but it might be too fast, don't you think?"

Her aunt shook her head. "Sweetheart, I don't think you're old but once you are over thirty you don't have the same kind of time or energy to mess around trying to figure things out. Besides, who says love has to adhere to some kind of schedule?"

"The heart wants what it wants."

"When it wants it, my dear niece."

"Being with him has been incredible. He's a real good guy."

"Of course he is. If you love him, he has to be. Just do yourself a favor and don't let all the size bull get to you. They have to sell papers." She stood up. "Just remember, today's news lines the bottom of tomorrow's bird cage."

She laughed. "That is too funny, Aunt Peg."

"And too true. I have to run my dear." She gave Cathy a kiss. "Tell your sister I will give her a call soon and we can talk wedding."

"I will. I know she'd like that."

"I won't tell her you told me the date. I'll let her spring it on me."

"Okay."

"So you take care, honey."

"I will, Aunt Peg. You do the same."

It never ceased to amaze Cathy how different her mother was from Peg. Her Aunt Peg always counterbalanced her mother and set her straight whenever it was necessary. Religion or not, she didn't let Elizabeth get away with anything. For Cathy and Anna it was nice to have someone in their corner.

CHAPTER 20

Done with the workday, Anna and Cathy busied themselves in the kitchen. Anna chopped vegetables while Cathy butterflied chicken breasts.

"You did what?" Anna was still laughing.

"You heard me. I chased her."

"The mental picture I'm getting is a hoot!"

"Mom was acting like she was playing dodge ball with the shopping cart. I thought she was losing her mind until she said we were being followed. All I could think was, 'What the hell is this about?' "

"I bet the woman was scared."

"I was an angry black woman with an attitude. Hell, I'd be scared, and it was me."

"I just think it's amazing that after that kind of scene, you had lunch with the stalker."

"Isn't that strange? We actually had a nice lunch and she gave me some valuable information about Cybil George."

"Really? What did she tell you?"

"She told me things I knew, like how long they went out. But she also told me the news link brief we saw last night was bull."

"What?"

"Not on Marcus's part but on Cybil's. She's shooting a film in Baltimore but the film's shooting in the same area where *The Wire* filmed."

"That's nowhere near Camden Yards," Anna said.

"Right."

"So she's putting herself in his face on purpose."

"She wants him back."

"What are you gonna do?"

"What am I going to do? What should I do? Slap her with my glove and challenge her to a duel at sunrise?'

"You could go to Baltimore."

"Why? We'll be in Tampa Friday afternoon. I can't live my life running after a man in the hopes of keeping another woman from him. That's not a life."

"You're right. I wouldn't do it either."

"I will tell you that your mother was in rare form today."

Anna rolled her eyes. "When isn't she? Did she ask you anything about my wedding plans?"

Cathy secretly wished she could say yes. Anna's first husband had been one selfish son of a gun, an overly critical, demanding liar. Somehow, Elizabeth had managed to remake his image as something better than what he actually was. Roger was the polar opposite: supportive, patient and unselfish. What more could a mother want? At least that was the way it was supposed to be.

"No. She did tell me she didn't approve of our conduct."

"Approve? She used the word *approve*?"

"Yep. Be happy you don't have children. Then you'd be flaunting your sex life in their faces."

"Cathy, your kids aren't babies, they're eighteen. It's ridiculous."

"Of course it is but we can't change her. I had a conversation about it with her today. Mom isn't getting mellow with age; she's getting more and more rigid."

"You talked to her about it?" Anna was shocked.

"Wonder of wonders, I know." Cathy threw her hands up. "It didn't change anything. There is no talking to her."

"Well, technically she's not supposed to talk to us. After all, we are demons."

"Oh, that's true."

"Why can't she just be our mother? That's what she was before 'the truth' entered our lives. Why is it so hard?" Anna had a hint of longing in her voice.

Cathy shrugged it off. "Anna, I don't think she knows how anymore." Cathy pounded the chicken breast harder.

"Cathy, are you trying to thin out the chicken breast or pulverize it?" Anna pointed to the chicken, which looked as if it had been through the food processor.

Cathy laughed. "I guess I'm more uptight about this subject than I thought." She paused. "Coming out of that religion was like getting off the space shuttle."

Anna shook her head. "It's a shame but it's true. We might as well have been from outer space it was such a shock."

Cathy butterflied another breast. "That's why I got out when I did."

Anna laughed. "But it still took you like four years before you'd put up a Christmas tree."

Cathy snickered. "I know. Wasn't that too much? I was celebrating Christmas but I was actually scared to put up a tree."

"Afraid you'd be struck down by lightning." Anna chuckled.

"Something like that, but I'm still standing."

"Mom thinks we don't believe in God anymore." Anna sighed.

"That's just silly. We didn't throw out the baby *with* the bathwater. We still believe in God. I just don't go to a building to prove it."

"That's why I'm so lucky to have found Roger. He really understood and he didn't pressure me about anything, including religion."

"To quote Martha, that's a good thing."

"His pastor is performing the ceremony."

"I guess that means Mom will be in the reception area until after the ceremony."

"You really think she'll do that? We're not getting married in a church."

Cathy put the knife down. "She stayed in the car for Alicia's ceremony and it was summertime in Baltimore. So you know she'd rather get heatstroke than sit for 20 minutes."

Anna sucked her teeth. "You're right."

"Don't worry, you'll still have a beautiful wedding and your marriage will be blessed." She paused to rinse the chicken. "By the way, I saw Aunt Peg today."

"Oh yeah? I didn't realize she was back from London."

"Neither did I. I saw her at Barnes and Noble this afternoon after lunch."

"How is she doing?"

"Really well. She looked good but she always looks good."

"That's true."

"She asked about your wedding plans and she wants you to call her."

"You didn't tell her the date, did you?"

"I resisted. She's excited for you, though."

"At least she's excited, which is more than we can say for Mom."

"You can't worry about it. She's not going to change. Sure, she'll put on a great show at the wedding but until then you know how she's going to be."

"I know Aunt Peg will put her in her place."

"They don't call her Peg for nothing. She's been known to knock quite a number of people down a few pegs."

"I used to wonder why they called her Peg when her given name is Yvette." "Now you know."

The phone rang. Cathy washed her hands and picked up.

"Hello?"

"Hey, Cathy. What's shaking?"

"Hey, Jim. How are you?"

"I'm great. I called to tell you about a gift I received today."

"A gift?" Cathy asked.

"Yeah, I got a box of premium cigars and Johnny Walker Blue."

"Really? Johnny Walker Blue."

Anna shook her hand. "Fancy."

"It came with a thank you card from Marcus Fox."

"Now wasn't that nice of Marcus?"

"What is he thanking me for?"

"You remember when you cancelled lunch the other day?"

"Yeah. We still have a rain check for that, right?"

"Yes. Anyway, I met Marcus that day. So if you hadn't cancelled the lunch we wouldn't have met."

"Oh. So you guys are dating?"

"It's so refreshing to talk to someone who hasn't read the gossip page."

"I never read that garbage."

"Then to answer your question, we are dating."

"Hey, I guess I can add accidental matchmaker to my curriculum vitae."

Cathy chuckled. "I guess you can."

"Well, I'm happy for you, Cathy."

"Thanks. Oh yeah, before I forget, I'm going away for a long weekend starting Friday."

"Good for you. When's the last time you took some real time off?"

"I have no idea. Still, better late than never."

"Right you are. Please tell Mr. Fox I said thank you."

"Will do."

"You have a good time, Cathy."

"Thanks, Jim. I will. Talk to you later."

Cathy hung the phone up. "Johnny Walker Blue and cigars. I know Jim is in hog heaven."

As she continued pounding the chicken, the phone rang again.

"Anna, would you get the phone please? I have chicken hands again."

Anna picked up.

"Hello? Hey, Madison. Are you dropping by for dinner?" Anna's tone suddenly changed from casual to distressed. "What? Where are you?" Cathy

saw concern on Anna's face.

"Okay we'll be right over." She hung up.

"What's going on?"

"Something happened at his apartment. Let's just go."

Cathy washed her hands and put everything away. Anna drove.

When they pulled up to Madison's place, there were a couple police cars there.

"What in the world?" Cathy was stunned.

They jumped out of the car. Madison was pacing on the front lawn.

"Madison! Are you all right?"

"I'm fine, Anna."

"What's going on? Why are the police here?"

"He cut my phone line, which disabled my security system, allowing him to get in and destroy my place."

Cathy noticed he was smoking a cigarette after quitting over a year ago.

"It was that guy, wasn't it?" "Yes. The guy's completely unhinged." "Are the cops looking for him?" Cathy asked.

"They didn't have to. He was still in there when I got home."

"Oh my God."

Just then two policemen brought him out in handcuffs.

"I have to go to the station to press charges." "We're going with you," Anna said.

"Thanks."

"Why don't you grab a few things from the house and stay with us."

"Thanks, Cathy. I'll bring my suitcase. I can use this weekend getaway more than ever now."

"I'll bet."

The three of them walked back into Madison's apartment. The destruction was unreal. The walls had holes and the furniture was spray-painted. Cathy stopped short of the bedroom; she didn't want to see any more. Madison went in, threw some things into the suitcase and they made a quick exit.

Madison, who normally talked a mile a minute, was quiet on the way to the station. He was shell-shocked. Fortunately, it wasn't a long car ride and they were soon sitting in the waiting area of the station. A detective called Madison to take his statement.

Cathy and Anna stayed in the waiting room for nearly an hour before Madison walked out. Raymond's ex-wife and center of the storm, Mary Gianni, ran into the station just as Madison came out of the squad room. She ran over and hugged him.

"Madison. I am so sorry. This is my fault." She was visibly shaken.

"It's not your fault. He did this. You're not responsible for his actions."

"But if I hadn't pressed him about the money…"

"Don't say that. You were married for 18 years and you have four children to think about. You only wanted your fair share."

"I thought you'd be angry with me."

"Not at all."

"Can I at least drive you home or to your cousins' place?"

"That's very sweet of you but my cousins are in the waiting room." He turned to toward Cathy and Anna. "That's Catherine on the left and Anna on the right." They waved.

"You have a great cousin."

"We know," Anna said

"Now you should go home to your kids," Madison told Mary.

She gave him a peck on the cheek.

Cathy and Anna stood up.

"All done?" Anna asked.

"Yeah. What time is it?"

Cathy looked at her watch. "It's eight-thirty." "It's that late already?" Anna was surprised.

"I know I interrupted your dinner stuff so how about we head over to Pete's?"

"Don't worry about the dinner stuff," Cathy answered. "We'll just cook tomorrow."

Anna agreed. "Right. Let's go to the diner."

***

Only a few people were scattered around the diner, having quiet conversations, reading books or working on laptops. After they were seated they quickly ordered. The eggshell silence continued.

"I certainly feel privileged this evening," Madison sighed.

Anna and Cathy looked at each other as if he was nuts.

"Cathy is actually missing a Yankee game." They broke up laughing.

"Thank God you broke the ice. It was getting to me," Anna said. "We're not used to being this quiet."

"I know. That's why I figured I would say something to get it over with."

"Good. But I am missing my Mr. Fox's game."

"I didn't think you cared," Madison clowned.

"Of course I care. However, I can also catch the rebroadcast tomorrow morning," she joked. "I should have figured that." The waitress brought the soup over.

"So are you feeling better?" Cathy asked, then blew on the hot soup.

"A little. I'm just glad this night will be over soon. Tomorrow is another day."

"True," Anna said.

"What happens next for you?"

"He gets arraigned and I wait for the D.A. to contact me about either a trial date or a plea bargain."

"So they might get in touch with you relatively soon?" Anna asked.

"Most likely."

"Good, the sooner you get this resolved, the better."

"Yeah." Madison looked distant. "I don't want to talk about it anymore. Let's talk about other things, happy things."

"Like our upcoming weekend." Anna smiled.

"Right. Have you booked the hotel yet, Cathy?"

"As a matter of fact, Marcus reserved three rooms for us at the Hilton."

"The Yankees stay in which hotel?"

"To be honest, Madison, I don't know."

"I guess we can assume it's the same one he booked us in."

"We'll find out soon enough."

The waitress brought their food to the table and they fell on it. Apparently spending time at the police station had increased the hunger factor for the three of them.

"Anyway, Madison, I didn't have the chance to tell you that Cathy had quite an eventful day."

"Really now?"

"Oh yes. She and a freelance reporter made quite a splash at Stop-n-Shop."

"What?"

"I'll let Anna fill you in. If you'll excuse me I need to go to the ladies' room."

Cathy could hear the game in the background, so she slowly walked to the ladies room so she could listen to the game on the way. She ducked into the hallway so Anna and Madison wouldn't see her as she lingered to hear the score. The Yankees were leading 7-1 heading to the top of the seventh inning. "Yes!" she whispered before she went into the ladies' room. Just to make sure they were still in the lead, she stopped again before going back to the table. The Yankees were up at bat with their lead still intact.

She sat back down at the table, confident of a Yankee victory.

"Cathy, I would have paid money to see you chase this woman in supermarket."

"It was rather comical but it broke the ice. We had lunch here this afternoon."

"Lunch with the enemy?"

"It wasn't as bad as all that, Madison. We talked and I got to know her a little. She's an Ivy Leaguer like us."

"Get out of here. What school?"

"She has a degree in journalism from Columbia University." Cathy twirled her fork.

"Wow, and she works freelance for gossip tabloids?" Anna asked.

"Hey, that's where the money is." Cathy shrugged.

"Can't knock the hustle," Madison said between sips of coffee.

"Not to mention she gave Cathy the scoop on Cybil."

"What did she say?"

"She told me Cybil is shooting a movie in Baltimore. However, her shoot isn't near Camden Yards. It's in another part of the city."

"So she made a special trip to Camden Yards to be near Marcus."

"So it appears."

"I wouldn't sweat it. We'll be in Tampa in two days."

"And so will Marcus."

"I know, guys. You don't have to try to make me feel better. I'm not worried about it."

"Good. So how about we order dessert then get the hell out of Dodge?" Madison said.

Cathy had avoided relationships for nearly three years for this very reason: They made her vulnerable. In this case, it also made her fodder for the gossip columns and entertainment news shows. Anna and Marcus knew better than to believe her.

After dessert they paid the check and went home. The evening's events had made Madison more tired than he thought so he went straight to bed. Anna had some numbers to crunch on her laptop for a little while before turning in.

As for Cathy, she had the Yankee post game report on. The final score was 9-3 in favor of the men in pinstripes, which made her very happy. The only thing that would have made her happier was a call from Marcus, especially in light of the information she had learned about Cybil over lunch. Knowing that she was in town and was making it her business to see Marcus drove Cathy nuts. So to take her mind off things she committed a cardinal bedroom sin: She grabbed a *Publisher's Weekly* from her office to read.

Just then the phone rang and in her rush to get it she slammed her toe on the desk. "Hello?"

"Hey, sweetie. Are you okay?"

Cathy sucked up the pain. "I'm fine, honey." Cathy was relieved to hear Marcus's voice. "So you guys won?"

`"Yeah. You didn't see the game?"

"I have to catch the re-broadcast tomorrow morning. We had a little family situation."

"Are the boys all right?" He said concerned.

Cathy was touched by his tone. "The boys are good.

My cousin Madison had something happen and Anna and I were with him for the evening."

"Oh, it sounds serious."

"It was. You know he's a divorce attorney, right?"

"Yeah."

"He had some trouble with a client's ex-husband. The guy was trying to hide money and property from the wife and Madison found it."

"I bet that didn't go over too well with the ex."

"Not at all. The guy went ballistic and tonight was the last straw. He broke into Madison's apartment and was still there when Madison got home."

"Oh my God. Was your cousin hurt?"

"No, thank God. He knew something was awry and called the police before going inside."

"Good. So they arrested the guy?"

"Yeah. We spent most of the evening at the police station. Then we stopped at the diner to get something to eat. It was too late to cook."

"Sounds like you had an eventful evening."

"Pretty much." She sighed. "I am really looking forward to Friday."

"Me, too. I miss you so much."

"I miss you, too."

"So you'll be touching down in Tampa around one or two?"

"Something like that. Oh, that reminds me, I'd better set up a car rental."

"I can take care of that for you. You want me to put it under your name?"

"Sure."

"Is Avis okay?"

"Perfect." She smiled even though she knew he couldn't see her. "So how did you do tonight?"

"I went 2 for 4, not exactly a stellar performance."

"I'm sure you performed quite well, you always do."

"Are we still talking about baseball?" Marcus said coyly. Cathy laughed. "Mr. Fox!"

"Well, are we?" he playfully insisted.

"That was the case a few minutes ago. Now I'm not so sure."

"It's not easy to concentrate on the topic at hand for me. I think about you all the time. After the game I can't wait to call so I can hear that sexy voice I love so much." He paused. "God, I miss you."

"I think about you all the time, too. And I love hearing your voice. It's so deep and sexy."

"So, Ms. Chambers, should we talk about it now or later?"

"Talk about what?" She wasn't sure what 'it' he was referring to.

"Us. We've talked nearly every night since I've been on the road but we have been avoiding a certain 'L' word and I don't mean the show."

"Thank God." Cathy breathed a sigh of relief. "I thought you meant phone sex."

He laughed. "Have you ever even had phone sex?"

"No," she quietly answered.

"You're kidding me. With your voice?" He was flabbergasted.

Unlike most people who explain why they had phone sex, Cathy had to explain why she hadn't. "I know. I have the voice of a 900-telephone sex operator. However, in my own defense, I was celibate for such a long time that I decided I preferred the real thing."

"When you put it that way, I get it."

"Good. So now I don't feel like too much of an odd ball. Anyway, honey, we're off the subject you wanted to talk about."

"Oh yes, the 'L' word."

"Frankly I'm really surprised you brought it up."

"Why?"

"In my experience, albeit limited, men don't bring up this topic much. Or at least that's what most women's magazines say."

"It's time to get rid of the elephant in the room. We both said 'I love you' Sunday morning. Granted, it was said in the throes of passion, but nonetheless we said it."

"I know."

"It's been on my mind ever since and I didn't want you to think it's something I take lightly or even say easily."

"I didn't want to bring it up just in case it fell under the category of spontaneous orgasmic utterances."

"Was it a spontaneous utterance for you?"

"No."

"It wasn't for me, either. I love you, Cathy. I'm in love with you."

She felt a tear roll down her cheek. "I'm in love with you, too, Marcus."

"Sure you can't change your flight to Thursday?"

"I wish I could but I've already booked the flight and I have a ton of things to do to get ready for the weekend."

"I guess I have to take another cold shower and go 3 for 4 at bat."

She laughed. "I'm making cinnamon rolls tomorrow morning."

"We both have energy to re-direct."

"Oh yeah."

"Game time is 7:00 P.M. on Friday and you're getting in around one or so."

"Right."

"I'd love to see you before the game."

"I'd love to see you, but don't you have to get to the stadium for the warm-up and pre-game?"

"Let me worry about that."

"Okay. How about we play it by ear then?"

"Fine, I'm cool with that. We'll play it by ear."

"Good. Well, it's almost the witching hour and you have an afternoon game to wrap up the series."

"Right."

"I'll be watching."

"I'll call you after the game. I love you."

"I love you. Talk to you tomorrow."

"Okay, babe."

Tonight was a first for Cathy; she cried happy tears over a man. Marcus Fox had said he loved her. His simple confession of love wiped away a lifetime of heartache. *Maybe God isn't punishing me after all,* Cathy thought.

CHAPTER 21

As promised, Cathy made cinnamon rolls first thing Wednesday morning. Her sister and cousin groaned and complained about their 'nonexistent' expanding waistlines. Out of the baker's dozen she made, five were gone by the time she got out of the shower.

Cathy had a lot of ground to cover for the office, which was why she called in her trusty sometimes assistant David to work with her for the day. He was one of the few people who could work with her in her home office. Cathy had tried to be very civic and community minded by offering the opportunity to young people in high school but it hadn't worked out. She could live with them singing the alphabet song to organize the filing system. What she couldn't live with was that the filing would still be out of order and it would take her twice as long to get anything accomplished.

David Macmillan was actually an attorney who did a lot of volunteer work for different charitable and political organizations. He and Cathy became friends during the Democratic Convention in '96. Deep down she thought he was going to eventually bring her the great American novel. In the meantime, he was a hotshot international corporate attorney who set his price and his own hours. At 6'4, a trim 200 pounds, with sandy brown hair and light brown eyes, he wasn't hard on the eyes. He was off limits, however. He was married to his work.

There was a knock at the door at nine. He was as punctual as ever.

"Come on in!" Cathy shouted from the living room.

"Mmm, it smells wonderful in here." He walked into the living room with coffee from Dunkin Donuts.

"There are cinnamon rolls in the kitchen, handsome."

He gave her a peck on the cheek. "You look different in a good way. What's going on, boss?"

"You don't know?"

"No. That's why I'm asking. I was in Europe for nearly two weeks. I just got back a couple of days ago."

"Oh, that explains it."

"Explains what? You're killing me here."

"Tell you what. Grab a couple of cinnamon rolls and I'll fill you in."

"Sounds interesting. I'll be right back."

When he returned, Cathy filled him in on everything that had happened in her little corner of the world.

He seemed astonished. "When you decide you're going to date again, you don't mess around."

She laughed. "I couldn't have found a better man if I'd planned it. No disrespect to you, my darling."

"None taken. Are you planning any legal action against the newspaper for running that full of crap article?"

"E.D. called Frank about it. I haven't heard anything since."

"Tell you what. I'll get in touch with Frank sometime this week or by Monday at the latest to see if we can get together to handle this for you. I can only imagine how you felt, retraction or no retraction."

"It was awful and I'd like to put it behind me."

"You should. But as long as you're dating a high profile baseball player like Marcus Fox, there will be no rest until the end of baseball season, we can only hope then."

"I love baseball season."

"I know you love your Yankees."

"I have to take the good with the bad."

He looked into Cathy's eyes. "You're not just dating him; you're in love."

"Is it that obvious?" Cathy wondered if she had something written on her forehead.

"I knew there was something different about you. I guess I'll just continue to pine away for you."

She playfully tossed her napkin at him. "You are so full of it. You're married to your career and if I'm not mistaken, you've had your share of beautiful women to keep you warm."

"True. But none of them are as warm as you."

Cathy scoffed. "That's because I weigh more than 110 pounds soaking wet. Bones tend to get cold and I am in no danger of that happening to me."

"You know I hate it when you talk about yourself like that. You've always been comfortable in your skin and that's what impressed me the most about you."

"Marcus said the same thing."

"See. Great minds think alike." He sipped his coffee. "So before we get into any more chatting, what's the project for today?"

"We're having a little power struggle problem."

"Beatrice and Sandra, right?"

"However did you guess?" she asked facetiously.

"I take it she needs another little call from counsel."

"Would you please?"

As an international attorney David knew his way around contractual negotiations. Legal insiders referred to him as the terminator, so having him assist in negotiations was a real plus for all of the agency's clients.

"Consider it done."

"Thank you."

"I'll give you a call to let you know how it went."

"Cool. I'll be around on Thursday but I'm leaving Friday for the weekend." David

pretended to faint.

"Ha, very funny. It hasn't been that long since I've taken a weekend off."

"You mean a real weekend? Dropping the kids off at college doesn't count."

Why does everyone keep saying that to me? She thought about it. "Okay, you win. It's been a long time."

"If ever."

"Now you're taking it too far. Can you do me a favor and get Jennifer's file from upstairs so we can work on making sure she's straightened out before the publisher gets the materials? Thank you, darling."

"Back in a minute."

He sprinted up the stairs. Within a minute he was back.

He sat down and opened the files. "There's a lot of stuff here."

"I know. I want to get it in order."

"Of course Jennifer has all this stuff, right? And this is your 'just in case' backup file."

"I am very well aware of just how anal I am. You are too."

He started sorting. "Ain't that the truth?" She threw a paper clip at him.

"Hey."

They worked quietly for a few minutes.

"How's your brother doing?"

He slowed down. "He's okay. He has his good and bad days. You know the story."

"Now ain't that the truth?"

"Now who's being a smarty pants?"

She chuckled. "All kidding aside, David, how are things really going?"

David's younger brother had MS. A few years ago his relapses had become more frequent and each time he was left a little bit worse off. David made sure his brother had the best care possible. He was a good big brother.

"The doctor says he thinks the physical therapy is helping."

"Good."

"Brian wants to join one of the programs at the Y. I'm not so sure about it."

"What did his neurologist say? I'm sure you asked him.

"He think it's a good idea for him physically and socially."

"He's right, you know. The programs are terrific and it will give him a chance to socialize."

"How do you know about the programs?"

"I used to take Alex and Andrew to the Y for swimming and I saw the classes in session. It looked like great fun to me. My Pilates instructor, Mo, works with MS patients too. She's really good."

"Really?"

"And she's on the north shore, which isn't far from you."

"Jot down the name and number before I leave."

"I will."

"So the programs are good?"

"Oh yes. Since he's in a wheelchair all he'll need is someone to go with him."

"Good deal."

David and Cathy worked the rest of the morning and into the afternoon. She threw together a little pasta Carbonara for lunch with mixed greens and apple fritters for dessert. She might not pay David with money but he was a bachelor, which meant he went months without a home cooked meal. This way they both got something good out of the deal. David had a date with one of his ladies, so they finished everything by the early part of the afternoon.

Cathy broke down and went to the mall a little later in the afternoon. If she had a choice, she preferred to shop during the week. Weekends at the mall were not her thing. She wasn't crazy about playing chicken with her car in the parking lot. In light of her scheduled trip, Cathy felt the need to visit Victoria's Secret to add a few more colors to her lingerie collection.

An energetic salesperson greeted her as she entered. She lingered over some pretty nighties and penoir sets, even though Cathy knew she couldn't get her left boob in one, let alone the rest of her body. So on to the panty displays she went. Though she was not much for bikinis, she refused to put on old lady underwear. Cathy perused the table of high cut briefs, which were a little sexy for her size, and picked up ten pair. While she was standing in line she noticed two young ladies picking over the same display.

"Do they have any in extra small?"

"They are some over here if you ladies would like to look." The salesperson led them away.

"Thank God," Cathy mumbled.

"I'm with you," the woman behind her said.

Cathy turned around. "I don't think I ever wore extra small, even when I was a kid."

"They are so obviously PBB. Pre-baby bodies."

She laughed. "I never heard that before."

"Everything about them at that age is perky, from their attitude to their boobs."

"I'm just happy the panties go up to a large and extra-large. Big girls like the little pink shopping bag, too," Cathy added.

The woman laughed and the cashier smiled. Cathy had been so centered on her size that she'd nearly forgotten that there were more women like her than women like Cybil. If there were more women like Cybil, Cathy thought, she'd probably be out of a job. Only in America could the media make women who are in the majority feel like second-class citizens.

***

On her way out of the mall Cathy slowed down long enough to notice there were a few new stores, including one for the younger plus size woman. She looked at the display window; it was good to see someone finally address this need. Girls needed to look like girls, young and pretty, not like little matrons. As she looked at the outfits, Cathy thought even she could get away with a couple of them.

"I think you'd look great in any of those," a male voice said.

"You don't think they're a little too young for me?"

"Not at all. You have a nice figure, you should show it off."

She thought for a moment. "Maybe I'll go in and try one on."

"You should."

"I need an objective opinion, Paul. Are you busy?" She turned around to see the look of astonishment on his face.

"I have some time."

"Good. I'm going away for the weekend and I need something fun like this to wear."

"A weekend getaway sounds like fun. Where are you going?"

"Florida. Let's go in, shall we?"

They were met by a salesperson/greeter.

"Hi, my name is Missy. Can I help you?"

"Hi, Missy. I would like to see that third ensemble in the window. It's the jeans and a halter top."

"The jeans are by Baby Phat. You'll like them."

"I'm sure I will."

"What size do you need?" Missy asked.

"I need a size 16 or 18, depending on the cut."

She looked at her. "I think you're more of a size 16." She took a pair from the rack. "Okay."

"What about the tops?"

"Well, I wear a 40DD, if that helps."

Paul looked uncomfortable. Cathy knew she was going to have fun with him.

"It does. You will probably need a 2X."

"I know. I've had big boobs for a long time." She laughed. "Can I try that hanky hem shirt, too?"

"Sure." The clerk handed her both tops. "The fitting room is over there." She pointed to the rear of the store.

Cathy handed Paul her Victoria's Secret bag and pocketbook as if he were her personal valet. "Hold these please. Thank you."

Cathy secretly enjoyed that fish out of water expression on Paul's face. Once in the dressing room she got out of her clothes and changed into the jeans, which fit nicely then she put her halter top on.

"How are you doing in there?" Missy asked.

"I think it's good." She stepped out of the fitting room and did a little twirl. "So what do you think?" "That looks hot," Missy said.

"What do you have to say, Paul?"

His face was red, which said it all. "You look good."

"Then I'm taking this outfit and the other top."

"You're not going to try the other top on?"

"No, Missy. I think I've tortured my former boyfriend long enough."

Missy smirked. "Gotcha."

Cathy went back into the fitting room.

Fifteen minutes later she was sitting in the food court with Paul.

"I think you picked the right outfits for the weekend. It's a shame that I'm not the one who's going to enjoy looking at you in them."

"Thank you for your help and for holding my stuff for me."

"That wasn't too uncomfortable."

She snickered. "Not too much."

A knowing look came over Paul's face. "Before I saw you I was on the fence but now I'm sure."

"Sure about what?"

"I wasn't sure if you were in love with him but now I can see it. Your whole attitude has changed. You seem happier, lighter and more at peace. Not to mention you didn't rip me a new one."

Cathy shrugged her shoulders. "What would that have accomplished? It's over and done with."

"That might be true for you but I will always regret how I took you for granted time and time again. I'm surprised you put up with me for as long as you did."

"I'm surprised about that too. God knows I should have dumped your ass much sooner."

"Why didn't you?" He genuinely wanted to know.

Cathy contemplated a moment. "In a way I was scared to let you go, which makes it as much my fault as yours since I let you get away with hurting me time after time. I was afraid I'd never find anyone else. It took finding you in bed with another woman to knock some sense into me."

"It took you catching me to get me to finally realize I blew the best thing I ever had."

He got up to hold her chair as she started to stand. "I guess we both learned a lesson," Cathy said.

He put the chair back. "You're never too old to learn."

Cathy turned to Paul. "Are you sure I won't look stupid in these outfits?"

"You looked great in them. Don't worry about it. You don't look 40 at all." She smiled. "You think not?" "I know not." He grinned

Paul walked Cathy to her car. She was glad that they'd reached a truce. She gave him a hug and headed home, having done one of the most grown-up things she'd ever done.

***

When Cathy got home she put her outfits to the side to pack up.

Just as she got settled in with a cup of decaf and a fashion magazine, the phone rang.

She looked at the caller ID. It was Andrew.

"Hello, Andrew."

"Hi, mom."

"This is a pleasant surprise. What's going on?"

"Not much, Mom. I wanted to see how you were doing."

"I'm good. I did tell you I was going to Florida this weekend, right?"

"I don't think so."

"I'm going to Tampa for the Yankees' weekend series with the Devil Rays."

"That's cool, Mom."

"I thought so, too. Be sure to tell your brother."

"Okay."

"What about you? Do you have any plans or a date this weekend?" Cathy knew she'd stepped into foreign territory. She normally preferred a don't ask, don't tell policy when it came to her sons' dating life, but today she made an exception.

"No."

"You don't like anyone up there in particular?"

"Well, there is one girl but she's in the Jane Austen Club."

"Now there's a girl after my own heart. Is she in one of your classes?"

"She's in my English class. We're reading novels by English authors this semester."

Cathy's inner nerd was very intrigued. "That sounds interesting. What authors are you reading?"

"Bronte and Austen are two I can think of now."

"*Wuthering Heights, Pride and Prejudice, Sense and Sensibility*, I love those books. I even re-read them every now and then. They are classics."

"You're a literary agent. You're supposed to read books. It just seems like we're reading the book versions of chick flicks."

Cathy tried to sway her son. "Well, the male characters are timeless and appealing to women of all ages."

"So what is it about those guys? They don't seem like nice men." He was perplexed.

Cathy couldn't help chuckling. "It's called brooding. Women find it intriguing.

"I don't get it. A guy snarls around all day making backhanded comments and girls go all gooey."

"In their defense the English countryside is beautiful but it does have its share of gloomy, overcast days, particularly in late fall and winter. They could be suffering from seasonal affective disorder. You know, not enough light."

"We've been to England, Mom. I think their disposition has more to do with the lack of dentists. I bet you they had some mean toothaches back then. They probably wandered around the moors until they got tired enough to sleep," Andrew said very matter of fact.

Cathy laughed in spite of herself. "You have a point, Andrew, but give Austen and Bronte a chance. You may get to like them."

"I'll try, Mom."

"You'll have to do better than that; you have a GPA to consider. Who knows? Maybe you can ask that young lady to study with you one day."

"I didn't think of that. Boy, Mom, going out again has really changed you."

"Really? How?"

"I would never expect you to give me advice about meeting a girl. Any other time you don't want to hear about it."

"I realize you and your brother are growing up. I can't stop you from being interested in girls or dating and I don't

"I realize you and your brother are growing up. I can't throw a wet blanket on girls or dating and I don't want to know the details. Your great-great grandmother said never to get too involved in your kid's love lives if you ever want to sleep again. Therefore TMI mean not enough sleep for me and I need my rest." She paused. "However the minimum age for grandparenthood age is over 52 and is subject to upward revisions."

He laughed. "I won't forget."

"Make sure you don't. I didn't have choices growing up, but I made damn sure you did."

"I know, Mom. Well, I'm getting a little hungry so I'm going to head over to the dining hall."

"All right, go ahead, I'll talk to you later. Don't forget I'll have my cell phone with me in Florida so I won't be out of reach."

"I got it, Mom. Have a good time and don't worry."

"Okay. Love you, beautiful child of mine."

He groaned. "Mom."

"I know. You're not a baby, but you two will always be my beautiful boys."

"Love you too, Mom."

Cathy looked at her sons' graduation photos on the dresser. As they grew up she'd allowed them the freedom to take part in many of the activities she hadn't been allowed to do when she was a teenager. They'd participated in school sports programs, belonged to clubs and gone on marching band trips all around New York State. They even went to the prom with dates. Why? Cathy didn't want Andrew and Alexander get such a late start in life doing *normal things*. In addition to talking about sex, she'd demonstrated how to use a condom. Cathy knew she could have asked her father or Madison to do that, but there was a method to her madness. Although she would prefer abstinence, she had to be realistic. There was a lot more at risk than unwanted pregnancies What's more, she figured the mental picture of their mother demonstrating the proper use of a condom would singe their minds just enough to buy her a little more abstinence time.

CHAPTER 22

The next morning Cathy tried to calm her nerves while waiting in the exam room for Dr. Adams. The last thing she needed was a high blood pressure reading to complicate her life and ruin her plans for the weekend. The Yankees had won 19-2 the previous night and she couldn't wait to get to Tampa. Her heart raced when Barbara came in to take her blood pressure.

"How are you, Cathy?"

"Good."

"Let's see what we have."

Stethoscope on, she put the cuff around her arm and began pumping. Cathy prayed for a decent reading.

She took the cuff off. "Have you been on vacation?"

"No, but I'm going away tomorrow. Why?"

"Your numbers look great. It's 110 over 70."

"Good."

"It really is." She noted it in her file and Dr. Adams walked in a few minutes later.

"Good morning, Cathy."

"Morning, Doc."

He sat on the stool. "So how are you feeling?"

"Overall, not too bad."

"How's your back?"

"I haven't been all that bothered in the last couple of days."

"Good." He made a few notations on her chart. "Okay, then. I'd say you were good to go for your trip."

She breathed a sigh of relief. "So I don't have to get undressed or get poked and prodded?"

"Not unless you were looking forward to that." His dry humor surfaced.

"Doctor Adams has jokes this morning," Cathy laughed.

He stood up. "I'm here all week. Don't forget to tip your waitress on the way out."

"You are too funny."

"Seriously, Cathy, just keep the meds up as needed, take frequent breaks and be sure to pace yourself in the warmer weather."

"I will." She slid off the table.

"Good. Be sure to make an appointment for two weeks from now."

"Will do."

"Have a good weekend, Cathy."

"Thanks, Doc."

Anna was reading *Ladies Home Journal* in the waiting room when Cathy walked out.

She stood up. "Are you all cleared and ready for takeoff?"

"I got the thumbs up. All I have to do is make another appointment for two weeks from now and we're out of here."

"Good, we can still make it to Magdalena's for a wash, set, blow and curl."

Cathy looked in the mirror at her hair. "Lord knows I need it."

Hair was a sacred thing for Cathy and Anna. Their dad had always said the hearings for Supreme Court nominees didn't hold a candle to choosing a hairdresser in the Chambers family. Over the years, Cathy, Anna and their mother had tried different salons with varying degrees of success. Cost was never an object but time was.

Magdalena's in Hempstead was their spot. Even though they had to travel and most of the beauticians spoke limited English, they did speak the international language of hair. With walk-ins accepted and enough operators to handle them, the only real problem was to sign in early. Otherwise, it was practically a roller derby without roller skates. When they arrived at the shop at 8:45 A.M. they immediately got out to wait in front of the shop for the doors to open.

Anna looked around. "I guess we're first."

Cathy peered in the window. "There's no one at the back entrance. Hopefully it will stay that way. What time do you have?"

Anna looked at her watch. "It's 8:52 give or take a couple of minutes."

A van pulled up next to their car and a group of teenage girls got out.

"I guess we got here just in time," Cathy whispered.

"We did. Antonio just walked in."

Magdalena's assistant, Antonio, unlocked the doors and held the crowd of women back for a minute. Once he had the sign-in book out, he quickly got out of the way of the stampeding women. Cathy and Anna signed in. As soon as they hung their jackets, they were called to the sink. An hour or so later they were ensconced under the dryer with the *CPA Journal* and *Publishers Weekly* to keep them occupied.

When a discussion turned louder at the front of the salon, Cathy looked up to see a teen girl sitting in the chair arguing about her style.

"I want it like this," the girl explained emphatically and pointed to a picture.

"She wants the spiral curls up here like this." Another girl pointed to her hair.

Cathy shook her head. *Thank God I have sons. I can't imagine having two girls with hair issues.*

Anna tapped Cathy on the hand. "See that?" She pointed towards the front.

"Yes, I see it."

"That's enough to change my mind about having a daughter."

Cathy chuckled. "I bet it is."

By the time ten-thirty rolled around Cathy and Anna were done. Anna had her hair wrapped and covered by a hat, while Cathy wore hers loose. They made a quick pit stop at Dunkin Donuts before heading home. Quietly sipping coffee, Cathy looked out the car window.

"I saw Paul when I went to the mall yesterday."

Anna was floored. "You saw Paul yesterday and you didn't mention it until now?"

"Yeah, it wasn't a big deal. I was looking in Torrid's display window and we started talking."

"You did?"

"Yeah. He even helped me pick an outfit for the weekend."

"Were you on medication yesterday?" Anna was being a little sarcastic.

"No. I had to drive to the mall myself so naturally I didn't take anything."

"So you were nice to Paul without any medicinal enhancements."

"I was. We even had a nice little chat over Cokes in the food court."

Anna was incredulous. "This is just too strange. So you've adopted this kinder, gentler attitude about Paul."

"I can't stay mad forever. I need to get rid of all the baggage in my life. Lisa did tell me that Marcus had nice girlfriends in the past and apparently there's no bad blood or anything, so I thought it was time I put Paul to rest."

"Wow, big sister, that's a really mature way to look at things."

"I know. I have to spread a little good karma out there."

"Oh, I see. Spread good karma and get good karma. I get it."

"At least that's the way I hope it works." Cathy looked out the window.

Cathy practically emptied out the contents of her closet to pack for one three-day weekend. At her wit's end, she tried to keep to a dressy casual theme. However, she finally gave up and chose another theme: whatever works.

When she finally finished packing, she put all the leftovers away. Underneath it all, she found her cell phone.

"Oh my God, I wondered what happened to that," she said out loud. Cathy picked up her phone to see she had a text message from Marcus.

Hey, baby. Call 555-3764 room 426 tonight for Intro to Phone Sex. There will be a quiz.

She laughed out loud. "He is too cute," she whispered.

"Cathy!" Anna shouted from downstairs.

Cathy walked to the top of the stairs. "Yeah?"

"Roger is coming over to stay the night. It will be easier for us in the morning."

"Makes sense."

"Have you called the car service for tomorrow morning?"

"Actually I emailed E.D. to contact them. It's the same people we use when we have to head out of town."

"Good. I'm heading to the drugstore. Do you need anything?"

"I've got all my meds. I packed lotion, shaving gel, bobby pins, rubbing alcohol. I'm not sure what else I might need."

"Condoms?"

"What?"

"You heard me. You do use them, right?"

"Absolutely."

"What size?

Cathy went cross-eyed. "Just get large or magnum or whatever the heck they call large."

"Lucky you."

"Are you picking up condoms?"

"No, Roger knows to have them."

"So does Marcus."

"You haven't seen each other in a couple of days; I'm picking them up so you have extras."

"Marcus isn't just playing baseball. He has batting practice, team meetings, pre and post-game press interviews. How much bumping and grinding do you think we'll have time for?"

"You're right. I'll get you two boxes."

"What?"

She left.

"Two boxes? Good grief. That's a lot of pressure."

***

A little while later Cathy decided to give Marcus a call. She knew she was a little ahead of schedule but she wanted to let him know she was looking forward to her lesson.

"Good afternoon," a man answered.

"Hi. May I have room 426?"

"Certainly."

It rang twice.

"Hello?" a woman answered.

Cathy was a little startled. "Yes, hello. Is Mr. Fox in?"

"May I tell him who is calling?"

"Yes. It's Catherine Chambers."

There was a pause. "I'm sorry, Ms. Chambers, he's busy at the moment. Can he call you back?"

"Yes, please."

"Does he have the number?"

"Yes, he does, thank you."

"All right then. Bye."

Cathy hung up the phone slowly. "Who in the world was that?"

Her mind went in a million directions. She'd dialed the right number and asked for the right room. Who was that woman? There was no way she was three for three in the cheated-on department. She was older, wiser, and her radar was much better. Cathy gave it some thought while she paced the floor. *For one thing, I don't know that Marcus was there to begin with. Why should I believe a woman I don't know? Didn't Marcus say they would be at the stadium in the afternoon before they checked in?*

She picked the phone up again. *Something is rotten in Denmark.* "Good afternoon." A woman answered this time.

"Yes. Good afternoon. Can you tell me if the guest in room 426 has checked in yet?"

"Certainly. Just a moment I'll check the computer."

"Thank you. Take your time."

"No, ma'am. We show no record of check in. According to the computer, he's set up for a late check in after eight A.M."

"Thanks so much. You've been very helpful."

"You're welcome. Have a good day."

"You do the same."

If Marcus hasn't checked in, who answered the phone?

Somebody is playing a game with me.

She called Marcus on his cell phone.

"Hello?"

"Hi, honey."

He was pleased to hear from her. "Hey, baby. Did you get my text message?"

"I most certainly did. I can't wait to be the teacher's pet."

"Sounds good to me. You'll be here tomorrow afternoon, right?"

"That's the plan."

"Your car service is coming to get you in the morning?"

"Yeah. E.D. took care of that for me."

"I can't wait to see you. I just took batting practice and I put a real edge on the ball, thanks to you."

"Thanks to me? What did I do?"

"You're all I can think about. I want you so bad it's driving me crazy," he whispered.

Cathy felt a rush through her body. "I can't wait to see you. I want you, too."

"Tomorrow can't come fast enough for me." He paused. "Anyway, baby, you called me. Is anything up?"

Cathy came back to earth. "I almost forgot. There is something."

"What's up?"

"I called your room a little earlier about your lesson plan."

"That was sweet, baby, but I haven't checked in yet."

"I know. A woman answered the phone."

"A woman answered the phone? How is that possible?" He was puzzled.

"She wanted me to think you were there and I'm positive it wasn't the maid."

"What did she say?"

"She said you were busy."

"Busy with what?"

"Like busy with her."

"This doesn't make any sense. Why would they connect you to my room from the front desk when I haven't checked in? I'm confused?"

"Me, too."

While they were talking, Cathy had logged onto her laptop to check the flight weather for travelers. As she was about to log onto The Weather Channel's site, she noticed an entertainment blurb about Cybil. She clicked on the story.

Her eyes popped. "Marcus. I found something interesting online."

"What?"

"According to this there's trouble on the set of Cybil George's debut film. Apparently she's walked off the set."

As soon as the words came out of Cathy's mouth, Marcus knew who was in his room.

He groaned. "I can't believe this crap."

"You think she was the one who answered the phone?"

"Now that you told me about her movie, I know it's her."

"You sound sure about that."

Marcus knew where this was going to go but he went ahead anyway. He reasoned he'd tell her now rather than later.

"She's done this before."

"Really? She's done this before?"

"Back when we were together, if she wanted to surprise me on the road she'd sweet talk the guy at the front desk into giving her the spare key card before I checked in."

Cathy put the pieces of the puzzle together. "That explains a lot."

"It does?"

"I called the hotel's front desk twice. The first time a man answered and connected me to the room. The second time a woman answered and she told me you hadn't checked in."

"I'm going to straighten this out, sweetie."

"I know you will."

"I'll give you a call a little later, okay?"

"Okay. I love you."

"I love you, Cathy."

Cathy should have felt better. Although she knew Marcus handled the Club Z incident, she couldn't shake the image of Cybil waiting for him naked in his room. She called the office.

"Good evening, Chambers-Stevens Agency."

"Hey, Sylvia. You're still there? It's getting late."

"I know, but E.D. was going over some things and needed me to stay."

"I'll talk to him. You go home to your handsome husband."

"Thanks, Cathy. Have a good weekend, okay? I'm ringing E.D."

"I will, thanks. You do the same."

"E.D. here."

"Hey, E.D. What's shaking?"

"Hey, Cathy. There's not much going on here. How about you?"

"Getting ready for the weekend," Cathy answered.

"Good." E.D. sounded tense.

"Now that we've gone through all the bull, what's got you in a tizzy? I sent Sylvia home."

"Shouldn't you be concentrating on your romantic weekend with Marcus?"

"We're not talking about me at the moment."

"Why not? What's going on there?"

"I'll tell you mine if you tell me yours, E.D." She heard him groan.

"It's Bill Bond. I checked in with the VP to see what was happening with the proposal we sent in to update his book for a third edition and I think they're jerking my chain."

"They're just pushing things closer to the timetable of ninety days delineated in the contract, which is just fine. If they don't give us an answer by the 90th day we can shop the proposal to other publishers and Bill gets the rights back to his book."

"So I'm getting worked up for nothing?"

"Yep. We're covered, don't worry."

"That's a load off my mind." He paused. "Now what's on your mind? What's going on with Marcus?"

"It's not really Marcus, per se. It's Cybil."

"What about her?"

"She walked off the set of her movie in Maryland and into Marcus's hotel room."

"She's where?"

"In his hotel room. She's making her play to get him back. I can't say that I blame her. Marcus is a wonderful man."

"You are far too calm. You're not behind the wheel of a Mercedes, are you?"

"That's foul, E.D. I'm not in Florida and I'm not planning to rent a Mercedes."

"Then why are you so calm?"

"I spoke to Marcus and he hasn't checked into his room yet. I know she's there because she answered the phone when I called."

"If Marcus isn't even checked in yet, how did she get into his room?"

"Like most pretty women, she sweet talked her way in. Marcus said he's going to straighten her out."

"I see. But you're worried she might be naked and his resolve may wane."

"I keep replaying a seduction scene over and over in my head."

"That's the real reason you called this evening. You need to keep your mind occupied."

"Guilty as charged."

"Trusting isn't easy for anyone, you know. Hey, I've been married twice."

"And I've been cheated on twice. I count my ex-husband in my overall number but Paul's cheating really scarred me."

"I know."

"I just have to relax, right?"

"It's easier said than done for all of us."

She sighed. "I know. Anyway, let's change the subject. Did you have a chance to call the car service for me?"

"It's a done deal."

"Thanks. That's one less detail for me to worry about."

"Anyway, my dear, I should get my tail out of here too."

"It's about time. Go home."

"Have a great weekend, Cathy, and don't think about the office or clients. This is your weekend."

"I promise. Have a good weekend yourself."

"Will do."

Anna called to say she and Roger were grabbing a bite out. With no one but herself to fend for, Cathy settled on yogurt. Before she could open it, she heard a voice at the door.

"Knock, knock, Cousin. I have pizza."

She put the yogurt back. "Good. Anna and Roger are having dinner out."

"I guess it's a good thing I only got one pie."

She took a couple of paper plates out. "What kind is it?"

He opened the box. "Half pepperoni and half plain cheese."

"Cool. You want a soda?"

"Yeah."

Cathy got a couple of Cokes from the refrigerator. "Here you go."

"Thanks." He grabbed a couple of slices and opened his soda.

"So have you told Aunt Peg about what happened at your apartment?"

He wiped his mouth. "Yeah. I went over there this afternoon."

"Good. She worries about you."

"I know. That's why I went over. I didn't want her to worry."

Cathy took a plain slice. "She's a pistol, that aunt of mine."

"Don't I know it? She had a good time in London, though."

"I always thought your mother and mine would travel together."

"So did I."

"It would have been a nice thing."

"True, but that ship has sailed."

She took a bite. "You got the pizza from Carmine's."

"Best pizza in town."

Cathy's mouth was full so she nodded in agreement.

"So are you jazzed about the trip?"

Cathy wiped her mouth. "Yeah, I am. I've never gone away for a baseball game."

"Don't you mean you've never gone away with or for a man?" His question was pointed.

"I did go away with my ex-husband on a mini honeymoon."

"Okay, let me rephrase that. You haven't been away with a man in more than a decade. I think that qualifies as never."

"Well, if you're going to split hairs." She rolled her eyes.

"All kidding aside, I am happy for you, Cathy. I don't think I've ever seen you this happy before."

"I'm not sure if I've ever felt like this before. It's all so new to me."

"That's a nice feeling. And yes I do remember what true love feels like."

"You think that's what this is?"

"Come on, Cathy, it's love. No doubt about it."

Cathy could have talked about what happened with Marcus and Cybil but for once she chose to let sleeping dogs lie.

"Well, I plan to enjoy it."

"You should. Aren't you going to have another slice?"

"In a minute. I can't put it away that fast."

"Are you trying to say something?"

Cathy looked at his tie. Most of the sauce was on it.

"I hope your tie enjoyed the pizza as much as you did."

He looked down. "Aw, damn it."

"You've never been able to master eating pizza or drinking coffee without getting it on your ties. God, sometimes I think you need a bib."

"You're probably correct about that." He took the tie off.

She laughed. Leave it to Madison to do something stupid to make her laugh, no matter how unintentional the laugh was.

One more slice of pizza later, Cathy was ready to relax upstairs in her room before calling it an early night. She couldn't afford to get bags under her eyes or sport a Rocky Raccoon look. She tried to put things out of her mind long enough to get a peaceful night's sleep.

The Yankees checked into their lodging late. Marcus told Ben about what had transpired when Cathy called and said he was wary of what other tricks Cybil had up her sleeve. As they left the desk, Ben took Marcus's suitcase from him and placed it on the cart.

Marcus was thrown off. "Ben, I can carry my own bag."

"I know you can. Just humor me, okay?"

Marcus threw his hands up. "Okay."

"Okay. We'll head up to your room first, Marcus."

The bellman just stood there quietly. The elevator bell rang.

Ben got in and held the door open for Marcus, John, Mark and Juan.

"Man, I am beat," John sighed.

"Thank God for travel days. There aren't many this time of year," Mark said.

"I think this is our last travel day," Juan added.

The elevator stopped on their floor.

Marcus turned to Ben. "We're going to my room first, right?"

"Right."

They walked up to his door and Marcus opened it.

Just as he was about to walk in, Ben stopped him. "No, Marcus, let the bellman put the bags in first."

He handed the bellman a tip. "Thanks, sir." He turned on the lights and went in. Immediately a woman screamed. White-faced and panicked, the bellman ran out. "I'm sorry. I didn't know anyone was in there."

Ben handed him another fifty. "Don't worry about it, son. That's what she gets for pulling this stunt again."

"Who the hell?" Sheet wrapped around her, Cybil came to the door ready to spit bullets.

"What are you doing in my room, Cybil?" Marcus was not amused.

"I wanted to surprise you."

"We're not a couple anymore, Cybil. Why would you want to surprise me naked when you obviously know I have a girlfriend?"

"I got to thinking about old times."

Mark yawned. "Listen, Marcus, I'm heading to my room. See ya in the morning for training." "Okay. Good night."

"I'm beat," John said.

"Same here. We'll see you tomorrow," Juan said as they walked down the hall.

Cybil looked at Ben.

"Look at me all you want. I am not going anywhere." He held his position.

She rolled her eyes at him.

Marcus was exasperated. "Okay, Cybil, fun and games are over. Get dressed and I'll meet you downstairs in the bar."

"We could have a drink in your room."

Marcus lost his patience. "The bar, Cybil. Ten minutes. I'll see you downstairs." He walked away.

She slammed the door.

"Was it something I said?" Ben chuckled.

Marcus sat at the bar with a club soda. He was tired. However, the situation needed handling and it wasn't something Ben could do for him; he had to straighten Cybil out once and for all. Ten minutes passed. Marcus was ticked off by her fashionable lateness.

Finally she appeared fully dressed. "Gin and tonic, please," she said to the bartender.

"Sorry I kept you waiting." She pulled up a stool.

"Coming right up, miss."

Marcus remained quiet and calm. He wouldn't begin talking until she had her drink in hand, even though he knew that he could wind up wearing it. "Here you go, miss."

"Thank you." She sipped her drink.

"Put it on my tab, please," Marcus said.

"Sure thing."

She smiled. "Thanks. I knew you still cared."

He rubbed his forehead. "Cybil, we have to get real here."

"Fine. You and I used to be a real couple."

"Cybil, you have to accept that I've moved on."

She fidgeted in her seat. "With your new girlfriend." "Yes, with Cathy. She's the one I want to be with." "Well, where is she? I'm here." She looked around. "That used to be a bone of contention with us."

"She'll be here tomorrow afternoon." He gulped back his club soda. "The fact is, I don't want this to get ugly, but you can't pull these stunts. First you show up in Baltimore saying you're filming a movie and now you're here in Tampa. I think it's a good bet that you're not shooting here."

"Okay, I wanted to see you and see for myself if you've really moved on."

"I have, Cybil. Cathy isn't just a girlfriend. I love her. I'm in love with her."

Cybil tried not to look as if she'd been punched in the chest. "I see."

"I'm not saying this to hurt you. It's the God's honest truth."

She looked at his face. "You're happy with her, aren't you?"

"Yes, I am. I hope you can find someone who makes you feel the way she makes me feel."

"Even with all the tricks and machinations, you hope I'll find happiness?"

"Sure. Why shouldn't I?"

She had a slight smile on her face. "That's nice of you." She rubbed her eyes. "You know, I never made the chubby chaser comment. The interviewer was asking all sorts of questions and my words got twisted."

"It happens. I was more upset for Cathy than me. She didn't deserve that. She has kids."

"I know that's a big thing for you. Have you met her kids?"

"Not yet. They're in college but I think I'll be meeting them during their early fall break in October."

"Speaking of October, I see you're really making the drive for the post season."

"We're trying."

"Good luck with that." She looked around for a clock. "What time is it?"

Marcus looked at his watch. "It's time for me to catch some sleep." He got up and put down cash for the bartender.

"Hold on, I'll give you change."

"Keep the change."

"Thanks."

"Well, Cybil, I'm going to say good night."

"Good night. I'm just going to finish my drink."

"Okay, then."

He walked out and back into the lobby. Ben was dozing near a potted palm. Marcus nudged him. "Hey, sleepy head."

Ben couldn't believe he'd fallen asleep. "So how did it go?" He stood up and stretched.

"Not bad. I think I made my point."

"Good. Now we can sleep." Marcus

pressed the elevator button.

"Damn!"

"What?"

"I told Cathy I'd call her tonight."

Ben squinted and rubbed his eyes to focus on his watch. "It's too late now to call her. Besides, she'll be here tomorrow."

The elevator bell rang.

Ben turned to Marcus. "I guess your workout is set."

Marcus sported a devilish grin. "Yep. I'm looking forward to extra innings," he said as they got on the elevator.

CHAPTER 23

All systems were go Friday morning. Cathy primped and fussed with her hair. The weather had cooled down in the North, but humidity was still king in the South. She gave her hair a spritz of holding spray and one last shake. "That's the best I can do."

Cathy studied the room to see if she had left anything out. She could hear Anna, Roger and Madison milling around downstairs.

Satisfied that she had everything, Cathy joined them.

"Good morning, Cathy."

"Good morning, Roger."

Roger was a tall, nice looking guy whose jovial personality balanced nicely with Anna's somewhat tougher demeanor.

"Cathy, you didn't set the coffee timer. There's no coffee," Madison whined.

"No, I didn't, Madison. We have to get to the airport and I wanted to keep the kitchen clean."

Bewildered by their cleaning habits, Madison nodded his head. "You two are obsessive when it comes to this clean thing."

"Shut up, Mad. Aunt Peg keeps a clean house, too. Don't act like you don't know," Cathy smirked.

"I certainly hope Alex and Andrew aren't keeping to the tenets at school. They're young men, they should be allowed to just let it hang sometimes," Madison asserted.

"This from the man whose cologne arrives two minutes before he enters the room." Cathy laughed.

"I did say sometimes."

"Listen, Mad, you can get a cup of coffee at the airport. Relax." Anna rolled her eyes.

"What time is the car coming, Cathy?"

"E.D. said it would be here between nine and nine forty-five."

Roger looked at his watch. "It's a little after nine now."

"You have only one bag, Cathy?" Anna asked.

"Yes, and everything is in it. I don't feel like pulling a caravan of luggage for three days."

The doorbell chimed, and Roger looked out the window. "Car's here."

Anna opened the door and there stood Louis.

"Good morning, Ms. Chambers. Nice to see you again."

"Good morning, Louis. Cathy didn't tell us you were coming."

Cathy walked to the door. "That's because Cathy didn't know."

"That's true. Mr. Fox sent me."

"But how? E.D. arranged for our usual car service." She stopped to think. "Oh, E.D. was in on this the whole time." Louis's smile said it all.

"I don't care how it came about. We're traveling to the airport in style," Madison said.

"Shut up, Madison," Anna and Cathy chorused.

"Damn."

"Louis, this is my cousin, Madison, and Roger, my future brother-in-law."

They shook hands.

"Nice to meet you both." Louis smiled, then turned to the bags. "Is this everything?"

Anna gave the room one last look. "Yes. That's everything."

Madison and Roger gave Louis a hand loading the bags into the trunk. Anna and Cathy walked outside. "Anna, you have our tickets?" Roger asked.

She checked her pocketbook. "I have them."

Although she'd already checked a million times Cathy looked to make sure her confirmation and e-ticket were in her bag. They were.

They climbed into the limousine and off they went.

Ham that he was, Madison stretched out like a movie star. "I could get used to this."

"Well, don't get used to it. Marcus didn't do this for you, he did it for Cathy," Anna said.

Cathy saw Louis smile in the rearview mirror.

Roger took out his palm pilot. "I checked the weekend weather and it's supposed to be on the warm side."

"At least the games are played in a dome so I don't have to worry about my hair," Anna said.

The conversation served as a background to Cathy's thoughts as she stared out the window. Distracted and tired, she hadn't slept much the night before, wondering what was happening in Tampa.

"Cathy, you're awfully quiet. Are you all right?"

"I'm fine, Anna. I was just thinking, that's all."

"Are you sure?"

"I didn't sleep that well last night. I'm just plain old tired."

"Okay. Maybe you can take a nap once we check into the hotel."

Although there were traffic pockets here and there, the car arrived at the airport in good time. When they pulled up to the hustle and bustle of the departures area, Louis gave them the star treatment, opening the door and loading the luggage onto the carts.

"Thanks again, Louis." Anna shook his hand.

"You're welcome. It was my pleasure."

Madison and Roger shook hands with Louis as well. They started to walk in.

"Cathy, are you coming?"

"Just give me a minute, Madison. I'll be right there."

She turned to Louis. "So how's your back?"

"Not bad, Ms. Chambers. What about you?"

"I'm fine. Thanks." She gave him a kiss on the cheek. "Oh, and please call me Cathy."

"I sure will, Cathy."

"Thanks again."

"You're very welcome. And by the way, you don't have anything to worry about. You are head and shoulders above her and he knows it, too."

She smiled. "Thanks, Louis. I needed to hear that."

***

I should have brought my dental records and blood type, Cathy thought as they waded through another flight check point. She was relieved when they finally cleared security and boarded the plane. *I just need to close my eyes for a minute*. Cathy sighed as she took her window seat.

"Cathy." Anna tapped her shoulder.

She opened her eyes. "Yeah?"

"We're here."

Her mind still in a fog, she looked around. "You mean I slept through the entire flight?"

"Yes, you did."

"Where's Madison?"

"He already de-planed. He's talking to a woman he met on the flight."

Cathy got up. "Okay, I'm ready."

By the time they de-planed Madison had retrieved the bags from the luggage carousel.

"Are you up now, sleepyhead?"

"As a matter of fact I am." She looked around for the Avis sign.

"What are you looking for?" Anna asked.

"The Avis car rental counter."

"I know where it is. Follow me."

They followed Roger to Avis. Cathy went up to the counter.

"Hi, can I help you?"

"Yes. My name is Catherine Chambers."

"Chambers? I have all your paperwork here. I just need to see some identification."

Cathy showed her driver's license. The clerk looked it over. "Thank you. Sign here please." Cathy read the paperwork over and then signed.

The clerk handed a young man the keys. "Evan will bring the car around. Enjoy your stay."

"Thank you." They

walked outside.

"That had to be the shortest time I've ever waited at a car rental counter," Anna said as she put on her sunglasses.

Evan pulled up in a Volvo. "Here are the directions to the Hilton. However, if you have any problems, the car is equipped with a navigational system. Have a nice stay in Tampa."

Madison and Roger loaded up the trunk.

"Are you sure you want to drive, Cathy? Roger or I can if you're not up to it," Anna said.

"Ahem. I am a licensed driver too. I can drive as well."

"Good grief, Madison, it's not a competition," Anna said.

"I'm all right to drive." Cathy looked at the map. "The hotel doesn't appear to be too far from here. I can handle it."

"Did you take anything on the plane?"

"No. I actually fell asleep because I was tired, not drugged."

"Okay. If you're sure then we'll go."

"I'm sure." She put her sunglasses on.

"Let's get going"

Check in was painless and Cathy was grateful for a little down time since her nap on the plane had been far from restful. She had an aching neck and shoulders to prove it. Still, this was one time she couldn't blame the accident for the pain; stress and worry were having their way with her.

There was a knock on the door.

"Hey, Anna."

"Listen, we're going to get something to eat. You want to come?"

"No. I'll pass. I'm still feeling tired."

"You want me to bring you something back?"

"No. I have a protein bar to tide me over. I'll be fine. You guys go ahead and enjoy yourselves."

"Okay. We'll see you later."

"All right."

After sending them on their way, Cathy unpacked and turned the television on as a distraction. It didn't help. There were 300 channels to choose from, but there wasn't anything of interest on a single one. Disgusted, Cathy turned the television off and decided to take a bath and soak her aching muscles. Not wanting to mess up her hair, she left the door open to let some steam out. Just as she stepped into the hot water, there was a knock at the door.

"Cathy?" Anna shouted.

"I'm in the tub, Anna!" she shouted back. "Okay.
We'll be back in the room around five-thirty." "Got
it! Five-thirty!" she called.

"I'll call your room when we're ready to head over to the stadium!"

"Good deal!"

Just as Cathy got comfortable again, there was more knocking.

"What's up, Anna?"

She waited for a reply and all she got was more frantic knocking.

"What's going on? I told her I was in the tub," Cathy mumbled as she wrapped a towel around her and slipped her robe over it.

"Okay, I'm coming to the door. Quit knocking so hard." She opened the door. "Okay, where's the…"

Before Cathy could get another word out, Marcus kissed her and nearly knocked her over. Cathy's hands frantically searched for the privacy sign. She hooked it with her two fingers and hung it on the door as it closed.

Cathy was breathless and towel-less in a matter of seconds. They didn't make it to the bed.

***

Curled up together in bed a little later, Cathy laid her head on Marcus's chest.

"So this is what the bed feels like."

"What do you think?"

"It's nice. I have to say, though, that I have a healthy new respect for recliners."

"Me, too."

She was quiet for a moment. "You know, I forgot to tell you something the other day."

He stroked her hair. "What did you forget to tell me?"

"I had lunch with Lisa Spellman."

His hair nearly curled. "You had lunch with her? She's a tabloid queen. Why on earth would you talk to her voluntarily?"

"Well..." She sounded like Samantha from *Bewitched*. "I was sick of her following me so I figured if you can't beat them, invite them to lunch. The way I see it, these tabloid reporters are able to write scandalous stories because they don't know their subjects. It's harder to write a hatchet piece when it's someone you know personally."

"You could have a point but I think the money commands greater allegiance for these folks." He was skeptical.

"Maybe so, but I thought there was just a little something different about Lisa so after I practically chased her through the supermarket, I invited her to lunch."

"You did what? You chased her?" He was dumbfounded.

"Yes."

"Through the supermarket in front of other customers?"

"Right. But that's beside the point. I learned a lot about her over lunch."

"Really? Like what?"

"For one thing, she has a degree in journalism from Columbia University."

"She's an Ivy Leaguer?"

"Yeah. I know, I was surprised, too. Apparently she fell into tabloid reporting by accident and it paid a lot more than her fact checker job."

"So she went where the money was."

"Can you blame her? Still, she seems like good people to me."

"You think so?"

"Yeah. For one thing, you haven't seen an article about the supermarket incident and that happened days ago. She could have skewered me."

"True. Maybe she isn't as bad as I thought. I'll take it under advisement."

"That's fine with me."

She rested her head on his chest and sighed.

"Penny for your thoughts, Ms. Chambers."

"It's not so much a thought as it is a question."

"Okay. Then it's a penny for your question."

"Seriously, Marcus, there is something I want to ask you about."

"Ask away."

She sat up. "You were supposed to call me last night after you talked to and/or handled Cybil. I just want to know what happened."

"I'm here. Doesn't that say it all?"

"Yes and no. What if the shoe were on the other foot? What if it was my former boyfriend who just happened to be a sexy actor? Would you let me get away with saying I'm here with you and that's it?"

"Yeah, that would be fine with me. I'm a guy. Most guys would rather know as little as possible when it comes to their girlfriend's old boyfriends. It's a girl thing to be curious."

He had a point. "Okay, so you're right." She sighed. "I know you're here and I feel good about that. But I still want to know what happened. I'll even take the bulldog version."

"The bulldog version?"

"A report that's three minutes or less."

Marcus saw a look of anxiety in Cathy's eyes. She was serious. He fluffed up the pillows behind him.

"Okay, then have it your way." He paused. "Naturally I told Ben what was going on. He's been through this with me before. Anyway, Ben figured we would teach her a lesson."

"Really?"

"Yeah. He sent the bellman in with the bags."

Cathy burst out laughing. "I guess the naked surprise was on her." She paused. "Remind me to thank Ben."

"Don't worry, I will. After she got over her embarrassment, I said for her to get dressed and meet me for a drink in the hotel bar."

"You weren't worried that you could have wound up wearing her drink?"

"The thought crossed my mind, but I had to let her know that I've moved on with my life, that I'd fallen in love with you." He brushed Cathy's hair from her eyes. "You're the woman I've been looking for all my life." They

kissed.

"So how did she take it?" Cathy asked.

"She seemed fine about it."

"Are you sure there isn't any underlying resentment?" Cathy was wary.

"Cybil's a grown woman. She'll live."

"You know her better than I do. I'll take your word for it."

"Good. Anyway, by the time I left the bar it was late. Now can I ask you a question?"

"Sure."

He reached over to Cathy's suitcase and took out two packages of condoms. "Why in the world do you have two packages of condoms? Talk about pressure."

Cathy turned beet red. "My sister Anna picked them up at the drugstore for me since I wasn't going out at the time."

"You told her to get this many?" He was surprised.

"No. I didn't tell her to buy two packages. I'm just glad I got the size right."

He had a cocky look on his face. "Yeah, large was right on the money. But she bought a regular and economy size box for a grand total of 48. Talk about performance pressure at the plate. This is a tall order."

Cathy laughed so hard her eyes watered. "Hey, I'm not putting pressure on you, okay?"

"The bar is set kind of high here. I have three games, three pre-game shows, three post-game shows, batting practices and at least three team meetings."

Cathy was insistent. "I repeat, I'm not putting pressure on you."

Marcus pretended he didn't hear her. "The way I see it, we have to go through at least a third of them for a respectable number."

Cathy's mouth fell open. "A third? Math isn't my strong suit but I know one third of 48 is 16. I think."

"Right."

"Sixteen times? We still have to eat, sleep and bathe in addition to all the baseball stuff. Not to mention we're leaving Sunday afternoon after the game."

"It's totally do-able. We have the rest of this afternoon and tonight after the game. Then we have Saturday morning and Saturday night. We even have Sunday morning."

"You're kidding?"

"No. I'm perfectly serious. We have to bring up our average."

"We have to what?"

"Bring our average up."

"What are you talking about? We're 2 for 2. Doesn't that mean we're batting 1,000?"

"Yes, if you look at it that way it does. However, we have 16 at bats which means our average is only 125."

"I don't think I've had sex 16 times in several months, let alone a weekend."

He moved closer to her. "Then it's time we changed that." Marcus hovered over her. "Really?" she asked.

"Oh yes. Really."

He planted little kisses all over her neck and breasts before he devoted his attention to her lips. She ran her hands through his hair and down his back. It was a perfect way to spend the afternoon and quite an accomplishment. They brought their average up to 250.

***

Marcus left around four, which left Cathy with some time to get ready for the game. She wanted to look nice and so she chose a skirt paired with a Yankee shirt with Marcus's name and number. Cathy noticed her skirt was a little loose, a pleasant side effect of being in love with such a gorgeous man.

There was a knock on the door.

"Cathy? Are you ready to head out?"

"Yeah. I'll be there in a minute." She checked her makeup and clothes in the mirror before stepping into the hallway.

"I'm caught up! I get lost in the afterglow!" Madison sang off-key.

Cathy put her key card in her purse. "Very funny,

Madison."

"You do have a glow about you, big sister."

"Yes, I must say your hair looks great, Cathy. Yours, too, Anna," Madison smirked.

They ignored him.

"It's nice to see you happy, Cathy."

"Thank you, Roger. It feels nice too."

"So what are we doing about tickets?" Madison asked.

"We have to go to the concierge desk."

"All right then, Yankee fans, let's boogie."

"Ahem. I'm a conscientious objector."

"That's right, Roger's a Mets fan." Madison laughed.

"But Marcus is a cool guy, so I'm rooting for the Yankees."

Cathy laughed. "Thanks, Roger. I guess we'd better get downstairs."

Anna pressed the button for the elevator. Just as the doors opened, Cybil and her entourage walked out. Cathy and Cybil stared at each other like fighters at opposite corners of the ring. Nothing was said and they simply let it pass.

Madison pressed the button. "Did you feel that cold wind?"

"Shut up, Mad," Anna shot back. "Are you okay,

Cathy? That was weird."

"I'm okay. Marcus and I talked about it and I'm fine."

"She doesn't look fine."

"Madison, shut up." Roger crossed his arms.

Roger had lightened the mood. They were laughing when the elevator doors opened. Cathy went up to the concierge desk.

"May I help you, ma'am?"

"Yes. I'm Catherine Chambers. I was told to come to the concierge to get our tickets for the game."

"Yes, ma'am. May I see some identification please?"

Cathy was a little taken aback as she opened her wallet for her license. "My goodness, who on earth would want to impersonate me for baseball tickets?"

The desk clerk checked her I.D. "Thank you, Ms. Chambers. I'm sorry if we offended you."

"None taken. You're just doing your job."

"We are. We certainly didn't want a repeat of what happened earlier." As soon as it came out of his mouth it was obvious he regretted it. "I'm sorry, Ms. Chambers. Here are your VIP passes for the game."

She took them. "Thank you, but what did you mean by a repeat of what happened earlier? Did someone else try to get the passes using my name?"

He spoke in a hushed tone. "I could get in a lot of trouble."

"I won't say a word. Just tell me what happened."

"A woman came to the desk earlier claiming to be you and she wanted the passes."

"What did she look like?"

"She didn't look like you at all. Although I hate to admit I read those rags, I'd seen your picture before so I knew it wasn't you."

"Why on earth would anyone impersonate me? I don't know anyone here."

He leaned forward. "Well, I saw her get into the elevator with the people of that model Cybil just a few minutes ago."

"Is that right?" She reached in her bag and gave him a tip. "Thank you. That was good looking out and I appreciate it. I really do." She looked at his nametag. "You've been a big help, Fred."

"Anytime, Ms. Chambers."

Madison, Anna and Roger were waiting for her.

"All set?" Anna asked.

"Yeah. I have everything."

"What's wrong? You don't look happy. Are they bad seats?"

"No, Madison, they're not bad seats at all."

"Then what's wrong? It's written all over your face."

"Apparently Cybil sent one of her cronies to try to get the passes earlier."

"How?" Roger asked.

"The woman tried to impersonate me but Fred there knew better."

Anna's face dropped. "You're kidding me. The nerve of that witch."

"I asked Marcus how Cybil took the news. He said she was fine, but I had a sinking feeling she was far to the left of fine."

"She can't change his feelings for you. They're a done deal."

"Maybe so, Anna, but that doesn't mean she has to like it or me." She stopped to take a couple of breaths. "Let's go. I don't want to be late."

Distracted, Cathy searched through her bag to find the keys.

"Give me the keys. I'll drive." Anna held her hand out.

She handed Anna the keys. "Thanks."

As they walked towards the exit she stopped. "Listen, I want us to have a good time at the game, so let's take Cybil and her antics off the discussion table for now." "I second that." Madison raised his hand.

"Good. Now the Devil Rays have been giving my boys a hell of a time this year and they need all the good thoughts and energy we can give them. Okay?" She smiled. Cathy could only imagine that she looked like a deer in headlights. God knows, she felt like one.

Even though Jonathan was no Melvin, he was just as sweet and helpful. He made sure he gave them the real VIP treatment. As for Cathy, she felt safe at the game. Marcus was on the field and the Yankees returned to form, beating the Devil Rays quite handily. By the seventh inning stretch, all was right with the world.

Madison returned from the bar with his third rum and Coke. "You know, I think I like baseball." "What's the matter with him?" Cathy asked.

"He's on his third rum and Coke." Roger smiled as he worked on his one and only beer.

Anna shook her head. "Can't take him anywhere, especially when top shelf liquor is concerned."

"Normally I would resent that statement but I don't care. I need to let my hair down and have a few drinks."

"Good thing we're the designated drivers," Anna said.

"True."

Cathy looked around the stadium and noticed Lisa. "Hey, Anna, that's Lisa over there. I wonder what she's covering."

"Don't worry, whatever it is it will be in on the supermarket stands before you know it," Anna answered.

"True again."

"From the looks of things I'd say you spend a lot of time in the supermarket." A voice came from over her shoulder.

Cathy turned around to see Cybil George standing there looking as if she were far more than half in the bag.

"Excuse me?"

"You heard me. You look like you spend a lot of time in the supermarket." She seethed.

"Ms. George, I think you're drunk and you should leave before you say anything else." Cathy tried to take the high road.

"Why?" She stepped towards me. "What are you going to do about it? Eat me?"

Anna stood up. "I think you should shut up.

"Anna, you don't have to stand up for me. I'm not paying her any attention." She turned her back to ignore her.

She was persistent. "What did you do to him? Huh? Did you put something in his food to make him love you? I mean, you are so not his type. You might have a pretty face but you're fat."

Angered, Cathy stood up. "I didn't do anything to him. I didn't drug him or anything like that. He wants me for me."

"You don't even know him. We were together for three years."

"So you're not together anymore and the only reason this bothers you is because you lost him to a fat chick and everybody knows it," Cathy shot back

"You are what you are."

"You know what? You can call me fat, large, obese or whatever label gets you through the night. I know that I love him and he loves me. It doesn't change the facts, and you know it."

She lunged towards Cathy. "You fat bitch."

Cathy moved out of the way and she fell flat on her face. Cathy bent down to try to help her up. "Don't touch me."

"Fine. Get up," Cathy said.

Cybil stood up and touched her split lip. "See what you did to me!"

"I didn't do anything to you."

Madison piped up. "It's not her fault! You lunged at her, not the other way around."

Although neither of them had noticed, Roger had gotten security.

The security guards flanked Cybil on both sides and she got indignant. "Take your hands off me!"

"Miss, you need to come with us."

"Get off me. You have no right to put your hands on me!"

"Miss, you are causing a disturbance and we need to remove you from the stadium. If you continue to resist, we will call the police who will then take you into custody."

"You can't arrest me! Do you know who I am?" Cybil insisted.

"I don't care if you're the queen of England. You're intoxicated and disorderly."

A third security officer appeared.

"Fine! I'll leave. Just don't touch me!"

She stumbled up the stairs and nearly fell again. When the guards caught her, she flew into a rage and they physically escorted her out. In the meantime, Cathy was in a daze.

"Cathy? Cathy are you all right?"

Her face felt flushed. "It's the ninth inning and I want to go. I have to go."

"Okay, we'll leave now. Roger, can you drive?"

"Yeah. Not a problem."

Cathy felt she walked past a firing squad of looks. Honestly, she would have preferred bullets; they would hurt less. She was the humiliated fat girl, whether she'd gotten a few good barbs in or not. As they walked out, Cathy saw Lisa out of the corner of her eye. She would have waved but she couldn't bring herself to look anywhere but straight ahead.

On the other side of the parking lot a group of reporters surrounded Cybil.

"What's going on over there?" Madison asked.

Roger looked over. "It looks like the police are taking Cybil into custody."

"I guess her manners didn't improve any."

"Could you two stop talking about this? Look at Cathy. She's in a daze and I can guarantee you that feeding frenzy will turn its attention to us if we don't get her to the car and out of here."

"You're right. Let's get the lead out." Despite three rum and Cokes, Madison picked up the pace.

No one wanted to draw attention. As nonchalantly as possible they picked up the pace to get to the car. Roger and Madison hopped into the front seat while Anna and Cathy scooted into the back. Cathy bent down in the back seat until they cleared the parking lot. Even once they were out of harm's reach, Cathy remained quiet in the car.

"What was the guy's name at the concierge desk again?" Anna asked.

"Fred," Roger answered.

"Madison, call the hotel and ask for Fred. Maybe he can help us get Cathy to her room."

"Why? Cathy's okay to walk. Aren't you?" "Yes, Madison, I can walk." Cathy sounded robotic.

"Idiot. I don't mean to help her to walk to her room. I'm talking about the media that's likely to be at the hotel."

While the car was stopped at a light, Roger looked at Anna. "You really think they'll be there? We left before them."

"Absolutely. The media is better organized than the military. Their strategy is to have an entrance and exit plan when it comes to news items. So you can bet there's someone at the hotel waiting for Cathy and there's another one down at the police station waiting for Cybil."

Madison dialed the hotel. Anna rubbed Cathy's hand. "You're okay, Cathy. You did a great job of standing up for yourself. This wasn't your fault."

Madison closed his cell phone. "I spoke to Fred and he said he'll meet us around the employees' entrance near the kitchen. This way we can take the service elevator up."

Just as Anna had predicted, reporters and photographers surrounded the front entrance.

Roger was mystified. "Even vultures take a while before they feed."

"Okay, Cathy, you're going to have to put your head down."

Cathy put her head down. "Is this low enough?"

"Yeah."

She couldn't believe she was reduced to hiding from reporters.

"Okay, we're clear."

Roger pulled into a space. Fred was waiting near the door.

"Fred, we can't thank you enough."

"Not a problem. Anything I can do."

Cathy forced a smile. "Thanks."

"I still can't believe all this commotion." Madison looked around.

They used the kitchen entrance to avoid prying eyes, and Fred used his key for the service elevator.

"Thanks, Fred," Anna said.

"We really appreciate it," Roger added.

"How in the world did those reporters find out so quickly? That's what I want to know," Madison said.

Fred piped up. "It was on the radio. They said a fight broke out between Marcus Fox's ex-girlfriend Cybil George and his new girlfriend Catherine Chambers."

"They over-hype everything. You would have thought it was the Thriller in Manila between Ali and Frazier," Madison scoffed.

When the elevators opened, Fred stayed behind.

"This is as far as I can take you. My break is over and I have to get back to the desk."

Anna reached into her bag and took out a hundred dollar bill. "Thank you."

"No, really. It was my pleasure."

Anna got back on the elevator and put the money in his pocket. "I insist. This was above and beyond the call of duty." She gave him a peck on the cheek.

"Thank you. Take care of yourself, Ms. Chambers. I hope to see you around tomorrow."

"Maybe so."

"Listen, I'm going to Cathy's room with her for a while. Why don't you two get something to eat and bring it back to her room?" Anna said.

"Yeah. We can do that. Come on, Madison."

"We'll be back, Cathy."

"Okay."

"Where's your key card?"

She handed it to Anna.

After Anna opened the door, Cathy only took two steps before collapsing into a sobbing heap in the middle of the floor. Anna didn't say a word. She knew Cathy had to let it go somehow, so she just hugged her while she cried for herself and anyone else who'd ever been the fat chick.

CHAPTER 24

After the game there was a bigger media presence than usual. A crush of reporters was trying to get to Marcus. A longtime pro at handling himself around the media, Ben managed to snake his way around them to an alternate exit.

Marcus stole away to another area to get away from the commotion.

Mark slid in the door. “It’s crazy out there.”

“I know. I have no idea what any of this is about.” “I do,” Ben interjected. “I have two words for you: Cybil George.”

“What?”

“That woman is bad news.” Mark shook his head.

“What happened?”

“As best I can tell, it seems that Ms. George was inebriated and caused a disturbance in the suite.”

“Wasn’t that where Cathy was seated?” Mark asked.

“Yes,” Ben answered. “It gets better.”

Marcus sat down. “I’m afraid to ask. How much better?”

“She exchanged words with Cathy and there was some sort of altercation.”

“They had a fight?”

“No, it was more like Cybil tried to start one but landed on her face.”

Marcus was frantic. “Where’s Cathy now?”

“No one has seen her.” Ben was sorry he didn’t have an answer.

There was a knock on the door. Tim stepped in.

"Sorry to intrude, but Lisa Spellman just handed me a note for you, Marcus." He handed him a piece of paper.

"A note for me?" He opened it and started to read.

"What does it say?" Ben was anxious. Marcus's expression changed. "Cathy was right." "What?" Mark asked.

"Cathy said she thought Lisa was good people and her instincts were on the money."

"What's in the note?" Ben asked.

"Read it for yourself."

Ben read the note while Mark read it over his shoulder. "Well, I'll be. I guess I have to take back what I was thinking."

"I can't believe it."

Ben chuckled. "I never thought I'd see the day I would say this."

"Say what, Ben?"

"I need to get Lisa Spellman on the phone so we can set the record straight. I think you should give her an exclusive."

"You have her number?" "I have everyone's number."

The men laughed.

After dozing for a little while, Cathy went from sad to mad as hell.

"What gave her the right to feel that she could say anything she wanted to me?"

Madison ate another French fry. "Because she's a supermodel. They believe they're above mere mortal women."

"I don't believe that. Not all models behave like Cybil."

"That's true, Anna. She did take salad witch to a whole new level." Roger drank his Coke.

An agitated Cathy paced. "What kills me is by now the story has been twisted in every direction like a bad game of telephone. Before this evening is out they'll have us dueling with pistols at twenty paces."

"Still no word from Marcus?" Madison asked.

"No. The game just ended a little while ago and there's still the post-game wrap up."

"I'm sure someone has informed him of the incident by now."

"It will be on the ten or eleven o'clock news, I'm sure."

"I still can't believe you didn't tell us about her being in his room."

"What was I going to say, Anna? I tried to put it out of my head."

"You could have talked to us about it."

"Lay off, Anna. I understand where she's coming from. It was enough she had to deal with the thought. Talking about it would have driven her crazy," Madison said.

Cathy was impressed. "When did you become so insightful, Madison? It almost doesn't sound like you."

"I went through a few things with Teresa I didn't talk to you two or anyone about. It was just too painful to talk."

"You had to see how it played out," Roger added.

"Well, I'd say you came out on top, which is much better than I did with Teresa."

Anna patted Madison on the back. "I know this is a tough subject for you to talk about."

"But it is in the past. Just like Cybil is in Marcus's past."

Cathy's cell phone rang.

"You want me to get it?"

"If you would please, Anna. Thanks."

Anna picked up. "Hello?" Oh hey, E.D. She's right here. Hold on." She handed Cathy the phone.

"Hi, E.D."

"Hey. Are you all right? I saw a blurb on television about a fight between you and Cybil George."

"I'm fine, E.D. It wasn't so much a fight as it was a drunken war of words on her part."

"What the hell is she doing in Florida? I thought she was doing a movie."

"I guess you didn't catch that blurb. She left the set to come to Florida."

"Don't tell me. She came to get Marcus back, right?"

"Yes, and when that didn't work, she got in my face."

"I hope you told her skinny butt off."

"It was too public to get into it like that, but I think I held my own."

"She sure did, E.D.," Madison interjected.

"Shut up, Mad," Roger admonished, taking both Anna and Cathy by surprise. "Hey, I'm practically a member of the family. I get to tell Madison to shut up, too."

Anna laughed.

"*Et tu Brute*?" Madison shook his head.

"Anyway, E.D., that's what happened."

"She got arrested, though."

"Not for what happened between her and me. Security was going to simply escort her out of the stadium. She got arrested because she resisted their peaceful attempts by kicking and screaming, not to mention she was plastered."

"Oh. It doesn't take long for models to get drunk; they're so skinny it goes straight to their heads," E.D. said.

"That's true. Anyhow, thanks for actually calling to find out the real story."

"Always. It didn't sound like anything you'd ever do. You've got far more class than that."

"Thanks, E.D. Lord knows I needed to hear that."

"Keep your head up and we'll talk after you get back next week."

"Okay, E.D. Later."

"Later."

"I'm surprised I haven't heard from Mom or Dad yet," Cathy wondered out loud.

"You were sleeping when they called."

"I should have figured. Do I have to call them back to explain?"

"I took care of it."

"So what was the verdict? I'm sure Mom said this happened to me because of my worldly lifestyle and Dad is ready to kick someone's butt."

"You know, you're right on the money."

Cathy was exasperated and flushed. "I'll be right back."

Flushed, Cathy went to the bathroom to splash cold water on her face. As she patted her face she stared at her reflection. "How did this happen to me?" she mouthed quietly.

"Cathy!" Anna shouted.

"Yeah?"

"Come quick or you're going to miss it."

She rushed out as fast as she could. "What's up?"

"You just missed the promo for the news."

"What did it say?"

"They have an exclusive interview with Marcus Fox tonight."

"Get out of here." She sat on the bed.

"It's almost time for the eleven o'clock news." Madison stretched out across the bed.

As her heart pounded, Cathy settled down to watch the broadcast. It was torture to sit through the local evening news waiting for the report. Finally the anchor announced the interview with Marcus.

In sports tonight the Yankees defeated the Devil Rays 12-3. However a real battle took place in the VIP section between Marcus Fox's former girlfriend, model Cybil George, and his current girlfriend, literary agent and author Catherine Chambers. Here to bring you our exclusive interview with Mr. Fox is Lisa Spellman. Lisa?

Lisa: Thank you, Hank. Tonight in addition to the action that unfolded on the field there was action in the stands when an apparently intoxicated Cybil George happened upon Catherine Chambers, who was quietly enjoying the game. Witnesses say Cybil was the aggressor while Catherine maintained her cool.

Woman: Yeah, she walked in like she was looking for a fight but she didn't get one.

Lisa: Some people said it got physical.

Woman: It looked like Cybil lunged at her but that Cathy was too quick for her. She stepped aside and Cybil fell on her face.

Lisa: After the game I spoke with Marcus Fox who had this to say.

Marcus: I'm very disappointed with Cybil's actions. I was told some of the things she said and frankly it made me sick. I love Catherine Chambers. I made it clear to Cybil that our relationship was over.

Lisa: According to witnesses she made some unflattering remarks regarding Ms. Chamber's size.

Marcus: That was completely uncalled for. I don't care about her size so why should anyone else? So what if I've dated thinner women in the past. She's warm, beautiful and caring and in my book that makes her exactly my type. She's the love of my life.

Lisa: As you heard, Marcus Fox stands behind Catherine, even calling her the love of his life.

Hank: So what's happening to Cybil George?

Lisa: According to the police, she was booked for public intoxication and disorderly conduct and will be arraigned in a few hours. Bail will likely be set at $1,000. She's expected to post it after the arraignment. In addition, there's talk of trouble with the studio since she left production on her debut movie to come to Florida. Back to you, Hank.

Everyone looked at Cathy for a reaction. Cathy stared at the screen.

"Did you hear that, Cathy? He just told the world how he feels about you."

"He doesn't have any commitment issues, Cuz. I'd say he's a keeper."

She started to cry again.

"What's the matter?"

"You can't take guys anywhere. Madison, those are happy tears."

"Isn't that an oxymoron?"

"It is when you say it," Anna said flatly.

There was a knock on the door.

"I'll get it."

"Roger, be sure it's not a reporter. They can be some sneaky little bastards."

"I'll take care of them if they are." Roger put his fists up.

"So this is good news, Cathy. I'm sure all the media outlets will pick this up and the world will know."

"As long as she knows I don't care about the world," Marcus said as he walked in.

Cathy turned around, surprised to hear his voice. "I just saw the interview with Lisa."

"What did you think?"

"Pardon us, but before you answer, we're going to take our cue and leave you two alone." Anna picked up her bag.

"Oh, you don't have to leave on my account."

"Thanks, but we should go and give you two your privacy."

"Come on, Madison," Roger urged.

"But I love happy endings."

"You're a divorce attorney. How can you love happy endings?" Anna asked.

"As a matter of fact, that's exactly why I love happy endings. I don't get to see too many of them."

"That's sweet. We'll take you to Friendly's instead." Anna winked.

"See you later." Roger waved.

Marcus sat down beside Cathy.

Marcus knew Cathy had been through the wringer since the two of them met. He was amazed that she'd been able to hang tough.

"And I thought it was tough on the baseball diamond," Marcus said.

"Yeah, those VIP seating areas are brutal," Cathy joked.

He took her hand. "How are you really? Are you feeling okay?"

"I'm fine. None the worse for wear."

"You know, in the past couple of weeks I've seen you handle whatever has been thrown your way with dignity."

"I couldn't afford to let them see me sweat."

"You've been the epitome of grace under fire."

"I don't think I would go that far. I did chase Lisa Spellman in the supermarket." The

two of them laughed.

"You know, I forgot about that."

She smiled. "I see you gave the interview to Lisa. How did that happen?"

"I decided to trust your intuition. You told me you thought she was good people and tonight she proved it to me."

"How?"

"She saw the whole thing go down between you and Cybil and instead of joining in the barrage of reporters and photographers asking questions, she slipped me a note."

"What did the note say?"

"She wanted me to know that you were with your family and you seemed okay to her, which said something about her character to me."

"I told you I had a good feeling about her."

"You were right. Ben called Lisa and arranged to give her an exclusive interview. She was there with a camera in record time."

"I'll bet. It was real a coup for her."

"So what did you think of the broadcast?"

"I was overwhelmed and happy." She kissed him. "Thank you. I was feeling a little beat up."

"I know and I'm sorry. That's why I had to set the record straight."

"Lisa told you what was said?"

"Yeah, and I was completely disgusted that even drunk Cybil would stoop to that level."

"She's embarrassed and her ego was bruised."

"So what? Big deal for her. I was more concerned with you."

Cathy looked away. "In a way she unburdened me."

He looked astonished. "How?"

"She said the words that have been living in my head for years and forced me to confront them out loud."

"You had an epiphany."

She nodded. "I finally decided to take Fil's advice and own the words so they don't have power over me anymore."

Marcus looked perplexed. "Who's Fil?"

"I'll tell you about her later. Trust me, you'll love her."

"If you like her, I'm sure I will, too." He took her hand. "I love you, Cathy. You are the best thing to ever happen to me."

Cathy caressed his cheek. "I love you, too, Marcus."

"I don't care about anything or anyone else as long as we're together." He pulled her close to him.

"Does that mean you changed your type?" Cathy asked.

"It means that I don't care what anyone else has to say. You're just the right type for me, now, tomorrow and for always."

Marcus sealed the declaration with a kiss that was one for the record books—a homerun with bases loaded.

Cathy could swear she saw fireworks going off and heard thousands of Yankee fans clapping and cheering.

Life was perfect.

ABOUT THE AUTHOR

Chamein Canton is the managing partner of the Chamein Canton Literary Agency. In addition to writing fiction, she writes non-fiction and has been moonlighting as a wedding planner for more than ten years. She attended Empire State College where she majored in Business Management and lives on Long Island with her twin sons.

CPSIA information can be obtained
at www.ICGtesting.com
Printed in the USA
LVHW02s1749280618
582188LV00009B/575/P

For New York literary agent and author Cathy Chambers, life is pretty good. She has a job she lives in a city she loves;things are even sweeter because New York is home to to her favorite baseball team, the Yankees. For years, Cathy has had a crush on Yankees superstar Marcus Fox. He's handsome, he plays for her favorite team, and, best of all for Cathy he's completely unattainable. That is until chance leads her to meet him in a trendy restaurant. Now, Cathy's dream is suddenly attainable...if she can overcome her self consciousness long enough to believe that Marcus, who is well-known for being surrounded by skinny models could really be interested in a full figured woman who is for all intensive purposes not his type.

ISBN 9781495238611
90000
9 781495 238611